Howard W



# A Practical Introduction to Conveyancing

Anatiposi

**Howard Warburton Elphinstone**

# A Practical Introduction to Conveyancing

Reprint of the original, first published in 1871.

1st Edition 2023 | ISBN: 978-3-38211-964-5

Anatiposi Verlag is an imprint of Outlook Verlagsgesellschaft mbH.

Verlag (Publisher): Outlook Verlag GmbH, Zeilweg 44, 60439 Frankfurt, Deutschland
Vertretungsberechtigt (Authorized to represent): E. Roepke, Zeilweg 44, 60439 Frankfurt, Deutschland
Druck (Print): Books on Demand GmbH, In de Tarpen 42, 22848 Norderstedt, Deutschland

# A PRACTICAL INTRODUCTION TO CONVEYANCING.

A

# PRACTICAL INTRODUCTION

TO

# CONVEYANCING,

CONTAINING THE

SUBSTANCE OF TWO COURSES OF LECTURES

DELIVERED BEFORE

The Incorporated Law Society

IN 1869, 1870, AND 1871,

BY

HOWARD WARBURTON ELPHINSTONE,

OF LINCOLN'S INN, BARRISTER-AT-LAW.

LONDON:
WILLIAM MAXWELL & SON, 29, FLEET STREET, E.C.
Law Booksellers and Publishers.
HODGES, FOSTER, & CO., AND E. PONSONBY, DUBLIN;
THACKER, SPINK, & CO., CALCUTTA; CHARLES F. MAXWELL, MELBOURNE.

1871.

# PREFACE.

THE bulk of this book consists of the lectures which the author had the honour to deliver before the Incorporated Law Society in the years 1869, 1870, 1871. In preparing them for the press he has made several additions, the most important one being Chapter III., "On the Interpretation of Legal Documents," which contains the substance of a paper read by him before the Juridical Society, and published by the Society.

The author has omitted those explanations which are to be found in "Williams on the Law of Real Property," and "Williams on the Law of Personal Property," except in cases where the omission would have rendered the context unintelligible. In composing a book addressed to students only, he has considered himself at liberty to make more use of the standard works of conveyancing than would have been proper had his book been intended for the use of the practising conveyancer. In acknowledging once for all in this place his obligations to

"Bythewood's Precedents," by Sweet, "Prideaux's Precedents," and "Davidson's Precedents," he thinks it right to add that many of the explanations in the text have been adapted with but slight modifications from the last-mentioned work. He is encouraged to hope that no serious error will be found of a nature likely to mislead the student, as the proof sheets have been kindly perused by his friends, A. C. Humphreys, Esq., and F. Thompson, Esq., both of the equity bar, to whom he is greatly indebted for the suggestions made by them.

The student is advised to read this book with a book of "Precedents" by his side, and to master the two works of Mr. Williams above mentioned, and to correct the errata, before he does so.

6, New Square, Lincoln's Inn.
*April*, 1871.

# CONTENTS.

## CHAPTER VIII.



## CHAPTER IX.



## CHAPTER X.



## CHAPTER XI.



## CHAPTER XII.



## CHAPTER XIII.

# ERRATA AND ADDENDA.

Page 19, line 18, *for* "in capital," *read* "*in capite.*"

27, line 8 from end, *refer to* Sanders on Uses, p. 67, 5th edition.

29, line 3, *for* "diverts," *read* "divests."

34, line 6, *for* "by the purchaser," *read* "to the purchaser."

47, line 5, *dele* , *after* "bear."

74, line 18, *insert* "of —— Esq." *after* "K. L."

91, line 3, *for* "use," *read* "*use.*"

96, line 2, *for* "in deed," *read* "in a deed."

101, line 8, *for* "by them," *read* "by a bargain and sale or a covenant to stand seised."

102, line 2, *insert* "of" *after* "use."

105, Want of space has prevented the Author from giving the promised explanation of the operation of Fines and Recoveries. *See* 2 Blackstone's Comm. (any old edition).

118, end of page, *add a reference to* "p. 234, *post.*"

125, line 3, *add a reference to* "Dart's Vendors and Purchasers, p. 503 (4th edition)," where it is stated that the proviso is now commonly inserted in practice.

159, line 4, *for* "*Smith,*" *read* "Smith."

164, line 17, *for* "s. 24," *read* "s. 23."

174, line 8 from end, *dele* ; *after* )

176, line 5, *for* "latter case," *read* "second case."

204, line 16, *for* "assignee," *read* "assignor."

208, line 12 from end, *insert* "in" *before* "the."

line 11 from end, *for* "p. 139," *read* "p. 141."

242, line 13 from end, *dele* (γ).

257, line 9 from end, *add, after* "lessor," "assuming that the latter has entered into the usual restricted covenant for quiet enjoyment."

296, line 7, *for* "of his," *read* "of the income of his."

b

Page 305, line 5, *before* "subject," *insert*, "that any exercise of the power would be."
321, line 10 from end, *after* "subclauses," *add* "and in the latter part of the third subclause."
line 8 from end, *dele* "three."
line 6 from end, *for* "The third," *read* "But the earlier part of the third."
341, line 8 from end, *insert* ) *after* "to."
344, line 4, *after* "marry," *insert* "for life."

# LECTURES ON CONVEYANCING.

## CHAPTER I.

### INTRODUCTORY.

It is the wish of the author to lay down the rules of Law in the broadest possible form, without in all cases stating the numerous exceptions; for, if he were to do so, the bulk of this book would be increased enormously, and it would become unintelligible to the student. The only safe course for the young practitioner to pursue, in seeking the law on any particular case, is to consider in the first place, to what results the general principles lead; and, in the second place, to search the reported cases, so as to ascertain whether the question under consideration falls under any of the exceptions to the rule.

The reader may possibly think that it is unnecessary for a conveyancer or solicitor to take any great degree of trouble for the purpose of becoming a good real-property lawyer, and that all that the mere draftsman has to do is to acquire a facility for adapting precedents to any particular case; this is an error. He may think that in all cases of difficulty, he can call in the assistance of some real-property lawyer of great experience. That is generally true, but unless the reader is a good lawyer, he will be unable to tell whether the case is one of difficulty or not. Again it must be remembered that for the purpose of giving sound advice to a client in by far the larger part of his business (*the non-contentious* part), the solicitor must have an accurate knowledge of what the law allows the client to do, and what it does not. Suppose, for instance, that a gentleman consults his solicitor about the arrangements to be made on his marriage; he may be owner in fee of one estate, tenant in tail of another, tenant for life with the usual powers of jointuring and raising portions of a third, they may all be subject to mortgages and annuities; he may desire to make a proper settlement, but will probably be entirely ignorant of what would be a proper settlement in such a case; he would certainly be unaware of the importance of clearing the property to be settled from incumbrances, and unless his solicitor were a good real-property lawyer, it would be most unlikely that the best arrangement would be made.

Again, the solicitor may be unable to obtain further assistance; he may be called in to make the will of a dying man; there may be no time to go to counsel; if he is a sound lawyer, he will know what dangers to avoid, and although he may not be a very skilful draftsman, he will at all events be able to make a will that will hold water. Suppose, however, that a solicitor has the draft settled by counsel, he has to peruse it not only for the purpose of correcting mere verbal inaccuracies, but for the purpose of seeing that it properly carries out the wishes of his client; and he cannot safely touch it for the purpose of correcting the most apparent error, unless he is a good lawyer.

An instance of the very serious consequences that may arise from a verbal error made by the draftsman, being erroneously corrected by another person, will be seen in *Newburgh* v. *Newburgh*, 5 Mad. 364. Here a conveyancer of great eminence, Mr. Butler, in settling Lord Newburgh's will, struck out by mistake the word Gloucester, in a devise of the testator's estates in the counties of Sussex and Gloucester; the copying clerk saw that something was wrong, and altered the word *counties* to county; a question arose as to what the devisee took. One is justified in saying that if the copying clerk had been competent to understand the will, he would either have altered it correctly, or would have seen that the error was of such a nature that he ought not to have touched it, as in the result the House of Lords decided upon the whole will that the intended devisee took the Gloucestershire property.

As an example of the importance of perusing a draft settled by counsel for the purpose of seeing that it carries out the client's wishes, the author need only point out that it is common for instructions for a will or marriage settlement drawn in haste to be imperfect in points of detail, which are not discovered till counsel settles the draft; he ought, and generally does, take care to call attention to them by a marginal note, but this may possibly be omitted, and in its absence nothing but a very careful and intelligent perusal will enable you to understand what he has inserted. (Post, p. 58.)

It must be remembered that if a solicitor, through ignorance of the law, gives advice that causes loss to his client, he may render himself personally liable in damages. (*Parker* v. *Rolls*, 14 C. B. 691; *Stannard* v. *Ullithorne*, 10 Bing. 491; *Taylor* v. *Gorman*, 4 Ir. Eq. Rep. 550; *Ireson* v. *Pearman*, 3 B. & C. 799.)

The best practical manner of discovering the meaning of a long and intricate draft is to make a careful analysis of it, affixing a number to each clause, and distinguishing the operative parts from the recitals by writing them on a different margin. [See post, p. 61.]

Difficulties in study of Law.

The study of the law of real property and conveyancing is full of difficulties, which arise from three different causes, viz.:

*First.* The inaccurate notions about Law that every man acquires before he commences the study of it in earnest.

*Second.* An inaccurate conception of the idea of property, in other words, not clearly understanding what is meant by that word.

*Third.* The manner in which changes in the law

of property, rendered necessary by the gradual changes in the customs of society, are effected.

It is hardly possible for any person to avoid picking up a few notions about Law from listening to ordinary conversation; but, unhappily, Law affords no exception to the general rule, that propositions in any science as stated in conversation are incorrect. While want of space forbids the discussion of the origin of the widely spread popular errors about Law, it is, perhaps, worth while to remark that as by very slow degrees the public learn some proposition of law correctly, so, when they have once acquired it, they are slow to learn that the law has been changed. For instance, most laymen believe that when land is entailed the entail can never be broken: this was the case from the time of the enactment of the Statute De Donis till the invention of common recoveries in the reign of Edward IV.; but since that time the law has been altered, and no estate can be rendered inalienable by any artifice for a time longer than a life or lives in being, and twenty-one years afterwards. As this is the first occasion on which the author has stated a general proposition without mentioning the exceptions, he suggests that it would be an instructive exercise for the reader in this and every subsequent case, when a general proposition is laid down, to consider what, if any, are the exceptions to it. First difficulty.

Another source of popular error as to English law is the great influence that Roman law and literature still retains on modern thought. Most of the common phrases used by people who talk about Law being ignorant of it, (phrases which have either no meaning, or are used in an incorrect meaning in English law,) are derived directly from Roman law. Thus the common belief that it is necessary to leave the heir at least a shilling in a will is derived from the Roman doctrine of inofficious testaments, and the phrase to make a man one's heir by will, which is absolute nonsense according to English law, is a proper technical phrase according to Roman law.

Second difficulty.

The second source of difficulty is an inaccurate conception of the idea of *property*, or in other words not clearly understanding what is meant by that word. The reader who has studied both Blackstone and Williams is extremely likely to fall into difficulties owing to the different senses in which these two authors use the word. The popular notion of property, a notion which I need hardly say is inaccurate, but contains some truth, is embodied in the proverb, "a man can do what he likes with his own."

Let us consider some examples. A loaf of bread belongs to me. I can (by which I mean the law allows me to) eat it, sell it, give it away, or if I choose to do that which is immoral, I can waste it, and lastly, no other person can do any of these things without my permission; on the other hand, I may not strike a man with it. So far as this example goes, it would appear that the maxim, "a man can do what he likes with his own," gives a correct explanation of the word property, if we add the restriction, so long as he does no harm to others. This, however, is not quite accurate, as will appear from another example. Suppose a horse belongs to me : I may ride him or drive him wherever I please, subject to the restriction that I may not go without permission on another man's land, even if I do no harm by doing so. Suppose, again, that a pickaxe belongs to me; I may use it on my own land, but not, without permission, on the land of any one else. I might even do him good by using my pickaxe so as to discover a valuable mine on his land, but I should not be the less a wrong-doer. Both the last-mentioned examples will show that the popular notion of property requires some modification.

True explanation of property.

The true explanation appears to be the following. One can act differently with respect to things of different natures; the possessor of a loaf and of a gun can act differently in many ways with respect to them, where by *can* act is meant, *has the physical power to* act. A little consideration will show that the number of ways in which the possessor of a thing can—*i. e.* can physically—act with respect to it, is quite indefinite. The law prohibits some of these ways of acting with respect to each particular thing, and vests exclusively the legal right of acting in all the ways which it permits in a particular person called the owner of the thing.

The reader can hardly expect to understand this at the first perusal, and as it is of great importance, it is repeated in another form of words:

"The owner of a thing is the person who can

exercise over it every right that the nature of the thing admits of, and the law allows to be exercised; where, by 'can' is meant 'can lawfully.'" It sometimes happens that more than one person can exercise an indefinite number of rights over a thing, in this case they are both properly called owners.

For instance, a person living in lodgings can use his rooms in an indefinite number of ways; he can eat in them, sleep in them, and so on; he is properly called the owner of them. The lodging-house keeper retains an indefinite number of rights over the rooms: he can enter them at certain times, sell his house including the rooms, and is therefore equally called the owner. The reader will note that the law so adjusts the rights of both parties that they cannot clash. The more correct description would be to call both the lodger and the lodging-house keeper partial owners, as, in fact, they jointly form the owner in the largest sense of the word.

Instances of more than one person being properly termed "the owner" of the same thing are common. Thus, in London, the same house may be sub-let half a dozen times; each leaseholder may properly call himself "the owner" of the house, while only one of them is the person who has the right of possessing it.

Where a man can exercise a definite number of rights over the property of another, the latter is still called the owner; the former is said to have a right, or a power over it; a common example is a right of way.

For instance, you are aware that many railway companies hire all their carriages; they can use them in any way that they think fit, subject only to this restriction, that they must not use them in any way not contemplated in the agreement for hiring; they are rightly called the owners, or, as we should say, partial owners. On the other hand, if you take a ticket to go by train, or even engage a whole carriage to yourself, you would not properly be called the owner; you have only very restricted rights over the carriage.

Another example of this is afforded by an ordinary settlement of land; it usually happens that some trustee who is not the owner of the property is able to sell it if he thinks fit: and although in strictness we ought to consider the trustee and the person who is commonly called the owner as jointly constituting "the owner," still the usage is to call the one the owner, and to say that the other has a power over it.

The third source of difficulty already pointed out, is the manner in which the changes which are rendered necessary in the law of property by the gradual changes in the customs of society, are brought about. Third difficulty.

These are effected in four different manners:

1st, by the jurisdiction of Equity.

2nd, by our respect for judicial decisions.

3rd, by the methods adopted for evading the Law.

4th, by Act of Parliament.

The Court of Chancery has always exercised a very beneficial influence by insisting upon men's acting up to a very high and pure standard of morality, so that it has often happened that when some knave has acquired possession of another man's property and refused to give it up, under such circumstances that the ordinary Courts of Law afforded no remedy to the rightful owner, the Court of Chancery interfered and made the knave act honestly and restore it. And by steadily insisting upon the performance of certain definite acts of morality, it gradually becomes settled law that they shall be performed. It will subsequently be shown that all modern conveyancing depends upon an elementary rule of morality, the performance of which was insisted upon centuries ago by the Court of Chancery, which declares that if a man contracts to sell land and receives the purchase-money, he shall do all necessary acts to vest the land in the purchaser.

The existence of the high standard of morality inculcated by the Court of Chancery has a very important practical result at the present day. The reader is aware that a man may have a legal right to do something which he has no moral right to do: for instance, a man has the legal right to disinherit a virtuous son, an extremely immoral action, and one that the Court of Chancery will not interfere with. But in all dealings between man and man it insists, as a general rule, that each man shall act quite honestly in the moral sense of the word. When, therefore, in advising a client one comes to the conclusion that he can legally do something which is not right morally, it is always well to reconsider the advice, so as to be certain that if the client follows the advice he will not offend against some rule of action laid down by the Court of Chancery.

The manner in which changes of Law are brought about by means of judicial decisions is well described in Mr. Maine's Ancient Law, p. 30. We always assume that whenever any particular facts come before a court, the law applicable to them is already existing. But really this is not the case. The decision is founded on the old principles and distinctions which are acknowledged, but the moment that the decision is pronounced we take it for a fresh starting point; and even when it has modified the law, we consider that it is law. As an example of this, the reader will find it extremely interesting and useful to compare all the cases on the doctrine of the wife's separate estate in chronological order; he will find that originally the husband had extremely large powers over the wife's real and personal property; and that the gradual effect of judicial decisions has been to place a wife in the position of a feme sole as regards certain parts of her property. (*Hulme* v. *Tenant*, 1 Tudor L. C.)

The modifications in the law introduced by judicial decision may arise either from the judge taking an incorrect view of, or reasoning incorrectly from, the existing law; or from his giving a decision on a doubtful point. Within the last few years a case was decided involving a question on a purely theoretical point of real-property law. A very learned conveyancer, the late Mr. Preston, had discussed it in a published treatise, and had expressed a strong opinion one way. The case ran through the Irish Courts; there the judges were divided in opinion. It came before the House of Lords; the judges who were called in gave an unanimous opinion agreeing with Mr. Preston's, while the House of Lords gave a decision the other way. One may fairly say, looking at the great weight of authority on both sides, that the question was unsettled prior to the decision which has, while in form declaring the law, really created new law.

Great difficulty has always existed in England, particularly in past times, in inducing the Legislature to make those changes in the law of property (as distinguished from the law of persons) that society requires. As the habits of society change, a corresponding change becomes necessary in the law of property, and we generally find that the ingenuity of lawyers is taxed to the utmost in endeavouring to evade the existing law, and that the legislature does not give its assistance till the evasion has become universal. As instances of this, consider the centuries that elapsed after the application of a common recovery for the purpose of barring an estate tail before the Act was passed which enabled this to be done by a deed enrolled. Or, again, the modern conveyance by lease and release was invented shortly after the passing of the Statute of Uses in the reign of King Henry VIII., for the purpose of evading the publicity which the then policy of the law insisted upon, while the necessity for the lease was only done away with in the present reign.

A few more words about *property*. The reader will observe that the word is used in two senses; it is sometimes used to denote the rights that a man exercises over a thing, and sometimes to denote the thing itself. Thus, Blackstone (2 Com. 1) says:—"the objects of our inquiry will be the *jura rerum*, or those rights that a man may acquire in and to such external things as are unconnected with his person. These are what the writers on natural law style the rights of dominion or property." Mr. Williams, on the other hand, without giving any definition of property, applies the word to the things themselves. Very little confusion will be occasioned by this ambiguous sense of the word, if the reader remembers its existence.

Property may be divided into moveables and immoveables: the distinction is important for legal purposes. If a stranger destroys my moveable the law cannot force him to restore the identical thing, because it no longer exists. On the other hand, he cannot entirely destroy an immoveable, and the law can replace the true owner who has been dispossessed. The distinction between moveables and immoveables exists in the law of every civilised nation, and has, owing to historical circumstances, been brought into great prominence in our own.

In English law, property is divided into real and personal, divisions which correspond very nearly with immoveable and moveable. Mr. Williams says that the reason of the names is this:—If you are deprived of your property, lands could be restored, the *real* land could be recovered; as to goods, the remedy was only against the *person* who had taken them away. (3 Austin, Lect. on Jurisp. 215.)

Real property is usually stated to be divided into:—

1. Land.

2. Tenements, *i. e.*, everything which is the subject of *tenure*, a term which I shall explain presently. This not only includes land, but certain rights connected with land, as an advowson, a franchise, a right of common, a title of dignity annexed to the land.

3. Hereditaments. This includes everything which passes to the heir on his ancestor's death intestate, such as a tenement, and certain personal property, as an annuity limited to the heir, not issuing out of land.

The reader will observe that this so-called division is really no division at all; for the word hereditament includes tenements, and tenements include land; while on the other hand certain interests in lands, *i. e.*, a term of years, are personal property. He will observe that hereditaments is the most sweeping word that can be used; when a man wishes to convey all his real property in a certain county, and the draftsman is not certain that he has properly enumerated all the particulars, it is advisable to add the words "and all other the hereditaments, if any, of the said A. B. in the county of," &c.

Hereditaments are divided into corporeal and incorporeal. (2 Austin, Lect. on Jurisp. 25.) Corporeal hereditaments are said to be those that can be actually seen and handled, incorporeal hereditaments such as cannot.

A considerable amount of confusion appears to exist in the distinction between corporeal and incorporeal hereditaments. Blackstone (2 Bl. Com. 17) says:—"Corporeal hereditaments consist of such as affect the senses—such as may be seen and handled by the body. Incorporeal are not the object of sensation, can neither be seen nor handled, are creatures of the mind, and exist only in contemplation." The distinction has very great historical importance, for the most common method of conveying corporeal hereditaments in old times was to actually take some part, as a sod of turf, and *deliver* it to the purchaser, in the place of the whole. This, of course, could not be done in the case of incorporeal hereditaments; the only method generally adopted to convey them was a deed of grant. Hence the distinction, corporeal hereditaments lie in *livery*, that is can actually be delivered; incorporeal hereditaments lie in grant. The reader will observe that land is the only hereditament of which the possession can be actually delivered, physically delivered to another. You cannot physically deliver an advowson or an annuity to another; you can deliver a gale or yearly payment to him, but that is not the annuity itself.

"Corporeal hereditaments," Blackstone goes on to say, "consist wholly of substantial and permanent objects, all of which may be comprehended under the general denomination of land only." Where, by land, he means not only the soil itself, but everything under it, as minerals, and everything situate, growing, or erected on it, as water in a pond, or in a watercourse, trees, or houses; and accordingly the word "land" in a conveyance includes all these things. You will observe that Blackstone has changed his language from that which he uses in describing property; he no longer speaks of the rights over things as being *property*, he speaks of the things themselves as *property*.

Remainders and reversions.

It may happen that while I have an indefinite number of rights over land, which the reader will remember amounts to saying that I am the owner of it, my enjoyment of *some* of these rights may be temporarily suspended. I may be a landlord, and properly called the owner, and yet I may have no right to the actual possession of the land; those rights which depend upon the right of actual physical possession of the soil cannot take effect during the existence of a lease granted by me; or, again, some other person may be entitled to the possession of the land during his life, and I may not be entitled to possess it till after his death. The reader will observe that in both of these cases I can exercise some of the rights of ownership before I become entitled in possession. In both cases the law allows me to enter on the land, and turn out the tenant (*i. e.*, the holder, the person in possession) in certain cases; or, again, I may sell the land, or, if we like to call it so, my rights over the land, subject to the existing lease or tenancy for life. The question arises, are my rights, or, in other words, is my property a corporeal or incorporeal hereditament? Property in land of the nature that we are speaking of, is called a remainder or reversion; the distinction between remainders and reversions is explained in Williams on Real Property.

The question for consideration is this, "Is a reversion or remainder in land a corporeal hereditament or not?" You will find that Blackstone does not include reversions and remainders among incorporeal hereditaments, while Mr. Williams properly does so; he adds the caution that they are somewhat of a mixed nature, being at one time incorporeal, at another not. By which he means that so long as they are reversions or remainders, they are incorporeal hereditaments, and that when they cease to be reversions or remainders, they become interests in possession, and become corporeal.

As the author has already said, the important distinction in conveyancing between corporeal and incorporeal hereditaments consists in this; viz., that in old times corporeal hereditaments could be conveyed by symbolical delivery, by physically delivering possession of part in the name of the whole, while this of course could not be done in the case of an incorporeal hereditament. There was one important exception to this rule. If the tenant in possession was tenant for a term of years only, the reversioner could with his consent convey the reversion by entry on the land, and making *livery* of it. Livery.

# CHAPTER II.

## HISTORICAL.

Tenures.

In the eleventh century of the Christian era, we find that all land in civilized Europe was regulated by one or other of two great bodies of law. In part of Europe, "the countries of written law," as they were called, the law was founded on, and closely resembled the Roman law; it was possible for a private man to have alone the entire ownership over land, in other words, to be the sole person who exercised any rights over it, and the land was called allodial. In other countries, called "countries of customary law," the sovereign was the only person who could have the entire ownership over land, no private person could alone be the owner of land; the ownership was always divided between two persons at least, in other words, at least two persons exercised rights over it, the one, called the tenant, had possession of the land, upon condition of performing certain services to the other called the lord, such as to follow him in battle, to sit in his court, to plough his fields, &c., while the lord had rights of seizing the land, or of resuming possession, in certain cases, into his own hands; the nature of the rights of property called *dominium utile* exercised by the tenant, and those called *dominium directum* exercised by the lord, varied in different places, and were regulated by the custom prevailing there. The land itself, or rather the rights of the tenant over it, was called a fief. The tenant was said to hold his fief of the lord, by service of—whatever the case might be. If the lord was a private person, he also held his interest in the land, *i. e.*, his fief, of another by services, so that he was at once lord in relation to his own tenant, and tenant in relation to his own lord; in speaking of the three, the terms used were lord or lord paramount, mesne, and tenant or tenant paravail. Ultimately all persons held their lands from the sovereign as the supreme lord, either directly as his tenants, in which case they were called tenants in capital or in chief, or indirectly as the tenants of a private person who held either directly or indirectly of the sovereign. Those lands of which the sovereign (using the word in the ordinary sense) retained possession, remained allodial. England is one of the countries in which the system of customary law prevailed. Those customs which prevailed all over England and affected everybody, were called common law; others, which had regard to the rights of the crown only, were called the prerogative royal; other customs, which prevailed in certain places only, were called customs, as the custom of gavelkind, the custom of borough English.

Originally fiefs were granted at the will of the

lord, to be held during his pleasure (this is stated by Mr. Butler, Co. Lit., 191, but is doubted by Hallam, Europe during the Middle Ages, vol. ii.); afterwards they were granted for the life of the grantee, and by degrees became hereditary in his family. By the reign of Henry III., they had become hereditary in England, and as a general rule, they descended to the eldest son; but the total exclusion of the younger sons is perhaps peculiar to England. In some countries the younger sons took a share for their lives, in other places this privilege was extended to their descendants. In Kent the custom called gavelkind was and is for the sons to inherit equally; in some parts of England the youngest son inherits, the custom is called borough English.

The possibility of the tenure in any particular part of England being gavelkind or borough English should not be forgotten. The author has heard of a case where a small squire had two sons. He bequeathed all his personalty to his younger son, believing that his land would descend to the elder. Unfortunately it was borough English, so that the elder son took nothing.

The relationship between lord and tenant appears to have been considered as a personal relationship annexed to the land, and therefore originally neither party could determine it without the consent of the other. The tenant's alienation, without licence from the lord, operated as an absolute forfeiture; a trace of this may still be seen in the customs of most manors, where a fine is due to the lord on alienation by a customary tenant; and the necessity for the tenant's consent to the lord's alienation still existed in Littleton's time. It will be observed that in troublous times it was a great advantage to the lord for his tenants to create sub-tenants, for when he summoned his own tenants to come to war, they would call upon theirs to come also, so that the lord would thus obtain a larger number of followers. The creation of a sub-tenancy was not considered as alienation, for the mesne tenant retained his old relationship to his lord.

In England, immediately before the passing of Magna Charta, we find the doctrine of tenures in full force. All land was held either immediately or mediately from the Crown; any tenant, except a tenant *in capite*, was at liberty to give his land, or any part of it, to be held of himself, but he might not give part of it to be held of his lord, as this, by dividing the services, was considered to prejudice the lord; it appears, however, that he could give the whole of it to be held of his lord. The use that is here made of the word "give" requires some explanation. At the time of which we are speaking, the most ordinary method of transferring or creating a freehold interest in land appears to have been by feoffment, *i.e.*, by delivering part to the alienee in the name of the whole. This act was called making a feoffment, or making "livery of seisin," where seisin means the possession of an estate of freehold. Hence the most formal method of stating that a man is entitled to an estate in fee simple, of property of

Alienation.

Feoffment.

which livery can be made, is to state that he is "seised in his demesne as of fee of and in" it, *i. e.* he has feudal possession of it in his demesne, that is dominion or possession held in fee. (Co. Litt. 17 a.) The feoffment was usually, but not always, accompanied by an explanatory writing; this was usually in Latin, and the operative words were usually *dedi* or *confirmavi*, or some equivalent. And hence, where one wishes to speak of the transfer of the feudal possession, one generally uses the word "give."

Quia emptores.

The important Statute of *Quia Emptores*, otherwise Westminster IInd, passed in 18 Edward 1, absolutely prohibited any one, except possibly a tenant *in capite*, from giving his land to be held of himself; but, in return, gave him power to sell the whole, or any part of it, to be held of his own lord. You will observe that the right that a freeholder has of selling his land at the present day depends on this statute. Similar power was extended to tenants *in capite* by the Statutes *de Prœrogativa Regis*, 17 Edward 2, stat. 1, and 1 Edward 3, c. 12.

There is another important effect of the Statute *Quia Emptores*. It prevents the creation of any new manor at the present day.* For, as the reader is probably aware, one of the tests of a manor is the existence of *freeholders* holding part of the land

* *Delacherois* v. *Delacherois*, 11 H. L. C. 62; S. C. 4 N. R. 501, where the opinions of some of the Irish judges are given. The advanced student will find this case worthy of very careful study.

comprised in it from the lord. Accordingly, in conveyancing, we sometimes speak of "the manor, or *reputed* manor of Dale;" where the words *reputed* manor have reference to the possibility that the number of freeholds held of the manor may be less than three, in which case it is no longer a manor strictly so called.

Principal tenures.

The principal tenures which existed at this time in England were,

1. Knight's service.
2. Socage.
3. Frankalmoigne.
4. Villenage.
5. By copy of court-roll.

Tenure by knight's service was abolished by 12 Carol. 2, c. 24; tenure by villenage, if it still exists, is probably confounded with tenure by copy of court-roll. Tenure by frankalmoigne, the tenure by which the clergy hold their lands, has been modified by the changes introduced into the Established Church at the Reformation; and the rest of this chapter will apply to socage tenures only.

Socage tenure.

In socage tenure (Williams on Real Property, 117), as modified by the 12 Car. 2, c. 24, the services due from the tenant to his lord are either fealty or fealty and a certain rent, called a quit rent; and in the latter case a relief or payment of one year's rent by the heir on his ancestor's death. As the amount of the rent must have been fixed before the Statute of *Quia Emptores*, it is always extremely small compared with the value of the land. Sometimes very small annual payments charged on land, the origin of which is not known, are improperly called quit-rents. The importance on a sale of providing against the necessity of accounting for the origin of them is shown in *Attorney-General* v. *Stephens*, 6 De G. Mac. & G. 111. Fealty is in practice never required. The form of the oath of fealty given in Co. Litt. 67*a*, is very quaint; the tenant holds his hand upon a book and says, "Know ye this, my lord, that I shall be faithful and true unto you, and faith to you shall bear for the lands which I claim to hold of you, and that I shall lawfully do to you the customs and services which I ought to do."

Prior to the passing of the Statute of Uses, in the reign of Henry VIII., the principal methods in which land was conveyed in possession were feoffments, fines, and recoveries; the germs of the modern conveyance by lease and release also existed. A fine was a fictitious suit brought for the recovery of the land by the person to whom it was intended to be conveyed against the tenant; the latter obtained leave to compromise the suit on paying a fine to his lord, in whose court the action was brought; and by the compromise acknowledged it to belong to the intending purchaser, who thus became owner by judicial decision.

Lease and release before the Statute of Uses.

As to the lease and release. The release is a deed which enlarges an estate already existing. Thus, if a man be tenant for life or for years, the reversioner may by deed release to the tenant all his (the reversioner's) estate, so that the tenant becomes entitled to it, and his own estate is merged in it. Suppose, therefore, that a man seised in fee granted a lease for years and the lessee entered (for before entry a lessee at common law has no estate in the land, he has merely what is called an *interesse termini*), the reversioner could afterwards by deed release all his estate to the lessee, who thereupon became seised in fee. No livery of seisin was necessary, as the tenant was already in possession.

In conveyances by feoffment, fine, or recovery, the change of possession was notorious; and in the case of lease and release the conveyance was made to a man who already had possession of, and was therefore known to have some interest in, the land.

**Bargain and sale before the Statute of Uses.**

By degrees a scheme came into use for making secret conveyances, as to which some doubts exist whether it was invented by some lawyer whose clients wished to evade the law, or whether it came into force by the desire of the Court of Chancery, that men should act uprightly.

Suppose that a man sold his lands for a pecuniary consideration to another, received the money, and refused to make any conveyance. This was clearly against morality. The common law courts could make him pay damages to the purchaser for the breach of contract, but it does not appear they had any power of making him perform his bargain. Chancery stepped in, and said that he must act honestly and perform his share of the bargain, and declared that he was seised "to the use;" or, as we should now say, "in trust" for the purchaser. The legal interest remained in him, he was still the tenant in the eye of the law, and as such liable to perform all the services to the lord, while the purchaser was put into possession by the Court of Chancery, and was entitled to receive all the profits. Under these circumstances the vendor was generally very willing to make a legal conveyance to the purchaser when called upon.

The next step was simple; when a vendor wished to convey secretly, he executed a deed, by which he bargained and sold his land to the purchaser. This, you will observe, created no legal interest in the purchaser, but gave him a right, called "the use," enforceable in Equity, to take possession of the land.

By degrees the plan was adopted of conveying the land at law—*i.e.* by fine or feoffment—to trustees, as we should now call them, or to feoffees, as you will find them called in the books, to the use of the rightful owner. The result was, that on the death of the true owner the use descended to his heir, while, as neither he nor the heir had *any legal* interest, the feudal incidents of tenure, which were very burdensome in the case of an heir being a minor and taking by descent did not apply. If one of the feoffees died, the surviving feoffees who were already seized of the land, and were persons of full age, escaped, if not all, at least the most burdensome incidents of tenure at the time of a death. At this time no man, except in some places by special custom, could devise his land, but he could devise *the use:* which gave the beneficial interest to the devisee.

The reader will find the whole doctrine of uses thoroughly explained in *Chudleigh's Case*, 1 Rep. 120*a*; also reported in Tudor's Leading Cases, 200. Uses.

The definition given is: "A use is a trust or confidence, which is not issuing out of land, but as a thing collateral annexed in privity to the estate, and to the person touching the land: *scilicet*, that *cestuy que use* shall take the profits, and that the ter-tenant shall make estates according to his direction."

In which he will notice,

1st. That the use is not annexed to the land.

2nd. That it is annexed to the person of the feoffee so long as he holds the legal estate. Any person claiming under the feoffee (except he were a purchaser for value without notice), or, as it is sometimes said, any one in "in the per," his heir-at-law, for instance, was liable to perform the use. On the other hand, any one taking by title paramount to the feoffee and those claiming under him, or, as it is called, any one in "in the post," such as his widow claiming her dower, his lord claiming by escheat, took the land discharged from the use. In "in the per." In "in the post."

Hence it became the custom to make several feoffees to uses, so that dower should not attach, and so that there should be no risk of escheat on the death of the feoffee. Lord Coke goes on to say, "He that hath a use hath not *jus neque in re neque ad rem*;" *i. e.* he hath neither any estate in the land nor title to the same.

Several Acts were passed (1 Ric. 2, c. 9; 4 Hen. 4, c. 7; 11 Hen. 6, c. 4; 1 Hen. 7, c. 1; 1 Ric. 3, c. 1, and others) for the purpose of restoring the ancient publicity of conveyances of land; but, without dwelling on them, we will pass to the Statute of Uses, 27 Hen. 8, c. 10.

Statute of Uses. It is impossible to over-estimate the importance of a thorough knowledge of this statute; it is the foundation of all modern conveyancing.

The 1st section recites the evils which, in the opinion of Parliament, had arisen from feoffments to uses. This recital is well worth perusing; and if the reader will take the trouble to understand each word contained in it (all of which he will find explained in Blackstone), he will have a very fair knowledge of old law. The section proceeds to enact in effect, "Where any person is, or shall be, seised of honours . . . . tenements, rents, services, . . . . reversions, remainders, or other hereditaments, to the use, confidence, or trust of any other person, that the latter shall be seised and deemed in lawful seisin, estate, and possession of and in the same honours, &c., to all intents and purposes, of and in such estates as they had, or shall have in the use, trust, and confidence. And that the estate, title, right, and possession of the former shall be in the latter after such quality, manner, form, and condition as they had before in or to the use, confidence, or trust that was in them."

The reader will observe that there are two branches of the clause: the first enacting part puts the *cestui que use* into actual seisin and possession of the land for the same estate as he had in the use. The second branch diverts the estate of the feoffee, and on the construction of the whole clause it is held that the *cestui que use* cannot take an estate more extensive than the estate of the grantee to uses. Thus a gift to A. for life to the use of B. in fee, gives B. an estate in fee determinable on A.'s death.

The 4th and 5th clauses of the statute enact that when a person is seised of land, &c., to the use that some one else shall take a rent-charge; the latter shall be in actual possession of the rent.

A common example is a jointure rent-charge.

The 4th and 5th sections are sometimes of use when one creates a rent-charge for the purpose of giving a qualification for the magistracy or to create a vote. The usual form is to make a grant at common law, then the grantee does not come into possession of his charge till some payment has actually been made. If it is necessary to put him into possession at once, and the state of the title affords no objection, this can be done by limiting the land "to the use that A. B. shall receive a rent-charge, issuing, &c., and subject thereto to the old uses." (*Heelis* v. *Blain*, 18 C. B. N. S. 90.)

Let us now consider the effect of the first section of the statute: it is necessary that there should be at least two persons, one seised to the use of the other. Thus, a feoffment "to A. and his heirs to the use of B. and his heirs," before the statute, made A. seised in fee, while B. took an equitable interest, which could be enforced in Chancery only. Since the statute, the same feoffment would vest the legal estate in B., who would, in the eye of the law, become immediately seised in fee.

In the common case of a conveyance "to A. and his heirs to the use of A. and his heirs," A. is seised in fee at common law, and the statute never has any effect at all; and if the conveyance be for value, the words are mere surplusage. The reader must not, however, suppose that it is suggested that he should leave them out. When a form of words has been sanctioned by long-continued usage, for the purpose of expressing some particular meaning, the very fact of changing the form raises a presumption that the draftsman wishes to express some other meaning: any alteration in a common form is therefore full of danger, and is to be avoided by every young practitioner. Although, *if the conveyance be for value*, the words "to the use," &c., are mere surplusage, this is not the case in a conveyance without consideration, for in such case, if there be no declaration of use, the law implies, as it would have done before the Statute of Uses, a use in favour of the person conveying.

In the fifth chapter we will discuss what amounts to a consideration, and will recur to the Statute of Uses.

Statute of Inrolments. We now come to the Statute for Inrolment of Bargain and Sale, 27 Hen. 8, c. 16. The reader will observe that, prior to the Statute of Uses, if A., seised in fee, bargained and sold his land to B., although no estate passed at law, the effect was to raise a use or trust for B. which the Court of Chancery enforced. The effect, therefore, of the Statute of Uses, which gave the seisin to the *cestui que use*, was to enable any one to convey his legal estate in land by a secret bargain and sale. For the purpose of preventing this, the Act of Inrolments (27 Hen. 8, c. 16) enacted that no estate of inheritance, or freehold in any hereditaments, should pass by reason only of a bargain and sale, unless the same be by writing, indented, sealed, delivered, and inrolled within six months of the date, as in the Act mentioned (see Williams, Real Property, p. 177).

Lease and release.

It appeared as if the Legislature had effectually provided for the publicity of all purchase-deeds relating to land; but the ingenuity of lawyers soon baffled them, and invented the celebrated conveyance by way of Lease and Release.

The operation of a lease and release before the Statute of Uses has already been described. Then a common law lease was made to the purchaser who actually entered on the land; a release operating at common law was then made to him by the vendor. It has also been stated, that courts of Equity held that a bargain and sale for value operated as a declaration of the use. The Statute of Inrolments applies to freehold interests only, and it follows that a bargain and sale of a leasehold interest took effect, notwithstanding the Act. But as it took effect as the declaration of a use, the Statute of Uses applied to it, and the lessee immediately after the execution of the bargain and sale, became in possession by virtue of the statute; being in possession, he could take a release of the reversion. A conveyance made in this manner by a bargain and sale for a term operating under the Statute of Uses, followed by a release operating at common law, forms the celebrated conveyance of lease and release, which may still be used, and has only recently become disused.

The operative part of the bargain and sale, or lease for a year, ran as follows:—"In consideration of five shillings paid by the purchaser to the vendor the vendor doth bargain and sell unto the purchaser his executors, administrators and assigns, all those [parcels] to have and to hold the same, with the appurtenances, unto the purchaser, his executors, administrators and assigns, from the day next before the day of the date of these presents, for the term of one whole year next ensuing."

Where, it will be observed, nothing is said about the use; but, as there is a valuable consideration, the use is implied for the purpose of carrying out the declared intention of the parties; and the Statute of Uses puts the purchaser into possession.

The operative parts of the release were—"The vendor, in consideration of      pounds, doth hereby release unto the purchaser and his heirs all those [parcels] to hold the same, with their appurtenances, unto the purchaser and his heirs." Stopping here, the purchaser is in by common law, and has a seisin, on which uses may be declared: and if the conveyance was to him himself, the use would be "to the use of the said purchaser, his heirs and assigns for ever."

Except in the very simple case of a conveyance in fee, the declaration of uses forms a most important part of a conveyance; and in order that it may take effect under the statute, it is necessary that some one should be seised to the uses (*Peacock* v. *Eastland*, L. R. 10 Eq. Ca. 17). In order to raise such seisin, the conveyance which vests the land in the grantee to uses must not operate under the Statute of Uses for, by a highly artificial construction of the statute, it is held that you cannot have a use upon a use. Thus, a feoffment or conveyance by release founded upon a lease for a year (which lease may either be a lease operating at common law, and perfected by entry, or a bargain and sale for years operating under the statute,) to A. and his heirs to the use of B. and his heirs, vests the legal estate in B.; but a bargain and sale inrolled, to A. and his heirs to the use of B. and his heirs, leaves the legal estate in A.; for the statute has produced all its effect in clothing the implied use raised in favour of A. with the legal estate. **Declaration of uses.**

It will be observed that the conveyance, if any, to the person on whose seisin the use is declared, may be by the same or a different instrument from that by which the uses are declared. Thus, in a conveyance by lease and release, the release contains the declaration of uses; but in the case of a fine or recovery, the declaration of uses was always made by an independent instrument, either before or after the fine was levied or the recovery suffered.

All conveyances which do not take effect by virtue of the Statute of Uses are said to operate by transmutation of possession, for the conveyance itself transmutes the possession of the land by the purchaser.

Bargains and sales and covenants to stand seised merely operate as declarations of use by the conveying party, and the possession of the land passes by force of the Statute of Uses.

Statute of Wills.

The Statute of Uses had another very important effect—an effect which aimed at producing so profound a social change, that it was actually put forward as one of the grievances sought to be redressed by the so-called Pilgrimage of Grace, the great northern rebellion, which took place shortly after the Statute was passed. As already mentioned, no man could (except in some places, by virtue of a custom) make a will of land. The plan adopted was to make a feoffment to the uses of the will, and then to devise the uses. The effect of the Statute of Uses was entirely to prevent this being done. For as there was no consideration for the use, a use resulted back to the feoffor, and by force of the statute he remained seised. Accordingly, one of the grievances alleged by the rebels was, that now no man could by will provide for his wife and younger sons. To remedy this, an Act was passed (32 Hen. 8, c. 1) which, *inter alia*, enabled a man to devise his lands held in socage tenure.

'equent

The subsequent changes in the law of real property that are of interest to conveyancers, appear to be principally the following :— changes in law.

1. The change of all tenures, except copyholds customaryholds, and leaseholds, into free and common socage. 12 Car. 2, c. 24.

2. The Statute of Frauds (29 Car. 2, c. 3), which renders it necessary for all conveyances of real property (excepting certain leases) to be in writing.

The effect of this was to render a feoffment with livery void, unless evidenced by writing, which now, by the Act to amend the Law of Property (8 & 9 Vict. c. 106), must be by deed.

3. The Abolition of Fines and Recoveries. 3 & 4 Will. 4, c. 74.

4. The Dower Act. 3 & 4 Will. 4, c. 105.

5. The Act to amend the Law of Inheritance. 3 & 4 Will. 4, c. 106.

6. The Wills Act. 7 Will. 4 & 1 Vict. c. 26.

7. Act abolishing Leases for a Year. 4 & 5 Vict. c. 35.

8. The Act amending the Law of Real Property. 8 & 9 Vict. c. 106, which makes all corporeal hereditaments to lie in grant.

The student may consult the following authorities on the subject of this Chapter.

1. Hallam's Europe during the Middle Ages—the chapter on the Feudal System.

2. Butler, Co. Litt. 191.

3. Coke's Second Institute, *passim*.

4. Blackstone's Commentaries, vol. ii. (any old edit.)

5. *Delacherois* v. *Delacherois*, 11 H. L. C. 62; S. C. 4 N. R. 501.

# CHAPTER III.

## ON THE INTERPRETATION OF LEGAL DOCUMENTS.

It is sufficiently obvious that no one is likely to become a good draftsman (*i. e.*, a person whose drafts are short and lucid) unless he understands the principles by which a person perusing them will be guided in interpreting them; or, in other words, in endeavouring to discover the author's meaning.

**Statement of the general problem.**

If a person has wishes or intentions which he wishes to communicate to another, he does so by means of physical signs addressed to the senses. There are many signs that he can make use of; they may be addressed to any of the senses. Thus a blow which is addressed to the sense of touch, affords strong indication that the person who gives the blow is angry with the person struck. The sign may be addressed to the eye, as in the common case, where a man nods to another, the nod may mean yes or no. The sign may be addressed to the ear, as in the case of speech; it generally happens that the signs are more readily interpreted when they are addressed to two senses at once; it is much more easy to understand a person speaking to us if he is in sight, so that we can see the expression of his countenance.

In all these examples the sign is fugitive, so that if we wish subsequently to discover what wishes a man expressed at a particular time, we cannot refer to the sign itself, it no longer exists; all that we can do is to endeavour to remember it, or to obtain such evidence concerning it as is afforded by the memory of others.

Sign should be permanent.

It is obvious that when a man wishes to preserve an accurate record of his wishes or intentions at a particular time, it will be convenient that he should express his wishes or intentions by a sign that has the character of permanence. Then there can be no question in the future as to what the sign was; the only question that can arise is what the sign meant. For example, it is not an uncommon thing to commemorate great national events by erecting monuments in stone. The sign itself, the monument, is palpable, the only difficulty is to discover what is meant by it. Some antiquarians, for instance, believe that Stonehenge is a monument raised to commemorate some particular event in our history; no doubt this may be so, but although the sign remains, we do not know what it means.

Writing, a permanent sign.

The art of writing affords a most convenient method of expressing one's intentions by signs which are readily saved from destruction. A person in the habit of expressing himself in writing can express himself as clearly as he does in ordinary conversation, add to which that he knows that if he becomes unintelligible in ordinary conversation, he will be able to repair his error on the moment; while, on the other hand, if he does not express himself intelligibly in writing, the error may be irreparable; he may never know of it, or if he does he may be prevented from stating what his true meaning was, so that it generally happens that the expression of a man's intentions as contained in writing is more accurate than that expressed in ordinary conversation.

Superior accuracy of writing recognised by the law of England.

The law of England recognises the superior accuracy of writing to conversation as a means of expression of intentions, when it declares that if a contract is reduced into writing, it shall be proved by that writing and nothing else. One word as to a source of confusion; we commonly speak of a writing containing the expression of a contract as "the contract." In strictness the phrase "the contract" applies to the engagement between the parties, while the writing is the expression of that engagement.

Again the Law (the Statute of Frauds) declares that no action shall be brought to charge a person who has entered into contracts of certain natures, unless they be reduced to writing: similarly a will must generally be in writing; the object in all these cases being to exclude the uncertainty and the risk of perjury, arising from trusting to men's memory of what has been said.

Expressed intentions.

In all these cases, where a written instrument is the only evidence that we may make use of for the purpose of ascertaining a man's intention when he wrote it, the sole question for our consideration is this, what are his *expressed intentions;* a different thing, it will be observed, from his intentions, as he may have had some intentions that he did not express; or his real intentions may have been something different from those expressed in the writing.

**The meanings of the words employed.**

The proposition that when we are interpreting a document we are seeking the writer's *expressed* intentions, is sometimes enunciated as follows: "In interpreting a document we have only to discover the meanings of the words employed." The latter form of expression is not very accurate, because as everybody knows, the same word may be used in different meanings. A sailor and a housemaid mean something very different by the word "sheet," and the words used to express the same thing will be different when used by different persons; they will depend upon the circumstances, character, and habits of the writer. A common instance is afforded by the use of slang terms, probably the language used by a professional thief, in describing his adventures, would be unintelligible to most educated men. If every word bore at this present time only one meaning, and had never borne a meaning different from that which it now bears, it would no doubt be correct to say that the meaning of the words employed by any writer were identical with his expressed intentions. But this is not the case, for, as already pointed out, the same word used by different people may mean different things. If we know accurately the circumstances, character, and habits of a writer, we can arrive with a high degree of probability at the meaning in which he used any particular word; and that (it will be remarked) will be sufficient for our purpose; for as it is evident from the fact of the document existing, that the writer desired to express some intention, we must put some interpretation on it, and we shall have done our utmost when we have discovered that it is more probable that the words used in it were used by the author in some particular meanings than in any others.

Unfortunately, although a writing may be preserved, still the longer the time that has elapsed since the author wrote it, the less certain can we be as to the meaning in which he used his words. We have difficulty in ascertaining his circumstances, character, and habits, and in default of being able to do so, we are forced to put upon his words the meanings which the ordinary usage of society affixed to them at the time when he used them, and possibly we may be in doubt as to what those meanings were, for owing to the gradual changes produced by the lapse of time, they may have been different then from what they are now. We are also uncertain whether the words did not at that time bear a technical or conventional sense, and whether they were not so used by him. The change which the lapse of time may make in the meaning of words may be instanced by the phrase, "the Scriptures." No phrase, perhaps, can now be cited of less ambiguous interpretation. Yet "search the Scriptures" in the New Testament does not include that part of them which, in the eyes of

Christians is the most important—the New Testament itself—simply because when that phrase was used the New Testament had not been written.

A word has generally more than one meaning.

These considerations show that we cannot generally speak of a word as having only one meaning: the problem that we have to solve is to discover in which of its meanings the author has used it. When we have solved this problem; when we have affixed to each word the meaning in which it was employed by the author; then, and not before, can we say that the meaning of the words used by the author is identical with his expressed intentions.

Two classes of evidence as to meaning of words.

We can call to our aid evidence as to the meaning in which the words were used of two different classes, *extrinsic* evidence and *intrinsic* evidence. Where by extrinsic evidence is meant evidence not contained in the document; intrinsic evidence is evidence derived from the inspection of the document.

From these considerations it will be apparent that when we wish to interpret a document, in other words, to discover the meanings in which the author used the words in it, we must endeavour to discover his circumstances, character, and habits at the time of writing. In other words, we must discover to what class of society he belonged, the time at which he wrote, in what meanings would his words have been used at that time by persons of that class; and, having regard to his character and habits, did he use them in a different meaning; is it probable, having regard to the subject matter of the document, that they were used in a scientific or technical sense; was the document in question a private document, by which is meant a document addressed to a limited class of persons only; and, if so, did the words bear a special meaning, having regard to the status of the persons addressed? We may properly admit both extrinsic and intrinsic evidence to enable us to ascertain any of these facts. We must not, however, admit extrinsic evidence to show the intention of the author, that any of his words should bear a special meaning in the document under consideration, for that would be to admit evidence to prove an intention on his part not expressed in the document, or, in other words, we should not be interpreting the document alone, we should be interpreting it together with other expressed intentions of the author. When, however, we admit extrinsic evidence for the purpose of showing that the words employed bear a special meaning having regard to the persons to whom the document is addressed, we are not seeking for evidence of intentions of the author not expressed in the document, for, as already stated, the status of the persons to whom the document is addressed forms an important element in determining the choice of words on the part of the author. For instance, a young man writing to another might address him as "My dear old boy," as a term of affection, while the very same phrase in a letter to one of his elders would be held very rude.

The reader will now be able to understand the rules for the application of extrinsic evidence to the interpretation of documents.

Rule I. When the words used in a document are in their primary meanings unambiguous, and when such meanings are not excluded by the context, and are sensible with reference to the circumstances in which the author was placed at the time of writing, including in such circumstances the status of the persons to whom the document was addressed, such primary meanings must be taken to be those in which the author used them. Rules for the employment of extrinsic evidence.

Rule II. Extrinsic evidence is admissible for the purpose of determining the primary meanings of the words employed, but not for any other purpose whatsoever.

These rules require the following explanatory observations:

1st. By "primary," sometimes called "literal" meaning, we mean not the primary etymological meaning, but the meaning usually affixed to the words at the time when the author wrote by persons of the class to which he belonged, as modified by his personal character, or the meaning in which the words would have been used by such persons, having regard to the circumstances in which the author was placed at the time of writing, or the meaning which it can be conclusively shown he was in the habit of affixing to them. Primary meaning.

2nd. If technical or scientific words occur in a document relating to the art or science to which they belong, the technical or scientific must be considered to be the primary meaning. For instance, if some word or phrase of ascertained meaning in law occurs Technical language. Example.

in a deed, such meaning must be conclusively affixed to it. Most laymen who are silly enough to draw their own wills offend against this rule. Instead of attempting to state their wishes in common language, they constantly go out of their way to employ technical words which they do not understand; a common blunder that they make is to use the word "issue" when they mean "children." "Issue" is a technical word, which exactly corresponds to "descendants;" so that the interpretation put on such a will generally is different from what the testator intended. One amusing instance has been handed down by tradition. A layman drawing his own will looked at his marriage settlement, and finding after every gift the words "but in trust only," considered that they were words of great efficacy, and inserted them in several places in his will, the result being to disappoint all the objects of his bounty.

Private documents.

3rd. If words occur in a private document having a special meaning, having regard to the persons to whom they are addressed, the special must be considered as the primary meaning.

This observation is sometimes of use in interpreting letters. It does not apply to ordinary legal documents which, in contemplation of law, are addressed to all the world. Consider the commencement of a deed-poll: "To all to whom these presents shall come;" and that an indenture "Witnesseth," *i.e.* preserves testimony for the use of any person who requires it.

4th. By the words "sensible with reference to

the external circumstances," it is not meant that the external circumstances render it more or less reasonable or probable that the primary meaning of the words used is that which the author affixed to them; it is enough if they do not exclude it, or, in other words, if they do not deprive the words of all reasonable application according to such primary meaning.

Incorporated public document.

Sometimes it happens that a public document is incorporated into another document; the questions arise, are we to consider the time of the adoption, or of the composition of the adopted document, as "the time of writing?" and are we to consider the circumstances of the original author, or of the person who has adopted it, as "the circumstances" under our rule?

Popular meaning.

It is evident that the person who adopts a public document does not necessarily employ the words in it in the same meanings as those in which he would have used them in an original document. There are two other meanings in which he may have used them, viz., in their primary meaning, as employed in the adopted document, or in their popular meaning. By popular meaning is understood the interpretation that has been put upon the words in that particular document by general consent; for we find that a public document is constantly interpreted by persons ignorant or careless of the true rules of interpretation until after the lapse of a certain time common usage may affix to some of the words or phrases contained in it a special meaning not necessarily the same as that which they bore when first written, or as that which they would have borne if used in an original composition by the person who has adopted them. The strong presumption is, that he has affixed the popular meaning to such of the words as have acquired it: for he knows that the document which he is composing will be interpreted by persons who are acquainted with the earlier document and the popular meaning of the words in it, and who are likely therefore to affix that meaning to them: while, if the words have acquired no such meaning, in other words, if the adopted document has habitually been interpreted correctly, the presumption still is that the person adopting it uses it in the sense in which it is habitually interpreted; in other words, he affixes the same meanings to the words as those at which he would have arrived had he applied our rules to the interpretation of the adopted document. These considerations lead to the 5th explanatory observation.

5th. The primary meaning of the words in an adopted public document is their popular meaning. But if they have acquired no such meaning, or if the circumstances of the person who has adopted them are such as to rebut the presumption of his acquaintance with them, their primary meaning is to be ascertained having regard to the external circumstances and time of writing of the author of the adopted document.

Statutes. The rule as to adopted documents has two important practical bearings. We very often find that a modern Act of Parliament adopts in great part the language of an older Act on the same subject which may have received judicial interpretation; such interpretation (even if incorrect) is an authoritative interpretation, and the meaning which the words bear, according to it is the "popular" meaning within the meaning of the last observation. When, therefore, we find clauses inserted in an Act taken from an older Act, we should endeavour to ascertain if there has been any judicial decision as to their meanings in the older Act, as if this be the case we must (subject to the application of Rule IV. *post,*) conclusively assume that the Legislature used the words in the meaning affixed to them by the decision. (*Ex parte Campbell,* L. R. 5 Ch. Ap. 706.) And, on the other hand, if we find the clauses slightly altered, it affords some presumption that they were not intended to bear that meaning.

Common forms.

The common forms used by conveyancers are public documents. They have been brought into their present shape by the efforts of generations of conveyancers, and while they have been modified from time to time in consequence of changes in the law, they remain substantially what they were many years ago. The meaning affixed to them by the usage of conveyancers, is the "popular" meaning in the sense in which that phrase is used in the fifth observation. It follows that where a draftsman wishes to express a meaning which can be expressed by a common form, he should always employ it, as he knows that all lawyers will put a correct interpretation on his language, without hesitation;

while if he endeavours to express the same meaning in a different form of words, he raises a presumption against that meaning being the correct one, owing to his employment of unusual language, and he causes an unnecessary expenditure of time and labour to the person perusing the draft. Many students beginning conveyancing object to the common forms on account of the apparently ungainly language in which they are expressed, but a more careful study will, in most cases, show the reason for the employment of every word in them; and even if the student could express the same meaning more concisely and elegantly, there would be danger in doing so, for the reasons above stated.

The author strongly recommends to the student to study the common forms very carefully, so as to understand the general scheme on which each one of them is founded, and the reasons which have led conveyancers to choose the words in which they are generally expressed.

Adopted private document. The case of an adopted private document is rather different, as, although we may be acquainted with the position of the person who adopts it, we may be ignorant of the existence of the earlier document, and of the position of its author; it follows, that in the interpretation of an adopted private document, we must take the time of adoption for "the time of writing," and must consider "the external circumstances" of the person adopting the earlier document, and not those of its original author. These considerations lead us to the sixth explanatory observation.

6th. The primary meaning of the words in an adopted private document must be ascertained, having regard to the person who has adopted them at the time of adoption.

The next question for our consideration is the following: "What intrinsic evidence, or, in other words, what evidence derived from the consideration of the document itself can we obtain as to the meaning which the author has affixed to his words?" It is obvious that intrinsic evidence will often give information as to the time of writing and circumstances of the writer, and that with greater certainty than extrinsic evidence, or, to use the language that we have hitherto adopted, intrinsic evidence will enable us to discover the primary meaning of the words employed. But the more important use of intrinsic evidence is for the purpose of removing apparent inconsistencies or contradictions. It may happen that when we affix the primary meanings to the words employed, we arrive at inconsistent or contradictory intentions on the part of the author, we are therefore led to suppose that he has employed some of his words at least in other meanings; for it is reasonable to suppose that he intended that the whole of the document should be consistent with itself, and that he has used each of his words in such a meaning as will cause this to be the case. To discover, therefore the author's intentions, we must endeavour to affix to some of the words employed such other of the meanings *which they properly bear* as will remove the apparent inconsistencies and con-

Intrinsic evidence.

tradictions. We must study, therefore, the whole of the document before we endeavour to place the final interpretation on any part of it, and must not consider any word or phrase isolated from the context. We must remember that the author may have employed the same word in a different meaning in different parts of the same document, and that the context will be our only guide to discover such an intention on his part. If a word occurs that bears a scientific or technical meaning, the context may alter or control it.

These considerations lead us to the following rules for the employment of intrinsic evidence :

Rules for employment of intrinsic evidence.

Rule III. Intrinsic evidence is admissible for the purpose of discovering the primary meaning of the words employed.

Rule IV. When the primary meaning of any word is excluded by the context, we must affix to that word such of the meanings which it properly bears, as will enable us to collect uniform and consistent intentions from every part of the document.

The rule which we have just considered is of special importance when we are interpreting an adopted public document. Although, as we have seen, the presumption in such a case is that the person who had adopted it intended to retain in their popular meanings such of the words as have acquired them, yet the context may show that he either intended them to bear the meanings which were their primary meaning at the date of the original composition of the earlier document, or the meanings which they would have borne if they had stood in a document composed by him at the time of adoption. The context may also rebut the presumption that he intended the words in the adopted document, which had not acquired a popular meaning, to bear the meanings which they bore at the date of the original composition of the earlier document, and may show that he intended them to bear the meanings which they would have borne if they had stood in a document composed by him at the time of adoption.

The difficulties that we shall encounter in the application of the foregoing rules are not caused by the author of the document, they arise solely from the difficulty of obtaining the necessary evidence. We now come to difficulties of a totally different class, viz., those caused by the author himself. He may not have had sufficient clearness of conception to form definite intentions, or sufficient mastery over language to express them, he may also have changed his purpose during the composition of the document, or again, he may have misled us through ignorance of the meanings that we should be led by our rules to affix to his words, and his language may, for one or other of these reasons contain contradictions or ambiguities. Difficulties caused by the author.

If the document under consideration has been in part adopted from an earlier document, ambiguities and contradictions may arise from the fact of the person who has adopted it being ignorant of the rules by which he ought to construe the adopted document, or from his being ignorant of the popular meaning which some of the words in it may have acquired.

Contradictions.

In cases where the documents contain apparent contradictions, we are sometimes able to reconcile them by the use of further evidence as to the circumstances and time of writing of the author; but when this is not the case, we must reject all but one of the inconsistent statements if we are to give any effect to the document. The question arises, which of them is to be rejected, which retained, and it is of importance to remember, in seeking the answer to this question, that it is not properly speaking a question of interpretation, but a question as to what is the subject matter to be interpreted. We have first to apply our rules of interpretation to ascertain what intentions are expressed in the document, and if we find that these intentions are inconsistent, we have further to consider which of them is most probably the intention which the author desired to express. The Law of England contains rules as to which of inconsistent intentions expressed in legal documents to reject, which to prefer; but they are hardly fit to be considered in an elementary treatise.

Ambiguities.

We now have to consider the case of ambiguities. Ambiguities may be divided into two classes. An ambiguity of the first class, called a "patent" ambiguity, occurs when the intentions of the author, as expressed on the face of the document, are ambiguous. An ambiguity of the second class, called a "latent" ambiguity, occurs when the intentions of the author, as expressed on the face of the document are free from ambiguity, and the ambiguity becomes manifest only when we consider some of his circumstances at the time of writing. In either of these cases the ambiguity may sometimes be removed by affixing to the words made use of their meanings as determined by our rules; but if this cannot be done, the author has expressed no intentions that we can take any cognizance of.

**Patent ambiguity.** As an example of a patent ambiguity, suppose that a man writes in a letter, "I give my dog Ranger to my nephew John or Thomas." Here the writer has on the face of his letter expressed ambiguous intentions. He appears to be halting between two intentions. The ambiguity may disappear when we consider the circumstances of the writer at the time of writing. It might, for instance, appear that John or Thomas were two names by which the same person was known to him at that time. But if, on the other hand, it should appear that John and Thomas were different persons, we should be unable to place any certain meaning on the words employed, or, in other words, we should be unable to ascertain the expressed intentions of the writer.

**Latent ambiguity.** As an example of a latent ambiguity, we suppose that the man had stated in his letter "I give my dog Ranger to my nephew Robert." He has expressed an intention free from ambiguity on the face of the document. We find, however, when we come to investigate his circumstances at the time of writing that he had two nephews, Robert Smith and

Robert Jones. If we cannot discover further evidence as to his circumstances, our rule fails to remove the ambiguity, and we fail to discover the writer's expressed intentions. But suppose that, on further inquiry, we find, that Jones had sailed for New Zealand many years before the date of the letter, that he had never been heard of again prior to that date, and that the writer of the letter had gone into mourning for him, though it had since been ascertained that he was living at that date. Suppose, further, that Robert Smith had, prior to and at the date of the letter, been on terms of intimacy with the writer, and had habitually been called "nephew Robert" by him, such evidence would be properly admissible under our rules to show that by the words "nephew Robert" the writer meant Robert Smith; we should not, however, admit direct evidence of the writer's intentions to benefit Smith, such as declarations made by him at the time of writing his letter, for that would be to admit evidence of an unexpressed intention. (*Grant* v. *Grant*, L. R. 5 C. P. 727.)

Exceptional case.

There is, however, one very important exception to our rules. Where there is a latent ambiguity in a will as to the subject of a gift, or as to the object of a testator's bounty, extrinsic evidence is admissible for the purpose of ascertaining in what meaning the testator used his words; or, as it is sometimes expressed, parol evidence is admitted to prove the testator's intentions.

It must be observed that much confusion has been

introduced into the theory of interpretation of wills from attention not having been paid to the fact that when a latent ambiguity can be removed by the consideration of all the circumstances of a testator at the time when he made his will, the necessity for having recourse to the exceptional rule as to the admission of parol evidence of intention does not arise, and that when a latent ambiguity cannot be removed by evidence admissible under our rules, and we admit direct evidence as to the testator's intentions, the case is, as already mentioned, exceptional, for we then admit extrinsic evidence to show that the testator affixed a special meaning to his words on the particular occasion when he made his will.

Interpretation is a tentative process.

The process of interpretation, as thus described, is a tentative process. When a document is placed in our hands, we at once obtain some information as to the time of writing from the character of the letters and the nature of the fabric on which it is written. But we can obtain no intrinsic evidence from the language employed till we have put some interpretation on it. In order to do so, we must seek the primary meanings of the words employed in conformity with the rules above laid down, assuming, in the absence of extrinsic evidence, such circumstances and time of writing of the author as shall not be inconsistent with the intrinsic evidence already obtained; so soon as we have affixed meanings to the words we are able to place some interpretation on the document, and from the intrinsic evidence that we derive from its perusal we are able to correct our opinions as to the circumstances and time of writing of the author, and are thus led to modify some of the meanings already affixed to the words; we are also led to modify them so as to endeavour to obtain a uniform and consistent sense from the whole document. If contradictions or ambiguities should now appear, we are thrown back on extrinsic evidence; but the very fact of reconciling contradictions and clearing up ambiguities may alter the intrinsic evidence and lead to some further modifications in the meanings which we affix to the words employed.

Preconceived opinions.

It is important to remember that if we wish to interpret a document correctly, we must dismiss any preconceived opinions as to the intentions of the author; we must be on our guard against the grave error of substituting the intentions which in our opinion the author ought to have held for those which we find expressed in the document before us. For the very reason of the author's having composed the document may have been to show that he did not hold certain opinions which he was generally to his own knowledge considered to hold. When the document relates to a subject in which we are deeply interested, the temptation to fall into this error becomes strong; and if it relates to a subject which is not only one in which we are deeply interested, but is one which we habitually talk about, this temptation may become irresistible. "Some ideas," it has been said, "are by frequency and strength of association so closely connected, that they cannot be separated." A man who habitually expresses certain intentions in a definite form of words, becomes at last unable to conceive the possibility of another man using that form to express any other intentions.

The advanced student, who wishes to pursue the study of interpretation, may peruse Hawkins on Wills; *Shore* v. *Wilson*, 9 Cl. & Fin. 255; Broom's Legal Maxims; The judgment of the Privy Council in "The Gorham Case;" Papers read before the Juridical Society, Vol. II., pp. 298 and 351, and Vol. III., p. 251.

# CHAPTER IV.

## ON THE PREPARATION OF ASSURANCES.

Duty of draftsman to express intentions of the parties.

THE duty of the draftsman is to express clearly and with conciseness the intention of the parties in technical language. It may appear superfluous to suggest that, in order to enable him to do so, it is necessary for him to form a clear idea of what those intentions are. It is, however, extremely difficult, in some cases, to discover what the parties wish, the instructions may be imperfect, obscure, or ambiguous, or they may offend against some rule of law. In all these cases the draftsman has nothing but common sense to guide him.

It is a convenient practice to put a note on the margin of those parts of the draft that are not strictly in accordance with the instructions, calling attention to the discrepancy. As an example: In most cases, where a lady takes the first life interest under a marriage settlement, it is intended to be settled to her separate use without power of anticipation, while in the instructions the words "separate use," without anything more, may occur. In this case the draftsman may follow the instructions strictly or he may (if he thinks that the words "without anticipation" have been omitted by error) add the restraint on anticipation, but in this case he would be acting most improperly were he not to call attention to the fact. As a general rule the young practitioner should follow the instructions exactly. It appears to be a convenient practice when the draft is finished to read the instructions over again, so as to be certain that it is in accordance with them.

Do the instructions offend against any rule of law?

When the draftsman has satisfied himself that he clearly understands the intentions of the parties, he should, in the next place, consider whether these intentions offend against any rule of Law. A testator may wish to tie up his property for a period that would offend against the rules against perpetuities, or he may wish to make an inalienable provision for an extravagant son, in both of which cases his intentions would be contrary to Law. In cases similar to these, where the instructions cannot be carried out, owing to their offending against some rule of Law, it becomes a subject for consideration whether the rule of Law can be evaded. For instance, in the second case that I have pointed out, the provision may be made by means of an artifice, that will be pointed out in the chapter on marriage settlements, while in the former case it would be a question for the draftsman whether he should settle the draft, differing from the instructions so far as necessary to make it lawful, or whether he should send back for fresh instructions. As a general rule, it appears the more convenient course to prepare the draft in the manner which will, in all probability be adopted, without waiting for further instructions, as, if it suits the client's wishes, time and expense will be saved.

When the draftsman has formed a clear idea as to what are the intentions of the parties, how far they are lawful, and if unlawful how they should be modified, he is in a position to begin to prepare the draft. His duty now is to translate the intentions of the parties (modified, if necessary, so as not to be illegal) into technical language, arranged in the order commonly adopted for the purpose.

The draft should be sketched mentally.

He will facilitate his operations by sketching out the frame of his draft in his mind before he puts pen to paper; before he does so, a perusal of drafts on similar subjects in any good book of precedents will generally enable him to hit upon the most convenient scheme. There is another advantage in perusing printed precedents at this stage of the work, as it lessens the risk of the omission of some clause which, though not stated explicitly in the instructions, should be inserted. For example, the instructions might be "To prepare a mortgage for £ at per cent. on the farm, the title to which is shown in the accompanying abstract." Nothing is said about a power of sale, but the draftsman would insert it as a matter of course.

Skeleton draft.

As soon as the general frame of the draft has been determined on, the draftsman may proceed to the actual preparation of it. A very good method is to frame a skeleton draft before he begins to draw in reality.

Thus, suppose the ordinary case of a conveyance by a mortgagor and mortgagee to a purchaser. (See Davidson's Concise Precedents, p. 72). The skeleton draft might run as follows:

Parties A. B. 1st—C. D. 2nd—E. F. 3rd.

Recitals.

1. Mortgage in fee for 1000*l.* C. D. to A. B.
2. Contract for sale for 1500*l.* C. D. to E. F.
3. Principal due, interest paid; principal to be paid off out of purchase-money. A. B. to join.

Witnessing clauses.

1. In consideration of 1000*l.* to A. B.; and of 500*l.* to C. D., paid by E. F.
2. A. B. and C. D. grant parcels unto E. F. and his heirs.
3. Habendum to E. F. in fee free from the mortgage.
4. A. B. covenants against incumbrances.
5. C. D. covenants for title.

In such a simple case as that given for an example it would hardly be necessary for any one, except a mere beginner, to prepare a skeleton draft, but the practice may, in difficult cases, be of use even to a person of experience.

The draftsman should mark in the margin of each clause of the instructions where they are complicated the number of the corresponding clause of the skeleton draft, so as to guard against the accidental omission of any thing intended to be provided for.

Begin each clause on a separate sheet.

It is a convenient practice to begin each clause on a separate sheet, to fold it up separately, and to endorse a reference to the skeleton draft.

These suggestions are of special value, when part of the draft has to be prepared by pupils or clerks. For when the skeleton draft has been carefully framed, it is unlikely that pupils of even small experience will adopt the wrong common forms when they draw the clauses; and if they should do so, the fact of each clause beginning on a separate sheet would facilitate the substitution of the appropriate clause.

Alterations in draft.

If the skeleton draft has been carefully framed it is unlikely that the frame of the draft will require much alteration; but if it should do so, the clauses already prepared should be resettled with the greatest care; for, bearing in mind the fourth rule of interpretation, it is evident that a slight change in the frame of the draft may alter the interpretation considerably.

For instance, suppose that as the draft originally stood, there were four witnessing parts which by a subsequent alteration were reduced to three, there would be a considerable risk of retaining a reference to "the hereditaments and premises fourthly hereinbefore expressed to be hereby conveyed."

Drawing at random.

It is hardly necessary to point out the impropriety of inserting or omitting anything without having a reason for it. The unnecessary insertion of a clause is likely to give a great deal of unnecessary trouble to any one perusing the draft; he will assume that there was some reason for the insertion, and will vainly try to discover what that reason was. On the other hand, the improper omission of a clause may either render the draft unintelligible, or may prevent it from having its desired operation.

Suppose, for instance, that the draft is a conveyance under a power of sale contained in a strict settlement on A. for life with remainders in tail to his sons and daughters in the usual manner, with remainder to B. for life, with remainders over, the power to be exercised by the trustees with the consent of the tenant for life for the time being, and that A. the first tenant for life having died without issue, B. the second tenant for life was in possession. In this case what we really want is to show that the power can now be exercised by persons who are parties to the deed, *i. e.*, by the trustees and present tenant for life. Our recitals should set forth the limitations of the settlement so far as, and including, the limitation to B., and the power of sale; the recitals would be continued by stating the death of A., and that he never had any issue. It would be unnecessary to set out any limitations subsequent to that to B., as the knowledge of such limitations would be useless to any one perusing the deed. Sometimes, indeed, they are shortly noticed as follows: "With divers remainders over, with an ultimate limitation to ——."

Suppose, on the other hand, the draftsman were to omit the recital of the death of the first tenant for life, the draft would be most incorrectly framed, as on the face of it it would appear that the necessary consent had not been obtained.

Draft not to be written too closely.

The young draftsman is warned against writing his lines too close together, for if he does so, he will have great difficulty in making any alterations which may become necessary. This is of special importance when the draft has to be settled by another person. Nothing is more annoying than having to settle a draft where the lines are placed close together. The author is acquainted with one counsel of eminence, who if a draft too closely written is sent to him to be settled, has it recopied on wide lines before he touches it. The practice is to put about two folios on a page. Should the draftsman have to resettle a draft prepared by some one else, he will find it convenient to make his alterations in pencil in the first instance, and afterwards to write them in coloured ink.

Common errors of unskilful draftsmen.

The most common occasions in which unskilful draftsmen make unnecessary statements, appear to be the following:

*First.* They state conclusions of law. This is unnecessary, for we presume that any one perusing the draft will know what the law is.

In the following examples, taken from 1 Davidson's Precedents, unnecessary words are printed in *italics*; the student is advised to discover for himself why they are unnecessary; if he is unable to do so, he will find the explanation in 1 Davidson's Precedents.

"A. B. died, leaving C. D., his heir-at-law, *him surviving*:"

"the said sum of £ [a mortgage debt] was not paid on the day appointed for the day of payment thereof, *whereby the estate of the said [mortgagee] became absolute at law, but redeemable at equity.*"

*Second.* They state conclusions as to facts. This statement may be either in a positive or negative form.

Examples taken from 1 Davidson's Precedents.

Stating that persons took "as tenants in common *and not as joint-tenants.*" Stating "the existence of several trustees, and the death of one of them *leaving his co-trustees him surviving.*"

*Third.* They deny that facts happened. It is obvious that, as a general rule, a negative statement is unnecessary, for we always presume that when a certain state of things is mentioned as existing, it remains the same unless some change is mentioned.

A negative event should, as a general rule, only be stated where the non-existence of a particular event is important for our purpose. Thus in the example (*supra*, p. 63), it is necessary to state that the first tenant for life died without issue, as if there were issue alive, B.'s consent would not be necessary to the exercise of the power.

In some few cases it is convenient to state a negative; as for example, where a power of appointment is to be exercised between children, we deny that any prior exercise has been made.

The student who desires to become a good draftsman, may turn any good book of precedents into an Book of precedents can be used as exercise book. exercise book, in the following manner: Let him make a careful analysis of a precedent, so as in fact to form the skeleton draft from which it might have been prepared. In a short time, when he has forgotten the actual wording of the draft, let him try to reproduce it from the skeleton draft and a book of common forms. Let him not be discouraged if his early attempts are failures, as nothing but practice can make an expert draftsman.

When he can reproduce the precedents with tolerable facility from the skeleton draft, let him frame the instructions on which, in his opinion, the skeleton draft might have been founded, and endeavour to reproduce the precedent from the instructions only. Two students working together might greatly improve on this method, one framing the skeleton draft, the other reproducing the precedent, as in this case no assistance would be given by memory.

Another excellent plan is to take some particular clause, a power of sale in a mortgage deed for instance, and having made a careful analysis of the variations in form that occur in the different precedents, to endeavour to discover the reason for them.

Endorse title. After the draft has had a back (or blank sheet) added to it, and has been tied and the pages have been numbered, the draftsman endorses a short title on the back, thus:

" Mr. A. B. and his mortgagees

to

Mr. C. D.

" Draft Conveyance of the Sutton Marsh Estate."

"Draft appointment by A. B. and C. his wife, in exercise of a power contained in their marriage settlement of 10,000*l.* consols to Miss D. B. on her marriage."

And, finally, he states his approval of the draft in some such form as the following:

"I have settled and do approve of this draft on behalf of Mr. ——." Approval.

"I have re-settled and do approve of this draft on behalf of all parties, in accordance with the verbal instructions given to me by Mr. —— in conference on the —— day of ——."

"I have re-settled and do approve of this draft on behalf of Mr. ——, in pursuance of the further instructions of the 18th July, 1870, subject to my notes in the margin."

He signs the approval, adding the date.

The young practitioner should be very careful when the draft is settled according to verbal instructions to call attention to the fact on stating his approval.

# CHAPTER V.

## THE FORMAL PARTS OF DEEDS.

Seal or mark used in old times.

In old times [see Williams on Real Property, p. 143] very few people could write, and accordingly when they wished to signify their assent to any document, they either put their mark to it in the form of a cross, as now done by the vulgar, or they affixed a seal to it. The former plan appears to have been a practice among the Saxons, the latter among the Normans; and as, after the conquest, the judges were Normans, they introduced the latter practice, *i. e.*, that of using a seal, into this country. As, in old times, writing was only used for matters of importance, the fact of sealing a document remained even after the art of writing had become common, a test of the document being of importance. And, accordingly, to this day a document under seal is considered in law as of greater importance than one not under seal.

Deed defined.

A deed may be defined as an instrument, not testamentary, written on paper, vellum, or parchment, sealed and delivered.

I need hardly remind the reader that it is necessary that the seal should have been affixed with the intention that the document should operate as a deed; that a seal affixed merely for the purpose of keeping the document secret, as in the case of a letter going through the post, will not render it a deed contrary to the wish of the person sealing it. In old times every man had his own distinctive seal, but in practice at present the seals are affixed by the law stationer, and only touched by the parties. Sometimes, indeed, in the case of a marriage settlement, some of the parties to the deed have a fancy for sealing it with their own seals. The solicitor witnessing the execution of such a deed will see that those people who use their own seals put them in the proper place, which is on the strings that tie the different skins of parchment, or sheets of paper, together. The reason of this place being adopted for the seal appears to be the belief that it throws difficulty in the way of a fraudulent substitution of one skin for another.

What amounts to delivery.

There is no need to make use of any particular form in the delivery (3 Bythewood, by Sweet, 13). "The usual custom is to touch the seal and say, 'I deliver this as my act and deed.'" But any words or sign showing an intention to deliver it will do. Thus actual physical delivering (handing over) to one of the parties or his solicitor is sufficient; or saying to him "take this," "this will serve," or the like, will suffice. Throwing the deed on the table in the presence of the other party, to the intent that he should take it up, would be sufficient. Merely throwing it on the table would not be a delivery, as the act would be equivocal; but throwing it on the table towards the other party, or allowing him to take it up, would clearly show the intention. In practice it often happens that a man delivers the deed in the presence of his own solicitor only, and possibly retains it in his own possession. The question whether this is intended to operate as an absolute delivery, or as a delivery to take effect on the performance of a condition, is entirely a matter of fact to be ascertained from all the surrounding circumstances. (*Xenos* v. *Wickham*, L. R. 2 E. & Ir. Ap. 296.)

Escrow. In the latter case, viz., when the deed is delivered to some person *not* a party to it, to take effect in certain events, it is called an escrow. A common example of this is where a person executes and delivers a deed to his solicitor to be exchanged against the purchase-money when paid by a purchaser, or against the counterpart of a lease when executed by the lessee. It would be monstrous, says Romilly, M.R., (*Walker* v. *Ware, &c., Railway Co.*, 35 Beav. 58,) for the purchaser to be allowed to say to the vendor, "You have executed the deed, I have got the legal estate, you may enforce payment of the purchase-money as best you can." His Honour was of opinion that in such a case the legal estate did not pass till the money was paid. In practice it would be a wise precaution for the solicitor, in cases where there is any serious doubt as to the ability of the purchaser, or as to the honesty of the intended lessee, to make his client deliver the deed as an escrow, to take effect as a deed upon the money being paid or the counterpart being delivered up. For Williams, J., in *Kidner* v. *Keith*, 15 C. B., N. S. 40, says, "in the common case of a deed executed, and left with a party's attorney, unless it is delivered to the attorney as an escrow not to be delivered until the consideration money is paid, or some other condition performed, it operates as a perfect deed."

Although, as a general rule, a purchaser cannot insist on the vendor executing the conveyance in the presence of himself or his own solicitor, still if such a request be made, the vendor will act wisely in acceding to it. The subject is fully discussed in the case of *Viney* v. *Chaplin*, 2 De G. & J. 468.

Deeds are divided into deeds poll and indentures (Williams on Real Property, p. 146; 1 Shep. Touch. 50).

By an indenture was originally meant a deed where the top of the paper or parchment is cut and indented. In old times when the deed was in two parts, they were both written on the same skin, which was afterwards cut through in a wavy manner, and generally a word was written along the line of division before they were cut asunder in such a manner that it was cut through, so that afterwards it could be seen that the two parts were what they professed to be by their fitting into each other. Gradually the custom of indenting a deed has died out; and now, by "an indenture" we only mean a deed that has parties of more than one part. The Indenture.

effect of 8 & 9 Vict. c. 106, is to render it unnecessary for a deed purporting to be an indenture to be actually indented. For some time before this Act was passed the rule as to an indenture being actually indented had been disregarded. Some judge, on its being argued that a so-called indenture could not take effect because it was not actually indented, asked to see the deed, took it, and looked along the top. He found, he said, that the top was not a mathematically straight line; he therefore determined that it was an indenture. Till the passing of 8 & 9 Vict. c. 106, every person who took any immediate benefit under an indenture was obliged to be named as one of the parties; that Act rendered this unnecessary, and now any person not named a party to an indenture can take an immediate estate or interest in any hereditament or the benefit of any condition or covenant respecting any hereditaments. This is, however, one of the many cases in which a change in the rule of law does not alter the rule of practice. It is still the proper and invariable custom to make every person a party who is intended to take an immediate estate or interest in hereditaments, or the benefit of any condition or covenant respecting them. (Co. Litt. 229 a.)

Deeds poll.

Deeds poll are so called because they were formerly *polled* or cut even at the head. The term is now applied to deeds where the persons executing are all of one part. The greater part of deeds poll are powers of attorney or deeds exercising powers in a settlement or will, as a deed appointing a jointure to a man's wife, or a portion to one of his children. Some of the statutory forms of conveyance to railway companies are very badly expressed deeds poll.

Date. It is the invariable custom to put a date to a deed; in indentures the date is placed at the beginning, in deeds poll at the end in the testimonium clause. As, however, "deeds in point of obligatory force with a view of priority of title take effect from, and therefore have relation to, the time, not of their date but of their delivery" (Shep. Touch. 72), it follows that if the date be impossible (Co. Litt, 46 b), or be omitted, or if the date stated in the deed be different from that of the time of delivery, the deed takes effect from the latter time. If several inconsistent deeds be executed, they take effect according to the several times of their delivery and not of their date.

Parties. As a matter of convenience the name of every person whose intentions are expressed by any instrument should be formally stated. When all the persons have identical intentions, they generally express them by means of a deed poll; but when this is not the case, they do so by means of an indenture, and are said to be made parties to it; those who have identical intentions being made parties of the same part. The phrase "identical intentions" requires a little explanation; in a common contract for sale from A. to B., although at first sight it may appear that the intentions of A. and B. are the same, yet this is not really the case: A.'s intention is to part with his property and receive money; while B. desires to part with his money and receive property; their intentions are different, and accordingly in the deed declaring their intentions they would be made parties of different parts; while, on the other hand, if the sale were made to two persons, B. and C., as trustees for instance, they would have identical intentions differing from those of A.; so that A. would be of one part, B. and C. of the other. In practice, every person who parts with any interest, or takes any *immediate* interest in property, or who enters into a contract contained in a deed, is made a party to it.

The date and names of the parties are stated at the beginning of an indenture in the following form:—

"This Indenture, made this third day of July, 1870, between A. B. of ——, Esq., of the first part, C. D. of ——, Esq., and E. F. of ——, Gent., of the second part; and K. L. of the third part."

The parties being expressed to be of as many parts as are necessary, the parties of the last part being introduced by the word "and." If the parties be of two parts only, they are said to be "of the one part" and "of the other part."

The formal method of stating the parties to a deed poll varies according as it does or does not contain recitals; in the former case it begins "To all to whom these presents shall come, A. B. of, &c., sendeth greeting;" in the latter case, it begins, "Know all men by these presents," the date being in each case mentioned in the testimonium clause.

In contracts not under seal the form appears to be

immaterial, but when they are prepared in a formal manner, the commencement is generally the same as that of an indenture, substituting the words "A memorandum of agreement," or "articles of agreement," for "this indenture." Where the contract is long, and is, according to a usual and convenient practice in such cases, divided into numbered paragraphs, the heading "articles of agreement" is more often used than "a memorandum of agreement," but it is entirely immaterial.

Additions.

The parties to a deed are always described by their names and additions, that is to say, by their dwelling-places and qualities. There is no strict rule as to the minuteness of description necessary; all that is required is to describe the parties with such a degree of accuracy that no confusion will arise. Generally, if a person lives in the country, a description, as "of the parish of ——," "in the county of ——," is sufficient. On the other hand, you generally state street and number in the street of any one living in a town. Thus, "of No. 118, John Street, in the parish of St. Mary, in the city of London." Sometimes it happens that a party to the deed was party to some former deed relating to the same property, in which he was described differently, in this case we generally give both the actual and the old description, thus:—

"John Smith, of No. 118, John Street, in the parish of St. Mary, in the city of London, but formerly of the parish of Tonbridge, in the county of Kent."

The quality of each party is stated after his dwelling-place with a reasonable degree of accuracy, but subject to the usual exception that a gentleman is generally called an Esquire, whether he be so strictly speaking or not: Examples—Sir John Dacres, of Dacre Hall, in the county of Middlesex, Baronet: William Lumley, of 152, Mount Street, in the city of Westminster, Esquire.

Peers.

In the case of a peer, peeress, or person holding a title by courtesy, the dwelling-place is usually omitted. The phrase "courtesy title" appears to require some explanation.

Courtesy titles.

The eldest son of a duke, marquis, or earl, is entitled by the courtesy of England to assume such one of his father's inferior titles that he thinks fit, while the younger sons of Dukes and Marquesses, and the daughters of Dukes, Marquesses, and Earls, are entitled by the courtesy to prefix the title Lord or Lady to their names.

A Peer is described by the proper prefix according to his rank, "the most noble" in the case of a Duke; "the most honourable" in that of a Marquess; "the right honourable" in that of any other peer; followed by his christian name and title, thus: "The most noble Arthur Duke of Wellington." There appears to be some difference of usage in the method of describing persons who bear courtesy titles. In all cases they are described both by their true description and by their courtesy title. Bearing in mind that every child of a peer is entitled to the prefix "honourable," and that the usage of conveyancers is to prefix the words "right honourable" to every person bearing a title by courtesy, the better plan appears to be to describe the person as "the right honourable," giving both christian and surname, adding "commonly called," and his title. Thus the Right Honourable Arthur Hill, commonly called Lord Arthur Hill, the Right Honourable Hugh Lupus Grosvenor, commonly called Earl Grosvenor; but some conveyancers describe persons having courtesy titles exactly in the same manner as they describe persons who are allowed by the usage of society to assume titles to which they have no legal right.

Titles assumed without any strict right.

This usage authorizes the assumption by the children of the eldest son of a peer who bears a courtesy title of the same titles as if their father had actually been a peer. But in this case they are not, strictly speaking, honourables, and it appears the better course to describe them first as if they had no title, followed by the title with the prefix right honourable. Thus the eldest son of Earl Grosvenor would be described as Victor Alexander Grosvenor, Esq., commonly called the Right Honourable Viscount Belgrave. Similarly the usage of society authorizes a commoner who marries a peer, and after his death marries a commoner, to retain the title that she acquired by her first marriage. Thus the widow of the late Duke of Manchester married Mr. Blackwood, and her proper description would be Harriet Sydney, the wife of Stevenson Arthur Blackwood, Esq., commonly called the most noble the Duchess of Manchester.

Privy councillors are entitled to the prefix "right honourable," and the younger sons of peers to that of "honourable." Example: the Right Honourable Benjamin Disraeli, of Hughenden Manor, in the county of Bucks.

Sometimes tedious genealogical recitals can be avoided by affixing a statement of relationship in the description of the parties, but this method is not to be recommended.

Order of parties.

The order in which the parties are arranged is very much a matter of custom, and will best be learnt by the student's carefully studying all the properly drawn deeds to which he can gain access. Usually in a conveyance the conveying parties come before those to whom the interest is conveyed; the persons having the legal estate come first; they are followed by incumbrancers, such as second mortgagees, annuitants, the person entitled to the beneficial interest subject to the charges, coming after his incumbrancers; the persons to whom the conveyance is made coming after those who convey; trustees, inserted for the interest of the persons to whom the conveyance is made, generally come last of all.

Thus, in the case of a conveyance to common uses to bar dower, the order is,—

1st, Vendor; 2nd, purchaser; 3rd, dower-trustee.

Here the vendor comes first, because he is the sole conveying party, and the dower-trustee last.

In the case of a conveyance by mortgagor and first and second mortgagee, the order would be,—

1st, First mortgagee; 2nd, second mortgagee; 3rd, vendor; 4th, purchaser.

Here the first mortgagee comes first as having the legal estate, and the vendor comes last of the conveying parties.

Occasionally, particularly in commercial and railway conveyancing, we annex to the description of each party the character in which they act, and afterwards call them by that name throughout the conveyance. Thus in a conveyance by a vendor, his trustees, and mortgagees, to a railway company, the parties might run as follows :—

"This indenture, made, &c., between A. B. of ——, Esq., C. D., of ——, Esq., and E. F., of ——, Esq., hereinafter called the mortgagees, of the first part; G. H., of ——, Esq., and K. L., of ——, Esq., hereinafter called the trustees, of the second part; M. N., of ——, Esq., hereinafter called the vendor, of the third part; and the North and South-West Junction Railway Company, hereinafter called the company, of the fourth part."

Then, wherever in the deed you would if you had not adopted this plan have used the names of the mortgagees, A. B., C. D., E. F., you would simply say "the mortgagees;" and so as to the other parties.

Nothing but practice will enable the student to determine when this artifice is likely to be of use or not.

The framing of recitals is the most difficult task in conveyancing. On the one hand they should be Recitals.

short, and, on the other hand, they must be intelligible; the draftsman must, above all things, aim at accuracy; this is of the utmost importance, not only for the purpose of making the deed intelligible, but also on account of the doctrine of estoppel. (See 4 Bythewood, by Sweet, 124; Co. Litt. 325*a*.)

Estoppel. "An estoppel is where a man hath done or permitted some act that the law will not allow him to gainsay."

The foundation of the doctrine rests partly on the duty of every man to speak the truth, and partly on the policy of the law, which will not allow a man to make a solemn statement on the faith of which he knows that another will act, and then to deny the truth of his statement. Every recital in a deed must be taken as a solemn statement, on which some of the parties are intended to act. Thus, for instance, in a common purchase deed, a recital that the vendor is seised in fee must be taken as his statement on which he intends the purchaser to act. And it would operate as monstrous injustice for the vendor afterwards to be allowed to allege that he was not seised in fee at the date of the deed, but that he had since become so, and to allow him to recover the land by his new title. Thus, he might allege that the land did not belong to him at the time when he professed to sell it, and that he had since bought it from the true owner. The purchaser from him would in an action of ejectment produce the deed, and although the vendor's present story might be quite true, he would be *estopped, i. e., stopped, prevented,* from setting up any title incompatible with that which he had solemnly asserted. But the recital would be no estoppel in an action between the parties not founded on the deed in which the question of the vendor's title incidentally came into dispute. Nor would it operate as an estoppel in the case of an action between the vendor and a stranger.

Recital restrained by operative part of deed.

In the chapter on Interpretation it was explained that we must, if possible, put such an interpretation on a document as will make every part of it consistent with the others, so that occasionally the generality of the recitals may be controlled by the operative parts. For instance, suppose that the contract is for a sale "free from incumbrances," and, that really the vendor intends to convey free only from incumbrances created by himself. The recital may in the usual manner state the contract for a sale free from incumbrances, while the covenant for title, framed in the usual form, where the vendor covenants only against his *own acts or omissions*, restrains the generality of the recital.

Recitals generally in chronological order.

In most cases it is convenient to arrange the recitals in chronological order. The exceptions may be ranged under the following heads:—

1st. Where the deed has reference to more than one distinct property: in this case it appears convenient to trace the dealings with each property separately down to the time when they first become dealt with together. Thus, in a deed of exchange, the dealings with the two properties would be kept entirely distinct.

2nd. Where the deed deals with more than one estate in the same property which have always been dealt with separately. Thus, where a term has always been kept distinct from the fee, and they are dealt with in the same conveyance, the recitals respecting them may very conveniently be kept distinct.

Two classes of recitals.

The recitals may be divided into *narrative* recitals, which are either general or particular, and *introductory* recitals.

Narrative.

The narrative recitals are so framed as to show the nature of the interest intended to be dealt with. They commence with the creation of the interest, and trace down all the dealings with it to the time of the execution of the deed in preparation. If the first of them be a deed, it is unnecessary, as a general rule, to show why or by whom the interest was created, and the recital is called a *general* recital.

*Example.*—"Whereas by an indenture dated, &c., and expressed to be made between —— and ——, the hereditaments hereinafter described and intended to be hereby granted, were, with the appurtenants, assured and limited unto, and to the use of, the said A. B., his heirs and assigns for ever."

All that appears from this recital is, that the hereditaments in question were at a certain date conveyed in fee simple to A. B.; no information is given as to who conveyed them, or as to what were his motives for doing so.

Now that the creation of A. B.'s estate is shown, we must, in the next recital, not only state that his interest became vested, or partially vested, in some one else, but show that A. B. conveyed it.

For example, the next recital might be,—

"And whereas by an indenture dated (&c.), and expressed to be made between [parties] in consideration of the sum of £—— paid by the said —— to the said A. B., the said A. B. did grant unto the said ——, his heirs and assigns, the said hereditaments with the appurtenances, to hold the same unto and to the use of the said ——, his heirs and assigns, subject to a proviso in the indenture now in recital contained for redemption of the same premises on payment by the said A. B., his heirs, executors, administrators, or assigns, to the said ——, his executors, administrators, or assigns, of the sum of £——, with interest thereon at the rate and on the day therein mentioned."

The following appear to be the principal exceptions to the rule, that the first of the narrative recitals should be general.

1st. Where the first recital is a will. Here, as everything that passes is derived from the bounty of the testator, it would be absurd to make the recital general in form.

2nd. Where the property dealt with is leasehold, and, for some reason, it is necessary to show who the lessor is.

3rd. Where the first recital is a recital of a mortgage deed: this exception is subject to the exception that where there were several conveying parties other than the mortgagor, the recital is left general in form.

Introductory recitals.

The introductory recitals are so framed as to explain what is intended to be done by the deed. Thus, in a purchase deed, the recital may be, "And whereas the said A. B. hath agreed to sell the said hereditaments to the said C. D. for the sum of £—:" taking care to avoid all reference to any preliminary contract or auction by which the bargain was made, so as to avoid putting them on the title.

If the deed were a marriage settlement, the introductory recital might run, "And whereas upon the treaty for the said intended marriage it was agreed that the said —— should assign the said sum of £—— and the interest for the same to the said [trustees], their executors, administrators, and assigns upon the trusts, and with and subject to the powers, provisoes, agreements, and declarations hereinafter declared and contained concerning the same." Care should always be taken to make the introductory recital correspond exactly with what is subsequently done in the operative part of the deed.

Where a power is to be exercised.

Where it is intended that the deed should operate as the execution of a power, the deed by which the power is created should be recited in the narrative recitals, so as to show the creation of the power, and the introductory recital should state that what is intended to be done is intended to be done in execution of the power. Thus, if a mortgagee sells under the power of sale contained in the mortgage deed, the conveyance would recite the mortgage deed, including the power of sale, and the introductory recital might run as follows :—

"And whereas the said [*mortgagee*] in exercise of the said power contained in the said indenture of the —— day of ——, has agreed to sell to the said [*purchaser*] at the price of £——, the fee simple in possession of the hereditaments hereinafter expressed to be hereby granted."

There are two very different schemes for framing recitals. In the one, which is by far the most usual and the easiest method, they commence with a clear root of title, and are thence continued down in a regular order to the time of the conveyance. In the other, which is infinitely more difficult and less usual, the draftsman states the effect only of the deeds and circumstances on which the existing state of the title depends. The latter method is very enticing to young practitioners, as when well done it gives rise to very concise and intelligible drafts. But the reader is warned against adopting it until he has considerable experience, as there is a very great danger of making some error in describing the effects of the deeds and circumstances.

Two schemes for recitals.

For example, suppose we have to prepare a conveyance of land, which had been conveyed to uses to bar dower in favour of the vendor, and had subsequently been mortgaged several times by him, the recitals framed according to the one scheme would run as follows :—

"Whereas by an indenture bearing date the ——

day of ——, and expressed to be made between A. B. of the first part, the said C. D. [*vendor*] of the second part, and E. F. [*dower trustee*] of the third part, the hereditaments hereinafter described and intended to be hereby appointed, were granted and assured to such uses for such estates and in such manner as the said C. D. should by deed appoint, and in default of and until any such appointment, and so far as no such appointment should extend to the use of the said C. D. and his assigns during his life, without impeachment of waste, with remainder to the use of the said E. F. and his heirs during the life of the said C. D. in trust for the said C. D. and his assigns with remainder to the use of the said C. D., his heirs and assigns for ever. *And whereas* by an indenture dated the —— day of ——, and expressed to be made between the said C. D. of the one part, and the said G. H. of the other part, in consideration of the sum of £——, paid by the said G. H. to the said C. D., the said C. D., in exercise of the power limited to him by the hereinbefore recited indenture, appointed and also granted and confirmed the hereditaments hereinafter described and intended to be hereby appointed unto and to the use of the said G. H., his heirs and assigns, subject to a proviso for the redemption thereof by the said C. D., his heirs, executors, administrators, or assigns, on payment by him or them to the said G. H., his executors, administrators, or assigns, of the sum of £——, with interest, on the —— day of ——. *And whereas* the said principal sum of £——, and no more, is now owing on the security of the lastly hereinbefore recited indenture, all interest thereon having been paid up to the date of these presents. *And whereas*, &c. [*recital of a mortgage to I. K. for £——*]. *And whereas*, &c. [*recital that principal sum is now owing on lastly recited indenture, but that interest had been paid.*] *And whereas*, &c. [*recital of a mortgage to L. M. for £——*]. *And whereas*, &c., [*recital that principal sum is owing on lastly recited indenture, but that interest had been paid*].

"*And whereas* the said C. D. has agreed to sell to the said Y. Z., at the price of £——, the fee simple in possession of the said hereditaments hereinafter described, and intended to be hereby appointed free from incumbrances.

"*And whereas* upon the treaty for the said sale, it was agreed that the sum of £——, part of the said purchase money of £——, should be paid to the said G. H. in satisfaction of the debt owing to him as aforesaid, and that the sum of £——, further part of the said purchase money of £——, should be paid to the said I. K. in satisfaction of the debt owing to him as aforesaid, and that the sum of £——, further part of the said purchase money of £——, should be paid to the said L. M. in satisfaction of the debt owing to him as aforesaid, and that the said G. H., I. K., and L. M. should respectively join in these presents in manner hereinafter appearing."

While, according to the other scheme, they might run as follows:—

"Whereas by the effect of the indenture, described in the first schedule hereunder written, the lands and hereditaments hereinafter described, stand limited to the usual uses to bar dower in favour of the said C. D., subject only to the several principal sums secured by way of mortgage mentioned in the second schedule hereunder written, and to the interest thereon, and to the securities for the same respectively, and all interest on the same several sums has been paid up to the date of these presents, and the legal estate in fee simple in the said hereditaments is vested in the said G. H. as mortgagee by virtue of the indenture first mentioned in the said second schedule. And whereas the said C. D. hath agreed to sell to the said Y. Z. at the price of £—— the fee simple in possession of the said hereditaments hereinafter described and expressed to be hereby appointed and granted with the appurtenances free from incumbrances, And whereas upon the treaty for the said sale it was agreed that the said several mortgage debts specified in the said second schedule should be paid off out of the said purchase money, and that the several mortgagees should join in these presents in manner hereinafter appearing."

The schedules would stand as follows:—

*The first Schedule above referred to.*

"An indenture, bearing date the —— day of ——, and expressed to be made between A. B. of the first part, the said C. D. of the second part, and E. F. of the third part."

*The second Schedule above referred to.*

"The sum of £—— secured by an indenture of mortgage, dated the —— day of ——, and expressed to be made between the said C. D. of the one part, and the said G. H. of the other part.

"The sum of £—— secured by an indenture of mortgage, dated the —— day of ——, and expressed to be made between the said C. D. of the one part, and the said I. K. of the other part."

[*Similar statement of mortgage debt secured to L. M.*]

Occasionally recitals are dispensed with, even where the conveyance is made by virtue of a power, reference being made to the power in the operative part. The operative part might run as follows:— **Recitals sometimes omitted.**

"The said A. B., in exercise of a power of sale contained in an indenture [*describing it*], and of every other power, him enabling, doth hereby appoint, &c."

Although this method of framing assurances is occasionally convenient in the hands of a skilful draftsman, it should be avoided by a beginner, as there is very considerable risk of its causing the draft to be obscure.

By the consideration for a contract or deed, we mean the motive that affects the parties.[1] **Consideration.**

No man ever acts without a motive; but all motives are not of equal weight in law. Thus, if I promise, even in writing, to give you £10 on account of my friendship for you, or on account of my admiration for your conduct, the motive or consideration which affects me, however laudable it may be, is not one which the law considers sufficient to render my promise binding. And, therefore, if I were to refuse to perform my promise, the law would give you no remedy.

This rule of law may be stated thus: "A simple contract, *i. e.*, a contract not under seal, requires a valuable consideration to support it."

On the other hand, a contract made under seal, that is, by deed, requires no consideration to support it.

Consideration necessary to raise a use.

Why, then, it may be asked, do we always express the consideration in a conveyance? There are two reasons; the first depends upon the doctrines of equity as to raising a use. Before the Statute of Uses, if a man enfeoffed another, the Court of Chancery held that unless the motive was one which was adequate, the feoffor remained entitled to the use; in other words, that the use resulted to the feoffor. On the other hand, if the motive was adequate, if the feoffment was made for valuable consideration, or for the benefit of relations, and on account of the feoffor's love for them, the use remained to the feoffee. It will be remembered that the statute has not altered the nature of a use; all that it does is to clothe the use with the legal estate. So at this day, if any conveyance operating by transmutation of possession were to be made without consideration, there would be a resulting use to the man who conveyed, so that he would retain the legal estate, though if it contained a declaration of uses, the *cestui que* use would by force of the statute take the legal estate. If a conveyance be made intended to take effect under the Statute of Uses, the use is not raised, and therefore it passes nothing, unless there is a consideration. The second reason for expressing the consideration in a deed is, that certain contracts not made for a valuable consideration may (though they are binding on the parties) be void as against third parties; and although you are always at liberty to prove the true consideration when it has not been expressed in the deed, the fact of its not being stated gives rise to the necessity of the proof.

**Contracts void as against creditors.**

The effect of the Statute 13 Eliz. c. 5, is to render any conveyance made by a man in debt to such an amount that he has not ample means to pay his debts void against his creditors, except the conveyance be *bonâ fide* and for a valuable consideration. And the effect of the 27th Eliz. c. 4, is to render any voluntary conveyance of land void as against a subsequent purchaser for value.

Thus if a man (3 Davidson's Precedents, 839,) after his marriage makes a settlement on his wife and children, and merely on account of his natural love and affection for them, which does not constitute a valuable consideration, it is liable to be set aside by his creditors whether it be of real or personal property; and if it be real property, the settlor can sell the property for value, just as if he had not settled it.

There is always a little difficulty in accepting a title depending upon a voluntary settlement; for on the one hand there is the danger that the settlor may subsequently have dealt with the property for value, and thus may have defeated the settlement; and, on the other hand, if you take as a purchaser for value against the settlement, it *may* turn out that there was a valuable consideration for the settlement, though it was not expressed, and thus the settlement may take effect against you.

Valuable consideration.

It requires some amount of thought to understand what amounts to a valuable consideration, or, as it might with greater propriety be called, a consideration valid at law. Money, marriage, doing something which is troublesome to oneself, or of use to the other party to the contract, are all valuable considerations. Thus if I agree with you, either verbally or in writing not under seal, to give you five shillings, there is no consideration for my promise, and the law will not interfere to make me perform my agreement, and will not give you damages if I omit to do so. If I were to agree with you to give you five shillings if you would walk half a mile, and you were to perform your share of the contract, there would be a consideration for my promise, viz., the trouble that you would have in walking the half-mile. If I were to promise to give you dinner at my house if you would come at a certain time, and you were to come, there would be a binding contract. The consideration for the dinner being the trouble that you would have had in coming. On the other hand, if we were to agree that I should at my expense send to you at your house a dinner from the cook's shop, there would be no consideration moving from you, and the law would not hold me to my promise.

But, in the latter case, if I engaged under seal, that is, by deed, to send you the dinner, the fact of the contract being made by deed would do away with the necessity of any consideration, and I should be bound. It must, however, be remembered that a Court of Equity will not decree specific performance of a contract entered into under seal without consideration; although damages can be obtained at law in respect of a breach of it.

Good consideration.

A good consideration merely means the motive of natural affection towards relations, it has no validity against creditors or purchasers; the only use of it is to raise the use in covenants to stand seised.

Recapitulation of the doctrine of considerations.

The doctrine of considerations may be stated, shortly, as follows:

Every simple contract requires a valuable consideration to support it.

A contract under seal does not require any consideration to support it as between the parties. But if there be no valuable consideration, it may possibly be void as against third parties under the 18 Eliz. c. 5, and 27 Eliz. c. 4.

Either a valuable or a good consideration is sufficient to raise a use or to prevent a resulting use.

The subject is explained in a very lucid manner in Leake's Law of Contracts, chap. iii. s. 1.

Nominal consideration.

Formerly it was the custom to make every conveying party accept a nominal pecuniary consideration. This foolish custom is now entirely abolished. It can never do any good, but in one instance may do harm. The effect of inrolling a disentailing deed under the Act for the Abolition of Fines and Recoveries is the same as inrolling a deed under the Act of Inrolments. Hence, if in such a deed you use the words bargain and sale, with a consideration of five shillings, the conveyance becomes a bargain and sale, so that the intended grantee to uses takes the legal estate, and the estates limited by way of use all become equitable.

The consideration is always stated in words at length; and till lately, under 48 Geo. 3, c. 149, ss. xxii. to xxv., on the sale of any property the purchase-money or consideration had to be set forth in words at length, under the penalty, on both purchaser and seller, of £50 and quintuple the duty on the consideration not set forth in that manner, while a solicitor who wilfully inserted any other than the true consideration was liable on conviction to a penalty of £500, and was rendered incapable of practising for the future.

These sections have been repealed by the Inland Revenue Repeal Act, 1870. The Stamp Act, 1870, s. 10, imposes a penalty of 10*l.* on any person who executes or is employed or concerned in or about the execution or preparation of any instrument in which all the facts and circumstances affecting the liability of the instrument to Ad valorem Duty or the amount of Ad valorem Duty chargeable are not fully and truly set forth. The effect of these two Acts appears to be to impose a penalty on the omission to state the consideration, but to allow it to be expressed in figures: owing, however, to the greater risk of error when the latter course is adopted, it is probable that the existing practice will be continued.

Witness.

It never appears to have been decided that the presence of a witness is necessary when either a deed or a contract not under seal is executed. But in practice a witness is always present, and signs his name to the attestation clause. The witness should add his name and quality, so that he can readily be traced if it should become necessary to prove the fact of execution. The case of a will is different, owing to the positive enactment of the ninth section of the Wills Act, which declares "that no will shall be valid unless it shall be in writing, and executed in manner hereinafter mentioned: (that is to say,) it shall be signed at the foot or end thereof by the testator, or by some other person in his presence and by his direction; and such signature shall be made or acknowledged by the testator in the presence of two or more witnesses present at the same time, and such witnesses shall subscribe the will in the presence of the testator, but no form of attestation shall be necessary."

The only safe method of executing a will is for the testator and the intended witnesses to be assembled before the testator begins to sign his name, and for the witnesses to subscribe immediately after him, without anyone leaving the room.

In all cases, any erasure or interlineation, either in deed, contract not under seal, or will, should be initialled immediately after the execution by the parties and witnesses.

The testimonium and attestation are rarely inserted by the draftsman, unless they are required to be of a special form. In cases where it is necessary to have the execution of the deed attested in some particular manner, it is improper to refer to it in the operative part of the deed; this is sometimes done in the manner following:—" doth hereby by this indenture, the execution and delivery whereof are intended to be attested by two credible witnesses:" the insertion of these words is quite useless; for the mere intention to have the execution of a deed witnessed in a particular manner is a different thing from having it actually done; and the words being useless should, according to the general rule, be omitted. In those cases where the deed has to be executed in a particular manner, attention should be called to the peculiarity by a marginal note on the draft.

The student may study—

Davidson's Precedents, *passim.*
Butler, Co. Lit. "Deeds," in Index.
Shepherd's Touchstone, *passim.*
Viner, Abridgment. "Additions."
Second Institute, 665.
1 Martin, by Davidson.
Bythewood, by Sweet, *passim.*

# CHAPTER VI.

## PURCHASE DEEDS OF INTERESTS IN LAND.

THE author purposes to discuss in this place conveyances; first, on the sale of freeholds, and second, on the sale of other interests in land, by a person under no disability; and to consider, subsequently, how the form of the conveyance depends on the status of the conveying parties.

Conveyances of the following natures are still to be met with in abstracts:— Kinds of conveyances.

1. Feoffment with livery.
2. Lease and Release.
3. Bargain and sale, enrolled under 27 Hen. 8, c. 16.
4. Covenant to stand seised.
5. Bargain and sale by executors,
6. A deed of grant.
7. An appointment under a power.
8. Fines.
9. Recoveries.

But although they may, with the exception of the two last, be used at the present day, conveyancers rarely employ any except a deed of grant, and an appointment under a power.

Feoffment. *First.*—A feoffment with livery. The livery alone conveys the land; the accompanying deed, called a charter of feoffment, was till lately of use only as bearing witness of what had already happened, and accordingly the operative words were in the past tense, but were repeated in the present tense, for the sake of confirming the feoffment. "The [*feoffor*] hath granted, enfeoffed, and confirmed, and by these presents doth grant, enfeoff, and confirm unto," &c.

The Statute of Frauds (29 Car. 2, c. 3) rendered it necessary that a writing should be signed by the feoffor or his agent duly appointed: and the Act to Amend the Law of Real Property (8 & 9 Vict. c. 106) renders every feoffment (except a feoffment made under a custom by an infant) void at Law unless evidenced by deed.

If a tenant for life or years made a feoffment, or even it is said (4 Byth. by Sweet, "Feoffment") if a person having no estate or interest in the land, having mere naked possession, made a feoffment; in either case the feoffee acquired a fee simple. This operation of a feoffment, called a "tortious" operation (*Taylor* d. *Atkyns* v. *Horde*, 2 Sm. Lead. Ca.) was made use of in conveyancing for various purposes, which are discussed in 4 Byth. by Sweet, "Feoffment," but as this operation has been abolished by 8 & 9 Vict. c. 106, s. 4, it is unnecessary to discuss it here.

It is, perhaps, necessary to remind the reader that

while a feoffment can be made of corporeal hereditaments only, still a feoffment of corporeal hereditaments will pass incorporeal hereditaments appurtenant to them.

As a feoffment is a conveyance operating at common law, uses can be declared on the seisin of the feoffee in favour of persons, who immediately become possessed of the land by virtue of the Statute of Uses.

In cases where the charter of feoffment is executed, but no livery is actually made, it sometimes happens that the land is passed by the charter; as, for instance, where the consideration expressed is natural love and affection, it is held to amount to a covenant to stand seised. If the land is in lease, or there is any outstanding estate, so that the feoffor's interest is really reversionary, the charter may take effect as a grant. Now that all corporeal hereditaments lie in grant, it is obvious that if livery be omitted, the charter of feoffment will take effect as a deed of grant and pass the lands. The word "grant" is generally used in addition to "enfeoff" in a charter of feoffment, so as to pass any incorporeal hereditament, such as a common in gross, which would not pass by the livery. (Butler, Co. Lit. 384 *a* (n.).)

*Second.*—A conveyance by lease and release. The operation of this has already been described (*ante*, p. 31). It was the most common form of conveyance until the year 1841, when it fell into disuse, as by 4 & 5 Vict. c. 21, a release expressed to be made in pursuance of the Act has the same effect as a release founded on a lease for a year. Lease and release.

Bargain and sale.

*Third.*—A bargain and sale enrolled under 27 Hen. 8, c. 16. The effect of this has been already explained (*ante*, p. 30). Occasionally, when it is desired to vest land in trustees, in contemplation of its being divided into lots and sold for building purposes, and the number of the lots is large, the value of each lot being small, it is desirable to avoid the expense of giving an abstract of title to each purchaser. In this case the conveyance to the trustees may be made by bargain and sale enrolled, in which the early title is very fully recited, and (as by 10 Anne, c. 18, s. 3, a copy of a bargain and sale enrolled, signed by the proper officer, and proved on oath to be a true copy, is admissible in evidence as well as the original) every purchaser can have an office copy of the bargain and sale delivered to him as a title deed; the property is sold under a condition precluding him from requiring any abstract other than a copy of the bargain and sale. It must be remembered that as the operation of a conveyance by bargain and sale enrolled depends upon the Statute of Uses, if any uses are declared on the seisin of the bargainee, the *cestui que use* will take an equitable interest only. But as under 11 & 12 Vict. c. 94, s. 17, an office copy sealed with the seal of the Enrolment office of a deed enrolled in Chancery is evidence without any oath, it appears that in the above-mentioned case the preferable method is to enrol the deed in Chancery, framing it according to circumstances, so as to take effect as a Bargain and Sale, or otherwise.

*Fourth.*—A covenant to stand seised. Here the consideration is natural love and affection, which, as already pointed out, is sufficient consideration to support a use.

Covenant to stand seised.

A bargain and sale enrolled, and a covenant to stand seised, differ in their operation from the other modes of conveyance. Before the Statute of Uses no estate passed by them; all that passed was "a use," that is a trust enforceable in Equity. A bargain and sale, it will be remembered, was simply a contract to sell land for money, while a covenant to stand seised was where a man wished to provide for his relations, and covenanted that on account of his "natural love and affection" he would stand seised to their use. In neither of these cases did any legal interest in the land pass, only the use passed; so that as soon as the Statute of Uses came into operation, it transferred the legal estate to the *cestui que use*, the person who was entitled to enjoy the use.

Soon after the passing of the Statute of Uses it was decided that a use could not be limited on a use. Thus, if you made a feoffment to A. and his heirs, to the use of B. and his heirs, to the use of C. and his heirs, the statute would transfer A.'s legal estate to B. his *cestui que use*, its operation would then stop, leaving B. seised of the legal estate as trustee for C. It follows from this decision that as in bargains and sales and covenants to stand seised, the use was clothed with the legal estate by the statute, no further uses could be declared, or at least if they were declared, they would merely give equitable interests, as the statute would have no further effect; it follows that a bargain and sale enrolled could not be made use for the purpose of making a conveyance to the ordinary uses to bar dower. Although it was unnecessary when the conveyance was by bargain and sale enrolled to declare any uses in favour of the purchaser, and the very fact of the bargain and sale raised them by implication, it became the common custom to declare them. The reason appears to have been the following: there was always the possible risk that the deed might not be properly enrolled; if this occurred it would take effect as a grant, provided that some estate was outstanding, such as an ordinary lease for years, and in this case the uses would properly be declared.

Bargain and sale by executor.

*Fifth.*—The bargain and sale at common law by executors is a very old form of conveyance. Although lands could not generally be devised by will before the Statute of Wills, 32 Hen. 8, c. 1, they could in some places be devised according to a custom. And wherever this custom existed it was allowable for a man to devise that his land should be sold by his executors. They had then a right or power by the custom to sell and convey the land; they could not make a feoffment, because they had no estate in the land; so they executed a deed conveying the land, which, it will be remembered, had not been devised to them, and therefore did not belong to them. After the Statute of Wills rendered lands generally devisable, the rule of law allowing executors to convey on a devise that they should sell the lands remained in force. The customary power became a common law power. As the bargainee or person to whom the land is conveyed is in at common law, uses can be declared on his seisin. The operative words generally used are, "bargain and sell." This conveyance is still occasionally employed.

The distinction between the case of a devise that the executors shall sell the land, and a devise of lands to the executors to be sold, is one of the utmost importance. In the first case there is merely a power operating at common law, which could formerly be exercised only by *all* the executors, so that if one executor renounced, the lands could not be sold; and the land descends to the heir-at-law until the sale takes place. In the other case, the property in the land passes to the executors (not in that capacity, but as trustees) as joint-tenants; the power is an equitable one only, and is annexed to the estate, so that if one renounces, the others can sell. (*Lane* v. *Debenham*, 11 Hare, 188.) In order to prevent the inconvenience of the naked power not being capable of being exercised by the acting executors, the 21 Hen. 8, c. 4, was passed—(see Butler, Co. Lit. 113*a*, n.)

*Sixth.*—A deed of grant, which is properly the method of conveying remainders and reversions and other incorporeal hereditaments, has now (owing to the Act to Amend the Law of Real Property, 8 & 9 Vict. c. 106, which enacts that all corporeal hereditaments shall lie in grant) superseded all other deeds Grant.

for the purpose of conveying freeholds, except a bargain and sale by executors at Common Law, and an appointment under a power.

In Stephens' Commentaries, vol. i. page 556, a grant to uses is classed among the deeds that take effect under the Statute of Uses. This is an error; the inaccuracy is twofold; no grant is ever made to uses; and the effect of the deed in conveying the legal estate in corporeal hereditaments depends upon the Act to Amend the Law of Real Property, not upon the Statute of Uses. No doubt it is the custom to declare uses on the seisin of the grantee, and then the Statute of Uses vests the legal estate in the *cestui que use*, if he be a different person from the grantee. But, according to the classification commonly adopted by conveyancers, a deed of grant is one that acts by transmutation of possession as distinguished from those which take effect under the Statute of Uses.

**Deeds construed as grants so as to take effect.**

Owing to the effect of a deed of grant in conveying remainders and reversions, it sometimes happens that when a charter of feoffment is made without livery (as already mentioned), or a bargain and sale is not enrolled within the proper time, or the lease for a year is omitted in a conveyance by lease and release, the conveyance, apparently imperfect, conveys the property; for it usually happens that some estate is outstanding, so that the vendor's interest is reversionary; the existence of a yearly tenancy is sufficient to render it so, and whenever this occurs, any deed which is intended to convey the freehold, but fails to do so, will be construed as a deed of grant, so as to pass the vendor's reversionary interest, if, by putting this construction on it, the intention of the parties can be carried out.

*Seventh.*—The method in which an appointment taking effect as a declaration of a use operates, is so fully explained in Williams's Real Property, 292, that it is unnecessary to add anything here. In preparing a deed to take effect as an appointment, the deed creating the power should be recited so as to show what the power is, and that it can be exercised. The operative words should follow strictly the words of the power. Appointment.

*Eighth* and *Ninth.*—The operation of fines and recoveries will be explained in the chapter on Disentailing Assurances. It suffices here to remark that each of them operated so as to convey the legal estate, and that it was the custom to execute either before or after the fine was levied, and before the recovery was suffered, a deed to declare on what uses the lands which passed by the fine or recovery should be held. The joint effect of the fine or recovery and deed was to vest the legal estate in the *cestui que use.* Fines and recoveries.

An ordinary deed of grant of freeholds consists of the following parts :— Deed of grant.

1. The date.
2. The parties.
3. The recitals.
4. The consideration.
5. The receipt.

6. The operative words.

7. The parcels, general words, and all estate clause.

8. The habendum and the tenendum.

9. The declaration of uses.

10. The covenants for title.

11. The testimonium.

12. The attestation.

13. The endorsed receipt.

Recitals. The principal questions arising on the four first and two last parts have already been discussed in Chapter V. It remains to consider whether recitals are necessary. Mr. Davidson's opinion (2 Davidson's Precedents) is, that in simple cases they may safely be omitted. Although this opinion is quite correct, it appears advantageous, in most cases, to recite the last conveyance by which the parcels were conveyed, for doing so greatly facilitates the identification of the property. In such recital the parcels may be described as "all those [——] and hereditaments hereinafter described and intended to be hereby granted."

In framing the narrative recitals the draftsman must show that the entire legal and equitable fee is vested in the parties who convey; or in cases where the sale is made by order of the Court of Chancery, or by trustees acting in exercise of a power of sale, he must show such a state of facts as gives jurisdiction to the Court to make the order, or enables the power to be exercised.

In the ordinary case the introductory recital

merely states that "the said [*vendor*] has agreed to sell to the said [*purchaser*], at the price of £——, the fee simple in possession, free from incumbrances, of the hereditaments hereinafter expressed to be hereby granted."

If the sale be made under a power, the recital may run, "the said [*vendor*] has agreed, in exercise of the said recited power, to sell," &c.

In cases where the purchase is made by trustees, and this necessarily appears on the face of the conveyance, it is more convenient to state the agreement as one, "for the purchase."

It should be noticed that the generality of the recital that the sale is free from incumbrances, is restricted by the covenant against incumbrances, and that, therefore, no vendor need fear to allow such recital to be inserted in the deed.

In cases where the property is intended to be conveyed, subject to incumbrances, their existence should be recited; it depends upon circumstances whether or not it is desirable to show how they arose; in these cases the contract should be stated for the sale "free from incumbrance, except the said ——."

Occasionally, in badly drawn deeds, no notice is taken of the incumbrances in the recitals; they are mentioned only in the covenants for title. The practice is extremely inconvenient, and should not be followed.

5. The statement of the consideration is followed (where the consideration is money) by the receipt Receipt.

clause, which was formerly followed by a formal discharge for the money; as this discharge is utterly useless, it is now gradually falling into disuse and had better be omitted. The effect of the receipt is to prevent or estop the person who states that he has received the money from showing at Law that the money was not paid. But in Equity this is not the case, for neither the receipt in the body of the deed, nor the endorsed receipt, prevents the person who acknowledges the receipt from showing in Equity that the money was not paid. This rule applies only between the original vendor and purchaser; it has been decided that a person purchasing from the original purchaser, and finding both the receipts in the usual form, is not obliged to inquire further. The reason is obvious, for if the rule were different no one would be safe in making a purchase.

6. As to the operative words.

Operative words.

It used to be the universal custom, and still is the custom of unskilful draftsmen, to use a great many words without having regard to their true meaning, and also to use them both in the past and present tense; thus, in a release founded on a lease for a year, the words used were: "He the said A. B. hath granted, bargained, sold, aliened, released, and confirmed, and by these presents doth grant, bargain, sell, alien, release, and confirm." The custom of using both tenses appears to have been adopted from the practice in a charter of feoffment, where, as already mentioned, this was commonly done. In the instance given all the words, with the exception of "grant and release" are simple surplusage; and in the recital of such a deed these would be the only operative words mentioned.

The occasions for the employment of the various operative words are the following; the list is slightly altered from that in Davidson's Precedents, vol. i.

"Assign," in a conveyance of personalty.

"Alien," absolutely parting with an estate.

"Enfeoff," in charter of feoffment.

"Confirm," where there has been a previous conveyance to the grantee, and it is intended to confirm it.

"Grant," the proper word for conveying freeholds not lying in livery.

As since the 1st October, 1845, all corporeal hereditaments lie in grant (8 & 9 Vict. c. 106), the word "grant" is the operative word now generally used in any conveyance of freeholds.

It is sometimes stated that at common law the word "grant" raised implied covenants for title on the part of the grantor. This broad statement of the effect of the word is erroneous. (See Butler, Co. Lit. 384 *a* (n.).) The error being prevalent, it was enacted by 8 & 9 Vict. c. 106, s. 4, that the word should not imply any covenant, except so far as it should imply a covenant by force of any Act of Parliament. When trustees are conveying parties, unskilful draftsmen constantly add to the word "grant" "*by way of conveyance only, and not by way of warranty.*" The words are utterly useless, and ought always to be omitted. However, when they are inserted by the advisers of the trustees, it is not worth while to strike them out. This is one of the many cases in which the practitioner will find it advisable to allow useless words to remain in a draft, where they have been inserted by a man who knows no better, simply on account of the time that would be wasted, and the expense that would be incurred in endeavouring to convince him of his error. Although in cases where a draft has been prepared by a pupil or a client, the draftsman will properly alter it till its frame and wording exactly suit his own views, the young practitioner should remember in cases where a draft is drawn on behalf of one party and submitted to him to settle on behalf of another, that his duty is simply to make those alterations in the draft which, in his opinion, are necessary for the purpose of carrying out the intentions of his client; that it forms no part of his duty to give the advisers of the other parties a lesson in conveyancing, and that for that reason he should abstain from making any alterations which are not absolutely necessary.

"Surrender," in the conveyance of a term to the intent that it may merge.

"Release," in the conveyance of a remainder or reversion to the person in possession, or to release either property or a person from any claim.

"Remise, release, and quit-claim," the old form of releasing property from a claim.

"Acquit, release, and quit claim," the old form of releasing a person from a claim.

"Demise," formerly "demise, lease, and to farm let," the word used in creating a term.

"Dispose of," used in a conveyance by a married woman by deed acknowledged, and by a tenant in tail in a disentailing assurance.

"Bargain and sell," where a pecuniary consideration passes, and it is intended to raise a use. If the deed be enrolled under the Statute of Enrolments, a freehold interest, otherwise only a term, can pass. Bargains and sales taking effect under the Statute of Uses, are but rarely used, except where a freeholder creates a mortgage term. If he uses the words bargain and sell, the mortgagee acquires possession for the term by virtue of the statute, without its being necessary to enrol the deed.

"Bargain and sell" used by executors selling under a common law power (ante, p. 102).

7. The parcels are generally inserted in the operative part of the deed, although in some few exceptional cases, as in the assignment or surrender of a lease, the transfer of a mortgage not by endorsement, a disentailing assurance, or the appointment of a new trustee, they may be more conveniently set out in the recital of the lease, mortgage, or settlement, and be conveyed by reference. They should be described according to their quality as arable, woodland and the like, quantity, *i. e.* according to the statute measurement, abuttals, and name of the occupiers. The description may either be given in the body of the Parcels.

deed, or, which is generally more convenient, by means of a schedule to the deed, and an endorsed map. In cases where intermixed or adjacent land, held on different titles, is dealt with by the same deed, the use of several schedules will generally be found to facilitate the draftsman's task.

The parcels are generally copied from the last conveyance; in this case if (as generally happens) the several parcels are described as being in the possession of A. B. and C., care should be taken that any changes of occupancy are noticed; generally it is unnecessary to retain the names of all the former occupiers—it is convenient to retain the name of the occupier mentioned in the last conveyance as well as that of the present tenant—the language may be, "late in the possession of A. B., but now of C. D.," or if there have been intermediate tenants, "formerly in the possession of A. B., but now of C. D." Attention to details of this nature is extremely irksome, but it is essential. In the case of a large property it may be desirable to have the parcels in the draft conveyance, compared with the existing rent-roll.

Sometimes the property has become so much altered since the last description in a conveyance, that an entirely new description has to be framed. In this case the new and old descriptions should be connected together, so as to preserve evidence of identity. The various methods of doing this will be found in Davidson's Precedents.

Where large properties are conveyed by an old

description, and also by a modern description, some words should be inserted for the purpose of showing that the generality of the old description is not to be limited by the new description.

Where the land is divided into farms, it is sometimes convenient to add columns in the schedule showing the amount of rent and the nature of the tenancy. This may conveniently be done, as follows:—

| Number referring to map. | Name. | Quality. | Acreage. | Name of Occupier. | Amount of Rent. | Nature of Tenancy. |
|---|---|---|---|---|---|---|
| | | | **Old Hall Farm.** | | | |
| 37 | Beaconfield ........ | Meadow ....... | 13 2 3 | Jesse Harmer | £35 | Yearly Tenant. |
| 38 | Beaconshaw ......... | Wood .......... | 7 1 0 | | | |
| 39 | Brookland .......... | Arable ......... | 6 3 2 | | | |
| 40 | Big Brookland...... | Pasture ....... | 7 3 2 | | | |
| 41 | Starve Crow Piece.. | Arable ......... | 5 1 13 | | | |
| | | | **New Hall Farm.** | | | |
| 53 | Spratsfield .......... | Meadow ....... | 7 3 2 | Mary Smith | £150 | Lease for seven years from Midsummer, 1868. |
| 45 | Spratsbarn ......... | Meadow ....... | 0 1 3 | | | |
| 54 | The Great Meadow | Arable ......... | 50 3 2 | | | |
| 56 | The Forty Acres .. | Do. ............ | 39 1 13 | | | |
| 57 | Leaseowes .......... | Do. ............ | 30 2 0 | | | |
| 58 | Ridge Field ......... | Do. ............ | 15 1 2 | | | |
| 59 | Great Ridge Field . | Do. ............ | 16 3 3 | | | |

It is convenient always to refer to the same set of parcels in exactly the same words. Thus, if they are described as "messuages and lands" in one place they should not be described as "farms and hereditaments" in another. If this is not attended to, a good deal of trouble may be occasioned to a person reading the deed hastily for the purpose of ascertaining what was done with any particular parcel.

On the purchase of a very large property it will often be found that different parts of it are held on different titles. Generally owing to the improvements that every new purchaser makes, by turning roads, grubbing fences, and the like, it soon becomes very difficult, or even impossible, to distinguish the different parts; a fact which may give rise to considerable trouble and expense on any future dealings with the property.

This may be avoided by procuring tracings of the parish maps in which the several parts of the property are delineated, and having them coloured with reference to the different titles on which the property is held. Unfortunately, the parish maps are not made on a uniform scale, so that they cannot often be used for the purpose of having a map of the property made with sufficient accuracy to enable the property to be conveyed by reference to it; but they will answer the purpose just mentioned.

It is hardly necessary to state that on the examination of an abstract with the deeds the parcels should be examined with most scrupulous attention.

Where in a subsequent part of the deed you wish to refer back to the parcels, the most convenient form is to refer to them as "the hereditaments and premises hereinbefore expressed to be hereby *granted*," or "first hereinbefore expressed to be hereby released," as the case may be.

Immediately following the parcels come the "general words." These are added for the purpose of passing easements, profits *à prendre*, and other rights which, though habitually enjoyed with the parcels, are not legally appurtenant to them. General words.

Easements and profits *à prendre* are generally rights enjoyed by a person as the owner of a particular land. I say *generally*, for it appears tolerably clear that a *profit à prendre*, *Shuttleworth* v. *Le Fleming*, 19 C. B., N. S., 687, and possibly an easement, can exist in gross [Gale on Easements by Willes, Introductory Chapter]; but as such existence is rare, the following remarks will not apply to easements or profits *à prendre* in gross. Easements, &c.

It sometimes happens that the owner of land has a right to do something on his neighbour's land, as to walk along it by a way not open to the public, or to pasture his cattle on it; or to prevent the neighbour from doing something on his, the neighbour's, land, as blocking up a ditch for instance.

Rights of the nature just mentioned are called easements or profits *à prendre*, the distinction being that a right (such as a right of way) in respect of which the owner derives no profit out of his neighbour's soil is an easement; while a right, such as that of pasturing his cattle, in respect of which he does derive benefit from his neighbour's soil; is a profit *à prendre*.

It will be remarked that it requires two tenements for the purpose of enabling an easement to exist. The tenement in respect of which the right of enjoyment exists is called the dominant tenement, the other is the servient tenement; an easement may be defined as "an incorporeal right imposed for the benefit of a tenement over corporeal property, but giving no right to the participation in the profits of it." A list of easements will be found in Gale on Easements, p. 19. An easement can exist only by virtue of a grant by the owner of the servient tenement, which may be either express or implied, or by prescription or custom, words which require some explanation.

Prescription and Custom.

It is evident that if any right of property is enjoyed uninterruptedly for a great many years, the presumption becomes very strong that the person enjoying it is lawfully the owner of it.

Where the right of property thus enjoyed is an incorporeal hereditament, and it has been enjoyed uninterruptedly for so long a time by the person claiming it and his predecessors in title, that the law recognises his right owing to the length of user only, he is said to have acquired a title by *prescription* or *custom*. The distinction being that a custom means a local usage, not a right annexed to a particular person; while a right by prescription is annexed to a particular person, or to the person seised of a particular estate. The examples given, Co. Litt. 113*b*, will render this clear. Where a man seised in fee of the Manor of Dale pleads that he and his ancestors, and all those whose estate he hath in the said manor, have time out of mind of man had and used to have common of pasture in such a place being land of another, as pertaining to the said manor, this is prescription. But where, on the other hand, a copyholder of the Manor of Dale pleads, that within the said manor there is and hath been such a custom time out of mind of man used, that all the copyholders of the said manor have had and used to have common of pasture in such a waste of the lord, parcel of the said manor: this is not prescription, but a custom; *Warrick* v. *Queen's College, Oxford*, L. R., 10 Eq. Ca. 105.

A profit *à prendre* can be claimed by grant or prescription, but not by custom; the reason, apparently, being, that the persons claiming by custom might become so numerous as to take all the profit of the soil.

It is easy to see how an easement may become destroyed; for if the servient and dominant tenements fall into the seisin of the same man the exercise by him of any right which, before the two tenements belonged to the same person, was an easement, is now only an exercise of one of the rights of property. If, therefore, when two properties belong to one person and one of them is sold, it is intended to grant along with it an easement or profit *à prendre* formerly belonging to it over the other property, it is necessary to make a grant *de novo*.

Occasionally, an equitable right, in the nature of an easement, is enjoyed by the owner of land. Such a right would possibly pass by the conveyance of the dominant tenement; but it appears safer to mention it.

The employment of general words is one of the many cases in which for greater safety words sanctioned by usage are employed, although we may possibly be unable to show the way in which each word of the form is directly applicable to the case before us. The draftsman will, however, be careful to use in each case the form of general words that is laid down in the books of precedents as applicable to hereditaments of the nature of those that he is conveying.

All estate. Following the general words comes the "all estate" clause. This, though invariably inserted except in appointments, wills, codicils, and in demises for years, appears to be absolutely useless. (*Neame* v. *Moorsom*, L. R. 3 Eq. Ca. 91.) At the same time the draftsman will, for reasons already mentioned, conform to the established custom and insert it.

If any exceptions are intended to be made out of the property assured, they follow the "all estate" clause.

The distinction between exceptions and reservations, which are constantly confounded, is the following. (Shep. Touch. 78—80.)

Exception. An exception is a clause whereby the vendor excepts something out of the thing granted; it follows that the thing excepted must be in existence at the time of the conveyance as part of the thing granted.

Reservation. A reservation is a clause whereby the vendor reserves some new thing to himself out of the thing granted: it follows that a reservation is not in existence at the time the grant is made.

Thus a grant of "all my lands in Essex, except my manor of Dale" (Dale being in Essex) affords an example of an exception. While a grant of land yielding a rose yearly or a rent quarterly is an example of a reservation. A reservation must be out of a corporeal hereditament, so that a distress can be taken in case it be not rendered; the exception being that it can be reserved out of a remainder or reversion, as, although no distress can be made during the continuance of the particular estate distress can be made for all arrears on its determination.

8. The clause beginning to have and to hold is the habendum and tenendum combined. The tenendum was of use before the passing of the Statute of *Quia Emptores* to state whether the purchaser was to hold of the vendor or his lord; it is now useless, but the words "to hold" are inserted from custom. The effect of the whole clause is to mark out the amount of interest taken by the purchaser, as to A. and his heirs. If the conveyance stopped here it would take effect at common law; if there was a consideration the purchaser would be entitled to the use; and if there was no consideration, there would be an implied, or as it is called a resulting, use to the vendor. But the invariable practice is to go on and declare uses on A.'s seisin. If the uses so declared do not exhaust the whole of A.'s seisin, there is a resulting trust for the vendor or the purchaser, according as there is or is not a consideration. Habendum and tenendum.

9. This appears to be a proper place for giving some explanation of the "uses to bar dower." If at any time Dower Uses.

during coverture a husband married on or before 1st January, 1834, is solely seised of any estate of inheritance in lands which any issue that he might (whether he did or did not actually) have by his wife could possibly inherit, she becomes entitled on his death to have an equal third part of the lands allotted to her, and to enjoy them during her life. This right of the widow was called dower. The instant that the right had once attached, it could not be defeated by any conveyance or act of the husband only. It could only be released by means of a fine, in which the wife joined, or by a recovery in which she was vouched. Both these methods were expensive and troublesome. Various plans were adopted to evade the law; the earliest was to take a conveyance of any lands which the husband purchased to himself and a trustee. Then the husband was not solely seised so long as the trustee lived, and therefore if he predeceased the trustee dower never attached. The disadvantages were that if the trustee died before the husband the latter became solely seised and dower attached, while if the trustee survived the legal estate remained in him and had to be reconveyed. And the husband could not make a conveyance during his lifetime without the trustee joining in it.

The next plan adopted was to limit an estate to the use of the husband for life with remainder after the determination of that estate by any means in his lifetime to a trustee and his heirs during the husband's life, with remainder to the husband in fee. In this scheme the husband never becomes seised of an estate of inheritance; true it is that he has the inheritance, but it is in remainder after his own death; this remainder is prevented from merging the life interest of the husband by the interposed estate of the trustee. Supposing that during the husband's life his estate becomes forfeited, then the trustee's legal estate vests in possession during the husband's life. The husband has in himself the whole beneficial interest, but if he attempts to sell, part of the legal estate is outstanding in the trustee, who has to join in the conveyance. In order to obviate the necessity of his joining, the plan was adopted of giving the husband a power of appointment overriding all these limitations.

The reader will remember that it was not necessary for a declaration of use to be made simultaneously with the raising of the seisin to feed the uses, or in other words with some person becoming seised to the uses. Thus, from the nature of the case, the uses declared on a fine or feoffment, must have been declared before or after the fine was levied or the feoffment made. And sometimes, instead of declaring all the uses at the same time, liberty was reserved by the instrument declaring the uses, for some person to declare uses in substitution for those then declared. This liberty was called a power, or power of appointment. The uses when declared were fed by the original seisin. The effect then of giving to a purchaser a power of appointment paramount to all the limitations in the deed was to enable him to declare a use in favour of any one else. He might declare the uses in favour of whomsoever he chose, and such person immediately took the legal estate, the use being fed from the old seisin. It was, however, the custom on a conveyance from the husband, who was entitled by virtue of the common uses to bar dower, not only to convey by appointment, but also to convey by some other method, such as lease and release, or bargain and sale, so as to convey all his interest.

Uses to bar dower should always be inserted in a purchase deed where the purchaser was married on or before 1st January, 1834, to a wife still living, but in no other cases. Where the husband was married after that day the dower uses do not bar his wife's dower, but he can dispose of his land by deed or will without her concurrence, and therefore a declaration that any widow shall not be entitled to dower should never be inserted, for if a man die intestate, his widow appears to be entitled, morally, to as much consideration as his heir.

Covenants for title.

10. The covenants for title are of considerable though, perhaps, of over-rated importance to the purchaser. Disputes constantly arise as to what covenants shall be entered into when the vendor is not absolute owner. The solicitor should always be careful to see that the proper covenants are inserted in the draft, for he may render himself personally liable in damages towards his client if, when acting for the vendor, he allow him to enter into unusual covenants [*Stannard* v. *Ullithorne*, 10 Bing. 491]; or if when acting for a purchaser he does not insist on the vendor's entering into those that are usual.

The purchaser is entitled to the four following covenants to be entered into by the vendor; for right to convey, for quiet enjoyment, free from incumbrances, and for further assurance; the vendor has a right to qualify them so that they shall not extend to guard against the acts and omissions of the whole world, but only against the acts and omissions of such of the people under whom he claims as have not themselves entered into proper covenants, and persons claiming under them; it follows, that a vendor who has received the property by devise or inheritance from his father, who was a purchaser for value, covenants against the acts and omissions of himself and his father and persons claiming under them, the purchaser being entitled, as "an assign," to the benefit of the covenants entered into with the father on his purchase. Formerly, these four covenants were preceded by a covenant that the vendor was seised in fee, but this is now always omitted.

The covenant for right to convey is qualified by the words, "notwithstanding anything by [*the vendor and those persons whose acts and omissions are intended to be guarded against*] done, omitted, or knowingly suffered;" where the word "done" has reference to positive acts of commission, as the execution of a deed, the creation of a charge; "omitted" has reference to such acts as the omission to execute a deed with required formalities, or the omission to bar an estate tail; "suffered" has reference to bankruptcy, or some wrongdoer having been allowed to take possession. It should be noticed, that if this covenant is ever broken, it is broken at the moment of executing the conveyance.

The covenant for quiet enjoyment is "without interruption or disturbance by the vendor, or any person claiming through or in trust for him." The word "lawful" is sometimes inserted before interruption, but it is unnecessary, as the covenant would not be held to guard against an unlawful disturbance.

The covenants against incumbrances and for further assurance require no particular remarks.

Where there is a grantee to uses the covenants should be entered into with him; they will then run with the land for the benefit of the persons for whom the statute executes the use.

Covenants by trustees.

On a sale by trustees they only covenant that they respectively have not incumbered. But there appears to be no valid objection to their covenanting for further assurance.

The question whether, on a sale by trustees with the consent of the tenant for life, the latter is bound to enter into the usual covenants for title, appears rather doubtful. The high authority of Mr. Davidson and Mr. Dart is in favour of his being allowed to insert a proviso restricting his liability as respects the estates in remainder after his own to the acts, &c., of himself and persons claiming under him. But the recent case of *E. Poulett* v. *Hood* before Lord Romilly, L. R., 5 Eq. Ca., 115, is a decision to the contrary. In the unsettled state of the practice a draftsman, acting for a purchaser, will probably insert the covenant in the usual form, while, if he be acting for a vendor, he will endeavour to obtain the insertion of the proviso.

Covenants for production.

Occasionally some of the muniments of title are not handed over to the purchaser; this happens when they affect other property of the vendor. In this case the vendor covenants that he will, at the cost of the purchaser, unless prevented, by fire, &c., produce them when required, and give copies of them to the persons entitled to the land sold, and will in the meantime keep them safe. Sometimes, by special agreement, the vendor is allowed to qualify his covenant by inserting a proviso to the effect that the covenant shall become void if he shall deliver them to any person lawfully entitled to the custody thereof, and shall, at his own expense, procure such person to execute and deliver a similar covenant to the purchaser. It may be remarked that in practice this proviso is rather to the advantage of the purchaser, as it is likely to enable him to trace the deeds on their changing hands.

If the covenant for production has to be entered into by fiduciary vendors, the usual form of covenant must be changed, so as to prevent them from incurring any personal liability under it; for this purpose each of them separately covenants, so as to bind himself and his representatives only while having the actual custody of the muniments of title, and so far as possible to bind them in the hands of other people; but not so as to incur any personal liability in respect of the covenant.

Whenever it is practicable, it is a very wise precaution to have notice of the covenant indorsed on the leading title deeds retained by the vendor. The purchaser cannot insist, without making a special agreement, that this should be done. But a vendor can hardly (in most cases) be recommended to stand on his strict right and object to it. This will prevent any difficulty occurring in case it should turn out that the covenants have been entered into by some person who had not the legal estate, so that they do not run with the land.

The practice in acting on covenants for production among some of the leading firms of solicitors in London is merely to write to the solicitors who hold the deeds, stating that they desire to inspect them on behalf of A. B., who claims under such and such a deed, at the same time offering to pay the costs of the inspection; an appointment to inspect the deeds is given as a matter of course: the actual production of the deed containing the covenant for production being dispensed with, unless there are suspicious circumstances.

The question sometimes arises whether it is desirable to insert the covenant for production in the conveyance itself, or to take it on a separate deed.

As a general rule, it appears to be proper to take the covenant for production by a separate deed whenever the covenant extends to any document not noticed in the conveyance. When the covenant is in the conveyance, it is, of course, notice to any subsequent purchaser of the deeds mentioned in it, and this is inconvenient, as it frequently happens after a lapse of time that it is very difficult to find the deeds; and in that case the fact of the covenant being in the conveyance would prevent the purchaser from being able to sell without restrictive conditions.

In very small purchases the covenant for production is generally inserted in the conveyance for the purpose of saving expense: but the practice is not to be recommended.

Where the property intended to be conveyed is reversionary, the recitals should show the origin and exact nature of the interests intended to be conveyed. There are two methods of describing the parcels: in the more common method they are described in the same manner as if the thing conveyed were an interest in possession, but the habendum is expressed to be "subject to" the particular estate; occasionally, however, the parcels are described as "all that the reversion, estate, and interest of the said A. B. expectant upon the determination of the estate created by the recited indenture of ——, of and in [*parcels*]." Reversions.

Till lately it was incumbent on the purchaser of a reversionary interest to show that he had given a full value for it, as in case he could not do so, the purchase was liable to be set aside by the Court of Chancery; the consequence was that reversionary interests were much depreciated in the market, as every purchaser knew that unless he purchased by public auction he ran the risk of a Chancery suit. The law has now been altered, 31 Vict. c. 4.

Contingent interests. The effect of the Act to Amend the Law of Real Property (8 & 9 Vict. c. 106) is to enable, as from the 1st October, 1845, "a contingent and executory and a future interest, and a possibility coupled with an interest in any tenements and hereditaments of any tenure, whether the object of the gift or limitation of such interest or possibility be or be not ascertained, also a right of entry, whether immediate or future, and whether vested or contingent, into or upon any tenements or hereditaments in England of any tenure," to be disposed of by deed.

Leaseholds. As a vendor of leaseholds, in cases where he is the original lessee, remains liable during the whole term to the landlord to perform the covenants contained in his lease, and in cases where he is not the original lessee, but has entered into the usual covenant with *his* vendor, to keep him indemnified against the covenants in the lease, he remains liable as between himself and his vendor (though not as between himself and the landlord), to perform during the whole term, the lessee's covenants contained in the lease, the purchaser has to enter into a covenant that he will pay the rent and perform the covenants in the original lease; this is of course unnecessary in cases where there is no liability remaining under the original lease, as, for instance, where it is a mortgage term at a peppercorn rent.

Where part only of the property comprised in a lease is to be sold the conveyance may be prepared in two different manners. It must be borne in mind that an assign of the original lessee is liable to the lessor during his ownership, to perform the covenants and pay the rent in the original lease, while an under-lessee is not liable. On the other hand, the assign of part of the property comprised in a lease is liable to eviction owing to the owner of the other part committing a breach of covenant, and an under-lessee is liable to eviction from the original lessor on the owner of the head lease committing a breach.

If, then, the purchase comprises a small part only of the property comprised in a lease, it is usually carried out by means of an underlease,. so as to cause the purchaser to incur no liability under the covenants comprised in the head lease: the vendor covenants with the purchaser to pay the rent, *i. e.*, the whole rent reserved by the head lease, and to perform the covenants comprised in it, so far as they regard the land which he retains; the purchaser entering into fresh covenants with his lessor, which should always be framed so as to comprise covenants similar to those contained in the head lease so far as regards the property contained in the under-lease. On the other hand, where the property sold forms a substantial part of the property in the head lease, the conveyance is made by assignment; the vendor and purchaser respectively entering into covenants with each other, secured by powers of distress, to perform the covenants contained in the head lease.

In this case, unless the lessor consents to an apportionment of the rent, it should be agreed on the contract for sale, whether the vendor or purchaser is to pay it, and the assignment should contain a covenant accordingly.

The covenants for title in an assignment of leaseholds are similar, *mutatis mutandis*, to those on a conveyance in fee, with the addition of a covenant confined to the acts of the assignor, his testators and intestates, that the lease is good and that the rent has been paid, and covenants have been performed up to the time of assignment.

Copyholds. The reader who has studied the chapters on copyholds in Williams on Real Property is recommended to read Butler, Co. Litt., 57b. to 63a. He will observe that the legal estate in copyholds passes by an admission founded on a surrender, but that a mere equitable interest can be passed by a deed. As the covenants for title form no part of the surrender, it is the custom to have a separate deed containing them, which may be executed either before or after the surrender. In the former case the operative part consists of a covenant by the vendor to surrender the land "to the use of [*the purchaser*] his heirs and assigns, according to the custom of the manor by and under the rents, fines, suits and services, therefor due and of right accustomed," then follow covenants for title similar, *mutatis mutandis*, to those contained in a conveyance of freeholds. If the deed follows the surrender, it recites it and witnesses that in consideration of the payment and receipt of the purchase-money, which are stated in the usual form, the vendor covenants for title.

It is improper to pay the purchase-money before the surrender is actually made, for if this were done (as an admittance made on a surrender takes effect as from the date of surrender) some person without notice might take a surrender for a valuable consideration during the interval that elapsed before the surrender on the original sale was made. If this were done, the second purchaser would, on his admittance acquire the legal estate, so that having an equal equity with the original purchaser he would be preferred to him, and the latter would get nothing.

For this reason the proper course is to take the surrender before the purchase-money is paid. It is understood that to save trouble the steward of the manor will generally appoint the purchaser's solicitor his deputy for the purpose of taking the surrender on his accounting to him for the fees. The actual surrender and admittances are usually prepared by the steward of the manor.

Where the object of the conveyance is to create an easement, it is hardly necessary to mention that it is proper to declare clearly what the easement is, and what are the dominant and servient tenements. For example, in the grant of a right of way, the owner of the intended servient tenement in consideration, &c., "for himself, his heirs, and assigns, hereby covenants and grants with and to the said [*owner of the intended dominant tenement*], his Easement.

heirs and assigns, that it shall be lawful for the said [*grantee*] his heirs and assigns, and his and their agents and servants, and the tenants and occupiers for the time being of the [*dominant tenement*], and all and every other persons and person for the respective benefit and advantage of the said [*grantee*], his heirs, and assigns from time to time, and at all times hereafter, at his and their respective will and pleasure, by night and day and for all purposes to go, pass and repass [*here state how, as on foot or on horseback*] in and over a certain road or way [*describing it*] intersecting certain closes called [ ]."

It should be clearly stated who, if any one, is to keep the way in repair.

Sometimes complicated arrangements have to be made as to water rights in the cases of mines or mills, and it may be at least open to a doubt whether the right intended to be granted is an easement, profit *à prendre*, or other right which can properly be annexed to the land. In this case the better course appears to be for the owner of the servient tenement to covenant with the owner of the dominant tenement, that the latter and those claiming under him shall enjoy the rights, and to endorse notice of the covenant on the leading title deeds, as doing so will render it impossible for any one to become entitled to the servient tenement, without having notice of the covenant, so that all future owners of the servient tenement will be bound in equity to permit the owner of the dominant tenement to enjoy the rights intended to be granted.

The purchaser of an equity of redemption is in a very dangerous position, for the following reasons: Equity of redemption.

First. Some mortgage may exist, the existence of which is unknown to him; in this case as he does not acquire the legal estate, such mortgagee has priority over him by virtue of the doctrine that where the equities are equal preference is given to priority of date.

Second. It is possible (*post*, p. 183,) that the vendor may have another estate, which is in mortgage at the time of the sale; if this be the case and the two mortgages either at the time of the sale or subsequently (*Beevor* v. *Luck*, L. R. 4 Eq. Ca. 537) become vested in the same person, the purchaser will not be allowed to redeem without paying off *both mortgages*. It appears, then, that in the absence of acquiring certainty that the vendor has no other estate in mortgage at the time of sale, it is desirable to procure the concurrence of the mortgagee to the deed conveying the equity of redemption, for the purpose of waiving as against the purchaser his right of consolidation.

Equitable interests in land are conveyed in practice in the same manner as if they were legal; but it should be remembered that any writing signed by a vendor expressing his intention to sell the property is sufficient to transfer the equitable interest. Equitable interests.

Freeholds belonging to a married woman are conveyed (by virtue of 3 & 4 Will. 4, c. 74, ss. 77 and following) in the same manner as if she were a feme Married woman.

sole by deed in which her husband concurs, and which is acknowledged by her pursuant to the Act. The form of the conveyance is the same as if she were a feme sole, with the following exceptions, viz., the purchase money is paid to the husband and wife who join in the receipt for it, and the wife, "with the concurrence of the husband, grants and disposes of, and the husband grants and confirms." The husband enters into the usual covenants for title, covenanting against the acts of his wife, her ancestors, &c., as the case may be, and his own acts.

As the purchase-money ought not to be paid till the deed has been acknowledged, it appears improper to state in the deed that it is intended to be acknowledged, or to make the husband covenant that the wife shall do so. The draftsman ought to call attention to the necessity for acknowledgment in the margin of the draft.

Married woman's separate property.

There has been a serious difference of opinion between the courts as to the proper method of conveying a freehold held in trust for the separate use of a married woman. (See *Adams* v. *Gamble*, 12 Ir. Ch. Rep. 102: *Lechmere* v. *Brotheridge*, 2 N. R. 219, 32 Beav. 353; *Taylor* v. *Meads*, 5 N. R. 348; *Hall* v. *Waterhouse*, 6 N. R. 20.)

The result of the cases appears to be that she can dispose of her equitable interest as if she were a feme sole; *i. e.*, by deed *without* acknowledgment, while the legal estate, if outstanding in trustees, must be conveyed by them in the usual manner, and on the other hand if there are no trustees, and the husband is at law seised in fee in right of his wife, the deed must be acknowledged for the purpose of passing the legal estate. In this case it appears on principle, in the absence of direct authority, that the purchaser is not entitled in strictness to any covenants for title from the husband, and that the latter can object to give them; but as in practice he rarely objects to give them, they should in the first instance be inserted in the draft on behalf of the purchaser. The wife is of course in strictness, unable to bind herself by any covenant, but as, if she enters into any engagement in which she purports to bind her separate estate, the latter will be bound, (*Johnson* v. *Gallagher*, 3 De G. F. & J. 494; *Mrs. Matthewman's Case*, L. R. 3 Eq. Ca. 785; *Butler* v *Cumpston*, L. R. 7 Eq. Ca. 16), it is proper to make her covenant "so as to bind her separate estate in equity."

Restraint on anticipation.

If the wife's separate estate is subject to a restraint on anticipation, she is unable during coverture to dispose of it in any manner by act *inter vivos*.

Wife's copyholds.

A wife's copyholds are generally conveyed by surrender by herself and her husband, she being first separately examined as to her consent by the steward, although in some manors the custom varies.

Wife's leaseholds.

A husband can assign or demise his wife's leaseholds without her concurrence.

Bankrupt.

The property (see the Bankruptcy Act, 1869, 32 & 33 Vict. c. 71), both real and personal, belonging to a bankrupt at the commencement of the bankruptcy, or acquired by or devolving on him during its continuance, including the capacity to exercise all powers (except the right of nomination to a vacant ecclesiastical benefice) that the bankrupt could exercise for his own benefit vests in the trustee under the bankruptcy. The certificate of the Court of Bankruptcy is conclusive evidence of the appointment of the trustee. The trustee can convey the bankrupt's freeholds exactly in the same manner as if he were an ordinary trustee. It is, however, the custom to procure the bankrupt's concurrence, if possible.

The recitals in the conveyance of any property which belonged to the bankrupt should state the adjudication of bankruptcy, the appointment of the trustee, and also that the property comprised in the conveyance belonged to the bankrupt at the date of adjudication, or (as the case may be) devolved on him after it. The trustee "grants" the bankrupt "releases:" the trustee covenants against incumbrances; the bankrupt gives the usual covenants for title.

The trustee (section 23) can, by writing under his hand, disclaim *inter alia* the bankrupt's leaseholds; and if he does so, the lease is deemed to have been surrendered at the date of the adjudication. If he sells them, the conveyance is in the usual form, with the exception that the bankrupt is not entitled to any covenant from the purchaser to indemnify him against the covenants in the lease as (by section 31), the bankrupt is freed from all subsequent liability. It appears that prior to the Bankruptcy Act, 1869, if the bankrupt was only the assignee of the original lessee he was not freed by his bankruptcy from his covenant to indemnify his vendor (2 Davidson's Precedents, 465, n.), but the practice was not to give him any covenant for indemnity. The practice remains the same under the Act of 1869.

The copyholds of a bankrupt can be dealt with by the trustee in bankruptcy in the same manner as if they had been surrendered to such uses as the trustee should appoint.

# CHAPTER VII.

## MORTGAGE DEEDS OF INTERESTS IN LAND.

**What a mortgage is.**

THERE is considerable difficulty in framing any definition of a mortgage which would be intelligible to beginners; for under the common name of mortgage we include things which operate in very different manners. But the typical form of mortgage, that of a mortgage in fee, may be described as a conveyance of land to a creditor subject to a proviso for reconveyance on payment of the debt and interest. The effect of such a mortgage *at law,* is to make the creditor (who is called the mortgagee) absolute owner of the land: on the other hand, in equity, the debtor (who is called the mortgagor) is considered the owner, and the rights of the mortgagee over the land are merely those necessary for enforcing payment of the debt. In old times a mortgage was defined (see Co. Litt. 205 *a*) as a feoffment in fee, upon condition to be void if the feoffor or his heirs should on a fixed day pay the debt and interest to the feoffee or his representatives. At law, the effect of performing the condition by payment on the day was to defeat the feoffment and to restore the mortgagor to his original estate, while non-payment on the day gave to the mortgagee an estate in fee discharged from the condition. As, however, at the present time mortgages are rarely if ever made by a conveyance upon condition, but are always made by a conveyance subject to a proviso for reconveyance, we will confine our attention entirely to mortgages made in the latter manner.

The doctrines of Equity have given a very different meaning to a mortgage from that which it bore in Littleton's time, when (as has been stated) the mortgagee would acquire the estate absolutely on non-payment of the money on the appointed day. Now, on the other hand, Equity lays down the rule that a mortgage cannot by any bargain entered into between the parties at the time of making the mortgage be made irredeemable—a doctrine sometimes stated as follows: "Once a mortgage always a mortgage."

On the other hand, you can convey land to a purchaser subject to a power of repurchase on the part of the vendor at a given time for a fixed sum. The distinction between a conveyance of this nature and a mortgage is very clear in principle. In the one case the contract is really for a sale, subject to a *locus pœnitentiæ* on the part of the vendor. In the other case, the parties do not contemplate that the property shall change hands, and it does not do so even on non-payment of the money on the appointed day: it only does so by the consequence of legal proceedings taken by the creditor for the purpose of procuring repayment of his money.

A mortgage is an example of vulgar errors about law.

A common mortgage affords a good example of the erroneous notions as to law entertained by most people. You will find the plot of novels turning on the supposed impossibility of redeeming an estate in mortgage after the appointed day for payment has passed; or, again, the villain of the story determines to ruin a mortgagor by buying up all the mortgages on his property, and then selling it under the power of sale contained in the mortgage deeds. Although the forced sale may probably cause the land to be sold cheap, the result is invariably to increase the income of the mortgagor. As an example: suppose the rent-roll of an estate to be £3000 a year, representing a selling value of £90,000, the interest of mortgages on it (amounting to £60,000 at £4 per cent.) is £2400, leaving a net income (subject to deductions by tenants) of £600. After the sale the mortgagor has £30,000, which, invested at £4 per cent., gives an income of £1200, or reinvested in land at thirty years' purchase, gives £1000 as the annual income. The author has been informed of a case where the mortgages absorbed the whole rental of the property, and, on the property being sold there remained, after paying off the mortgages, over £200,000 for the mortgagor.

Mortgage effected by indenture.

A mortgage of an estate in fee simple may be regarded as the typical form of mortgage; it is effected by an indenture, the narrative recitals in which are framed so as to show the nature of the interest intended to be mortgaged, and are similar to those which would be inserted in a purchase deed; the introductory recitals state the agreement for the loan and security. Sometimes, when brevity is of importance, the deed is framed without any recitals at all; but this is extremely rare.

The clauses forming the operative parts of a mortgage deed are usually arranged in the following order:— Arrangement of clauses.

I. The clause converting the loan into a specialty debt. (*Post*, 143.)

II. The mortgage proper. This consists of the conveyance and the proviso for reconveyance.

III. The provision for payment of interest if the debt be not paid on the appointed day.

IV. Clauses altering the primary contract between the mortgagor and mortgagee.

V. The provisions for keeping up the value of the mortgaged property.

VI. The clauses giving additional remedies to the mortgagee.

VII. The covenants for title.

It appears to the author that the arrangement here suggested, which is that most usually adopted, should, as a general rule, be adhered to (see Dav. Prec., *passim*); otherwise, there is a risk that a person perusing the mortgage in haste may not have his attention attracted by a clause in an unusual place. Sometimes, however, other arrangements are adopted.

Group I.

Group I. consists of a single clause, a covenant by the mortgagor with the mortgagee for the repayment of the loan on a certain day, generally six months from the date of the mortgage, with interest in the meantime after a specified rate. Where this covenant forms the first witnessing clause, we follow the usual practice of stating the consideration in it, referring back to it as "the consideration aforesaid" in the clauses by which the conveyance is made. The consideration in the simple case of one mortgagor and one mortgagee may be expressed as follows, "in consideration of the sum of £——, upon the execution of these presents, paid to the said [*mortgagor,*] by the said [*mortgagee*];" and is generally followed by a simple receipt clause in a parenthesis, "the receipt of which said sum of £—— he, the said (*mortgagor*), doth hereby acknowledge." Till lately it was customary to follow the receipt by a formal discharge; but as this is unnecessary, it is better omitted. It has been suggested to substitute the word "now" for "upon the execution of these presents," and there appears no objection to this being done.

In old mortgages this covenant was sometimes omitted, and in its place a bond of even date with the mortgage deed was given for the payment of the mortgage debt and interest: but when inserted, it usually followed the conveyance, which thus became the first operative part, and contained the statement of the consideration and the receipt clause. Occasionally the bond is retained in modern practice in cases where the mortgaged property affords an insufficient security; for on a sale of the property under the power contained in the deed, the mortgage deed has to be handed over to the purchaser as a title deed, and therefore after a sale the mortgagee would be unable to enforce his personal remedy on the covenant if it were contained in the deed unless the purchaser would lend him the deed.

If no covenant or bond for payment of the debt be given, the mortgagee becomes a simple contract creditor of the mortgagor, though even where there is no such covenant or bond it may be held on the construction of the whole deed that a specialty debt is created by implication. In some few cases, however, the mortgagor is by a proviso inserted in the deed freed from personal liability, the land forming the sole security; as, for instance, if trustees acting under a power raise money on mortgage, and there is no cestuique trust able or willing to enter into the usual covenants; although in the case of a mortgage by trustees under a power, an adult tenant for life generally enters into the covenant, but a proviso is inserted declaring that as between the tenant for life and the remainderman the land should primarily be charged with the debt, so as to render the former a surety only.

Specialty debt.

A debt secured by an instrument under seal is called a specialty debt; it is binding on a man's heirs if they are mentioned, in which case it is called a specialty debt in which the heirs are bound. As specialty debts in which the heirs are not bound are unknown in practice, the following remarks are confined to specialties in which the heirs are bound.

Formerly, if a man died without paying his simple contract creditors, they had no remedy against his land.

The heir was bound to pay the specialties of his ancestor to the amount of the lands which he inherited; but the devisee was not bound.

By the 3 & 4 Wm. and M., c. 14, all devises were made void as against creditors by specialty in which the heirs were bound, except devises for payment of debts.

If a man charged his debts on his land, or directed his land to be sold for the payment of his debts, the simple contract creditors and specialty creditors were entitled to be paid out of the land without any priority *inter se*.

In 1803 the lands of traders, and in 1833 the lands of all persons not devised for the payment of or charged with debts, were rendered liable to be administered in Equity for the payment of simple contract debts, reserving the priority of specialty debts in which the heirs are bound.

The effect of 32 & 33 Vict. c. 46, is to place the creditors, whether simple contract or specialty, of persons dying after 1st January, 1870, on the same footing in administration; so that now the only practical difference between debts of the two classes consists in the difference of time allowed by the Statutes of Limitation for the recovery of them.

Group II. comprises, Group II.

*First*, a conveyance of the mortgaged property. This is in a form similar to that which would be adopted in the case of an absolute conveyance, repeated as often as the nature of the case requires; but the *habendum* is made "subject to the proviso for redemption hereinafter contained." And *Second*, a proviso for redemption (which, if there be more than one clause of conveyance, follows the last), and is to the effect that "if the [*mortgagor*], his heirs, executors, administrators, or assigns shall on the said day of" [namely, the day on which the principal is covenanted to be paid] "pay to the [*mortgagee*], his executors, administrators, or assigns, the said sum of £—— [principal], together with interest thereon in the meantime at" the rate mentioned in the covenant; "then [*the mortgagee*], his heirs or assigns, shall at any time thereafter upon the request and at the cost of the said [*mortgagor*], his heirs, executors, administrators, or assigns, re-convey the said premises hereinbefore expressed to be hereby granted to the use of the said [*mortgagor*], his heirs, or assigns, or as he or they shall direct."

Proviso for redemption.

The old practice of naming the hour and place for repayment has long since been discontinued: and the day mentioned in the proviso is not now considered as fixing a date after which the mortgagor cannot redeem, but as fixing a date before which the mortgagee cannot foreclose. Although the mortgagor has a strict right to pay off on the day appointed, he never does so in practice. In the absence of special stipulation he has to give the mortgagee six months' notice of his intention to pay him off, and is entitled to six months' notice from a mortgagee calling in his money.

Foreclosure. If the mortgage deed were to stop here, it would entitle the mortgagee to his most characteristic remedy for the nonpayment of the mortgage debt and interest, namely, foreclosure. This is obtained on application to a Court of Equity, which orders the mortgagor to pay principal and interest on a given day, generally six months from the time of the decree, and declares that "on default he shall be foreclosed from all right or equity of redemption;" in other words, that the land shall belong to the mortgagee, free from redemption. The right of foreclosure is incident only to a mortgage properly so called. It does not apply to a conveyance on trust for sale, or to a mortgage by deposit of deeds. Under the 15 & 16 Vict. c. 86, the Court is authorised to direct a sale instead of foreclosure at the request of any party interested.

Right to redeem reserved incorrectly. "It sometimes happens" [But. Co. Lit. 208*a*, n.] "that by the language of the proviso for redemption the right to redeem is limited to a person who had either no interest, or a partial interest only, in the land at the time of the mortgage: and that from the circumstance it becomes doubtful *whether the person to whom the equity of redemption is thus limited does not acquire under the limitation* the beneficial ownership of the equity of redemption; or at least a greater interest in it than he had in the land before the mortgage:" as, for instance, if the mortgage is made of the wife's land to secure the husband's debt, and the equity of redemption is limited to the husband: the question, which is sometimes of great nicety, arises, is the title to the equity of redemption altered or not?

If it is really intended to change the title to the equity of redemption, an appropriate recital should always be inserted; on the other hand, there is but little risk of transferring the title to the equity of redemption contrary to the intention merely by reserving the equity of redemption to the mortgagor, his heirs or assigns, when he is not really owner in fee.

**Group III.**

*Group* III. consists only of a covenant for payment of interest on so much of the principal as shall for the time being remain unpaid after the appointed day.

**Covenant for payment of interest.**

It should be noticed that occasionally a person is willing to covenant for the payment of the interest for a certain time only. Thus, when a mortgage is made by trustees under a power, it sometimes happens that the tenant for life objects to covenant to pay the principal, but is willing to covenant to pay the interest accruing due during his life. Sometimes where a reversioner mortgages his interest the tenant for life covenants to pay interest during his own life. In the former of these cases the tenant for life would, in the absence of any covenant, be bound as between himself and the remainderman to keep down the interest during his life to the extent of the rents, which in the absence of any notice from the tenant for life to the remainderman, would be pronounced to be sufficient for that purpose. (*Lord Kensington* v. *Bouverie*, 7 H. L. C. 557). In the latter case a provision should be inserted in the deed declaring that notwithstanding the covenant by the tenant for life, the interest shall, as between him and the other *cestui que trusts*, or the reversioners, be primarily charged on the land, so as to render him a surety only.

Group IV. *Group* IV. The propriety of the insertion of the clauses in this group depends upon the circumstances of each particular case; the more important clauses of this group provide,

(*a*). For reduction of interest on punctual payment.
(*b*). For the continuance of the loan for a time certain.
(*c*). For payment by instalments.
(*d*). For putting the mortgagees, if more than one, on the footing of joint tenants as regards the receipt of the mortgage-money.

Reduction of interest on punctual payment. (*a*). The intention of inserting a provision for reduction of interest on punctual payment is to secure punctuality: such a provision is extremely convenient, and its insertion should generally be stipulated for by a prudent mortgagee. It is in the form of a covenant by the mortgagee, that if the mortgagor shall (so long as any part of the principal remains unpaid) pay interest at *the reduced rate* within thirty days from the day appointed for payment of interest, then the mortgagee shall accept the amount in satisfaction of the interest due. For example, if it be intended that interest should be paid at 5 per cent., the mortgage would be drawn making it payable at 6 per cent., while the proviso would make 5 per cent. alone payable on punctual payment.

The converse agreement, that a higher rate of interest shall be paid if the interest be not paid punctually, is regarded in the light of a penalty, and is relieved against in Equity.

Care should be taken to make it apparent whether the reduced interest is to be accepted as often as paid within the appointed time, or whether the neglect on any one occasion is to deprive the mortgagor of the benefit of the reduction on all future occasions.

**Continuance of loan for a time certain.**

(*b*). The provisions for the continuance of the loan for a certain time are always made conditional on the regular payment of interest and performance of covenants by the mortgagor, and are generally followed by a declaration that the mortgagee shall not be compelled to receive his money before the time fixed.

On the question which sometimes arises, whether trustees who invest on mortgage are justified in lending the money for a time certain, see *Vickery* v. *Evans*, 33 Beav. 376.

**Loan payable by instalments.**

(*c*). The intention of the provisions for payment of the loan by instalments is, that the instalments should be regularly paid, and that in default of regular payment the mortgagee should be at liberty to call in the unpaid part of the mortgage-money. For the purpose of carrying this intention into effect, the proper course appears to be to covenant as usual for the payment of the principal and interest in six months, and to insert a proviso in this place that if the instalments be paid punctually on certain days, together with interest on the part not paid off, the mortgagee will not call in the part not paid off.

Sometimes a different plan is adopted. The primary covenant for payment is for payment by instalments; the proviso for redemption is that the mortgaged premises shall be redeemable upon payment of the principal money and interest "by the instalments, at the times, and in manner hereinbefore mentioned, and pursuant to the covenant in that behalf hereinbefore contained." Then follows a proviso giving power to the mortgagee to call in the money in case the instalments and interest are not regularly paid.

The advantage of the former scheme appears to consist chiefly in this, that when the draftsman adopts it, he can use all the usual clauses, provisoes, and power of sale, the meanings of which are well known, and qualify them by a single proviso.

Declaration that monies belong to mortgagees on a joint account.

(*d*). *As to the declaration that the moneys are advanced on a joint account and shall belong to the survivor.*—Suppose several persons to join in lending money on mortgage. At Law they are joint tenants of the mortgage debt, but in Equity they are tenants in common, so that after the death of one of them, the mortgagor paying off the debt would be obliged to get a discharge from the personal representatives of the person dying in respect of his share.

This rule is inconvenient when trustees lend money on mortgage, for as the surviving trustees are the persons to perform the trust, they are the persons who ought to be able to give discharges for the mortgage-money. If the mortgage deed were to show the trust, and that in accordance with the trust the survivors could give receipts, this difficulty would not arise; but there is a formidable objection to this course, as, owing to the notice that the mortgage-money was trust property, the title of the mortgaged property would become encumbered with the deeds relating to the trust. To avoid this, the trustees lend as if they were absolute owners, and insert a declaration that the money belongs to them on a joint account, and, accordingly, "that the receipt of the said" [*mortgagees*], "and the survivors or survivor of them, or of the executors or administrators of such survivor, or their or his assigns, shall be a discharge for" the principal and interest and every part thereof.

It may be objected that as the mortgage deed is never executed by the mortgagees the declaration would fail in effect, as never having been actually made by the trustees. But the effect of the declaration is not to confer a legal right, it is only to prevent the operation of an equitable doctrine: and Equity would hold that if mortgagees advance their money on a deed containing a certain stipulation, none of them could afterwards refuse to abide by it.

Purchase by joint tenants.

The case of persons advancing money jointly for a purchase is different. If the conveyance is made to the purchasers as joint tenants, they are presumed to have intended to take their chance of survivorship, and accordingly they are joint tenants at Equity as well as at Law. The rule is, however, controlled by the presumed intention of the parties: and although the conveyance is made to them as joint tenants, they are considered as tenants in common in Equity if the purchase-money was advanced in unequal shares, or if the property was purchased for trading purposes, or out of moneys belonging to a partnership.

Mortgage money advanced by several.

It often happens in practice that several persons join in lending money which does not belong to them on a joint account as one sum on the same mortgage: for when a large sum is to be borrowed, the solicitor who negociates the loan may be unable to find any one person who is willing to advance the entire sum; while several smaller sums may readily be obtained. In this case several plans may be adopted. The most usual plan is for the intending lenders to nominate some persons as trustees who appear by the mortgage deed to advance the money in the usual manner, as if it belonged to them on a joint account, and who by a separate deed declare that they hold the mortgage moneys on trust for the persons actually advancing it. It will be observed that there is an obvious risk in this course, for as the trustees can give a receipt for the mortgage-money, they can get it paid off, and thus make away with it. The risk may be reduced to a minimum by taking proper precautions. In the first place, if three or more trustees of respectable position are chosen, the risk of their combining to appropriate the mortgage-money is but small. In the next place, the persons advancing the money should see that the title deeds are not left in the actual possession of the trustees. They should be deposited at a solicitor's or a banker's. A very prudent person might leave a request with the solicitor or banker that the deeds should not be given up to the trustees without his knowledge; but in practice the latter precaution is omitted.

In a very small case, where only two or three people advance the money, the mortgage may be framed as if they advanced the money on a joint account, with a declaration that the survivors or survivor shall hold the mortgage-moneys in trust for all the mortgagees as tenants in common. The objection to this scheme is, that ultimately one person alone will be able to give receipts for the mortgage-money, a situation giving him considerable facilities for committing frauds. It appears, however, a convenient plan to adopt where all the parties are above suspicion, and the amount of the mortgage-money is but small.

In a case where the property was large, the following plan was adopted for making a mortgage to three persons, A., B., and C., as tenants in common.

The property was divided into three lots, proportional in value to the several amounts to be advanced. Each lender took a first mortgage on his own lot, and a second mortgage on one of the other lots, and a third mortgage on the remaining lot. To avoid the necessity of having more than three deeds, the lot on which A. took the first mortgage was limited to A. for 1000 years, remainder to B. for 1000 years, remainder to C. in fee; the limitations of the other lots being similar, *mutatis mutandis.*

Group V.

*Group* V. The clauses providing for the management and preservation of the mortgaged property.

(*a*). Insurance against fire.
(*b*). Covenant to keep in repair.
(*c*). Renewal of leaseholds.
(*d*). Power to lease.

Insurance against fire.

(*a*). The clause providing for insurance against fire should always be inserted when a substantial part of the mortgage consists of buildings, machinery, ships, or personal chattels.

An existing insurance, if any, may be assigned to the mortgagee; but the common and better plan is, to effect a new policy in his name. Generally, the mortgagor covenants to produce when required the last receipt for the premiums, but is allowed to pay them himself: in case of doubt as to the honesty or solvency of the mortgagor, a proviso might be inserted authorising the mortgagee to pay the premiums in the first instance, and to add the amount to his security.

In either case, whether a new policy be effected or not, the policy should be handed over to the mortgagee; or, if this be impossible, the mortgagor should covenant to produce it on demand.

If the policy be assigned, it must be done with the consent of the office.

The questions which arise as to the application of the moneys receivable under the policy in case of fire, are very important, but they are of too intricate a nature to be discussed at length here.

The proper course is to avoid all such questions and to make the mortgagor covenant to insure; or if he has assigned an existing policy, covenant to keep it up: with power to the mortgagee to insure on his default, and to charge both the mortgagor and the mortgaged property with the premiums and interest. It appears that when this is done, either mortgagor or mortgagee will be able to require the mortgage-money to oe employed in reinstating any house or building insured, 14 Geo. 3, c. 78. *Ex parte Goreley*, 13 W. R. 60, 5 N. R. 22; but, on the other hand, if the property consists of machinery, ships, or personal chattels, it will be proper, having regard to *Lees* v. *Whiteley*, L. R., 2 Eq. Ca. 143, to make some provision for the application of the moneys either in payment of the mortgage debt or in reinstating the mortgaged property. It appears proper in all cases in which the insurance is not effected in the name of the mortgagee, for him to give notice to the office that the policy belongs to him.

In the absence of any special contract, the mortgagee can, under the Trustees and Mortgagees Act, 23 & 24 Vict. c. 145, in all cases where the principal money is secured by deed on hereditaments of any tenure, at any time, after the expiration of a year from the time when the principal becomes payable, or when any interest shall have been in arrear for three months, insure the whole or any part of the property, and add the premiums to his principal money.

As the statutory power does not arise except in the contingencies mentioned in the Act, it is clear that it does not obviate the necessity of inserting the usual insurance clauses in the mortgage deed.

(*b*). The discussion of the covenant to keep in repair will be found *post*, in the chapter *On Leases*.

Renewable leasehold.

(*c*). If the subject-matter of the mortgage be a *renewable* lease, it is of importance to the mortgagee that it should be renewed if possible, and that the renewed lease should form part of the security. Accordingly, the mortgage contains a covenant on the part of the mortgagor that he, his heirs and assigns [or executors, administrators, and assigns], will from time to time, so long as any money remains due on the mortgage, procure, or endeavour to procure, the renewal of the existing lease and of any renewed lease, and will assign the property comprised in the renewed lease to the mortgagee, subject to the then existing equity of redemption; and that on neglect by the mortgagor, the mortgagee may renew and hold the renewed lease as a security for the original loan and the costs of renewal.

In the absence of special agreement the mortgagor cannot be forced to renew; but the mortgagee may renew in his own name, and hold the renewed lease as security for the mortgage debt and the costs of renewal. It appears, therefore, that it is not positively necessary to insert the covenant under consideration. But, on the whole, the balance of advantages appears to be in favour of inserting it.

Whether there be any stipulation for renewal or not, the mortgagor or mortgagee renewing the lease holds it under the old title.

Power of leasing.

(*d*). Sometimes a power of leasing is inserted. A lease granted by a mortgagor is good as against himself, but not good as against the mortgagee, unless he concurs in granting it. It generally is not the intention of the parties that the mortgagee should interfere in the management of the property, and for this reason power is sometimes given to the mortgagor to lease. The power takes effect as an appointment under the Statute of Uses, and is to be exercised only before sale or foreclosure. The mortgagee is the person seised of the reversion expectant on the term, and as such is entitled to the benefit of the proviso for re-entry contained in the lease; and after he has given notice to the tenant to pay rent to him, he can distrain for non-payment, while at any time until the mortgagee has given notice to the tenant to pay rent to him, the mortgagor can distrain for non-payment of rent and justify as the mortgagee's bailiff.

Where a

It is convenient here to consider the remedies of a

lease is made not under power.

mortgagee or mortgagor for obtaining payment of rent in cases where a lease is made not under the power.

1st. Let the lease be made before the mortgage.

In this case the effect of the mortgage deed is to transfer to the mortgagee the reversion expectant on the term demised, and with it the rent; and if he chooses he may give notice to the tenant to pay the rent to him, and after giving notice, may enforce payment by distress. But suppose that instead of giving notice he permits the mortgagor to go on receiving the rent, the tenant is safe in paying it to the mortgagor (4 Anne, c. 16, s. 10); and the mortgagor may distrain for it as the bailiff of the mortgagee (*Trent* v. *Hunt*, 9 Ex. 14).

The mortgagee can, whether he has given notice to the tenant to pay rent to himself or not, take advantage of the proviso for re-entry contained in the lease if the tenant pays neither mortgagor nor mortgagee.

2nd. Let the lease be granted after the mortgage by the mortgagor alone.

Here the mortgagor can distrain or bring ejectment, until the mortgagee has given notice to the tenant to pay rent to him, and the tenant has acquiesced. The tenant cannot set up the mortgagee's title against the mortgagor on account of the estoppel arising by his acceptance of the lease. The mortgagee may eject the tenant by his title paramount, or after he has given notice to the tenant to pay rent to him, and the tenant has acquiesced, in which case a new contract, not necessarily on the terms of the existing lease, is constituted between the mortgagee and the tenant (Notes to *Moss* v. *Gallimore*, *Keech* v. *Hall*, *Smith*, L. C.); he may distrain for non-payment.

The practical result is, that if a mortgagor having no power to lease grants a lease out of his estate after the mortgage, the mortgagee can always evict the tenant. This renders it desirable in the case of building properties to insert a power of leasing. It is quite true that even without any power the mortgagor and mortgagee could jointly grant a valid lease. But this is inconvenient, as the mortgagee generally does not wish to be troubled with the management of the property.

*Group* VI. The clauses of this group consist of— Clauses of group VI.

(*a*). The power of sale.

(*b*). The attornment clause.

(*c*). The clause giving a power of distress to the mortgagee.

(*d*). The clause appointing a receiver.

Of these the power of sale is invariably inserted, but the adoption of the last is a matter of special agreement.

Bearing in mind that the better the security is the lower is the rate of interest, and that the effect of the insertion of these clauses is to give to the mortgagee more complete remedies for the recovery of his principal and interest than he has without them, it follows that the insertion of them is in part for the benefit of the mortgagor, as it may induce the mort- Give additional remedies to mortgagee.

gagee to lend at a lower rate of interest than he would otherwise.

The effect of the first of these clauses, the power of sale, is to extend the remedies of the mortgagee for the recovery of his principal and interest, while the effect of the other three is to secure punctual payment of the interest only.

(*a*). The power of sale when properly framed contains eight clauses.

The permission to sell.

By the first of these power or liberty to sell the mortgaged property is given to the mortgagee; this power or liberty of sale differs entirely in its *modus operandi* from the powers already considered. These are (as the reader will remember):—1st, a bargain and sale by executors, which is a power operating at Common Law: 2nd, an appointment of a use, which is a power taking effect by virtue of the Statute of Uses: 3rd, a power of attorney, or liberty to make use of the name of the person creating the power. At Law the mortgagee is absolute owner, and therefore can sell. But his sale would be bad at Equity, where he is considered as having a charge only. We give him, therefore, *liberty*, or as it is usually called, a *power* to sell, the effect of which is to prevent the mortgagor or any one claiming under him from disputing in Equity the mortgagee's right to sell. The reader will observe how greatly this differs from the other powers already described. It does not operate at Law like a bargain and sale by executors; it does not operate as the declaration of a use. All that it does is to declare that Equity shall not interfere with the strict legal rights of the mortgagee, and it may therefore be called an *equitable* power.

The power of sale should always be given to the person or persons who from time to time are entitled to the mortgage debt; that is to say, to the mortgagee, his executors, administrators or assigns, or if there be several mortgagees, to them or the survivors or survivor of them, or the executors or administrators of such survivor, their or his assigns, and never to the mortgagee, his heirs and assigns. The heir of the mortgagee has nothing to do with the money, all that he has to do with the mortgage is to be trustee of the legal estate for the persons entitled to the mortgage debt. To whom given.

The word *assigns* should never be omitted from the power of sale, as otherwise a transferree of the mortgage will not be able to exercise it.

If the mortgage be made subject to any existing charges, power should be given to sell either subject to or free from existing charges, and in the latter case with power to pay them off out of the purchase-money, or on any other terms of indemnity against them.

As in the absence of any special direction in the power of sale, it is the duty of the mortgagee in selling under his power to sell under proper conditions, it is unnecessary to give him special permission to do so, but such express permission is always given in practice; similarly express permission is always given to sell either by public auction or private contract, although under a general power the mortgagee might sell in either manner; this appears to be one of the many cases where the common forms include some words not actually essential to the operation of the deed, but convenient as pointing out the rights or duties of the parties acting under it.

Heir to concur in conveyance.

If a mortgagee dies intestate, his administrator becomes entitled to the mortgage debt, while the legal estate in the land descends to his heir-at-law. The administrator is the person to sell, but he cannot convey the legal estate to the purchaser; it is therefore proper to declare by the second clause in the power of sale that, on any sale under the power, the person having the legal estate "shall make such assurances of the same for the purpose of carrying the sale thereof into effect as the person or persons by whom the sale shall be made shall direct."

When power may be exercised.

If the interest be paid regularly to the mortgagee, and if the principal be paid off on proper notice, there would be no reason for allowing him to sell the property, and accordingly a clause (the third in order) is inserted which provides that the power shall not be exercised—*first*, till default shall have been made in payment of "some principal and interest," [*i. e.* not before the day named in the covenant for payment;] and notice shall have been given in writing to the mortgagor to pay off the monies due for the time being, and default shall have been made in doing so for six months; or *secondly*, until some half-yearly payment of interest shall have been in arrear for three calendar months.

It is of importance that the mortgagee should not

be hampered when he wishes to give notice by any difficulty in finding the person to whom it is to be given, and for this reason it is usually provided that the notice should be sufficient if left on any part of the mortgaged premises, or sent by post to the mortgagor at his last known place of abode in England; and that it should be sufficient if not addressed to any person in particular; for after the death of the mortgagor the mortgagee may not know to whom it ought to be addressed.

In some few cases, chiefly when the mortgage is an extremely insufficient security for the debt, and sometimes in a mortgage to secure an account current at a banker's, the whole of the clause under consideration is omitted, so as to enable the sale to be made without any notice to the mortgagor, whenever the mortgagee thinks fit; in this case the clause giving liberty to sell may expressly declare that the power may be exercised without any notice to the mortgagor at any time after the execution of the mortgage deed.

It might sometimes be extremely difficult to produce satisfactory evidence to the purchaser that the events had happened provided for in the last clause. For this purpose a clause (the fourth), is inserted expressly declaring that every sale purporting to be made under the power of sale should be valid as regards the purchaser, and that the remedy of the mortgagor in respect of any improper sale should be in damages only, *i.e.* leaving him to his personal remedy against the mortgagee. **Purchaser protected against improper sale.**

Receipt for purchase-monies.

The receipt clause (the fifth), provides that the mortgagee, his executors, administrators, or assigns may give a receipt for the purchase-money arising on any sale.

This clause is inserted to prevent the application of the rule of equity which provides that a person paying money to another who is not to his knowledge the absolute owner of it is bound to see that the latter applies it properly. This would cause considerable difficulty in carrying out a sale under the power, as a purchaser would be obliged to investigate the state of accounts between the mortgagor and mortgagee, and to see that the latter paid to the former that part of the purchase-money that belonged to him. The effect of the accidental omission of the clause appears to be guarded against by Lord St. Leonards' Act, 22 & 23 Vict. c. 35, s. 24.

Application of purchase-monies.

By the sixth clause the mortgagee is directed to apply the purchase-money in the first place in defraying the expenses of the sale; in the next place, towards paying off the monies due on the mortgage, and to pay the surplus, if any, to the mortgagor. Where the mortgage is of realty only, the surplus is made payable to the mortgagor, his heirs or assigns; if it be of personal estate, to the mortgagor, his executors, administrators or assigns; and if it be both of real and personal estate, to the mortgagor, his executors, administrators and assigns, with a distinct declaration that it is to be paid as *personal estate*, so as to prevent the mortgagee from being incumbered by any dispute between the real and personal representatives of the mortgagor as to whom he ought to pay the surplus.

By the seventh clause it is declared that any one entitled to give a receipt for the mortgage monies, may exercise the power of sale.

By the eighth clause it is declared that no person exercising the power of sale shall be liable for any involuntary losses.

(*b* & *c*). The attornment clause, or the clause giving a power of distress, is inserted when part of the property is in hand.

The effect of the former, the attornment clause, is to make the mortgagor tenant of the mortgagee, so as to enable the latter to distrain for rent—the rent being made equal in amount to and payable on the same days as the interest—so that if the interest be not punctually paid, the mortgagee can distrain for an equal sum as rent. (*Morton* v. *Woods*, L. R. 3 Q. B. 658; *Hampson* v. *Fellows*, L. R. 6 Eq. Ca. 575.) If a receiver be appointed, the attornment should be made to him. The clause should go on and provide that in spite of the tenancy created by the attornment, the mortgagee may exercise his right of entry on the mortgagor without notice. Attornment.

The clause giving a power of distress appears to have less efficacy than the attornment clause. It creates no tenancy between the mortgagor and mortgagee. It only operates as a license, enabling the latter to distrain for his interest on the goods of the former; and as no tenancy exists, he cannot distrain on the goods of a stranger which happen to be on Distress.

the premises, nor on the goods of the mortgagor after his bankruptcy, while this can be done if a tenancy is formally created. (*Jolly* v. *Arbuthnot*, 4 De G. & J. 224, see p. 236.)

A mortgagee can always make the tenants of any part of the property which is in lease pay their rents to him, as he is the legal owner of the property, and as such has the ordinary remedies of a landlord; but he has not, where the mortgagor himself is in possession, any means of getting at the profits of the land, without bringing ejectment, unless one or other of the clauses just mentioned be inserted.

Appointment of receiver.

(*d*). The appointment of a receiver may be included in the mortgage deed, but the more usual practice is to make it by a separate deed, called "An appointment of a receiver." The advantage of this course is, that the deed can conveniently be placed in the custody of the receiver, and produced by him when necessary to the tenants, while possibly the mortgage deed may be kept by the mortgagee in his own possession.

The case where it is desirable to appoint a receiver, is where the property is *not* in the mortgagor's own possession, but is let to several tenants. The receiver, who, though formally appointed by the mortgagor, is really the nominee, generally the solicitor, of the mortgagee, does nothing so long as the interest is paid regularly, but as soon as any one payment becomes in arrear for the time specified in the deed, usually one calendar month, he acts, and by virtue of the deed collects the rents, and after deducting his salary, keeps down the interest, and pays the surplus to the mortgagor. The deed itself contains a recital of the mortgage deed, so far as to show when and what amount of interest is to be paid, and that on the treaty for the mortgage it was agreed that a receiver should be appointed.

I give an analysis of the operative part of an appointment of a receiver.

By the operative part ;—

Analysis of deed of appointment of receiver.

(α). The mortgagor, with the privity of the mortgagee, appoints "the said A. B.," his attorney, to collect the rents, and to use all lawful remedies for recovering them, and directs the tenants to pay accordingly.

(β). The receipts of the receiver, or of any future receiver for the rents, are declared sufficient.

(γ). The trusts of the monies received are for the receiver, after payment of all outgoings and insurances, and keeping down the interest on any charges prior to the mortgage debt, to retain such sum, not exceeding £5 per cent., as the mortgagee shall allow for his salary, and then to pay the interest falling due on the mortgage-money; and lastly, to pay the surplus to the mortgagor.

(δ). The receiver covenants to do his duty.

(ε). The mortgagor covenants—

1st. Not without the consent of the mortgagee to revoke the powers given to the receiver, or any future receiver.

2nd. To concur with the mortgagee when

requested, in the appointment of a new receiver.

(ς). Power to the mortgagee to appoint a new receiver on the mortgagor's neglect to do so when requested.

(η). The mortgagee is declared not to be liable for any loss occasioned by the receiver.

(θ). The mortgagor is to bear any losses occasioned by the receiver, and to pay his salary.

(κ). The receiver is not to act till some interest is in arrear for one calendar month.

If any tenant refuses to pay rent to the receiver, the latter can distrain in the name of the mortgagee. On the other hand, he cannot grant leases or manage the estate, and apparently cannot enter for non-payment of rent, unless express power be given to him.

Covenants for title.

*Group* VII. The covenants for title. These differ from those contained in a purchase deed, mainly, in their being absolute instead of qualified.

The only points worthy of notice, are, that the covenant for quiet enjoyment is made to commence after default in payment of the mortgage money; and the covenant for further assurance does not now follow the old form, which postponed its operation till default had been made in payment of the mortgage money. For it is clear that it might be desirable to have some act of further assurance done before default is made.

The better form of the covenant appears to be to throw the expense of the further assurance after foreclosure or sale on the persons by whom the further assurance is required.

Lastly, a receipt by the mortgagor is always endorsed on the mortgage deed. Receipt endorsed.

We have now considered all the ordinary clauses in a mortgage deed, and will mention shortly the statutes which are intended to supply any accidental omission. Statutory remedies of mortgagee.

As before stated, the proper remedy for a legal mortgagee is foreclosure. Whether a power of sale is or is not contained in a mortgage, the court has power, under "The Improvement of Jurisdiction in Equity Act," 15 & 16 Vict. c. 86, s. 48, on a foreclosure suit, to order a sale instead of foreclosure.

Lord Cranworth's Act, 23 & 24 Vict. c. 145, contains provisions intended to supply the place of the ordinary powers of sale, insurance, and the appointment of a receiver. The usual practice of the profession is to consider these provisions as supplementing only the ordinary provisions in a mortgage deed, and to insert all those clauses that they were intended to supersede. If, however, the ordinary clauses have been omitted, the remedies given by the Act may sometimes be valuable.

We now pass to the consideration of the frame of mortgage deeds of interests in land, as modified by the tenure of the land.

A mortgage of copyholds is effected by a surrender, conditioned to be void on payment of the debt and interest on a certain day. The surrender is accompanied by a deed, which contains Copyholds.

clauses similar to those which would be contained in a mortgage of freeholds, with the exception of the conveyance and proviso for redemption. If the surrender precedes the deed, it will be recited in it; if, as is usually the case, the deed precedes the surrender, the deed contains a covenant by the mortgagor to surrender the property to the use of the mortgagee, subject to a proviso for making void the surrender, on payment on the appointed day. It is desirable to add a declaration by the mortgagor, that he will stand seised of the premises until surrender upon trust for the mortgagee, his heirs and assigns, "subject to such equity of redemption as the same premises would have been subject to if the same had been so surrendered as aforesaid." The effect of this will be to enable the mortgagee to get in the legal estate, by an order under the Trustee Act, if a surrender be not made. [See 2 Dav. Prec., 960, note.] Sometimes a power of attorney is given by the mortgagor to the mortgagee, to effect the surrender. But neither of these plans appears of much use, as the money ought never to be advanced till the surrender is actually made for the reasons stated above (p. 131).

The mortgagee is not usually admitted, because fines and fees would be payable on his admittance, and also on the surrender to the use of the mortgagor, and his admission thereon, when the debt was paid off. The mortgagee incurs no risk by not being admitted, for on his admittance his title becomes perfect, against all persons except the lord, as from the time of the *surrender*.

When the mortgagee has not been admitted, it is the practice, on the mortgage being paid off, to enter an acknowledgment of satisfaction on the court rolls, which is considered to be sufficient evidence of the repayment of the mortgage money to vacate the surrender. A receipt should also be endorsed on the deed accompanying the surrender.

If the copyhold be held for lives, the deed should contain the usual provisions for renewal and payment of the fines.

The form of a mortgage of leaseholds depends upon the amount of the rent and the nature of the covenants to which they are liable. Leaseholds.

As before stated, the assignee of a leasehold is liable to pay the rent, and to perform the covenants, while, on the other hand, he incurs no danger of the term being forfeited by any act of the original lessee. An under-lessee is not liable to pay the rents or perform the covenants contained in the head lease, but the head lease may become forfeited, and therefore the under-lease destroyed by the act of his lessor the head-lessee.

It follows that if the rent be nominal, and the covenants not onerous, the mortgage had better be made by assignment, as in this case the lease cannot be forfeited by any act of the mortgagor. While, if as usually happens, the liability that may be incurred under the head lease be considerable, the mortgage should be made by under-lease, so that the mortgagee may escape liability.

Where the mortgage is made by way of under-lease, a clause should be inserted in the power of sale, in either of the forms following, *i.e.*: 1st, a clause authorising the mortgagee, on any sale being made under the power, to assign, as the attorney of the mortgagor, the nominal residue of the term to the purchaser; or 2nd, a clause by which the mortgagor declares himself a trustee of the nominal reversion for a purchaser.

Care must be taken not to insert any covenants as to insurance or otherwise repugnant to those in the original lease. Thus, if the covenant in the original lease is to insure in the name of the lessor, the covenant in the mortgage must not be to insure in the name of the mortgagee, for then the mortgagor would have to keep up two insurances instead of one.

It is worth noticing, that although it is the invariable custom for the mortgagor to pay the costs of the mortgagee, even if the negotiation goes off, so that no mortgage is ever effected, there is, in the absence of any special agreement, no such privity between the mortgagor and the mortgagee's solicitor, as to enable the latter to recover his costs as against the former; he has a remedy against his own client, who has his remedy over against the mortgagor. (*Rigley* v. *Daykin*, 2 Y. & J. 83; *Wilkinson* v. *Grant*, 18 C. B. 319; *Pratt* v. *Vizard*, 5 B. & Ad. 808.)

# CHAPTER VIII.

## MISCELLANEOUS DEEDS RELATING TO MORTGAGES.

### PART I.—TRANSFERS OF MORTGAGES.

A TRANSFER of a mortgage is made use of in either of the following cases:— When made use of.

*First.* The mortgagee may want to have his money in a hurry, so that he cannot wait during the interval allowed to the mortgagor after notice is given to pay off. In this case the only course that the mortgagee can adopt is to find some person willing to pay him off on having the debt and securities assigned to him.

*Second.* The mortgagee may call in his money, and the mortgagor may be unable to pay him off: in this case the latter is forced to borrow it from some one else. In this case a transfer of the mortgage and securities is generally taken by the person lending the money, as he thereby gets the same priority for his charge as the original mortgagee had.

*Third.* When a mortgage is vested in trustees and new trustees are appointed.

It must be borne in mind (*post*, p. 198) that as a debt cannot be assigned at law, the effect of the transfer of the mortgage debt is not to enable the transferree to Effect of transfer of debt and of land.

bring an action for it in his own name: on the other hand, the land can be transferred to him at law, and if the original mortgage be properly framed, he becomes, as the assign of the original mortgagee, entitled to prosecute in his own name all the remedies as against the land that the latter could have prosecuted during the continuance of his security. In cases where it is desired to enable the transferree to sue for the original mortgage debt, a power of attorney is given to him by the original mortgagee authorising him to sue in the name of the latter.

**Mortgagee generally assigns if requested by mortgagor.**

Although it is the usual custom for a mortgagee who is paid off to assign the mortgage debt if requested so to do by the mortgagor to any one advancing the money for the purpose of paying him off, still, occasionally, this course is objected to by the mortgagee on the ground that if he gives a power of attorney to the transferree he may render himself liable in costs (*post*, p. 201). In practice, however, although no mortgagee can be compelled to make a transfer however ruinous the consequences of his refusal may be to the mortgagor (*Dunstan* v. *Patterson*, 2 Phill. 345; *James* v. *Bion*, 3 Swans. 241; *Smith* v. *Green*, 1 Coll. 563); still the risk which he would incur by making a transfer is so infinitesimally small, that the most prudent person may incur it without hesitation.

There are three cases which may vary the form of the transfer.

1st. Where the mortgagor is not a party to the transfer.

2nd. Where he is a party to the transfer and has incumbered the equity of redemption.

3rd. Where he is a party and has not incumbered the equity of redemption.

It will be convenient to point out the difference between the operative parts in these three cases before we consider the difference between the recitals. In each case the mortgagee assigns the mortgage debt and the interest thenceforth to become due thereon and the benefit of all securities for the same to the transferree; but the object of doing so is different in the different cases. In the 1st case, where the mortgagor is not a party, the object of assigning the debt is that of enabling the transferree to sue in the name of the mortgagee, and therefore in this case the assignment is followed by a power of attorney enabling the transferree, his executors, administrators, or assigns, to sue and give receipts for the principal and interest in the name of the original mortgagee, his executors, or administrators. In the two latter cases, where the mortgagor is a party, the only object of the assignment is that of showing that the debt is intended to be kept alive for the protection of the transferree; and, as I shall point out, a fresh covenant will be given to him enabling him to sue in his own name, and therefore the power of attorney is omitted. The power of sale and other powers and remedies against the land should not be expressly assigned; for if they were properly framed in the original mortgage deed, they will pass to the transferree as the assign of

Assignment of mortgage debt.

Power of attorney when required.

When not required.

Power of sale.

the original mortgagee: while, on the other hand, nothing that the mortgagee can do will give the transferree the right to exercise them unless they pass to him by virtue of the original mortgage deed. In the latter case, however, where the mortgagor is a party to the transfer, it appears proper to recognise their existence (*Young* v. *Roberts*, 15 Beav. 558); this is done not by assigning them but by adding a few words, "with the benefit of the power of sale and of all other powers and remedies contained in or given by the hereinbefore recited indenture for securing or recovering payment of the said principal sum and interest."

**Conveyance of mortgaged property.**

Next follows, in each case, a conveyance by the original mortgagee of the mortgaged property to the transferree. If the mortgagor is a party, the conveyance is expressed to be made at his request; and if he has not incumbered the equity of redemption he joins as a conveying party. The parcels are generally set out in the recital of the original mortgage, and in the conveyance they are usually described as "the hereditaments and premises in the hereinbefore recited indenture comprised or expressed to be thereby granted, or which now by any means are vested in the said [*mortgagee*], subject to redemption, by virtue of the hereinbefore recited indenture." It sometimes is more convenient, particularly when the mortgagor is a party and has not incumbered the equity of redemption, to refer in the recitals to the parcels as "the hereditaments hereinafter described and intended to be hereby granted," and to set out their full description in the operative part. In either case the mortgagee is not bound to trouble himself as to any new description; all that he is bound to do is to convey by the description in his mortgage.

Subject to old equity of redemption.

Bearing in mind that where the mortgagor is not a party to the transfer, the mortgagee cannot alter the equities affecting the land, and that even where he is a party, but has incumbered the equity of redemption, he and the mortgagee cannot alter the equities affecting the land as against subsequent incumbrancers, the habendum in either of these cases must be made "subject to such right or equity of redemption as the same premises are now subject to, by virtue of" the original mortgage deed; but for the purpose of showing that the debt is now charged on the land in favour of the transferree, the form continues "on payment to the said [*transferree*], his executors, administrators, or assigns" of the mortgage debt and interest.

Free from old but subject to new equity of redemption.

Where the mortgagor is a party to the transfer, and has not incumbered the equity of redemption, the case is different, he and the mortgagee together having the entire legal and equitable interest in the land can affect it with any equities that they think fit, and accordingly in this case, where, it will be remembered, the mortgagee conveys at the request of the mortgagor, and the mortgagor conveys and confirms, the habendum is made free from the existing equity of redemption, but subject to a new proviso for redemption on payment to the transferree.

Whether the mortgagor is a party or not, a cove-

Covenants by mortgagee. nant is inserted by the mortgagee that he has not incumbered, and according to the practice of some conveyancers, a covenant for further assurance; but it appears that the transferree cannot insist upon the insertion of this latter covenant. By mortgagor. If the mortgagor be a party, he covenants for payment of principal and interest, so that the transferree may have his own covenants to sue upon. If the equity of redemption has been incumbered, covenants for title by the mortgagor or a new power of sale would be useless; but where this is not the case, covenants Power of sale. for title by the mortgagor, a fresh power of sale, and other powers and remedies, are inserted for the benefit of the transferree.

Recitals. To return to the consideration of the recitals; the mortgage is recited so far as to show the conveyance, proviso for redemption, and (in cases where the mortgage debt is to be assigned with a power of attorney) the covenants for payment of principal and interest. Then follows a recital that the principal is still due, either with interest from a certain day, or that no interest is due. And, according to circumstances, a recital that the transferree has agreed to pay off the mortgage debt to the original mortgagee, "upon having such transfer as is hereinafter contained," of the mortgage debt, and interest, and securities; or that he has agreed to do so at the mortgagor's request, "upon having such transfer, &c., and upon having repayment of the same with interest after the rate hereinafter mentioned, further secured in manner hereinafter appearing."

Where the mortgage is vested in trustees, and has to be transferred upon an appointment of new trustees, care must be taken to frame the transfer so as not to disclose the trusts. The better course appears to be to recite that the mortgage debt now belongs in equity to the continuing and new trustees, and that they had requested the trustees in whom it was vested to make such transfer of the mortgage debt and securities as hereinafter appeareth, which they had agreed to do: the rest of the transfer will present no difficulties. Transfer to new trustees.

Whenever circumstances admit, it is most desirable to make the transfer by a deed endorsed on the original mortgage deed. Where both mortgagee and transferree are clients of the same solicitor, there is but little difficulty in doing so; but when they are not, it is not an easy thing to manage, for it is the duty of transferree's solicitor to engross the transfer; while the mortgagee may and probably will refuse to allow his mortgage deed to pass out of his hands for that purpose. Transfer by a deed endorsed.

It is hardly necessary to observe that in all cases in which it is possible, the mortgagor should be made a party for the purpose of being bound by the recital as to the state of the debt: for if he were not a party and had no notice of the transfer, he might set off against the claim of the transferree all moneys paid by him towards the discharge of the mortgage debt before the assignment, or after the assignment and before notice of it, the rule being that when the mortgagor is not a party to the trans- Mortgagor should be a party if possible.

fer, the transferree represents the mortgagee, and can only claim what is actually owing on the mortgage (see *post*, p. 201).

Simultaneous transfers of mortgages on property of different people.

Occasionally it happens that the same mortgagee holds mortgages on the property of different mortgagors, and wishes to transfer them all to the same person. This is a case which often happens when the mortgagees are trustees and a new trustee is appointed. Care must be taken in this case to transfer each mortgage by a separate deed: as, if this is not done, inconvenience will be occasioned to the mortgagors when the mortgages are paid off, as the same deed—the deed of transfer—will be a title deed of each of them. And it appears that whichever mortgagor is the first to redeem has a right to the custody of the joint deed of transfer, on executing, at the expense of the transferree, whose bad conveyancing has caused the inconvenience, a covenant for production. (See 2 Dav. Prec. 834; Morgan & Davey, Costs in Chancery, 167, 168.)

Costs of transfer.

There appears to be but little authority as to the costs of a transfer. It appears from *Re Radcliffe*, 22 Beav. 201, that when the interest is paid regularly, and the mortgagor has never been called upon to pay off the mortgage, he will not be liable to pay the costs of a transfer made without his concurrence.

Transfers of mortgages of copyholds.

The method of making the transfer of a mortgage of copyholds depends upon the manner in which the mortgage has been effected.

The mortgage may have been made—

(α). By covenant to surrender.

(β). By conditional surrender.

(γ). By conditional surrender followed by admission.

In each case I shall only point out the peculiarities in the conveyance of the land, the forms of the assignment of the debt being the same as in the case of a transfer of mortgage of freeholds.

In the first case, where no conditional surrender has been made, the mortgagee has an equitable interest in the copyhold, which he can pass by assignment (*Rex* v. *Hendon*, 2 T. R. 484), and accordingly all that is necessary in the absence of the mortgagor is an assignment of the copyhold and benefit of the covenant to surrender, with power to sue in the name of the covenantee, habendum to the transferree, his heirs and assigns, subject to the existing equity of redemption, on payment to the transferree. In this case the conditional surrender should, if possible, be actually made to the transferree by the mortgagor. No surrender made.

In the second case, where the mortgage was effected by means of a conditional surrender; here, if the mortgagor will join, and there is no subsequent surrender on the Court Rolls, the best course is to make a fresh conditional surrender by the mortgagor, to the use of the transferree, and to enter up satisfaction of the old conditional surrender on the Court Rolls. If the mortgagor does not join, or if he has made subsequent incumbrances, the proper method is for the mortgagee to be admitted, and to surrender to the use of the transferree, subject to Surrender but no admission.

the existing equity of redemption. The deed will contain a covenant on the part of the mortgagee that he will be admitted, and immediately make a surrender to the use and at the costs of the transferree subject to the existing equity of redemption, followed by a declaration that in the meantime the mortgagee will be a trustee for the transferree.

The objection to this plan is, that it entails additional fines and fees on the admission and surrender of the mortgagee, and if the transferree be admitted, on his admission, and whether he be admitted or not, on the surrender to the mortgagor when the mortgage is paid off, and his admission. If the transferree be admitted the admission of the mortgagor must be founded on a surrender by him; if he be not admitted it must be founded on a surrender by the mortgagee and be followed by a release from the transferree of his bare legal right to be admitted. (*Steele* v. *Waller*, 28 Bea. 466.)

For the sake of avoiding this expense, the transferree sometimes remains satisfied with a covenant from the mortgagee to surrender if required.

Mortgagee admitted.

In the third case, where the mortgagee has been admitted, he will surrender to the use of the transferree, subject to the existing equity of redemption.

Reconveyance.

The re-conveyance, on payment of the mortgage-money, may be made in the three cases above mentioned, by a deed of release, by entering up satisfaction of the conditional surrender, and by surrender respectively.

## PART II.—CONSOLIDATION OF MORTGAGES.

Consolidation of mortgages.

It sometimes happens that the same mortgagor has made several mortgages to different people. It is convenient to him to get them all into the same hands, as he is then less likely to be harassed by constantly having to pay off or find a transferree. In this case the practice is to take a separate transfer from each mortgagee to the transferree, so that each mortgagee has only a deed relating to his own charge to peruse. The deed contains an assignment of the mortgage debt and security, with the benefit of the powers of sale, &c., a transfer of the mortgaged property, subject to the old proviso for redemption on payment to the transferree, and lastly a covenant by the mortgagee that he has not encumbered. No power of attorney from the mortgagee, and no covenants by the mortgagor, are inserted. Then another deed, a mortgage for the aggregate sum advanced, is framed, containing the covenants by the mortgagor, a new power of sale, &c. The frame of this last-mentioned deed is rather difficult to understand.

Form of deeds of transfer.

Remedies of transferree before execution of consolidation deed.

Before we pass to the consideration of the consolidation deed, a word as to the position of the transferree before the execution of it. He is entitled, whether the property contained in each of the original mortgages is the same or not, to hold all the property comprised in each mortgage as a security for the aggregate debt, and that even if subsequent mortgages exist on some of the property. This right is not lost by the fact that the equity of redemption in one of the properties has been sold before all the mortgages have become vested in the same person. See 2 Dav. Prec. 839, and *Beevor* v. *Luck*, L. R. 4 Eq. 537.

This right of consolidation is one reason of the danger that there is in purchasing an equity of redemption (*ante*, p. 133), or in taking a second mortgage.

The right of consolidation is sometimes confounded with that of tacking, but they are very different.

Tacking. Tacking is where a third mortgagee, who has advanced his money without notice of a second mortgage, takes a transfer of the first mortgage. By thus acquiring the legal estate, he obtains priority as to the whole of his debt over the second mortgagee. To enable a subsequent mortgagee to tack, it is necessary, *first*, that the money should have been advanced by him without notice of the second mortgage; *secondly*, that the advance should have been originally made on the security of the land, a judgment debt, for instance, cannot be tacked; and *thirdly*, that he should acquire the legal estate.

The explanation of the doctrine usually given is this: the third mortgagee advancing his money without notice of the second mortgage, has an equal equity with the second mortgagee to be paid, not equal, strictly speaking, as the equity is really to be paid after him, but as he knew nothing of the second mortgage, he acted in good faith, and when, by getting in the legal estate he acquires an advantage at law, equity will not take it from him. (See *Marsh* v. *Lee*, 1 White & Tud. L. C. Equity.) The reader will observe how widely this differs from the doctrine of consolidation; when a mortgagee consolidates mortgages he does not oust a prior mortgagee as he does in tacking. Consolidation takes place in respect of mortgages of different estates; tacking in respect of mortgages of the same estate. A mortgagee can consolidate without obtaining the legal estate; to enable him to tack he must get in the legal estate.

Form of deed of consolidation.

We now return after this long digression, to the consideration of the deed of consolidation. In the absence of any such deed, the transferree has the right to hold all the property comprised in the several mortgages as security for the aggregate debt. He has, however, no power of sale over the aggregate property; but he can sell the property comprised in each mortgage deed by virtue of the power of sale contained in it. He has no covenants enabling him to sue in his own name. All that would be absolutely necessary would be a deed containing the covenants for payment of principal and interest, and giving him liberty to sell all the property comprised in the several deeds as a whole. But in practice the deed is prepared as if it were a mortgage for the aggregate sum subject to the original debts. It may be asked, Does not the mortgagor render himself liable to pay the aggregate debt twice over, once in detail under each separate mortgage deed, and the second time under the consolidation deed? This is provided against as follows: —The consideration is not stated to be the aggregate sum now advanced by the transferree, but the transfers are recited very shortly, and the consideration is stated to be the aggregate sum so "owing as aforesaid;" also, although the conveyance is made subject to the original mortgage debts and interest, and to the securities for the same, it is also made discharged from all rights of redemption under the original mortgages, and subject to a new proviso for redemption on payment of the aggregate sum. Having regard to the possibility of the mortgagor having in some manner charged his estate so as to prevent him from granting a proper power of sale, a distinct declaration is inserted that nothing contained in the consolidation deed shall hinder the transferree from exercising the power of sale, &c., contained in any of the prior mortgage deeds.

## PART III.—DEEDS OF FURTHER CHARGE.

Frame of deed of further charge.

A deed of further charge contains covenants for the payment of the further advance with interest, and for payment of interest during the currency of the security, the first day of payment being such of the days appointed for payment of interest in the original mortgage deed as follows next after the date of the deed of further charge. No conveyance of the land is necessary, as it is already vested in the mortgagee, but a covenant is inserted, on the part of the mortgagor, that it shall stand as a security to the mortgagee, not only for the original debt and interest, but also for the fresh advance and interest, and that it shall not be redeemable until payment to the mortgagee of both sums and interest. Then follows an agreement and declaration that such of the clauses of the 4th, 5th, and 6th group as are contained in the original mortgage, and are intended to apply to the further advance shall do so. It is convenient to endorse a deed of further charge of this nature on the original mortgage, as it saves a recital. The inconvenience pointed out (*ante*, p. 179) attending the engrossing of an endorsed deed will not apply in this case, as the solicitor whose duty it is to engross the deed is the mortgagee's solicitor, the person who probably has the custody of the original mortgage deed.

Made on occasion of a transfer.

If, as often happens, a fresh advance is made on the occasion of a transfer, it is charged by means of the proviso for redemption. For assuming, as is most probable in such a case, that the mortgagor has not incumbered, the land is conveyed to the transferree subject to a new proviso for redemption on payment of the aggregate sum, consisting of the original debt and further advance.

## PART IV.—RECONVEYANCES.

Reconveyances.

When the mortgage debt is paid off, the mortgagee ceases to have any equitable interest in the property. It was conveyed to him merely as security for his debt, and for no other purpose: as soon as his debt is paid off, it becomes his duty to reconvey it to the mortgagor.

Reconveyance should be endorsed.

It is desirable to make the reconveyance by a deed endorsed on the mortgage. In this case unless there have been dealings with the mortgage, all that is required is a conveyance without any recitals to the mortgagor, free from "all principal moneys and interest intended to be secured by the within written indenture," and a covenant against incumbrances by the mortgagee.

When, however, circumstances render it inconvenient to endorse the reconveyance, the mortgage must be formally recited, and a recital must be made, stating the dealings, if any, with it, and the existing state of the debt. The rest of the deed presents no peculiarity.

**Mortgagor may keep debt alive for his own benefit.**

Although, as already stated, no mortgagee can, strictly speaking, be forced to transfer his mortgage, it appears that the owner paying him off can insist on having the debt kept alive for his benefit; and if he have but a limited interest, if he be tenant for life only, the presumption will be that he intended to have the charge kept up; while if he be tenant in fee or in tail in possession, the presumption will be the other way. But following the usual rule of preventing any doubts arising, it is always proper in either case to insert a few words stating clearly the intention of the person who pays off the debt; the general rule being if it is intended to keep up the charge to take a transfer, although if that method should be objected to, it need not be adopted.

**Sub-mortgages.**

Occasionally a mortgagee wishes to receive part of his money only, and is unwilling to disturb his original investment. Suppose, for instance, that he has advanced 20,000*l.* on mortgage of land, and wants 500*l.*, it might be disadvantageous to him to call in the 20,000*l.*; while if he were to ask the mortgagor to pay him 500*l.*, the latter not having 500*l.*, and being unable to find a person willing to advance him 500*l.* on a second mortgage, might be compelled to borrow the whole 20,000*l.* from another person, and thus discharge the whole debt. In such a case, a *sub-mortgage*, or mortgage of the mortgage-debt and securities, is resorted to. The subject-matter of the sub-mortgage being the mortgage-debt and securities, they have to be transferred to the sub-mortgagee, subject to redemption (in our example on payment of 500*l.*), with liberty to him to sell them.

The transfer of the debt will be made by an assignment and power of attorney, habendum "to the sub-mortgagee, his executors, administrators, and assigns, subject to the proviso for redemption hereinafter contained," *i.e.*, to redemption on payment of 500*l.* and interest. Notice of the assignment must be given to the original mortgagor for the reasons already pointed out (*ante*, p. 179). The subject-matter of the original mortgage will be transferred to the sub-mortgagee in the appropriate method, "subject to such right or equity of redemption as the said premises are now subject to by virtue of" the original mortgage, "and subject also to the proviso for redemption hereinafter contained." The proviso for redemption in our example would be on payment of 500*l.* and interest by the original mortgagee to the sub-mortgagee.

The effect of the two provisoes for redemption in

the original mortgage and the sub-mortgage appears to be the following:—

Under the proviso contained in the original mortgage, the mortgagor can redeem that which he mortgaged, viz., his land, on payment of 20,000*l.*; that is, 19,500*l.* to the original mortgagee, and 500*l.* to the sub-mortgagee; and on doing so, he becomes entitled to a reconveyance of the land from both of them. Under the proviso contained in the sub-mortgage, the original mortgagee can redeem that which he mortgaged, viz., the debt of 20,000*l.* and securities to the sub-mortgagee; and on doing so, he becomes entitled to a reassignment of the 20,000*l.* and a reconveyance of the land, subject as to the latter to the proviso for redemption contained in the original mortgage.

Bearing in mind that the original mortgagor may wish to pay off his 20,000*l.*, trusts are declared concerning it in the sub-mortgage similar to those contained in a mortgage of a chose in action (*post*, p. 206), and power is given to the sub-mortgagee to give a receipt for the whole 20,000*l.* The power of sale authorises the sub-mortgagee to sell the subject of his security, *i.e.*, the mortgage-debt of 20,000*l.*, and the land subject to redemption on payment of 20,000*l.*; if the original mortgage-deed is properly drawn, he can also, as assign of the mortgagee, exercise the power of sale contained in it. Let us consider the method in which the two powers of sale work. The power contained in the sub-mortgage is only to be exercised if the original mortgagee makes default, *i.e.*, if he does not keep down the interest on the 500*l.*, or neglects to pay the principal after due notice; but, on the other hand, it can be exercised without reference to the defaults of the mortgagor; when exercised, it passes the 20,000*l.* and securities. The power contained in the original mortgage is only to be exercised if the original mortgagor makes default, *i.e.*, if he does not keep down the interest on the 20,000*l.*, or neglects to pay the principal after due notice; when exercised, it passes the land.

freeholds, the essential difference being, that there is no declaration of uses.

Volunteers. A Voluntary Bill of Sale, made by a person in insolvent circumstances at the time of making it, will be void against creditors under 13 Eliz., c. 5.

Assignor remaining in possession. Although no delivery of the goods is necessary for the purpose of changing the ownership as between the parties, it used to be considered that if the assignor remained in possession of the goods, even where there was a valuable consideration, the deed would be void against creditors, as being fraudulent under 13 Eliz., c. 5; but the modern doctrine is, that the fact of the assignor remaining in possession of the goods does not necessarily render the deed fraudulent and void as against creditors, and that where the remaining in possession is consistent with the terms of the deed and the nature of the transaction, the deed is valid. For example, if I, being insolvent at the time, assign the furniture in my house to you absolutely by Bill of Sale, and remain in possession, the deed is void as against creditors, under the 13 Eliz., c. 5; but if I assign the furniture to you by way of mortgage, this is not the case, for my remaining in possession is consistent with the terms of the deed and the nature of the transaction.

Order and disposition. Personal chattels in the possession, order, and disposition of a trader at the commencement of his bankruptcy pass to the trustee in bankruptcy: it follows that where any trader, whether insolvent or not, executes a Bill of Sale, and remains in possession of the property comprised in it till his bankruptcy, the trustee in bankruptcy can sell it as against the persons claiming under the Bill of Sale. (See 15th Section of Bankruptcy Act, 1869.)

The rule as to order and disposition has many exceptions, the principal being that, in cases where, according to the ordinary custom, it is usual for traders to have in their possession the goods of others, they will not pass to the trustee in bankruptcy. (1 Prid. Prec. "Bills of Sale.") **Exceptions.**

Another exception of considerable importance is the case of fixtures, which requires some discussion. It is clear, *first*, that any conveyance of the land, whether by way of absolute sale or by way of mortgage, by any person who is owner both of the land and fixtures, passes them, as they are annexed to the land, and that whether the deed expressly mentions them or not, and that such a conveyance, whether registered under the Bills of Sale Acts or not, confers a good title, both as against creditors claiming under the stat. of Eliz. and the trustee in bankruptcy; —*secondly*, that where a sale or mortgage is made of the fixtures apart from the land and is registered under the Bills of Sale Acts, the mortgage at least, and probably the sale, will prevail against the trustee in bankruptcy. (*Whitmore* v. *Empson*, 23 Beav. 313.) **Fixtures.**

Although the execution of the Bill of Sale transfers the property to the assignee as against the assignor, it is necessary to perfect it by registration under 17 & 18 Vict., c. 36; otherwise the transfer is void as against the trustee in bankruptcy, a trustee under any assignment for the benefit of creditors, **Registration.**

and execution creditors. There are several exceptions to the rule, for which the reader is referred to the Act itself.

It follows from the rules above laid down, that where a Bill of Sale is made by way of mortgage of personal chattels which remain in the possession of the mortgagor, it is necessary in order to protect the chattels against the persons above mentioned, that it should be registered under the Bills of Sale Acts, and that the mortgagor's possession should be consistent with the terms of the deed, and having regard to the doctrine of reputed ownership, that it is desirable, for the purpose of securing the chattels against the trustee in bankruptcy, in cases where the mortgagor is a trader, to enable the mortgagee to take possession and sell at very short notice.

The following is an analysis of a mortgage of furniture by way of Bill of Sale, where the clauses are arranged in an order which, though often adopted, is, in my opinion, not so convenient as the order suggested above (p. 141) :—

1. Assignment subject to redemption.
2. Proviso for reassignment on payment on demand, or within twenty-four hours after demand.
3. Proviso for mortgagor retaining possession until default in payment.
4. Declaration that mortgagor will not remove furniture, and that mortgagee may enter the house where it is and inspect and take a schedule of it.

5. Power to mortgagee, in default of payment, to enter into house and take possession of the furniture.
6. Power of sale comprising—
    - (α). Liberty to sell.
    - (β). Receipt clause.
    - (γ). Trusts of purchase-money.
    - (δ). Declaration that purchaser should not be bound to enquire as to default.
7. Covenants by mortgagor—
    - (α). To pay on demand the principal.
    - (β). To pay interest half-yearly in the meantime.
    - (γ). For right to assign.
    - (δ). That mortgagee may exercise the powers given him without interruption.
    - (ε). Further assurance.
    - (ζ). To insure—
    - (η). Power to mortgagee to insure if mortgagor does not.
    - (θ). That mortgagor shall repay moneys expended by mortgagee in insurances, and that in the meantime they shall be charged on property.
    - (ι). That insurance-moneys received shall, at option of mortgagee, be applied either in reinstating the premises or in repayment of moneys due on the security.
    - (κ). A declaration that demand for payment may be made by notice affixed to premises on which the chattels are.

The reader is referred to 1 Prideaux's Precedents in Conveyancing, tit. "Bills of Sale." Seton on Decrees, 408.

## PART II.—OTHER PERSONALTY.

Blackstone (2 Comm. cap. 25) defines a chose in action as being:—

1st meaning of phrase.

"Where a man has not the occupation, but merely a bare right to occupy the thing in question, the possession whereof may, however, be recovered by a suit or action at law; from whence the thing so recoverable is called a thing or chose in action." This definition does not extend far enough, as the term chose in action extends to the right to recover damages; and, on the other hand, the term is not, generally speaking, applied to specific chattels in the occupation of a person other than the true owner, though probably the principal propositions of law laid down in the text-books with respect to choses in action apply to specific chattels which are recoverable by action by the true owner. In the more limited sense of the word in which I shall employ it, by a chose in action is meant a right to take legal proceedings for the purpose of recovering money or obtaining damages. For instance, if I sell a horse to a man, and he does not pay me, I have a right to recover payment of the price from him; this right is called a chose in action.

2nd meaning.

By a common confusion of language the money itself that can be recovered, whether on a contract or by way of damages, is also called the chose in action. Where the money can be recovered by action at law, as in the common instance of a debt, it is called a *legal* chose in action; Legal. where it can be recovered by suit in equity, as, for instance, where money is in the hands of trustees, it is called an *equitable* chose in action; where the money Equitable. is not payable at the present time, but there is a present right to its future payment, as in the case of the money secured by a policy of assurance, which does not become payable till the death of the person whose life is insured, it is called a *reversionary* Reversionary. chose in action.

By a further confusion of language, lawyers some- 3rd meaning. times speak of a document evidencing the title to a chose in action as itself being the chose in action; the reader will often hear a bond or a policy of assurance called a chose in action, while really the bond-debt or the policy-money, or if we like to vary the language, the right to recover the money secured by the bond or policy, is the chose in action.

According to the doctrines of the common lawyers, Not assignable at law. no chose in action is capable of being assigned (10 Rep. 48), on the ground that if it could, "that would be the occasion of multiplying of contentions and suits, of great oppression of the people;" on the other hand, Courts of Equity recognise such an as- But in equity. signment. This doctrine is sometimes expressed broadly, as follows: "a chose in action is assignable in equity, but not at law." (2 Tudor's Leading Cases in Equity, note to *Ryall* v. *Rowles*. Dicey: Parties to Actions, 66—382.)

The student will feel some difficulty in grasping the distinction between an assignment which operates at law and one that operates in equity only; an example will render it more clear. Suppose that a leasehold which is assignable at law is assigned to me, I can (as soon as the assignment is completed) take in my own name any proceedings at law which may be necessary for the purpose of fully enjoying the property; I can bring ejectment for the purpose of obtaining possession of it if I am wrongfully kept out; or, to take an example of a chose in action assignable at law, if a cheque, originally drawn in favour of another person, be delivered to me, I can bring an action on the cheque in my own name; on the other hand, suppose that a creditor to whom a bond-debt (which is assignable at equity only) is due, assigns it to me, and the debtor refuses to pay me, I cannot bring an action in my own name to compel payment, as the court of law would refuse to recognise the assignment; I must resort to one of two courses; I must either induce the original creditor to bring an action at law in his own name, which he can still do, as the assignment is not recognised by the Court in which the action is brought, and to hand over the money to me when received; or I can take proceedings in my own name in a Court of Equity where the assignment is recognised, either against him, to compel him to allow me to bring an action in his name, or, in some cases, against the debtor himself.

Exceptions to rule.

The reader may raise this objection—a debt is a chose in action; it is not the less a chose in action because it is secured by a bill of exchange; such a debt is assigned by endorsing the bill, and the assignee can bring an action on the bill in his own name. This is one of the very many exceptions to the rule that a chose in action is assignable in equity only. Unfortunately, no general rule can be laid down as to what choses in action are assignable at law; they consist chiefly of debts which, by the custom of merchants, are assignable by the endorsement or delivery of the document evidencing the right to them, such as Bills of Exchange, Promissory Notes and Cheques, and other debts, such as the Bonds and Debentures of Companies, which can by statute be transferred in some particular manner. A policy of life assurance, though formerly assignable in equity only, can be assigned at law by following the formalities prescribed in the "Policies of Insurance Act, 1867." The student will do well to bear these exceptions in mind, as many of the propositions laid down in the text-books with reference to choses in action require modification when applied to choses in action transferable at law.

Assignments usually made by deed.

To return to the assignments of choses in action assignable at equity only; no special form of assignment is necessary (*Morrell* v. *Wootten*, 16 Beav. 197: *Rodick* v. *Gandell*, 1 De G. M. & G. 763), but the assignment is usually effected by a deed similar in its general form and arrangement to an ordinary purchase deed of freeholds. Bearing in mind the importance, where a legal chose in action is assigned, of being able to sue the debtor at law in the name

Power of attorney.

of the original creditor, a power called a power of attorney is always inserted in the assignment of a legal chose in action, enabling the assignee "to demand, sue for, recover, receive, and give effectual discharges for the debt, in the name of the assignor." In cases where the assignment is for value, the original creditor cannot revoke the power.

Costs of action.

It should be borne in mind that if the power be acted upon, and an action be brought in the name of the original creditor, the latter being the plaintiff on the record, may, on judgment going against him, be liable in costs; for this reason, if trustees (who ought never to incur any liability) make an assignment, with a power of attorney, a declaration is sometimes inserted that no action shall be brought in their names until sufficient security for costs has been given to them, or a covenant is inserted by the assignee to indemnify them against any costs that may be incurred. It is, perhaps, necessary to warn the reader that as the assignee of an equitable chose of action can take proceedings in his own name to recover it, the power of attorney should *never* be inserted where the chose in action is equitable only.

Assignment of chose in action subject to all equities.

As the assignee of a chose in action takes it subject to all the equities affecting it (*Rolt* v. *White*, 31 Beav. 520), or in other words, takes only what the assignor could recover by action or suit, it follows that the assignee ought before completion to enquire from the original debtor, whether he has notice of any assignment of, or charge on the chose in action, and what is the state of accounts as between himself and the assignor: if he be informed of the motive of the enquiry, he will, as between himself and the assignee, be bound by his answer.

**Enquiries to be made before completion.**

For example, let the subject of assignment be a simple contract debt and interest. It may happen that part of the principal has been paid off, but in this case, if the original creditor conceals the fact of the repayment, the assignee might not, unless he had made enquiries from the debtor, discover the attempted fraud until he endeavoured to enforce payment. He might also find on enquiry that the original creditor had already assigned or mortgaged the property, a fact which he would have no other method of discovering.

**Notice to be given after completion.**

When a chose in action can be assigned at equity only, the assignee must immediately after the assignment has been executed, give notice of the assignment to the debtor, for the two following reasons: *first*, if no notice was given, the debtor might pay the original creditor; *second*, courts of equity have established the rule, that as between two assignees of a chose in action, he who first gives notice has priority. A rule which has been expressed as follows, by Wood, V. C.; *Lee* v. *Howlett*, 2 K. & J. 535, he "who first makes himself master of a chose in action, by giving notice to prevent its being handed over by the person in whose hands it is to any other claimant—in other words, who first divests the title of the owner by giving notice to the person through whom the owner must derive the fund—arrests that fund and acquires the property for himself, whether the fund be a trust fund held by A. in trust for B., or a debt payable by A. to B.; if B. assigns, and his assign requires A. to pay the money over to him, that gives him priority over a previous assign of B., who has not given such notice."

It appears from the large number of cases that come into court, that sufficient attention is not paid to giving notice, and that considerable losses are incurred in consequence. Sometimes an appeal is made from the assignor to the assignee not to give notice to the debtor, on the ground that he might be injured by its being known that he had parted with, or incumbered, his property; it must be remembered that if his request is acceded to, the assignee is trusting entirely to the honour of the assignee not to make another assignment behind his back, and that if such an assignment be made, the subsequent assignee can, by giving due notice, obtain priority over the earlier one. There was until lately another reason for giving notice of the assignment. It will be observed that till the assignee has completed his title by notice to the debtor, the debt could be disposed of by the assignor, or in other words, was within "the order and disposition" of the assignor; and in all cases before the present Bankruptcy Act, 32 & 33 Vict. c. 71, would therefore have passed to his assignees in bankruptcy. The law is now partially altered; the rule is now only applicable to such choses in action as are trade debts, in the order and disposition of the trader himself.

Order and disposition.

An example will render this more clear. We will suppose that on his marriage a gentleman proposes to settle a reversionary interest expectant on his mother's death in the trust funds comprised in her settlement. Enquiry should strictly speaking be made before the marriage from the trustees of the mother's settlement, whether they have had notice of any assignment of or charge on the gentleman's interest, and also what is the amount of his reversionary interest, though to the author's belief the former enquiry is often omitted in this particular case. Immediately after the execution of the settlement notice of it must be given to the trustees.

Let us take another example: A. B. proposes to mortgage a policy on his own life to C. D. Here the debtor is the Insurance Office, and the enquiry must be made from it immediately before the money is advanced, and notice given to it on completion.

Stop order.

In cases where the chose in action is a fund in the Court of Chancery, there is no person to whom notice can be given; it is, therefore, necessary to obtain a stop order. This is an order which can be obtained by summons where the party whose interest is affected joins in the application, otherwise by petition only; for this reason the assignment should contain a power of attorney to apply by summons in the name of the assignor. The title of the assignor must either appear from the proceedings by virtue of which the fund is in Court, or be proved by affidavit. The order made, the stop order itself, is that the funds "shall not be transferred, sold, paid out, or otherwise disposed of" without notice to the assignee. It appears (*Macleod* v. *Buchanan*, 33 Beav. 234) that an incumbrancer who has obtained a stop order on a particular fund cannot safely make a further advance without obtaining a fresh stop order.

Exception to rule as to notice.

There is, however, one important exception to the rule of equity, that as between several assignees of a chose in action, he who first gives notice obtains priority, and that is the case of a mortgage debt charged on land. Here the mortgagee has an interest either legal or equitable in the land, and although the assignee of such a mortgage debt ought (*ante*, p. 179) to give notice to the mortgagor for the purpose of preventing him from paying the original mortgagee, no priority is gained by notice; on the other hand, where the subject matter of the assignment is a share of the proceeds of real estate directed to be sold, or in money directed to be raised by the sale or mortgage of land, priority is obtained by notice. (*Lee* v. *Howlett*, 2 K. & Jo. 531; *Re Hughes' trust*, 2 H. & M. 89.)

Analysis of assignment of bond debt.

To give an analysis of an absolute assignment of a bond debt.

Parties: A. B. vendor (1); C. D. purchaser (2).

Recitals: (1.) Bond.

(2.) Principal and interest due.

(3.) Contract for sale.

Operative clauses:

(1.) In consideration of —*l.*

(2.) Receipt clause.

(3.) A. B. "doth hereby assign unto C. D.,

his executors, administrators, and assigns, all that principal sum of —*l.*, secured by the said recited bond, and all interest now due, and henceforth to become due, on the said bond, and the full benefit and advantage thereof."

(4.) All estate clause.

(5.) Power of attorney.

(6.) Habendum to "C. D., his executors, administrators, and assigns absolutely."

(7.) Covenants by vendor for

(*a*) Right to assign.

(*β*) Further assurance.

(8.) Testimonium.

**Mortgage of chose in action.**

When the assignment is made by way of mortgage only, it must be remembered that possibly the original debt may be paid off before the mortgage debt. To provide against this contingency, clauses are inserted authorizing the mortgagee to give receipts for the whole debt, as otherwise the original debtor would have to pay part to the mortgagee, and part to the mortgagor, and might have at his own risk to ascertain the state of accounts between them; and declaring that the monies when received by the mortgagee shall be held by him upon trust, after retaining his costs, and all monies due on the security, for the mortgagor; the two clauses being similar to clauses 5 & 6 in the power of sale in a mortgage of freeholds (*ante*, p. 164).

It must be also remembered that the mortgagee would be bound in the absence of a stipulation to the contrary to do everything in his power for the purpose of obtaining payment of the chose in action mortgaged; he may generally speaking be trusted for his own sake to do so, as if he neglects to do so he may lose his mortgage debt, but a provision ought to be inserted for the purpose of guarding him against the consequences of his accidental omission to do so.

Mortgage of life policy.

Where money is to be advanced on the security of a policy of life assurance, an existing policy may be assigned to the mortgagee, or a new policy may be effected in the name of the mortgagor, and assigned to the mortgagee, or it may be effected in the name of the mortgagee; in which latter case the mortgage deed necessarily contains no assignment, but contains the proviso for redemption and other usual clauses of a mortgage deed. In either of these cases it is necessary that some provisions should be made for the purpose of keeping up the value of the policy; for this purpose a series of clauses are inserted, the 5th group (*ante*, p. 139) to the following effect.

Covenants by the mortgagor.

(α). That he will not do anything by which the policy may become void, as, for instance, by his going to the tropics contrary to the terms of the policy.

(β). That he will restore it if it becomes voidable.

(γ). That he will effect a new policy in the name of the mortgagee if it becomes void.

(δ). That the new policy shall be subject to the present security.

(ε). That he will pay the premiums on any new or substituted policy and deliver the receipts to the mortgagee.

(ζ). That if the mortgagor neglects to pay premiums, the mortgagee may do so; that the mortgagor will on demand repay the moneys so paid by the mortgagee and his expenses with interest, and that until repayment the moneys shall be a charge on the premises assigned.

Although a newly-effected policy of assurance is not of much value as a security by itself, still it is of considerable value when it is combined with the mortgage of something else, such as a life interest, which will afford a fund out of which the interest and premiums may be paid.

**Case of creditor insuring debtor's life without any bargain.**

Occasionally a creditor insures his debtor's life without any bargain on the subject, and in this case the question may arise whether the policy belongs to him absolutely or is redeemable by the debtor. The general rule is, that in the absence of contract express or implied, a policy effected on the life of another will belong to the person who effects it. But this presumption is rebutted if the debtor pays the premiums, or is with his assent (*Bruce* v. *Garden*, (L. R. 8 Eq. 430, 5 Ch. Ap. 33) charged with them in an account; and in either of these cases the policy becomes the property of the debtor on payment of the debt.

**Mortgage of choses in action**

As already pointed out, there are some exceptional cases in which choses in action can be trans-

assignable at law.

ferred at law: no remarks appear to be necessary in this place with respect to absolute assignments of them; but mortgages of them and of certain other interests in personal property, which are not strictly choses in action, will present some difficulties to the student.

Where liability is not incurred:—

If the property be of such a nature, as for example, if it be a railway debenture, that the owner can incur no liability in respect of it, the mortgage is effected by a transfer in the appropriate manner to the mortgagee, and a deed containing the proviso for redemption, the power of sale, and, if necessary, the trusts of the moneys to be received in respect of the mortgaged property.

Where it is incurred by the owner.

On the other hand, if the property be one in respect of which liability may be incurred by the owner, a different course is adopted: in this case the mortgagee is not made the legal owner, and consequently he incurs no liability; but provisions have to be made for the purpose of enabling him either to become the legal owner without any further act on the part of the mortgagor, or to make a transfer at law without himself first becoming the legal owner to any person to whom he may sell under the power of sale.

The first object is carried into effect in different manners according to the subject-matter of the security. If it be of such a nature that the mere execution of the deed of transfer by the mortgagor does not cause the transferree to become the owner, or to incur any liability until some additional act is performed by him, a formal deed of transfer is executed by the mortgagor; but the additional act is not performed. For example: Suppose that the subject of the mortgage be a share in a company, the transfer is executed by the mortgagor but not by the mortgagee, and the name of the mortgagee is not entered on the register of shareholders; so that although he does not become the owner of the share he can, if he think fit, complete his title by registration at any moment. Notice of the transfer should be given to the company so as to preserve priority as against any subsequent assignment by the mortgagor (*Ex parte Shelley*, 5 N. R. 200), and the share certificates should be delivered to the mortgagee. The mortgage deed will, in addition to the usual clauses, contain a declaration of trust by the mortgagor in favour of the mortgagee; and a power of attorney authorising the mortgagee on any sale of the shares to execute transfers of them to the purchaser in the name of the mortgagor, by which means the mortgagee can make a transfer direct to the purchaser without becoming the legal owner and thus incurring any liability. The mortgagor remaining the registered owner, can receive the dividends, but power should be given to the mortgagee to do so should he think fit.

In cases where the transfer does not require any additional act, such as registration, for the completion of the title of the transferree, no transfer is executed by the mortgagor, but a power of attorney is inserted in the mortgage deed enabling the mortgagee to execute a transfer to himself in the name of the mortgagor.

The student may have some difficulty in seeing how the mortgagee can enforce his security: he may act in two different manners; he may complete his title either by registration or by executing a transfer to himself in the name of the mortgagor, as the case may be, a process somewhat analogous in its effects to an ejectment by a mortgagee of freehold; in this case he will, by completing his legal title, render himself liable for calls, &c., and will have to account to the mortgagor as mortgagee in possession. On the other hand, he may, without completing his own title, sell under the power of sale: in this case he can call upon the mortgagor, as his trustee, to execute a transfer to the purchaser; or, if he thinks fit, he can execute a transfer to the purchaser in the name of the mortgagor by virtue of the power of attorney.

Professional incomes.

It is worth pointing out that certain professional incomes which present some analogy to choses in action are not assignable either at law or in equity, such as judicial salaries, the pay and half-pay or pension of an officer in the army (46 Geo. 3, c. 69), or of his widow (47 Geo. 3, sess. 2, c. 25), or apparently of an officer in the navy (though not of an officer formerly in the service of the East India Company, *Carew* v. *Cooper*, 4 Giff. 619), see 5 Byth. by Sweet, 225, and the cases of *Flarty* v. *Odlum*, 3 T. R. 681; *Lidderdale* v. *The Duke of Montrose*, 4 T. R. 248.

Officer's

Although an officer cannot lawfully part with his

commission by way of pledge or mortgage (*Colyer* v. *Fallon*, 1 T. & R. 468), he can assign the proceeds of the sale of it. In the ordinary course of business the proceeds come into the hands of the army agent, and, subject to certain regimental deductions, belong to the officer or his assigns. If the army agent has made advances to the officer, he has a right to repay himself such advances out of the proceeds of the sale of the commission when they come to his hands, or rather he may set off the debt due from the officer to himself against that which becomes due from him to the officer, so that any assign of the proceeds can only take subject to the claims of the army agent. As between different assigns, no priority is obtained by giving notice to the army agent before the proceeds are actually in his hands (*Somerset* v. *Cox*, 33 Beav. 635, S. C. 5 N. R. 682; *Buller* v. *Plunket*, 1 J. & H. 441), and consequently a charge on the proceeds is a most ineligible security.

commission.

If a married woman be entitled to a chose in action, and the husband is able to "reduce it into possession," in other words to obtain payment of the debt during the coverture, he can give a receipt for it, which is binding as against the wife: on the other hand, if the chose in action is not reduced into possession during the coverture, it remains the wife's property if she survives her husband, and passes to him as her administrator if she dies in his lifetime. Suppose, for instance, that the wife is the obligee in a bond; if her husband can, during the

Married woman. Reduction into possession.

coverture, obtain payment of the whole, or any part of the money secured by the bond, he can give a receipt for it which binds the wife. On the other hand, anything that the husband can do short of actually obtaining payment, as, for instance, an assignment by him, is absolutely void as against the wife surviving him, and that even if she joins in the assignment. (*Prole* v. *Soady*, L. R. 3 Ch. Ap. 220.) If, however, the assignee can obtain payment of the bond debt during the coverture, this operates as a reduction into possession by the husband, and is effectual against the wife surviving.

The question as to what amounts to a reduction into possession by the husband is sometimes one of considerable difficulty; the reader is referred to the note in 2 Dav. Prec., "Agreement for settling the construction of an obscure will."

Wife's mortgage debt.

There is one case of importance in which the student who reads the note referred to, without looking at the cases cited, may be led into error. Where a mortgage debt is due to the wife, it is clear that the mortgagor may pay off the debt if he thinks fit to do so. The payment must be made to the husband, whose receipt will discharge the mortgagor, while the whole transaction will operate as a reduction into possession by the husband. It also appears from the case of *Rees* v. *Keith*, 11 Sim. 388, that a payment to the husband by a third person on behalf of the mortgagor will have the same effect. The reader must not, however, rush to the conclusion that a husband alone, or a husband and wife together, can make a transfer of a mortgage debt which will bind the wife, if it be not reduced into possession during the coverture.

The case of *Rees* v. *Keith*, 11 Sim. 388, shows that where the mortgage debt is paid to the husband by a third person on behalf of the mortgagor, that the husband's receipt discharges the mortgagor, and that the wife becomes a trustee for the latter of any interest that she has in the subject of the mortgage. It appears to follow that in this case a transfer of the mortgage debt and securities, which would bind the wife surviving, could be effected by the husband making an assignment of the mortgage debt by the direction and at the request of the mortgagor, and by the husband or husband and wife, as the case might be, making a transfer of the subject matter of the mortgage.

The reader may ask, how could the transferree obtain a good title to the subject of the mortgage, if that itself were a chose in action, assignable at equity only, and the wife were to survive the husband, who were to die before it had been reduced into possession. It must be remembered that as the wife becomes, after the payment to her husband, a mere trustee for the mortgagor, she would be obliged, after the husband's death, to assign the chose in action to the transferree.

It appears, however (*Michelmore* v. *Mudge*, 2 Giff. 183), that where the payment to the husband is not made by the mortgagor, or on his behalf, the assignment of the debt does not operate as a payment by the mortgagor, nor as a reduction into possession, and therefore does not bind the wife should she survive her husband and the debt not have been paid off.

It must, however, in all cases be borne in mind that where the mortgage debt is secured on land, and the wife is willing to concur in the transfer, no difficulty will arise, for the debt is an interest in land, which the wife can pass by an assurance perfected according to the provisions of the Fines and Recoveries' Act. (*Williams* v. *Cooke*, 4 Giff. 343.)

If the mortgage debt is secured on leaseholds, the husband can convey the leaseholds without his wife's concurrence; and if the transfer is made at the request of the mortgagor no difficulty will arise; but on the other hand, if this should not be the case, and the wife is willing to join, she had better acknowledge the deed, so as to fall within the reasoning of *Williams* v. *Cooke*.

Reversionary interests of wife.

If the wife's chose in action be reversionary, and consists of pure personalty, there was, till lately, no method by which it could be dealt with, so as to bind the wife surviving, as from the nature of the case it could not be reduced into possession: attempts have been made to get over this difficulty by inducing the persons having the prior interests to assign them to the wife, so that they could coalesce with hers, and render it a present interest that could be reduced into possession; but Courts of Equity have decided that in such a case the wife's interest remains reversionary for the purpose of affording her protection. The effect of Malins' Act, 20 & 21 Vict. c. 57, is to enable a married woman to dispose by deed acknowledged of reversionary interests of this nature, to which she becomes entitled under any instrument made since 31st December, 1857 (other than her own marriage settlement), unless such instrument contains a restraint on alienation.

The wife's reversionary interest in money charged on land, or in the proceeds of real estate directed to be sold, can, and could even before the Act, be passed by deed acknowledged (see the cases referred to in the note above-mentioned, and *Bowyer* v. *Woodman*, L. R. 3 Eq. Ca. 313; *Franke* v. *Bollans*, L. R. 3 Ch. Ap. 715; *Tuer* v. *Turner*, 20 Beav. 560).

# CHAPTER X.

## LEASES.

A LEASE may be made for a term of years, or for a life or lives, or for a term of years determinable on lives.

A lease for a term of years, or for a term of years determinable on lives, gives a chattel interest to the lessee, but a lease for a life or lives gives him a freehold interest. Leases for lives were formerly very common, but they are gradually falling into disuse. I shall, therefore, discuss leases for years only.

Agreement for a lease.

Lessor's title.

To consider in the first place the points that arise on the negotiation for a lease. It is the usual custom to dispense with any investigation of the lessor's title, except in cases where the lessee intends to lay out a considerable sum of money on the land. Curiously enough, the question whether in the absence of stipulation to the contrary, an agreement for a lease implies that the intending lessor will deliver an abstract, and show a good title, appears never to have been decided: though it appears clear that he cannot enforce specific performance of such an agreement without having a good title (*Fildes* v. *Hooker*, 2 Mer. 424; *Bashcomb* v. *Phillips*, 29 L. J. Ch. 380); and that if he has no title, an action will lie against him by the intending tenant. (*Stranks* v. *St. John*, L. R. 2 C. P. 376.) For these reasons it should always be distinctly agreed on the treaty for the lease, whether the intending lessor is to show any and what title. Where the title is not investigated, the intending tenant should, if the property be situated in a town, enquire whether the lessor is restricted from using it in any particular manner, as, for instance, whether he is prohibited from using it as a shop; for if the landlord be restrained from using it, the tenant cannot put himself into a more favourable position than his landlord, merely by omitting to enquire into the title, and although if the lessor falsely states that there is no restriction, the tenant gains no right to use the property in the forbidden manner (*Clements* v. *Welles*, L. R. 1 Eq. Ca. 200; *Feilden* v. *Slater*, L. R. 7 Eq. Ca. 523), still he would have his remedy over against the lessor.

It may be remarked that on the sale of a leasehold interest, the vendor entering into an open contract is bound to show his lessor's title (*Souter* v. *Drake*, 5 B. & Ad. 992); the exceptions to the rule are stated in Dart, Vendors and Purchasers, cap. viii. s. 3.

Entry by lessee before lease is granted.

Sometimes on the treaty for a building lease it is stipulated that the tenant may enter upon the property for the purpose of erecting the proposed buildings before the actual execution of the lease. In such a case it is sometimes intended that instead of granting one lease of the whole ground, separate leases of the different houses should be granted to the builder or his nominees as the houses are completed. The latter is perhaps the most usual plan, as it is the safest for the tenants. For if all the ground was included in one lease, and the builder were to grant underleases to the purchasers of the several houses, then if any one of the latter were to break the covenants in the head lease so that it became forfeited, the tenant of every house would become liable to eviction.

It is desirable not to grant the actual lease till the houses are finished, so as to render it unnecessary to put the covenants as to building, which are sometimes long and elaborate, into it; if this were done, every sub-lessee or purchaser would have to ascertain that they had been performed, while by granting the lease after the buildings are completed, this is rendered unnecessary.

"Ground-rent."

Rent reserved on a building lease, which is small compared with the rack-rent, is commonly called "a ground-rent." If the lease is granted directly to the builder's nominee, the builder joins in the lease for the purpose of acknowledging the receipt of the purchase-money of the house, and of requesting the head landlord to make the demise; if the builder takes the lease to himself, he generally does not sublet at rack-rent, but takes from the sub-lessee a fine of a sum not much less than what he has expended on the house, not under the name of a fine, but as the purchase-money of the house, and lets the house at a rent a little larger than the ground rent: this is generally called an improved ground-rent.

Agreement for lease.

The agreement should specify the commencement and duration of the term, the amount of rent, and when it is to be payable, and the nature of the covenants to be entered into both by lessor and lessee. The importance of specifying what covenants are to be inserted is pressed strongly on the reader, for in the absence of special agreement the insertion of the "usual" covenants can alone be insisted on, and unfortunately it is very difficult to say what the "usual" covenants are: 5 Dav. Prec. 46 (n.). See a list, Dart, Vendors and Purchasers, cap. iv. s. 4.

Having regard to the fine distinctions between agreements for leases and leases themselves (which are fully discussed in 5 Dav. Prec. 1, *et seq.*), it appears desirable to state distinctly in the agreement that "these presents are to operate as an agreement only, and not as an actual demise of the premises, or to give the tenant any legal interest therein, until the said lease shall be executed."

Lease must be by deed.

The effect of 8 & 9 Vict. c. 106, s. 3, is to render every lease which was at the date of the Act required by law to be in writing, to be void at law, unless made by deed. And as by the Statute of Frauds all leases are required to be in writing, subject to the exception of leases "not exceeding the term of three years from the making thereof, whereupon the rent reserved to the landlord during such term shall amount unto two third parts at the least of the full improved value of the thing demised," it follows that all leases must now be made by deed, except those falling within this exception: and that in cases where the agreement is not under seal, and the lease does not fall within the exception, the last mentioned clause is not absolutely necessary.

It is also proper to agree that "until the lease be executed the rent, covenants, and agreements to be therein contained shall be paid and observed, and the several rights and remedies shall be enforced in the same manner as if the same had been actually executed."

Costs of lease.

It should also be provided that the lessor shall execute and deliver to the lessee a counterpart of the lease; and it should be declared who is to pay the costs of the lease and counterpart. As, however, in the absence of any special stipulation, the solicitor of the lessor prepares the lease at the cost of the lessee (*Smith* v. *Clegg*, 27 L. J. Ex. 300), and the lessor pays for the counterpart, the last-mentioned stipulation is not absolutely necessary, though, if inserted, it may save disputes. If there be any difficulty in getting the costs of the lease, the lessor's solicitor has his remedy against the lessor, who has his remedy over against the lessee. (*Grissell* v. *Robinson*, 3 Bing. N. C. 10.)

Entry by lessee before lease is granted

As a general rule, subject to the exception already mentioned in the case of building leases, the tenant should not be allowed to enter until the lease is actually granted, for in that case until rent has been actually paid by him the landlord cannot distrain for rent, but is left to his remedy by action; and, on the other hand, the tenant cannot be advised to enter until the lease is executed, for, as he has no legal interest, the landlord can at any time bring ejectment against him, an action to which the tenant would have no legal defence, though he would have an equitable defence.

To pass to the consideration of the lease itself: the intention of the parties is that so long as the lessee pays the rent regularly, and performs the covenants on his part, he shall not be disturbed by the landlord; but that, on the other hand, on his omission to do so, the landlord shall have a speedy remedy against him.

The law gives to the landlord two remedies for his rent (Co. Litt. 43 b), distress (*post*, p. 237) and action; in addition to this, the lessee always enters into an express covenant to pay it, so as to turn it into a specialty debt. **Remedies of landlord for rent.**

The landlord can bring an action for damages in respect of the breach of the other covenants by the lessee, and in some cases a Court of Equity will restrain a contemplated breach by injunction. **For breach of covenant.**

A clause has been invented called the proviso for re-entry, which is always inserted in leases, and which gives to the landlord the right of actually evicting the tenant for non-payment of rent or other breach of covenant. In the case of a lease for a short term at rack-rent, this clause does not exercise the same deterrent effect on a tenant contemplating **Proviso for re-entry.**

a breach of covenant as it does where the lease is for a long term, and is a beneficial one; for in the former case the pecuniary loss to the tenant on eviction is small, in the latter case it may be large. For this reason, in the prudent management of house property it appears to be desirable to let the houses at a rent slightly below the rack-rent, causing the tenant to lay out a small sum of money on the property; as, when this is done, it is tolerably certain that he will not run the risk of eviction for breach of covenant.

By the proviso for re-entry it is provided that the lease is granted "upon this express condition, that if the rent be in arrear for twenty-one days, whether the same shall have been legally demanded or not, or if, and whenever, there shall be a breach of any of the covenants by the lessee herein contained, the lessor, his heirs, and assigns may re-enter upon any part of the said premises in the name of the whole, and thereupon the said term of —— years shall absolutely determine." It is obvious that the proviso can be extended so as to guard against any act or omission on the part of the tenant, as, for instance, against his becoming bankrupt, or allowing any execution to be levied on the premises. The words in the proviso, "whether legally demanded or not," are inserted to avoid the necessity of demanding the rent with all the formalities prescribed at common law, which can be found in Woodfall, Landlord and Tenant, p. 282. Care should be taken to frame the proviso so as to apply to the breach of a negative covenant, such as the covenant not to assign. (*West* v. *Dobbs*, L. R. 5 Q. B. 460.)

Sometimes the proviso, instead of authorising the landlord to enter, declares that in the specified events the lease shall be "deemed null and void to all intents and purposes." The effect of the proviso being thus framed is to render the lease voidable only at the option of the landlord, otherwise, on an action being brought for the rent, the tenant might show that he had committed a breach of covenant, which had rendered the lease void, and thus claim to take advantage of his own wrong.

Breach of covenant (effect of).

It will be remembered that a breach of covenant in respect *of any part* of the property demised, renders the tenant liable to be ejected from *the whole* (*ante*, p. 220).

License to commit breach of covenant.

Occasionally the question arises whether a landlord can allow the tenant to commit a breach of covenant without prejudice to his right of re-entry in case of any future breach of covenant. There are two cases for consideration: *first*, where the landlord is asked to pardon a past breach of covenant, as, for instance, where the tenant has not kept up the insurance in conformity with his covenant, and on the discovery of his omission makes a proper insurance, and asks the landlord to condone his omission; *second*, where a tenant applies beforehand for leave to commit a breach, as, for instance, if he wishes to insure in an office different from the one in which he ought to insure according to his covenant.

Forgiveness of past breach.

In the first case, where he applies for pardon for a past breach of covenant there is no difficulty; all that the landlord has to do is to accept rent knowing of the breach of covenant, the acceptance of rent precludes him for ever taking advantage of the breach afterwards. No writing of any sort is necessary, but occasionally it may be advisable to mention in the receipt for rent that the landlord is aware of and has forgiven the breach of covenant. The reason of the rule appears to be the following:—When ejectment is brought, the plaintiff's case is that on a certain day he had a right to the possession of the land, or, in the case of ejectment against a tenant, that the latter had ceased to be tenant on that day; and by the acceptance of rent the landlord admits that the tenancy still exists.

The rule, that acceptance of rent by a landlord knowing of a breach of covenant operates as forgiveness of that breach, should always be borne in mind when it is intended to bring ejectment against a tenant for breach of covenant; in this case no rent accrued due after the breach has been committed must be accepted.

Probably one of the most efficacious methods of frightening a troublesome tenant is to take notice of any breach of covenant committed by him, at the same time informing him that in consequence of it the landlord will refuse to accept his rent. He will probably apply to his solicitor to know the meaning of his landlord's conduct, and will be informed that it is the preliminary to an ejectment.

It may be remarked that actual waiver of the benefit of any covenant or condition in a lease by the landlord only operates as a waiver with respect to the particular breach to which it has reference. (*Doe* v. *Bliss*, 4 Taunt. 735; see 23 & 24 Vict. c. 38, s. 6.)

**Licence to commit future breach.**

In the second case, where the landlord wishes to grant permission beforehand to the tenant to commit a breach of covenant, the permission, to be effectual at law, must be granted under seal.

It should be remarked that a landlord who has given permission not under seal to commit a breach, will be restrained in equity from taking advantage of the breach, and that (as before stated) when he has, with knowledge of the breach, accepted rent accruing due after the breach, he cannot take advantage of the breach at law; except, therefore, in cases of importance, a licence under seal need not be used, as a permission in writing to commit the breach, followed by acceptance of rent accruing due after the breach, will operate as a waiver of the breach both at law and equity.

**Defeazance.**

Formerly, if a covenant or condition was once dispensed with, it was entirely gone, and could never be enforced for the future; to avoid this inconvenient result the practice was adopted of the tenant executing a deed of defeazance at the time when the licence was given to him. By the defeazance the tenant granted to the landlord a new power of re-entry on breach of the condition mentioned in the defeazance, a condition which was a copy of that in the original lease, *mutatis mutandis.* The effect of 22 & 23 Vict. c. 35, ss. 1, 2, and 23 & 24 Vict. c. 38, s. 6, is to alter the rule of law and to dispense with the need of a defeazance.

**Who is bound to perform lessee's covenants.**

The next questions for our consideration are—Who is bound to perform the covenants contained in the lease, and who has the benefit of them?

The original lessee and his representatives are always, even if they have assigned the term, bound to perform the covenants. This is sometimes an important practical question where the lease contains onerous covenants, as for instance to rebuild a house in case of fire; the original lessee of the lease might have long since parted with it, still he or his representatives would be bound to perform the covenant. To guard against this liability as much as possible, the assignee of a lease always covenants with his assignor to perform the covenants in the lease, so that if the latter is compelled by the landlord to perform them, he may have his remedy over against the assignee; but as it is obvious that the value of such a covenant must depend upon the means of the assignee, care should always be taken before entering into an agreement to assign a lease, to ascertain that the proposed assignee is a man of substance.

The question whether the assigns of the original lessee are bound as between themselves and the landlord to perform his covenants appears to depend on the nature of the covenant. (*Spencer's case*, 5 Rep. 16.) A covenant which extends to "a thing *in esse* parcel of the demise," binds the assigns whether they be named or not; as an example of this take a covenant to repair in a lease of an existing house —here the tenant for the time being is bound to repair according to the covenant, whether assigns are named or not.

A covenant which concerns something to be newly done on the thing demised, will bind the assign if he be named in the covenant, but not otherwise. Suppose that in the lease of a piece of land the lessee covenants to build a house on it, his assign is bound to perform the covenant if the lessee covenants for *his assigns*, but not otherwise.

A covenant which has nothing to do with the thing demised, or, to use technical language, which is *simply collateral*, does not bind the assign, even if he be named in it. As, for instance, if the lessee of a farm covenants for himself and his assigns to pay a sum annually to the churchwardens, or to build a wall on land not parcel of the demise, his assigns are not bound to do so.

The position of the assignee of a lease containing onerous covenants is, however, better than that of the original lessee; the former is only liable for breaches of covenant committed while he holds the land, the latter is liable for all breaches during the term. When I say that the assign is only liable for breaches of covenant committed while he holds the land, I must be understood to be speaking of the remedy by action only; for the landlord can distrain for rent due, or bring ejectment for any forfeiture committed before the assignment. As soon as the assign assigns over the land his liability as between himself and the landlord with respect to any future breach ceases, even if he assign to a pauper.

In cases where it is intended that the assign should perform the covenants, he will, even if he be not liable to perform them at law, if he takes the land with notice of them, be forced to perform them in Equity. (See *Tulk* v. *Moxhay*, 2 Phill. 774.)

Who has benefit of lessee's covenants.

The question, who is entitled to the *benefit* of the lessee's covenants, or, bearing in mind that the due performance is secured by the proviso for re-entry, who is entitled to enter on breach, is rather difficult.

At common law the rule was extremely inconvenient; the doctrine being that though an estate could be assigned, a contract could not; or, as it is expressed in the preamble of the statute (32 Hen. VIII. c. 34) passed to remedy the evil, "no stranger to any covenant, action, or condition shall take any advantage or benefit of the same by any means or ways in the law, but only such as be parties or privies thereto." To consider an example: the lessee of a house covenanted to keep it in repair; the lessor sold his property, but he could not assign the benefit of the covenant, so that on breach of covenant by the tenant, the new landlord could not bring an action in his own name—the only method that he could adopt would be to obtain permission from the original lessor to bring it in his name. At the time of the Reformation, when a large part of the Church lands fell into lay hands, this inconvenience attracted notice, and an Act was passed (32 Hen. VIII. c. 34) which in substance gave the landlord for the time being the same remedy against the tenant as the original lessor had against the original lessee; and in like manner gave the same remedy to the tenant for the time being against the landlord in respect of the covenants entered into by the original lessor as the original lessee had against him.

The doctrine just stated is sometimes expressed as follows:—the assignee of the reversion is entitled to the benefit of the lessee's covenants. The student may find some difficulty in understanding who is the reversioner in certain cases which occur in practice. Fortunately, however, the inquiry has now little more than theoretical interest, as in most cases the person entitled to the next vested estate after the lease has all the remedies of the reversioner. (8 & 9 Vict. c. 106, s. 9.) See on this point *Williams* v. *Hayward*, 1 El. & El. 1046.

The nature of the provisions usually inserted in a lease varies so materially with the nature of the property that it is difficult to give any detailed analysis of a lease that would be of use to the reader, The usual clauses may perhaps be arranged as follows:—

Analysis of lease.

1. Parties.
2. Recitals (when necessary).
3. Consideration.

4. Demise by the lessor to the lessee, his executors, administrators, and assigns.
5. Parcels—general words—licence.
6. Exceptions, if any.
7. Habendum.
8. Reddendum.
9. Lessee's covenants.
10. Proviso for re-entry.
11. Lessor's covenants.

To consider these in order:

Parties. 1. It appears unnecessary to make any remarks about the parties to a lease.

Recitals. 2. It is generally unnecessary to insert any recitals in the lease. Even where the lease is granted by virtue of a power contained in a will or marriage settlement, we break through the ordinary rule, and instead of reciting the instrument creating the power, we refer to it in the operative part of the lease. Where the property is in mortgage both mortgagor and mortgagee must concur in the lease (*ante*, p. 157). But even in this case no notice is taken of the relationship between the parties—the mortgagee "demises at the request of" the mortgagor, who "demises and confirms." Where an under-lease is to be made, and the original lease contains a covenant not to underlet without licence, the usual method is for the landlord to give his licence to underlet by a separate document, but he may be made a party to the under-lease; in this case the head-lease is recited in the under-lease, so as to show that it could not be granted without the concurrence of the landlord.

3. The consideration is generally stated to be "the rent (or rents and royalties) hereinafter reserved, and the covenants by the lessee hereinafter contained." Consideration.

4. In old leases several operative words are employed; as "demise, set, lease, and to farm let," but the only operative word used in modern practice is "demise," except in the case of a lease under a power, where the words of the power should be followed. Demise.

5. The parcels should be carefully expressed; in the case of the lease of a house in a town, or of a villa, or anything of that sort, or of mines, it is extremely convenient to describe the parcels by reference to a plan. Parcels.

After the parcels follow the general words—these are generally shorter than those in a conveyance of freeholds. If the property comprised in the lease has not been usually severed in enjoyment from the adjoining land of the lessor, so that it can have acquired no easements over it, care should be taken to specify *nominatim* the easements if any which the lessee is to enjoy over such adjoining land. No "all estate clause" is inserted in a lease. General words. "All estate clause."

The lessee, being only a tenant for years, has no right to commit waste; if therefore it be intended that he should be at liberty to do so, it should be distinctly specified what waste he is to be at liberty to commit. A list of the various forms of waste will Liberty to commit waste.

be found in Co. Litt. 52 b, and in Woodfall's Landlord and Tenant, 481.

Perhaps the best definition of waste is doing or permitting anything which causes a lasting damage to the inheritance. Thus, cutting timber, opening mines (but not working mines already open), pulling down or erecting permanent buildings, turning arable into pasture land, and the contrary, are all examples of waste.

Mining lease.

In a mining lease liberty is given to the lessee to "dig, work, and get," or "search for, sink to, unwater, ventilate, work, and get" the specified minerals.

Bearing in mind that erecting permanent buildings is waste, as it changes the inheritance, it is usually necessary in mining leases to give express liberty to erect engine-houses, &c., and sometimes to make railways, wharfs, and other permanent buildings.

Grants of the nature of which we are speaking are called *licences*. Occasionally a licence is given without any estate in the land—for example, in some parts of the country it is the custom, instead of granting mining leases, to grant a mere licence to enter upon the lands, and win and take away the minerals. Where this course is adopted it must be carefully stated whether the licence is to be exclusive or not, *i.e.* whether the licensee is to be the only person entitled to win minerals. (*Newby* v. *Harrison,* 1 Jo. & Hem. 393 ; *Carr* v. *Benson,* L. R. 3 Ch. App. 524.)

6. Following the grant of licences to the lessee come the reservations and exceptions, and the *privileges*

or licences granted to the lessor (*ante*, p. 118). The student may find some difficulty in understanding the proper situation for a reservation in a purchase deed or a lease. The word "reservation" comprises both rights, such as easements and profits *à prendre*, and rents. The reservation of rights of the former class operates, strictly speaking, as a regrant of such rights to the vendor or lessor by the purchaser or lessee, and is inserted immediately after the general words, while the reservation of rents follows the habendum.

**Right of sporting.** Thus, when the right of sporting is retained by the lessor, it is expressed in the lease to be "reserved;" but such a right operates as a regrant by the lessee to the lessor of the right to enter and pursue the game, which right is a profit *à prendre*. (*Doe* d. *Douglas* v. *Lock*, 2 Ad. & El. 743; *Wickham* v. *Hawker*, 7 M. & W. 63; *Ewart* v. *Graham*, 7 H. L. C. 331; *Hooper* v. *Clark*, L. R. 2 Q. B. 200.)

**Habendum.** 7. The *habendum* is "to the lessee, his executors, administrators, and assigns, for the term of —— years, from the —— day of ——." The term of years may be made to commence from a day already past, from the date of the lease, or *in futuro*. Sometimes the term is made determinable at the option of one or either of the parties—this is the common case of a lease for seven, fourteen, or twenty-one years. In the case of an under-lease which is intended to comprise practically all the interest of the original lessee, the term is made to determine a few days before the original lease, so as to leave a reversion in him. As to the effect of an under-lease which by mistake comprises the whole term in the head-lease, see *Beardman* v. *Wilson*, L. R. 4 C. P. 57; *Williams* v. *Hayward*, 1 El. & El. 1041, and the cases there cited; see also *Pluck* v. *Digges*, 5 Bli. N. S. 31.

Reddendum. 8. The *reddendum* specifies the amount of rents and royalties, and the times at which they become payable. An additional rent is sometimes made payable on the committal of some particular act by the tenant. Thus it is not uncommon to reserve an additional rent of 10*l.* per acre if the tenant ploughs up old meadow land; the object being to prevent the tenant from committing the act, the additional rent is placed so high as to render it extremely improbable that it would be to his advantage to incur it.

Penal rent.

Royalty. A rent is an ascertained sum, but the amount of a royalty, which is a sum to be paid in respect of every ton or other certain quantity of minerals raised, or in respect of every 1000 bricks sold, or the like, depends on the act of the tenants. It is obvious that the amount of a royalty depending entirely on the amount of minerals, &c., worked by the tenant, it is desirable that there should be a fixed minimum payment. This is generally effected by reserving a rent as well as a royalty.

Render. A "render" is where a certain proportion of the minerals themselves are to be delivered to the lessor.

Time of payment. The days on which the rent and royalties are to be paid must be stated; it is generally proper to stipulate for the payment of the last quarterly or half-yearly payment to be made a short time (say a calendar month) in advance, as it enables the lessor to distrain for the rent before the determination of the lease. It is also convenient to stipulate that if the lease be determined by re-entry by the landlord for breach of covenant, a proportionate part of the rent up to the day of entry should be paid.

To whom reservations are made.

Where the lessor is seised in fee, the reservations should be to him, his heirs and assigns. If the estate be in settlement, and the lease be made under a power contained in the settlement, or under any of the statutory powers, there is an apparent difficulty in seeing to whom the reservations should be made, as the person who becomes entitled by virtue of the settlement on the death of the lessor may not be his heir. It is settled, however (*Whitelock's case*, 8 Rep. 69 b), that if the reservation be made to the lessor and his heirs, or to the lessor, and to every person to whom the inheritance or reversion shall appertain during the term, it shall in either case be good, for the law will distribute it to any one to whom any limitation of the use is made. But in the same case it was agreed that the best way is to reserve the rent generally, *i. e.*, not to any particular person, and to allow the law to make the distribution.

Power of distress.

When land is let, the act of letting creates a tenure between the landlord and tenant—the rent reserved is one of the services by which the land is held, the other being fealty, which is now never exacted in practice. At common law, if a tenant neglected to perform his services, his lord might enter on the land in respect of which they were due, and distrain. It follows that in the ordinary case of rent being reserved on the lease of land, the landlord has a right to distrain if the rent be in arrear; the right of distress extends, with some exceptions, over all chattels which are found on the premises, whether they are the property of the lessee or a stranger? It will be observed that the right of distress being a consequence of tenure, does not arise at common law where the thing demised is not a tenement—where it is furniture or machinery for instance. In these cases a clause called a power of distress is inserted in the lease, being a clause declaring that if the rent be in arrear for so many (generally twenty-one) days, the landlord may enter, distrain, and dispose of the distress, for the purpose of discharging the arrears of rent and costs.

It appears that the effect of such a clause is not to enable the landlord to distrain in the strict sense of the word. It operates as a licence to him to enter and act exactly in the same manner as if he were distraining in the strict sense of the word, while the tenant is estopped from denying that the distress is lawful, owing to the licence being contained in a deed; the difference between a distress in the strict sense of the word, and a distress made under such a licence, would appear if a stranger's goods on the premises were distrained. In the former case the distress would be lawful, in the latter case it would not.

It may be asked—Is it necessary to insert a power of distress in the lease of a furnished house, where the house in respect of which a tenure is created, and furniture in which this is not the case, are comprised in one demise? It is settled that in this case the whole of the rent issues out of the land (*Spencer's case*, 5 Rep. 17; *Newman* v. *Anderton*, 2 Bos. N. R. 224; *Farewell* v. *Dickinson*, 6 B. & C. 251), and accordingly the whole rent can be distrained for, and the insertion of an express power of distress is unnecessary.

In cases where chattels are let with the land, and there is no reason for letting them and the land at separate rents, the clause giving a power of distress is unnecessary; but where it is convenient to let the chattels and the land at separate rents (as, for instance, where a lessor is tenant for life of a house and absolute owner of the furniture, so that on his death the house and furniture will pass to different people), it is necessary to insert the clause.

There is another case in which the power of distress should be inserted. Suppose that the land to be leased is in mortgage, and that the mortgage deed contains no power of leasing. In this case neither mortgagor nor mortgagee can make a valid lease without the concurrence of the other. They both join in making the lease, and as the mortgagee has the legal estate, the tenure is created between him and the lessee—he therefore can distrain, while as no tenure is created between the mortgagor and the lessee, the mortgagor cannot distrain. As it is never intended that the mortgagee shall have anything to do with the actual management of the property, it would be extremely inconvenient for the mortgagor to have to procure his concurrence in making a distress, and accordingly a distinct power of distress is given to the mortgagor, until the mortgagee shall have given notice to the tenant to pay the rent to him.

Covenants by lessee.

9. As already stated, the nature of the covenants contained in a lease depends entirely upon the nature of the property. I intend, therefore, only to discuss a few of the more important.

I. Covenants for payments by lessee.
- (α). Rent.
- (β). Rates and taxes.

II. Covenants having reference to keeping up the value of the property with respect to
- (γ). Repairs.
- (δ). Insurance.
- (ε). Waste.
- (ζ). Using premises in a certain manner only.
- (η). State in which property is to be delivered up.

III. Miscellaneous.
- (θ). Not to assign or underlet.

Accounts.

(α). The covenant to pay rent appears not to require discussion: but it should be remembered that in all cases where the lessor is to receive royalties the lessee should covenant to keep accounts of the working of the minerals, and to allow the lessor to inspect them, or an abstract of them, and to take copies of them. If there are extensive underground workings, the lessees should be bound to keep accurate plans, and to deliver copies free from expense (or at cost price) to the lessor.

Rates and taxes.

(β.) It often happens that it is intended that the tenant should pay all rates and taxes: it appears that a stipulation that the tenant should, as between himself and the landlord, bear the landlord's share of the property-tax, would be void; but the same end might probably be attained by reserving a larger rent than that actually intended to be paid, with a proviso for a variation in amount with the variation of the property-tax. (*Colbron* v. *Travers*, 12 C. B., N. S., 181.) The most sweeping words for including all rates and taxes are "all existing and future taxes, rates, assessments, and outgoings of every description for the time being payable either by landlord or tenant in respect of the premises." Occasionally the lessor covenants to pay the rates and taxes; in this case, if the rateable value of the property is larger than the rent payable to the landlord, the tenant who pays the rates, &c., in the first instance, is only allowed to deduct so much as is payable in respect of the rent payable to the landlord, and not the total sum payable. (*Smith* v. *Humble*, 15 C. B. 321.)

Covenants as to repair or against permissive waste.

(γ.) Before the passing of the Statute of Marlebridge, lessees for life or years lay under no prohibition of waste at the common law because they came in by the act of the lessor, and he might have provided against it in the lease. (2nd Instit. 145.) By that statute, an action for damages was given to the landlord; and by the Statute of Gloucester, the land wasted was made liable to forfeiture. In the absence of covenant, the tenant of a house is bound to refrain from actual waste (see the question discussed at Co. Lit. 53a), and probably he is bound to refrain from permissive waste. (*Harnett* v. *Maitland*, 16 M. & W. 257; Tudor's Leading Cases, note to *Lewis Bowles' case.*)

The covenants with respect to repairs inserted in the lease of a house are—

1st. To repair and keep the premises in good repair.

2nd. To paint the outside and inside at certain times in a prescribed manner.

3rd. To allow the lessor to enter and view the premises, and on his giving written notice of want of repair, to repair within three months.

Repairs. (γ). It should be remembered that giving notice to repair under the last covenant is a waiver of any forfeiture that may have happened under the general covenant to repair (*Doe* d. *Morecraft* v. *Meux*, 4 B. & C. 606): while a notice to repair "in accordance with the covenants" of the lease is not so. (*Few* v. *Perkins*, L. R. 2 Ex. 92.) The corresponding covenants in the case of a farm, mines, or quarries, would be very different, and would depend upon the special circumstances of each case. In the case of a farm, these covenants are sometimes inserted with reference to the farmhouse; but more usually this is not the case, but the tenant covenants to keep hedges, ditches, roads, &c., in repair. In a quarry, where the nature of the working is to make use of open pits, so that the whole of the soil above the stone removed has to be removed, thus leaving a large hole, it is sometimes specified that the hole shall be filled up, and the surface soil replaced after the stone has been worked, so as to leave the surface fit for agricultural purposes; it might also be necessary to insert covenants about repairing the roads leading to the quarry. In a mining lease, the lessees should covenant to keep in repair all buildings used in connection with the workings, and all engines, &c., belonging to the lessor, or which by the terms of the lease are to be left for his benefit at the expiration of the lease; and possibly to leave certain parts of the minerals unwrought as support to the surface, or as bulwarks against water from the neighbouring mines. It may be necessary to make some special provisions as to tramways, and as to the disposal of rubbish by way of spoilbanks or otherwise.

Destruction by fire.

Where the covenant to repair is general, the lessee must repair if the premises be burnt down. (*Bullock* v. *Dommitt*, 6 T. R. 650.) It has been decided that when there is a covenant of this nature on the part of the lessee, and the lessor has voluntarily insured in his own name, the lessee has no equity to compel the lessor to expend the moneys received from the Insurance Office on the premises being burnt down in rebuilding, or to restrain the landlord from suing for the rent till the premises are rebuilt. (*Leeds* v. *Cheetham*, 1 Sim. 147; *Loft* v. *Dennis*, 1 El. & El. 482.) It appears, however, that if either lessor or lessee has insured without having covenanted to do so, the other of them can, IF THE PROPERTY INSURED BE A HOUSE OR BUILDINGS, require the Insurance Office to cause the insurance moneys to be laid out in rebuilding the premises. (*Ex parte Goreley*, 5 N. R. 22; 13 W. R. 60.)

Reason for inserting the lessee's covenants.

The reader may ask—why is it necessary to insert a covenant for the payment of rent, or against the commission of waste, as in the absence of any covenant the landlord has his remedy by distress or action against the tenant for the time being. The advantage of the insertion of a covenant is, that thereby the lessor has, in addition to his other remedies, a personal remedy against the lessee. Suppose that the lessee assigns the land, and that the tenant commits waste, the landlord may, if he thinks fit, bring an action against the lessee on the covenant. The personal remedy against the lessee is of additional use, for the following reason: "Where the law creates a duty or charge, and the party is disabled to perform it, without any default in him, and hath no remedy over, there the law will excuse him. As in the case of waste, if a house be destroyed by tempest or by enemies, the lessee is excused. But when the party, by his own contract, creates a duty or charge upon himself, he is bound to make it good, if he may, notwithstanding any accident by inevitable necessity, because he might have provided against it by his contract: and therefore, if the lessee covenant to repair a house, though it be burnt by lightning, or thrown down by enemies, yet he ought to repair it." (*Prince Rupert's case*, Aleyne, 26, cited at 1 Macq. 677.) It is also convenient for the lessee to know the principal obligations thrown on him.

(*b*.) Where the lease comprises buildings, machinery, furniture, or other property that is likely to be damaged by fire, it is a common practice for the lessee to covenant to insure, and keep them insured, for a certain sum in an office to be approved by the lessor, either in the joint names of lessor and lessee, or of one of them only. The custody of the policy may be left with the lessee, he covenanting to produce it and the last receipt for the premiums on demand, and to lay out all moneys received under the policy in rebuilding. Insurance.

By the effect of 22 & 23 Vict. c. 35, and 23 & 24 Vict. c. 126, the Court of Chancery, or any Court in which ejectment is brought, under a proviso for re-entry on breach of the covenant to insure, can relieve against the forfeiture if no loss or damage by fire has happened, if the breach of covenant has occurred through accident, and if a proper insurance is existing at the time of the application to the Court. Notice of the relief having been granted is to be indorsed on the lease, and relief cannot be given to the same person twice in respect of the same covenant. It requires some consideration to see what is the best plan to adopt in the management of building estates as to requiring the tenants to produce their policies. If the houses be let at a ground-rent, it appears hardly necessary, during the early part of the term, to require the production of the policy, as in the case of a fire the tenant would usually rebuild for his own sake. Probably in such a case it would be sufficient to send an occasional notice reminding the lessees that they ought to insure. Notice to that effect is printed on the receipts given for rent in respect of the Crown Property in London. In other cases, the production of the policy and receipt should be occasionally asked for. The better plan is occasionally, at uncertain intervals, to require the production on the rent day. The fear of being detected will prevent most of the lessees running the risk of letting their insurances lapse. Occasionally the plan is adopted of the landlord insuring, and entering into covenants with the lessee, to keep up the insurance and for the production of the policy and receipts, similar to those usually entered into by the latter.

In all cases it is advisable, and where part of the property demised consists of machinery and the like, it is essential, that this covenant should also provide for the application of the insurance money in reinstating the property. (*Lees* v. *Whiteley*, L. R. 2 Eq. Ca. 143.

The covenants that we have hitherto considered are *positive* covenants by the lessee, *i. e.*, covenants that he will do some particular thing; the covenants of the next two classes are chiefly *negative* covenants, *i. e.*, covenants that he will abstain from doing some particular thing.

(ε.) The covenants intended to restrain the lessee from committing waste are— **Covenants against committing actual waste.**

*In the case of a house and pleasure grounds:*

(α.) Not to alter the frontage of the house.

(β.) Not to destroy timber.

(γ.) To keep up the ornamental plantations.

*In the case of a farm:*

(α.) Not to break up meadow or pasture.

(β.) Not to cut trees.

(γ.) Not to sell manure nor certain crops.

*In the case of mines:*

(α.) Not to remove any engines, engine-houses, buildings, &c.

(β.) To remove any buildings built by the lessee that the landlord may require him to remove, and other covenants of a like nature, varying with the circumstances of each case.

(ζ.) In cases where the lessor of a house carries on any particular trade or business in the neighbourhood, he often stipulates for the insertion of a covenant on the part of the lessee not to carry on the same trade or business: the reason is obvious—he wishes not to have a rival. **Covenants in restraint of trade.**

Where the lessor has many houses in the neighbourhood he often insists on the insertion of a general covenant against carrying on any trade or business, or certain specified trades; for he may think that trade being carried on in any one house would lower the rentals of his adjoining property. There is, perhaps, no clause in leases which has given rise to so much litigation as the clause under consideration: the contest being between the lessee carrying on a particular trade which he alleges not to be prohibited, and the lessor who contends that it is. (See the cases collected at 5 Dav. Prec. 139 n., and Woodfall's Landlord and Tenant, c. xiii. s. 3.)

In the older forms of this covenant the plan adopted was to specify prohibited trades. There is an obvious objection to this course if the lease be for a long term, as new trades are constantly invented. In a lease made at the beginning of the present century no one would have introduced a prohibition against refining petroleum; but that particular trade is now one of the most dangerous known. The different forms that are now in use are, *first*, a prohibition against using the premises as a shop or warehouse, or suffering any profession, trade, or business to be carried on thereon, with an engagement on the part of the tenant to keep and use the same as a private dwelling-house only—a form which appears to prohibit any profession, business or trade being carried on. *Second*, a prohibition of offensive businesses or trades. *Third*, a prohibition of certain specified trades or businesses only; and *fourthly*, a prohibition against any trade or business without the licence of the lessor.

"Free" public-house.

Where the lease is of a public-house and the landlord is a brewer, a covenant is commonly inserted to force the lessee to purchase his beer, &c., from his landlord: this is so generally inserted as to give rise to the term "free" public-house, meaning one in the lease of which no such covenant is contained, so that the tenant can purchase his beer where he will.

Cultivation of a farm.

In the lease of a farm it often happens that covenants are inserted to compel the tenant to cultivate in some particular manner: the nature of these covenants depends entirely on the method of farming generally adopted in the district. In the absence of any such covenants there is an implied covenant by the lessee that he will use the farm in a good and husbandlike manner according to the custom of the district, or, as it is called, "the custom of the country." In like manner leases of mines or minerals contain covenants as to the manner in which they are to be worked, depending entirely upon the particular circumstances of each case.

Covenant not to hold an auction.

Sometimes a covenant is inserted that no auction shall be held on the premises; the object is twofold: in the first place it is intended to save the adjoining property of the lessor from the annoyance occasioned by the concourse of persons if sales by auction were habitually carried on, and, in the second place, it is intended to guard against the damage that might be occasioned to the property on which the auction was held by a concourse of persons on one occasion only.

Covenant to deliver up in particular state.

($\eta$.) A covenant is often inserted as to the state in which the premises are to be delivered up at the end of the term.

In the case of a house, the tenant covenants to deliver it up in "such good and substantial repair as aforesaid (*i. e.*, as provided for by the covenants to repair, &c.), and in such state and condition as shall be consistent with the due performance of the several covenants hereinbefore contained." The co-

Fixtures.

venant sometimes goes on to provide that all fixtures shall be delivered up. In the absence of express stipulation, every fixture put up by the tenant belongs to the landlord (*Gibson* v. *Hammersmith & City Railway Co.*, 2 Dr. & Sm. 608), with the exception of "tenant's fixtures," *i. e.* fixtures put up by the tenant for ornament, or for his convenience, or for the purposes of trade, which are but slightly attached to the freehold, and can be detached without doing any serious injury to it. If, however, the tenant neglects to remove the tenant's fixtures during the term, they belong to the landlord. (*Pugh* v. *Arton*, L. R. 8 Eq. Ca. 626.) Lists of fixtures removable by the tenant will be found in Woodfall's Landlord and Tenant, and in Smith's Landlord and Tenant. In the case of a lease, for a short term, of a house already completed, it appears sufficient for the covenant to provide for the delivery up of "the said premises, and all new fixtures and additions thereto, in such good and substantial repair and condition, and so preserved as aforesaid, and in such state and condition as shall be consistent with the due performance of the several covenants hereinbefore contained." It will be observed that this form of covenant is quite general; everything that is a fixture on the premises at the date of the lease, at any time during the term, and at the end of the lease, must be delivered up.

Sometimes it is preferred to have a schedule of the existing fixtures annexed to the lease, and the tenant covenants to deliver them up, or sometimes to deliver them up together with any other fixtures that may be on the property at the end of the lease.

Where the lease is for a long term, so that the original fixtures may presumably be worn out before the expiration of the lease, the better course is to provide that the lessor may enter within the last seven years of the lease and take an inventory of the fixtures, or of fixtures of certain specified classes (lists of which will be found in any book of forms of leases), and that the lessee shall deliver them up in good condition, &c., to the lessor at the end of the term.

In the case of a farming lease, it is rarely necessary to provide for the delivery up of the fixtures in the farm-house, the value of which is generally small; the important thing is to provide for the state in which the ground is to be left as regards cultivation, and as to what manures, &c., are to be paid for by

Farming lease.

the incoming tenant. In the absence of any special agreement, the latter part of the covenant is regulated by "the custom of the country." In a formal lease, it appears, however, convenient to state precisely whether the lessor or the succeeding tenant is to be allowed to enter upon the farm before the expiration of the lease for the purpose of sowing some particular crop (5 Dav. 199); whether the outgoing tenant is to be allowed space in the barns for his wheat, &c., for a limited time; whether he is to be paid for manure actually put into the ground by him; for manure *not* put into the ground, but left on the premises; and whether he is to be bound to leave any crops for the use of the incoming tenant, to be paid for at a valuation.

Mining lease.

In leases of mines and quarries, the stipulation generally is that all works or erections of a permanent nature, such as buildings, railways, and water-courses, shall be delivered up in good repair; while pumps, machinery, and working plant are generally to remain the property of the tenants, with an option on the part of the landlord to purchase them at a valuation.

Not to assign or underlease.

(*θ*.) The covenant not to assign or underlet is intended to prevent the premises falling into the possession of an insolvent or man of bad character; in cases where the property comprised in the lease is adjoining to other property of the lessor, it may be of great importance to him to have a veto on the occupation of the premises by any person whom he dislikes, or whose business he objects to. This can be effected by inserting a covenant on the part of the lessee "not to assign or underlet the premises without the licence, in writing, of the lessor, his heirs and assigns." The clause is often inserted in other cases, such as the lease of a farm, where the manner in which the occupier uses the property may be of importance to the lessor. The covenant should extend to the assigns of the lessee, as otherwise it is doubtful whether they will be bound by it. (*West* v. *Dobbs*, L. R. 4 Q. B. 637 note.)

The author suggests that the covenant not to assign without licence should now generally be inserted in leases at rack-rent: for suppose that the lessee assigns to a person who becomes bankrupt, and the trustee in bankruptcy disclaims, it appears very doubtful whether the effect of the 23rd section of the Bankruptcy Act, 1869, may not be to release the original lessee from his covenants, so that the landlord would have the property thrown on his hands, and probably, owing to its having been in the possession of a bankrupt, in a depreciated condition.

The following points have been decided upon the construction of the covenant:—

Under-letting.

*First*, that if the covenant is *not to assign*, underletting is not prohibited.

Deposit of lease by way of mortgage.

*Second*, that the covenant not to assign or underlet is not broken by the deposit of the lease so as to create an equitable mortgage.

It should be observed that the mortgagee in such case holds a security of very doubtful value; his only remedy is sale, and that cannot be done without the consent of the lessor. If, however, the lease be a head-lease, out of which under-leases have been granted with the licence of the lessor, a security may be created in the manner following:—The lessee deposits the lease with the mortgagee and simultaneously executes a deed, containing the ordinary mortgage covenants, by which he appoints the mortgagee his attorney, with power to appoint a substitute to collect the rents. Trusts are declared of the rents similar to those contained in a common receivership deed, with the exception that if default is made in payment of the principal after notice to that effect, the mortgagee shall be entitled to apply the surplus rents after keeping down the interest for that purpose. The outline of the deed above given is similar to that indicated at 6 Bythewood by Sweet, 404.

Lease taken in execution.

*Third.* The restriction against assignment does not cause a forfeiture on the lease being taken in execution, or on the bankruptcy of the lessee; it appears also that the assignees, now the trustees in bankruptcy, can sell without licence. The very important question remains—can the purchaser from them sell without licence? The question appears to be undecided. (See 5 Dav. 178.) On the whole it appears that an assignment without licence by the assign of the trustee in bankruptcy would be too doubtful a title to be accepted. The safer plan is to frame the proviso for re-entry, so as to render the lease determinable on the bankruptcy

Trustee in bankruptcy can sell without licence. Can his assign do so?

of the lessee, his executors, administrators, or assigns.

It appears very doubtful whether a bequest of the term by the lessee is not a breach of the covenant not to assign, and therefore it may be advisable expressly to allow bequests. Bequest of term.

The marriage of a woman by which the term passes to her husband is no breach of the covenant. Marriage of female lessee.

*Lastly.* Where an under-lease is granted, the sub-lessee covenants to perform the covenants and conditions contained in the head-lease so far as they apply to the property in the under-lease, except the covenant for payment of rent. This covenant is of importance to the original lessee, for in its absence the sub-lessee might by his acts cause a forfeiture of the head-lease, leaving the head-lessee without any remedy. It is, however, the better plan for the under-lessee to enter into express covenants similar to those contained in the head-lease. In either case the head-lessee covenants on his part to perform the covenants in the head-lease so far as they apply to the rest of the property. Covenant in under-lease.

We now pass to the covenants on the part of the lessor. Lessor's covenants.

In the absence of any express covenant the word "demise," "let," or any similar word which actually creates a term, creates an implied covenant by the lessor for quiet enjoyment during the term. (Co. Litt. 348 a (n.).) Such covenant is unqualified, *i. e.*, it is against the lawful acts of all the world; but, on Covenant implied by the word "demise."

the other hand, it ceases with the estate of the lessor, for the term necessarily does so, unless the lease be granted by virtue of a power. This appears to require some explanation. Suppose a tenant for life to grant a lease and then to die within the term; on the eviction of the lessee after the lessor's death, *i. e.*, after the determination of the estate of the lessor, the lessee cannot bring an action against his representatives on the covenant implied by the word "demise." The nature of the covenant, its being unqualified, *i. e.*, against the acts of all the world, is a little hard on the lessor; and, on the other hand, the possible case that I have pointed out is hard on the lessee.

Express covenant for quiet enjoyment.

Owing to the unsatisfactory nature of the implied covenant for quiet enjoyment, it has become the custom to insert an express covenant for quiet enjoyment by the lessor, qualified, however, as only guarding against the acts of himself "or his heirs, or any other person or persons claiming by, from, or under him, them, or any of them." Such a covenant is a "usual" covenant. The insertion of such a covenant, according to the rule of construction, "*expressum facit tacitum cessare*," discharges the lessor from his liability under the covenant implied by the word "demise," and substitutes the liability expressed in the covenant, which is of a much less onerous nature, only extending against his own acts and those of persons claiming under him, instead of extending against the acts of all the world. It may be remarked that such a covenant may be safely entered into by a person who has no title to the property comprised in the lease, for if the true owner claiming by title paramount to the lessor's disturbs the tenant, the disturbance is *not* "the act of the lessor or his heirs, or any other person or persons claiming by, from, or under him, them, or any of them."

Although the express covenant is less beneficial to the lessee than the implied covenant, owing to his liability to eviction by a person claiming by title paramount, on the other hand the lessor's liability does not cease with his interest; so that if a tenant for life grants a lease for years, and dies within the term, and afterwards the lessee is disturbed by some one claiming under him, his representatives are liable to an action on the covenant.

**Danger to lessee who does not investigate lessor's title.**

It may be remarked that a lessee who does not investigate his lessor's title is in a very dangerous position; as in the case of ejectment being brought against him by a person claiming by title paramount to the lessor, he has no means of defending his title, and if ejected, he has no remedy against his lessor. The risk is one which may fairly be run where the lease is at rack rent, but where the lessee intends to lay out a considerable sum on building or improvements, he ought either to investigate the lessor's title, or, at least, to see the conveyance to him, or, if possible, to get him to enter into an unqualified covenant for quiet enjoyment, *i. e.*, a covenant on which he would be liable to the tenant on his being evicted by anybody. The learned Editor of Woodfall's Landlord and Tenant, p. 543, is of opinion that "the lessor ought not to refuse to enter into such covenant where no investigation of his title takes place," but the Author believes that such a covenant is never given in practice. The reason is obvious; if a lessor granting a building lease enters into such a covenant, and the lessee be evicted by title paramount, the lessor would not only lose his rent, but would be under a liability to the lessee which would be measured by the loss of the latter, *i. e.*, the improved value of the land. Where a building lease is to be taken of part of a larger property which is habitually let for building, the title of which is known in the neighbourhood, the lessee is often willing to run the risk, and neither to investigate the lessor's title, nor to require the unqualified covenant for quiet enjoyment.

If the lease is granted by a tenant for life under a leasing power, the covenant may be qualified, so as to bind the persons claiming under the settlement only while they shall be respectively entitled to the reversion.

Occasionally, although the lessor does not show his title, he covenants to produce his title deeds when necessary to support the tenant's title.

Covenant to sell property to lessee at a fixed price.

Sometimes the lessor covenants to sell the premises to the lessee at a certain price if required to do so before a certain day. This covenant is not uncommon in leases granted by persons who have built houses on building leases in a new neighbourhood. The option of acquiring a long term thus given to the sub-lessee is an inducement to him to take the lease; and, on the other hand, the price being fixed, saves him from having to pay an extravagant sum should the neighbourhood become fashionable. A similar covenant may, of course, be inserted in the lease from the freeholder. Where such a covenant is inserted, some provision should be inserted as to the title to be shown by the lessor in case of the tenant electing to purchase: in the former case, where the lessor is himself a lessee, he must be careful to guard himself from being bound to show his landlord's title, unless he can do so.

**Covenant by lessor to use his own property in a particular manner.**

Occasionally the lessor covenants to use or abstain from using his property in the neighbourhood of that comprised in the demise in some particular manner. For instance, if the lease be a building lease, he may covenant not to allow houses of an inferior class to be built on it; or that if any private roads be made over it, the occupiers of houses to be built on the land comprised in the lease shall be allowed to use them. There appears to be considerable doubt as to how far covenants of this nature run with the lessor's land so as to bind it in the hands of those claiming under him. But it is clear that every person claiming under him who is affected with notice of the covenant will be bound to perform it. (*Tulk* v. *Moxhay*, 2 Phill. 774; *Western* v. *Macdermott*, L. R. 2 Ch. App. 221.) The difficulty for the conveyancer is to discover the most convenient manner of reudering it certain that everyone claiming under the lessor will have notice of the covenant. Possibly the most convenient plan is to indorse notice of the lease on the leading title-deeds of the inheritance.

Where the lessor contemplates very large building operations, the plan is sometimes adopted of vesting the whole property in trustees for a long term upon trust not to allow any buildings other than those of a specified class to be erected, to lay out and maintain roads, &c., with power to grant leases.

In all cases where the occupiers of houses have rights of way granted to them over carriage roads some arrangement should be made as to how and at whose expense the roads are to be kept in order. The better plan, perhaps, is for the burden of doing so to be thrown on the landlord, he having the right to recoup himself by levying a rate, not to exceed a certain amount, on every house having the use of them. In this case it should be provided that his remedies for the recovery of the rate should be the same as if it were rent in arrear.

Some such plan may be adopted for keeping up a square or ornamental garden. In one case that occurred in practice, the lessee of each of the several houses round the square covenanted with the lessor to keep it up in common with the others of them, and to defray the necessary expenses. It would have been an improvement on this plan if the lessor had covenanted, at the request of any tenant, to sue any other tenant for a breach of the similar covenant contained in his lease.

Fortunately, however, in such cases it usually happens that it is so clearly for the benefit of all parties to keep up the roads, &c., that if the sums demanded for that purpose are not excessive, they are paid without much investigation into the strict legal right of demanding them.

Copyholds.

A copyholder cannot, generally speaking, grant a lease for more than one year without license from the lord of the manor.

Sometimes, where the lessor is a copyholder and wishes to grant a long lease, the lord is unable, by the custom of the manor, to grant a license for a lease for a term exceeding twenty-one years: the lessor may grant a lease of twenty-one years with a covenant for renewal if the lord will grant a license for a fresh lease, which he covenants to endeavour to procure.

Renewal.

The covenant for renewal should always be subject to a proviso that all the rent should have been paid, and the covenants on the part of the lessee performed, at the time for the renewal. If the covenant be in this form the lessor can, on the tenant committing a breach of covenant, refuse to renew, and eject the tenant at the expiration of the term originally granted, even if there be no proviso for re-entry. (*Job* v. *Banister*, 2 K. & J. 374.)

Covenant for renewal.

Three points require consideration in framing the covenant for renewal:

1st. On what event the renewal is to take place.

2nd. What are to be the terms of the renewed lease.

3rd. Is the renewed lease to contain a covenant for renewal,—in other words, is the renewal to be perpetual.

Covenants of this nature are often inserted in leases for lives. Where this is the case it must be carefully specified whether the renewal is to take place on the death of the *cestui q. vie* first dying, or whether it is to take place on the death of the survivor of them. The difference may be very great: in the former case the tenant can put in one young life on the death of the *cestui q. vie* who dies first; in the latter case he can put in three young lives (if the lease be for three lives) on the death of the *cestui q. vie* who dies last.

Sometimes, where the lessor himself holds the lands on lease, he covenants to renew in case his own lease is renewed. In this case, if a fine becomes due on the renewal of the head-lease, it must be carefully pointed out whether any fine is to be paid on the renewal of the under-lease, and if so, whether it is to be calculated with reference to the fine paid on the renewal of the head-lease, and whether the under-lessee is to pay any part of the expenses of renewing the head-lease. It may also be convenient (*Postlethwaite* v. *Lewthwaite*, 2 J. & H. 237), having regard to the fact that a large portion of Church property held on leases renewable by custom has now fallen into the hands of the Ecclesiastical Commissioners, who, as a rule, refuse to renew, but will sell the reversion, to provide for the case of the purchase of the reversion in fee by the owner of the head-lease instead of renewing. It must also be stipulated whether the benefit of the covenant is to run with the land, or be personal to the lessee.

It should be remembered by the holder of a renewable leasehold (either for years or on lives) that if he neglects to renew at the proper time the right of renewal is gone, and that a Court of Equity will not help him; unless his neglect to renew is occasioned "by ignorance not wilful, or by unavoidable accident. Ignorance is considered to be wilful where a person neglects the means of information which ordinary prudence would suggest; and accident is not unavoidable which reasonable diligence might have prevented." (*Harries* v. *Bryant*, 4 Russ. 91.)

The most important question, when the renewed lease is actually granted, is whether it is to contain a covenant for renewal; and if so, whether the renewal is to be perpetual. The strong leaning of Courts of Equity is against perpetual renewals, and accordingly a proviso that the renewed lease should contain the same covenants as the original lease does not extend to the covenant for renewal, but it is more prudent to exclude it expressly; on the other hand, if the covenant be clearly one for perpetual renewal, its performance will be enforced by the Court. Thus, a proviso that the renewed lease should contain "the same covenants as are herein contained, including this present covenant," would operate as a covenant for perpetual renewal.

# CHAPTER XI.

## SETTLEMENTS.

As to insertion of powers which are also given by statute.

SOME of the clauses which till lately were always inserted in a settlement, such as the "maintenance" and "investment" clauses in settlements of personalty, and the "power of sale" in settlements of realty, are now sometimes omitted, in reliance on recent Acts of Parliament, which vest in the trustees of a settlement powers similar to those intended to be given to them by such clauses. The expediency of omitting them is a moot point in the profession. In the author's opinion they should always be retained where the thing authorized to be done does not require the employment of a solicitor, and they may be omitted in safety where the contrary is the case. It must be remembered that generally one at least among the trustees of a settlement is a man of business habits, competent to read and understand such a clause as the maintenance clause. If, then, the necessity for maintenance arises, and the clause is in the settlement, no necessity for taking professional advice will arise; on the other hand, if it be omitted, the prudent trustee who is not a lawyer will insist on acting under the advice of a solicitor, and expense will thus be incurred. On the other hand, if the question be whether a new trustee can be appointed or not, even supposing that the clause is inserted, it will be necessary to employ a solicitor for the purpose of preparing the appointment ; and very little extra expense will be caused by making inquiries from him whether it is possible to make the appointment. The author considers it proper to add that this distinction between the clauses of the two classes does not seem to be generally received in the profession, the ordinary rule being to insert all the clauses as to which the question arises if the property settled be large, and to omit them all if it be small; with the intention of saving expense in the first instance in the latter case, by having a short deed.

### *Settlements of Personalty.*

The arrangement of the clauses of a settlement of personalty sometimes differs slightly from that given in the following analysis, the principal variations being in the place of the investment clause, and the covenants for title.

1. Parties.
2. Recitals.
3. Assignment of property by intended husband to the trustees, habendum to the trustees in trust for him till the marriage, and afterwards upon the trusts after declared.
4. Similar assignment by intended wife.

5. Declaration of trusts after marriage, *i. e.*
6. Trusts for investment, with power to vary securities.
7. Trusts for payment of income of property brought into settlement on the part of the intended husband.
8. Trusts for payment of income of property brought into settlement on the part of the intended wife.
9. Trusts for the issue of the marriage.
10. Ultimate trusts of property.
11. Miscellaneous clauses, such as covenant by husband's father to pay an annuity.
12. Covenant to settle after-acquired property of the intended wife.
13. Power to invest in land.
14. Power to apportion blended trust funds.
15. The receipt clause.
16. Power to arrange and compromise.
17. Power to appoint new trustees.
18. Indemnity clause.
19. Covenants for title.

Sometimes the respective covenants for title follow the assignments by the intended husband and wife, while the trust for investment with power to vary securities immediately precedes the power to invest in land.

It will be more convenient, instead of considering the clauses in the order in which they occur, to divide them into the classes following:—

*First.* Those having reference to the preservation and management of the settled property.

*Second.* Those stating the interests taken by the husband and wife.

*Third.* Those stating the interests taken by the children of the marriage.

*Fourth.* Those stating the ultimate destination of the property on the failure of the persons primarily intended to be provided for; *i. e.* of husband, wife, and issue.

*Fifth.* The trustee clauses.

Subdivisions of first class.

These *Clauses of the first Class* may be subdivided as follows:—

1. The clauses, if any, by which the property is assigned to the trustees.
2. The clauses authorizing investments, sales, and re-investments, of the trust property, the power to give receipts.
3. The power to apportion blended trust funds.
4. The power to arrange and compromise.

The assignment to the trustees.

When the property is transferred by delivery or in a statutory form.

1. When the property to be vested in the trustees consists of money or other personal chattels which pass by delivery; property, such as consols, which can be transferred in some statutory manner; or such as railway debentures which are properly assigned by deed in statutory form, it is transferred to the trustees in the appropriate manner. The settlement contains a recital "that, in pursuance of an agreement entered into upon the treaty for the intended marriage, A. B. transferred the stock (*or*

*as the case may be*), with the approbation of the intended husband and wife, into the names of" the trustees, upon trust that "the trustees, and the survivors and survivor of them, should stand possessed thereof upon trust for the said A. B. until the said intended marriage, and from and after the solemnization thereof upon the trusts and with and subject to the powers, provisoes, agreements, and declarations hereinafter declared and expressed concerning the same."

When by a common deed, should the assignment be contained in the settlement.

But in cases where the proper method of assigning the property is by a deed in the ordinary form, the question arises, should the assignment be contained in the settlement itself, or should it be carried into effect by a separate deed? In cases where the property consists of furniture, or something of that sort, which passes by delivery, and it is desirable not to transfer the ownership to the trustees by delivery only, but to employ a bill of sale, it does not signify whether the settlement itself is the bill of sale or not; for on any sale of the furniture by the trustees, the bill of sale will not be one of the title-deeds of the purchaser. But where the property is of such a nature that every instrument of assignment is a necessary link in the title, the answer to the question above proposed appears to depend upon whether the property may have to be parted with in the exercise of the trusts of the settlement or not; for in the former case inconvenience would arise if the settlement were to become one of the title-deeds of the property. Thus, if a mortgage is to be trans-

Mortgage.

ferred to the trustees, the transfer ought to be effected by a separate deed (*Capper* v. *Terrington*, 1 Coll. 103; *Dodson* v. *Lund*, 4 De G. & S. 575); otherwise, when the mortgage was paid off the settlement would become one of the title-deeds of the mortgagor.

The transfer of the mortgage to the trustees would be in the usual form, with the following exceptions: it would contain a recital of the intended marriage; the transfer would be expressed to be made "in pursuance of an agreement in this behalf, entered into upon the treaty for the said intended marriage, and in consideration of the said intended marriage, with the approbation of the intended husband and wife," or, if one of them was the transferror, with the approbation of the other: the habendum of the mortgage debt would be, "to the said E. F., and G. H." (the trustees), "their executors, administrators, and assigns," in trust for the [transferror] until "the said intended marriage, and after the solemnization thereof upon such trusts, and with and subject to such powers, provisoes, agreements, and declarations as are declared concerning the same by an indenture" (meaning the actual settlement) "already engrossed and intended to bear even date with these presents, and expressed to be made, &c." Powers are inserted for the trustees to give receipts for the mortgage money, and for the appointment of new trustees.

The settlement recites the mortgage; or, if it has been dealt with since it was made, recites that the settlor "is entitled to a mortgage debt of £—— secured, together with interest at the rate of ——, on hereditaments at ——, by an indenture, dated, &c." The contemporaneous deed of transfer is also recited.

Where the thing assigned is not to be disposed of.

On the other hand, suppose that the property assigned is not intended to be disposed of: as, for instance, where the property assigned by the intended wife is her reversionary interest expectant on her father's death, in the funds comprised in his settlement. Here it is not intended that the reversionary interest should be disposed of. The trustees are intended to hold it till it becomes payable, and there is no objection to the assignment to the trustees being made in the settlement itself.

Covenants for title.

Where the assignment is contained in the settlement itself, most practitioners insert covenants for title: there is some discrepancy of opinion as to what the proper covenants are. Some practitioners omit them altogether; others insert merely a covenant by the husband for the further assurance of property assigned by him, and separate covenants by the husband and wife for further assurance of property assigned by her, except where the property assigned is a policy of life assurance, when they insert all the usual qualified covenants for title: while others insert a qualified covenant against incumbrances, as well as the covenant for further assurance. Sometimes the intended husband is made to covenant "for the acts and defaults of himself and of every person claiming under him, and also for the acts and defaults during the intended marriage of [*the intended wife*];" while the intended wife covenants for "her own acts and defaults, and after the determination of the intended marriage for the acts and defaults of every person claiming under her."

Land.

Occasionally land is put into settlement, with the intention that it should ultimately be divided among the children of the marriage. Here the proper scheme is not to settle the land itself, owing to the inconvenience of land being held by tenants in common: it should be conveyed, by a separate deed, to the trustees of the settlement, upon trust for the original owner "until the said intended marriage; and afterwards upon trust, that they, the said [trustees], or the survivors or survivor of them, or the heirs of such survivor, shall, at the request, in writing, of the intended husband and wife, during their joint lives, and afterwards of the survivor of them during his or her life, and after the death of the survivor at the discretion of the trustees or trustee for the time being, sell;" the power of sale being similar to the first clause in the power of sale in a mortgage deed (*ante*, p. 160); the trusts of the proceeds being declared by reference to the marriage settlement, in a manner similar to that given above (*ante*, p. 270), where a mortgage debt is settled. By the adoption of this scheme the land cannot be sold against the wishes of the husband and wife, so that they will as certainly enjoy it as if it had been settled in specie; while, on the other hand, where the property has to be divided, no one child can prevent the sale; and further, the artifice of settling the proceeds only allows us to make use of the ordinary clauses and provisions of a settlement of personalty.

Wife's after-acquired property.

Having regard to the fact that at the time of a marriage no one can tell what the lady's fortune may eventually amount to, it is a usual custom to insert a covenant to settle any property acquired by her during the coverture. Occasionally, when the covenant is improperly framed, it extends in terms to all the property acquired by the wife, both during her husband's lifetime and after his death. The tendency of the Courts, where the expressions are ambiguous, is to construe the covenant, on the broad general ground of intention, as applying only to property acquired during the husband's lifetime. (*Dickinson* v. *Dilwyn*, L. R. 8 Eq. Ca. 546; *Carter* v. *Carter*, L. R. 8 Eq. Ca. 551; *Re Mainwaring's Settlements*, L. R. 2 Eq. Ca. 487; but compare *Prebble* v. *Boghurst*, 1 Swan. 309.)

The questions that arise on the construction of the covenant are difficult, and the author will therefore pass them over. The clause itself may be divided into the following sub-clauses:—

(*a*). A description of what is to be settled. This is generally stated to be—(a), any property to which the intended wife "now is" entitled; (b), any property which she or her husband in her right shall during the coverture become seised or possessed of, at the same time and from the same source, of more than a minimum value (often £200); (c), except certain articles and furniture, jewels, plate, &c., which excepted articles are to belong to the wife for her separate use.

(β). The husband and wife shall convey the property to the trustees, at the cost of the trust estate.

(γ). The trustees are to sell and convert into money any part not properly invested, and not being an annuity for the life of the wife.

(δ). The trusts of the sale moneys, and of the unconverted property, are declared by reference to the trusts declared in the settlement.

(ε). Trusts of the annuities are declared by reference to the trusts declared of the income of the trust moneys in the settlement, with power to sell the annuities with the consent of the intended wife, and to hold the proceeds on the trusts of the principal moneys which become subject to the covenant.

(ζ). It is very commonly and properly declared that if there be not more than a certain number of the children of the intended marriage, or sometimes whatever be the number, the wife should have power to appoint a life interest in her after-acquired property to any future husband; it is sometimes even provided that her children by any future marriage shall take some interest in the fund.

Occasionally neither husband nor wife may have any property in possession; it may all be subject to prior life interests, and in this case it becomes necessary to provide an immediate income for the new married pair; or if that should be considered unnecessary owing to the husband having a large professional income, still some provision should be made for the case of his death before the settled funds fall into possession. This can only be done by the relations on one side or the other agreeing to pay an annuity until that time.

The most desirable plan would, of course, be to charge some property belonging to the family on one side or the other with the annuity. But this will very rarely be agreed to, as it might cause difficulty in providing for other children; or might, for other reasons, be inconvenient. Sometimes the father on one side or the other proposes to make a voluntary allowance. This should, I think, be always resisted as far as possible, because circumstances may arise which may make him change his mind, and (even if he wishes to fulfil his promise honourably) may, in his opinion, be such as to release him from his promise. Annuity.

The most usual course under these circumstances is for the father to enter into a covenant for the payment of an annuity.

The covenant should usually be entered into with the trustees of the settlement, and the trusts of the annuity may generally be declared by reference to the income of part of the settled funds. The annuity should be made payable quarterly or half-yearly, and till lately it was necessary to make it accrue from day to day. The words "accrue from day to day" require some explanation. The general intention is to provide for the payment of the annuity during an uncertain period, such as till the husband's father dies; or till the husband attains a certain rank in the army, and the like. The probability is that that period will not end on one of the days on which the annuity is payable, and it becomes, therefore, necessary to provide for the payment of a proportional part of the annuity up to the day on which it determines. There are two methods of doing this: in the one method we provide for the payment of a certain annuity, say £100, by equal quarterly payments of £25 each, so long as (the father, suppose, be alive), and direct that on the quarter-day next after his death a further payment should be made proportional in amount to the number of days that he survives the quarter-day. By the other method, that referred to above, we cause a proportional part of the annuity to become a debt daily, but not to be payable till the following quarter-day, which, it will be observed, comes to exactly the same thing, but is a more convenient method of expression. The effect of the 1st and 2nd sections of the Apportionment Act, 1870, 33 & 34 Vict. c. 35, appears to be to obviate the necessity for expressly stating that the annuity is to accrue from day to day, but as the words employed are very few, "to be considered as accruing from day to day," it appears better to retain them, for it is unwise for the young practitioner to frame his draft in such a manner that it will fail in effect unless his own interpretation of the statute is correct.

Sometimes it is intended that the annuity shall vary in amount according to circumstances which may arise. In this case the most convenient course is for the draftsman to insert a covenant for the payment of the full amount, followed by provisoes qualifying the original covenant.

Life insurance.

Sometimes the husband may have no funds that can conveniently be settled, and at the same time he may be in the receipt of a large income derived from his business or profession. In this case he generally insures his life and settles the policy and the money insured. He may effect the insurance either in the names of the trustees or in his own name, and in the latter case he must assign the policy to the trustees; the assignment may conveniently be made in the settlement itself, as it is not intended that the trustees should part with the policy.

The trusts of the policy-moneys are generally declared by reference to the trusts of the other trust funds. The husband should enter into covenants with the trustees for the purpose of keeping the policy up and renewing it if it should become void or voidable, the covenants being of the same general nature as those in a mortgage of a policy (*ante*, p. 208).

Sometimes there is a power enabling the trustees to apply any part of the income or even of the capital of the trust funds in paying the premiums on the husband's default. It is desirable to leave a good deal of discretion to the trustees as to whether they should keep up the policy or not on the husband's default. They ought to be empowered, if they think fit, to surrender it, and to hold the sum received on the surrender upon trusts for accumulation during the husband's lifetime, and to hold the total sum accumulated upon the same trusts after the husband's death as the policy-moneys. But the propriety of inserting such a power must depend on the circumstances of the case. If the policy be for a large amount, and the other settled funds be but small, the burden of keeping up the policy might, if the husband became unable to pay the premiums, be very serious, and might leave a very small income for the wife and family to live on. Having regard to the fact that a bonus is an accretion to the principal sum secured by a policy (*Roberts* v. *Edwards*, 33 Beav. 259), and that consequently it cannot, in the absence of an express power, be applied in reducing the premiums, liberty is sometimes given to the trustees at the request of the husband to apply the bonus for that purpose.

Next presentation.

Sometimes, when the husband is a clergyman, a next presentation is purchased out of the settled funds. In this case the intention is that the sum advanced for the purchase should be ultimately repaid to the trustees, and, for perfect security, the husband's life ought to be insured immediately for the amount. Generally, however, as his income will be but small till he succeeds to the living, this is not insisted on; but he covenants to insure as soon as he obtains possession of the living. There exists in this case a difficulty which occurs in all cases where a man covenants to insure his life at some future time, viz., the risk that when the time comes for effecting the insurance his life may not be insurable, or may be insurable only at an extravagant premium. To guard against this, a proviso should be inserted enabling the trustees to dispense with his insuring his life on his paying them a certain annual sum to be accumulated at compound interest.

If an advowson be purchased, it is generally arranged that it should be sold as soon as the husband has been presented. In this case the insurance must be effected for the amount of the loss on the resale, which is often considerable, as the purchase is made, if possible, while there is an old incumbent, and the sale is made immediately after the husband has been presented. Advowson.

A similar scheme may be adopted where it is wished to enable an officer to apply part of the settlement funds towards the purchase of a commission. Commission.

(2.) Clauses of the second sub-class consist of—

(a). The investment clause.
(β). The power to invest in land, and its accompanying trusts and powers.
(γ). The receipt clause.

(a). A well-drawn investment clause directs the trustees either to allow the property (but as regards any reversionary interests after the same shall have fallen into possession) to remain in its actual state of investment, or to sell it and invest the proceeds in certain specified securities, with power from time to The investment clause.

time to vary the securities. As a general rule, every power given to the trustees of a settlement of personalty is made exerciseable "by the said A. B., C. D., and E. F. (the trustees), and the survivors and survivor of them, and the executors or administrators of such survivor, with the consent of the intended husband and wife during their joint lives, and of the survivor of them during his or her life, and after the death of such survivor at the discretion of the trustees or trustee for the time being."

The reader will observe that the power is not in terms given to the assigns of the trustees, thus differing from the powers in a mortgage deed, which are expressly given to the assigns of the mortgagee. The reason is obvious; it is not intended that the persons to whom the trust fund may be assigned on any sale should exercise the powers; and in the clause providing for the appointment of new trustees, it is declared that any new trustee shall act in the exercise of the trusts and powers of the settlement exactly as if he had been a trustee originally.

How consent is given.

The consent to the exercise of any power should be given in writing, if no particular method of giving consent is prescribed; the writing should, for the security of the trustees, be carefully preserved. The reasons why it is necessary to insert an investment clause would more properly come into a treatise on equity. But it may be stated shortly that till lately it was the duty of trustees, in the absence of directions to the contrary, to invest in a 3 per cent. Government Stock; while the effect of the Acts 22

& 23 Vict. c. 35, and 23 & 24 Vict. c. 38, and of the general order of the Court of Chancery of the 1st February, 1861, is to enable trustees, having cash in their hands which it is their duty to invest, to invest it in Bank Stock, *East India* Stock (30 & 31 Vict. c. 132), Exchequer Bills, £2 10s. per cent. Government Annuities, on mortgage of freeholds or copyholds in England and Wales, in Consols, Reduced and New 3 per Cents., and to change the investments from time to time. It may be observed that no authority is given by the Acts to sell property which is settled without any power of sale or power to vary investments. The Acts only apply where the trust property is already or may properly be converted into cash.

The reader may inquire why, when by law trustees have such large powers of investment, we habitually insert an investment clause in settlements. There are two reasons. In the first place, the range of investment usually given in a settlement is rather larger than that given by law; and in the next place it appears to be desirable, in those cases at least in which the greater economy obtained by brevity is not of primary importance, to state clearly in the settlement itself, for the information of the trustees, what they are to be at liberty to do (*ante*, p. 265).

It is quite impossible to lay down any precise rule as to what is a fair range of investments. It must be remembered that the safest investments invariably give the lowest rate of interest: and that the poorer the family is the more important it is, on the one hand to render the trust funds absolutely safe, and on the other hand to obtain a large income from the settlement funds. The following appears to be a fair range: Government Funds or Securities of the United Kingdom, or India, Bank Stock, Real Securities in England, Wales, or Ireland, Debentures or Debenture Stock of any railway in the United Kingdom or India, and possibly stock or shares of any railway company in India, the interest on the capital whereof is guaranteed by the Government of India, and mortgage debentures issued under 28 & 29 Vict. c. 78, and if the parties are connected with Ireland, Land debentures issued pursuant to 28 & 29 Vict. c. 101, as amended by 29 & 30 Vict. c. 99. A solicitor acting for trustees will be careful to see that no investments are authorized under which they might incur any personal liability; such, for instance, as shares in a company where they would be the owners on the register, and therefore liable to calls, &c.

Duties of trustees lending money on mortgage.

When trustees are authorized to lend trust moneys on real securities, they must be careful to have the title of any property proposed as a security properly investigated. They must not, as a general rule, lend more than two-thirds of the actual value of freehold land, or more than half the actual value of freehold houses or of leaseholds. (*Vickery* v. *Evans*, 33 Beav. 376, and the cases there cited; Lewin on Trustees, Cap. XIV. § iv.)

They should be careful not to consider the proposed security to be of the value placed on it by a valuation made on behalf of the intending mortgagor. "It is a matter of constant observation," says Lord Romilly, M. R., in *Ingle* v. *Partridge*, No. 2, 34 Beav. 412, "that nothing is more uncertain than a valuation; and the Court has constantly had occasion to observe upon the great discrepancy between valuations made by those persons who want to enhance, and by those persons who want to depreciate, the value of property. They are so great, that it is very difficult for the Court to come to a satisfactory conclusion on the subject; and it sometimes leads to most singular results. In one case, a plaintiff was compelled to compromise his suit, in consequence of his valuer mistaking the side for which he was employed. Valuations are mere matters of opinion, on which a person cannot be indicted for perjury. A man *bonâ fide* forms his opinion, but he looks at the case in a totally different way when he knows on whose behalf he is acting."

When the power does not authorize an investment on leaseholds, *eo nomine*, but is merely a power to invest in real securities, there is, to say the least, a doubt whether leaseholds come within the words of the power. But, on the whole, the better opinion appears to be, that chattel interests in land, such as long terms of years, not burdened by rent or covenants, are within the power, while ordinary leaseholds are not: 3 Dav. Prec. 27, n.

**Trustees lending trust-moneys as**

It is improper for trustees to join with others in a mortgage, so as to mix up the trust fund with the rights of strangers; nor should they take a joint mort-

part of an aggregate sum.

gage in the name of a common trustee (*ante*, p. 152). The attention of the reader is called to this, as the practice is by no means uncommon. It will be observed that the breach of trust consists in the fact that the trustees do not advance the money on the real security: they advance it to another person as the common trustee, and have not the land itself as a security, for the common trustee can get paid off and discharge the land.

Transferred mortgage on appointment of a new trustee.

Trustees who lend money on mortgage, lend it as if it belonged to them absolutely: with a declaration that it belongs to them on a joint account, and that the receipt of the survivors, or survivor, &c., shall be an effectual discharge. If a new trustee is appointed, the mortgage is transferred in the usual manner, founded on a recital that the mortgage money and interest have become the property of the continuing and new trustees nominatim. Doubts have been suggested whether a future purchaser would not be entitled to know how the new trustees became entitled. But the better opinion is, that the statement by the continuing trustees (who have become, both at Law and in Equity, the owners of the mortgage debt) as to the change of ownership confers an equitable title, to which they are bound to add the legal estate. Whatever may be the theoretical doubts as to the validity of such a transfer, it is constantly adopted in practice.

Power to invest in land.

($\beta$). Sometimes it is thought desirable to enable the trustees to invest the trust funds in the purchase of land. The propriety of the insertion of this clause, which, with the accompanying powers, is rather long, must depend on the circumstances of the particular case. If the sum put into settlement is large, it should always be inserted. When the property is small, it appears to be unnecessary; unless, indeed, it be thought desirable to do so for the purpose of enabling a house to be purchased as a residence for the married pair. If, however, the husband has some unsettled property of his own, it can hardly be necessary to insert the clause for this reason only, as the trustees could, under the power to lend money on mortgage, advance him part of the value of the house.

The power generally extends to freeholds, copyholds, and leaseholds having, at the time of purchase, at least sixty years to run. Trusts are declared for resale at the usual request or discretion, with a declaration that the produce of the sale shall be subject to the same trusts as the money laid out in the purchase would then have been subject to if no purchase had been made. Then follows a declaration that the rents of the purchased land shall, till resale, be applied in the same manner as the income from the moneys laid out would have been applied if no purchase had been made: a power of leasing, at rack-rent, for twenty-one years is usually added.

When land is purchased under the power now being considered, or when land is vested in the trustees on trust for sale, and the proceeds are settled, it is intended that until sale the person who would be entitled to the income of the proceeds of the sale had the sale been effected, should be entitled to the possession, or the receipt of the rents and profits of the land. In many cases it is proper, in the prudent management of the estate, to commit waste by cutting timber, or opening mines and quarries; and although the trustees are the legal owners of the fee, it appears that in equity they have no power to commit waste, except it be for the benefit of all their *cestui que trusts.* It would follow that, whenever it became proper to cut a tree, they would be bound to sell it and invest the proceeds. The rule is extremely inconvenient; as, if rigorously carried out, it would render it necessary for the trustees to interfere in the management of the estate. In most settlements, it is not attempted to guard against the difficulty; but where it is probable that a timber or mining property will be bought, or where such a property is settled on trusts for sale, this should be done. One scheme (2 Prideaux Prec. Conv. 220) is, to make the person entitled to the receipt of the rents and profits legal tenant for life, without impeachment of waste; but to declare that if a sale be made in his lifetime, the property shall be sold, with possession. The better plan appears to be to adopt the usual form, adding a short clause which gives to the trustees very general powers of management and of committing waste, with a declaration that the proceeds of the waste, amounting to over £      in any one year, shall either be laid out in improving the property, or shall be invested as capital; and that the proceeds of waste amounting to less than £ in any one year shall be treated as income. By a subsequent clause, the trustees are authorized to delegate their powers of management and committing waste to the person entitled to the rents and profits, and are made not accountable for his acts. The result, according to the proposed scheme, is, that so long as things go on well, the husband manages the property as if he were absolute owner; while, if he gets into difficulties, the trustees manage it themselves. On the other hand, if he were made tenant for life without impeachment of waste, and became bankrupt, the trustee in bankruptcy would be able to cut every tree on the property.

When trustees purchase land in pursuance of the trust, the conveyance is usually made to them upon the trusts of the settlement; but occasionally it is made to them as joint tenants, concealing the fact of their being trustees. In this case a declaration of trust should be made by a separate document: it may conveniently be effected by a memorandum endorsed on the settlement, and signed by the trustees. This latter plan may possibly give rise to a little difficulty on a sale. For, as when it is adopted there must generally be some reason which renders it undesirable to disclose the trusts, the trustees sell as absolute owners; in which case the purchaser is entitled to the usual covenants for title, covenants which the trustees may be unwilling to enter into. Difficulties on re-sale.

It will be observed, that if no change of trustees

has taken place since the purchase, the usual covenants for title really extend only to the acts of the covenanting parties; and the trustees may, therefore, not be unwilling to enter into them. The solicitor acting for the trustees must, however, be careful not to allow a trustee to enter into such covenants, without clearly explaining to him the nature of the liability that he takes upon himself, and that he is not bound to do so.

The most usual method, perhaps, of getting over the difficulty is, to sell under a condition that the purchaser shall not be entitled to any covenant of title, except that the vendors have not incumbered saying nothing about their being trustees.

If one of the trustees should die, a difficulty would occur on the sale of the property in respect of succession duty, in cases where the fact of the purchase having been made with trust moneys is intended to be concealed; for, although no duty is due on the death of a trustee, in order to prove to a purchaser that none was payable, it would be necessary to show that the person dying was a trustee, which is exactly what we do not wish to do.

It should, perhaps, be observed, that if an unauthorized investment is made in land, care must be taken to keep the trusts off the title: for, as the *cestui que trusts* have a right to elect to proceed against the trustee either for the land or the money, if this be not done, it will be impossible to make a good title to a purchaser so long as any of the *cestui que trusts* are not *sui juris*.

(y). The object of the receipt clause is to enable payments to be safely made to the trustees notwithstanding the rule of Equity that renders persons liable for the proper application of moneys paid by them to any persons other than the true owner. The question when a power to give receipts is implied, forms a most prominent head in Equity, which cannot be discussed here; but it may be mentioned that the principal cases where the power to give receipts is implied are:—1st. When the trust is for payment of debts, for seeing to the application of the moneys would in this case be an unreasonable burden on the person paying the trustees. 2nd. When the trust is of such a description that the performance requires time and discretion. 3rd. Where trustees have a power of investing and varying securities. (*Locke* v. *Lomas*, 5 De G. & Sm. 329.) Receipt clause.

The Act 7 & 8 Vict. c. 76, "for simplifying the transfer of property," rendered the receipts of trustees sufficient discharges, unless the contrary should be declared by the instrument creating the trust. This was repealed by "the Act to amend the law of Real Property," 8 & 9 Vict. c. 106; and the power to give receipts under the former Act extends only to trusts created between the 1st January and the 1st October, 1845. Other statutory powers of giving receipts will be found in Lord St. Leonards' Act, 22 & 23 Vict. c. 35, and the Trustees and Mortgagees Act, 23 & 24 Vict. c. 145. The power contained in the latter Act, which applies only to instruments executed after the 28th August, 1860, appears to render the insertion of a receipt clause unnecessary. But it is generally inserted in practice, not only for the reasons before stated (*ante*, p. 265), but also to save trouble on the sale to a purchaser ignorant of the law.

When money has to be paid to several trustees, the proper course is for them all to attend to receive it. If this cannot be done, the money had, in Lord St. Leonards' opinion, be better paid by their direction to an account in their joint names in a bank. Notwithstanding doubts that have been entertained, it appears now to be law that payment by their written direction to their agent duly authorized will discharge the purchaser. (*Hope* v. *Liddle*, 21 Beav. 183.)

Power to apportion blended trust funds.

(3). Sometimes it may happen that ultimately different parts of the settled property become payable to different persons, and that owing to the manner in which the property is invested at the time of division it is doubtful which part has been produced from each original fund. To avoid this inconvenience, power is given to the trustees to apportion the trust funds between the parties entitled thereto, and it is provided that the division, made by them, shall be binding.

The power to arrange and compromise.

(4). The power to arrange and compromise consists of the following powers:—First, to compromise or submit to arbitration any dispute about the trust property; secondly, to settle any legal questions as advised by counsel; third, to settle accounts; fourth, to determine whether any particular sum is income or capital; fifth, and lastly, to deal with the trust premises as if they were absolute owners, without being responsible for any loss occasioned thereby. The only part of the clause that appears to require any observations is the last. It appears at first sight as if the trustees were thereby authorized to deal with the property as they pleased, that is to say, *inter alia* to invest it as they pleased. But the generality of these words must be restrained by the words in the earlier part of the clause—so that, in reality, they only mean that the trustees may *for the purposes of the clause*, deal with it as if they were absolute owners.

This clause should always be inserted where part of the property settled consists of a reversionary interest under an earlier settlement: for when it falls into possession, there may be some confusion in the accounts of the earlier settlement, so that the amount to be transferred cannot be correctly ascertained, or loss may have occurred owing to improper investments; and in either of these cases the trustees of the new settlement would hardly be justified, in the absence of the clause, in accepting the amount offered to them as being that to which they were really entitled; and they might be forced, for safety, to take proceedings in equity.

## *Clauses of the Second Class.*

The wife generally takes the first life interest in

The question whether the husband or wife should take the first life interest in the property brought into settlement on the part of the wife is fully disher own property

cussed in 3 Dav. Pre. 53. The author may, perhaps, add that to his belief the opinion most generally held in the profession is that when it is proposed, on the part of the intended wife, that she should take the first life interest, it is improper, in ordinary cases, to raise any serious objections on the part of the intended husband; and that the real risk intended to be guarded against by the settlement is not that of disagreement between husband and wife, but that of the husband falling into pecuniary difficulties.

When the wife takes the first life interest in any part of the trust funds, the income is given to her for her separate use during the joint lives of herself and her husband, and generally with a restraint on anticipation.

Separate use.

If the income be given to her for her separate use only, she is exactly in the position of a *feme sole* in respect of it; she can dispose of her interest during the joint lives, and is exposed to pressure on the part of her husband or his creditors to do so; but when the restraint on anticipation is added, the income becomes practically inalienable.

Without power of anticipation.

There is considerable difficulty in understanding the phrase "without power of anticipation": for, as the only place where it is used with a technical meaning is in the clauses under consideration, it is erroneously supposed by those who have not thoroughly grasped its meaning to mean "*inalienable.*"

Suppose that the owner of consols, immediately after he has received his dividend, goes with the money in his pocket to a shop and makes a purchase, which he pays for out of it, he applies his dividend not by way of anticipation. On the other hand, if he makes the purchase before he has received the dividend, and promises to pay out of the dividend when received, he disposes of it by anticipation. So if he sells his stock he disposes of the whole of the future dividends by way of anticipation. Generally speaking, the law does not allow a restraint on anticipation to be imposed on income; if income be given to a man with a restraint on anticipation, the restraint is absolutely void: he can dispose of it as absolute owner. How, then, does the restraint on anticipation protect a woman? It will be remembered that, in cases not coming within the Married Women's Property Act, 1870, 33 & 34 Vict. c. 93, a wife is absolutely unable to contract; and that all income coming to her during the coverture belongs at law to the husband. Equity, which gives to her the rights of property over her separate estate, gives her also a power of contracting with respect to it; but when the words "without anticipation" are added, Equity modifies the power of contracting, so that it does not apply to contracts made by way of anticipation, and her common law incapacity of contracting comes into play; hence, as she cannot dispose of her income by way of anticipation either at common law or by virtue of any power given to her by Equity, no part of the income can be disposed of before it becomes due, or, in other words, the *corpus* becomes inalienable.

Although the restraint from anticipation is generally inserted, there are some few cases—as, for instance, on the re-marriage of a widow of mature years—where it may properly be omitted.

Income generally paid to husband.

In most cases, the income of property settled to the wife's separate use without power of anticipation is paid by the trustees to the husband by the tacit permission of the wife. The question has to be considered whether the trustees are justified in acting in this manner, or whether it is not their strict duty to obtain the wife's consent for each such payment. In other words, can the wife charge them as for a breach of trust in making such payments. The older opinion, decided, on the analogy of the cases on pin-money, was that the wife was entitled to recover one year's arrears of income. But the modern doctrine appears to be, that the wife is not entitled to any account. Although most of the cases which are collected in a note to 26 Beav. p. 5, relate to separate estate where the restraint on anticipation does not apply, still the *ratio decidendi*, the grounds of the decision, appear to apply equally to the cases where that restriction is imposed. The case of *Rowley* v. *Unwin*, 2 K. & J. 138, confirms this view. Trustees acting in this manner will be careful not to continue the payments to the husband if circumstances arise (such as the husband's pecuniary embarrassments or grave dissensions between husband and wife) which would probably cause the wife to wish to have the payments made to herself.

The modern form of the trust for separate use without power of anticipation consists of directions to the trustees—first, to pay the income to the wife during the joint lives of herself and her husband; second, for her sole and separate use, independent of her husband and his debts, control and engagements; third, that her receipts alone shall be sufficient discharges; fourth, that she shall not have power to dispose or deprive herself thereof by way of anticipation. In which it will be observed that the second and third clauses show that the property is to go to the wife's separate use, and that the restraint upon anticipation is imposed by the fourth.

The doctrine of separate estate is discussed in the notes to *Hulme* v. *Tennant*, 1 Tudor's Leading Cases in Equity. A collection of cases as to what amounts to a gift for separate use will be found in 2 Jarman on Wills. See also the important cases of *Massy* v. *Rowen*, L. R., 4 E. & I. Ap. 288; *Taylor* v. *Meads*, 5 N. R. 348.

**Payment of income to the survivor.**

But to return to the general frame of the settlement. The trust for the wife during the joint lives of herself and her husband is generally followed by a trust for the payment of the income to the survivor during his or her life; but sometimes the property is still further protected by making the interest of the husband, in case of his surviving the wife, determinable on alienation or bankruptcy.

**Trusts determinable on bankruptcy.**

In framing such a trust, we have to bear in mind—first, that it is impossible to give to any person a continuing interest in property after bankruptcy;

second, that property cannot be so settled on any person except a married woman as to take away the power of alienation to the extent of his interest in it; but third, income can be settled on a man *till* he becomes bankrupt, or *till* he attempts to alienate it. This third rule is subject to the exception that a settlement on a person of his own property till BANKRUPTCY is considered as a fraud upon creditors, and the trustee in bankruptcy takes the whole interest originally given. It was till recently considered that in the case of a settlement on a person of his own property till ALIENATION the restriction was void, but this is not the case. (*Knight* v. *Brown*, before V.-C. Wood, 7 Jur. N. S. 894.) It follows that the income of all the property comprised in the settlement can be settled on the husband till he attempts to alienate it, and that the income of all the property except that *belonging* to him originally —(*belonging to him*, not that brought into settlement on his behalf,) can be settled on him till his bankruptcy; so that the life interest of the husband in the whole of the property can be made inalienable, and his life interest in the whole of the property, except that which originally belonged to him, can be secured as against his trustee in bankruptcy. In a settlement of this nature, we have to provide for the destination of the income at the determination of the husband's interest; we may give it to the wife or children, whose enjoyment of it will, for most purposes, be substantially equivalent to his own.

There is, however, a plan slowly coming into use which appears to give a still greater protection to the husband's interests—the plan of a discretionary trust. Protected life interest.

When this is adopted, the trustees are authorized to apply the income at the determination of the husband's interest, "if in their absolute discretion they shall think fit, after the same shall become payable, but not by way of anticipation, towards the maintenance and personal support of the husband and his wife (if any), and his children in existence (whether by his then intended or any after-taken wife), or for the maintenance and personal support, of one or more, to the exclusion of the others, of the objects of the power, in such shares and during such time as they shall think fit."

I have given an outline of the clause as usually framed; but as the object of the clause is to make an inalienable provision for the family—and, subject thereto, for the husband—it appears advisable to add to the objects of the power, every person who after the death of the wife and children may become interested in the settlement funds in any manner. So long as the wife or children are alive, the trustees will be able to keep up a house for them, which the husband can share. But after the death of the wife and failure of children, there would, in the ordinary form, be no object of the power other than the husband; and the protection to him would fail. (*Snowdon* v. *Dales*, 6 Sim. 524; *Davidson* v. *Chalmers*, 33 Beav. 653.) If, however, the words which I have suggested be adopted, there would still be other objects of the power—viz., in the ordinary form of settlement, the deceased wife's next of kin. And, although the husband would probably not live with them, still the trustees could pay them the money; and it is probable that some of it would find its way as a gift to the husband. In such a case, the trustees should most carefully guard against using any expressions when they pay the money which would tend to cast any obligation on the person to whom they pay it to hand it over to the husband; for a trust for the husband might thus be raised, which would enure for the benefit of the trustee in bankruptcy, or for the alienee.

In the author's opinion, the free use of determinable life-interests and discretionary trusts appears to be one of the most fertile fields for improvement in modern conveyancing. Suppose, for instance, that in the case where the wife's property was very large, the husband's advisers objected to her taking the first life-interest in the whole, they could not object to any interest that the husband took during the wife's lifetime being made determinable on his bankruptcy or alienation, particularly if it was followed by a discretionary trust for him or his wife.

If the husband objects to take a determinable life interest, a certain degree of protection may be obtained by making his life interest subject to the obligation of maintaining and educating such of his children as shall for the time being be minors; and, it might be added, subject to the obligation of lodging and maintaining his wife. The insertion of such provisions would render it difficult for him, unless his wife were to die leaving no children, to raise money on mortgage of his life interest; and, in the event of his bankruptcy, the children, or wife and children, would have a right to have their maintenance, &c., provided for out of the funds passing to the trustee in bankruptcy.

### *Clauses of the Third Class.*

These consist usually of the following clauses :—

(α). The power of appointment among the issue of the marriage.

(β). Trusts for the children in default of appointment.

(γ). The hotchpot clause.

(δ). The advancement clause.

(ε). Maintenance.

(ζ). Accumulation.

(α). The power of appointment confers on the donees an equitable right of selection among the objects of the power. The donees are the husband and wife, and the survivor. The objects should always be the issue, and not the children only of the marriage; for, when this is the case, provision can be made for the issue of a deceased child, or of a child who has become bankrupt, or alienated his interest under the settlement. The power of appointment.

The power should be made exclusive—*i.e.*, so as to allow an appointment to be made in favour of one or more of the issue, to the exclusion of the others; so as to be able to exclude an improvident child.

Generally, the class of issue who form the objects of the power is restricted to those born during the lives of the husband and wife, or the survivor, or within twenty-one years after the death of the survivor. This restriction is made with reference to the rule against perpetuities; but it is not necessary. A power to appoint among issue generally would be good; the exercise of it would be bad if an attempt were made to offend against the rule.

If the power be general in terms, it must be borne in mind that the test of the validity of any exercise of it is the following. Could the appointed interests have been inserted consistently with the rule against perpetuities into the settlement itself? (See, on the general question of perpetuities, *post*, p. 341.)

The power should be very wide in its terms; it should authorise the appointment to be made at any age or time, in any shares, with any future executory or other trusts, for the benefit of the issue; with provisions for their maintenance, education, or advancement, at the discretion of the trustees of the settlement, or otherwise; and, generally, upon any conditions, with any restrictions, and in any manner.

The joint power of husband and wife is generally made exerciseable by deed, *or writing sealed and delivered;* the latter words having reference to the alleged disability of a married woman to execute a deed. It is inadvisable to require the appointment to be exercised in any particular manner, though this was often done in old settlements. By the provisions of 22 & 23 Vict. c. 35, s. 12, execution of the deed of appointment in the presence of two witnesses is sufficient, notwithstanding that some special formalities are required by the power. But, in practice, the terms of the power are complied with.

In default of joint appointment, or so far as such appointment does not extend, the power of appointment among the issue is made exerciseable by the survivor of the husband and wife, by deed, or writing sealed and delivered, or by will or codicil, or other testamentary instrument. The latter words being inserted with reference to the incapacity of the wife making a will, properly so called, during any subsequent coverture.

When, however, brevity is of importance, the words "writing sealed and delivered," and "other testamentary instrument," may safely be omitted.

**Appointment of aliquot share of trust funds or sum of money.**

When the power of appointment is to be exercised, the questions for consideration are the following:—Is the intention to appoint an aliquot share of the trust funds, or a particular sum of money or stock? And, if either husband or wife be dead, does the survivor intend to relinquish his or her life interest in the appointed funds?

There appears to be no objection to appointing either an aliquot share of the trust funds, or a particular sum of money. In the former case, although the appointed funds are, till they become payable, subject to the power of varying securities contained in the parent's settlement, care should be taken to distinctly show the intention of keeping the power alive; for it is obvious that a change of investment, made under the power contained in the settlement, may change the value of an aliquot share at the time of distribution. When a sum of money is appointed, this difficulty appears not to arise.

Appointment of specific part of trust funds.

A specific part of the trust funds—such as a certain sum of stock—should never be appointed, unless it is intended that the parent should relinquish his or her life interest in it to the appointee; as this would cause confusion in case the power for changing investments was exercised. If it be wished that the object of the power should really take a certain sum of stock, the proper course appears to be to appoint "all those £5000 consols, or, in the event of the trust funds being then otherwise invested, such a sum of money as according to the market value of stock on the day of the death of the survivor of the" [father and mother] "shall be equal to the then market value of £5000 consols."

An exception to the rule against appointing a specific part of the trust funds occurs when an investment has been made in land. In this case, it is sometimes wished to preserve the land as a family estate, and it is accordingly appointed specifically.

Appointment to daughter — her mar-

When an appointment is to be made to a daughter on her marriage under age, to the intent that she shall resettle it, the following difficulty occurs. As

riage under age.

she is under age, she cannot assign her reversionary interest; and accordingly, if she survives her husband, and the appointed fund does not become payable till after her husband's death, she is not bound to hand it over to the trustees of the settlement; but may keep it for herself. One method of getting over this difficulty is, to make an application to the Court of Chancery under the Infants' Settlement Act, 18 & 19 Vict. c. 43. By this Act, an infant (being a male not under twenty, or female not under seventeen) is enabled to make a binding marriage settlement, with the approval of the Court. The objection to the adoption of this plan is the delay and expense that it entails.

The author calls particular attention to the following method for getting over the difficulty, invented by a gentleman of great eminence; and which he believes is not generally known to the profession:—

In this scheme the father does not appoint directly to the daughter; but he appoints "upon such trusts as the daughter, in case she shall attain the age of twenty-one years, shall, within two years after she shall have attained that age, by deed, with the consent of A. B. and C. D., or the survivor of them, or the executors or administrators of such survivor, appoint" (where A. B. and C. D. are the trustees of the daughter's settlement); and in default of "appointment, and if the power shall not become exerciseable, or shall not in fact be exercised, then upon trust for the daughter absolutely."

The settlement contains an assignment to the

trustees by the intended husband, and a settlement, of all the interest which on the solemnization of the marriage will accrue to him in respect of the appointed share.

This plan gives the daughter absolute power over the appointed share, with the consent of her own trustees. But the risk of the power being exercised for any purpose other than that of confirming the settlement is extremely small—as the trustees have to concur in any exercise of it.

As soon as the daughter attains the age of twenty-one, she, by deed, to which her trustees are parties, makes such an appointment of her appointed share as will vest it in the trustees upon the trusts declared by her settlement concerning the husband's interest in it.

The general effect of this scheme will be, if the appointment by the daughter be made in due time, to place the share appointed to her in exactly the same position as if she had attained her age of twenty-one at the time of the marriage; while, if she omits to appoint, no harm is done; matters remain the same as if the special power had not been inserted.

Immediate provision for a child.

Sometimes, when it is wished to make an immediate provision for a child, the father and mother wish to relinquish their life interests, so that the fund may be rendered immediately available for that purpose. Although the father can do so, it must be remembered that where the mother's life interest is subjected to the usual restraint on anticipation, she cannot do so. In this case we are obliged to resort to the power of advancement.

The instrument of appointment is a deed-poll containing a recital of the settlement, so as to show the existence of the power, subject to the prior interests of the father and mother, the marriage of the latter; and that the intended appointee is one of the objects of the power. If, as is often the case, the appointment is endorsed on the settlement, the power need not be recited.

Illusory appointment.

In cases where the power does not authorize the exclusion of any object of the power, this may practically be done by appointing the bulk of the property to those objects who are intended to be benefited; leaving a mere nominal sum unappointed in cases where the objects intended to be excluded take in default of appointment; but appointing a nominal sum to be divided between them equally where this is not the case. Formerly, an appointment of a nominal share, or one by the effect of which a merely nominal share was given to one of the objects, was bad in Equity, under the name of an *illusory* appointment; the law is now altered by 1 W. 4, c. 46, which enacts, in effect, that no appointment made after the passing of the Act shall be invalid on the ground that an illusory or nominal sum "shall be thereby appointed to, or left unappointed to devolve upon any one or more *of the objects of the power*."

Trusts for children.

($\beta$). There are two different methods of declaring the trusts for the children in default of appointment, both having for their ultimate effect the giving of the trust funds to such of the children as being sons attain twenty-one, or being daughters attain that age, or marry under that age.

In the method which is more usually adopted at the present day, the trust is declared directly for such of the children as are ultimately intended to take—that is to say, for sons who attain twenty-one, and daughters who attain twenty-one or marry under that age.

Formerly the same result was arrived at in a more circuitous method—a trust was declared for every child; so that every child took a vested interest at birth, subject, of course, to be divested by any exercise of the power of appointment, and subject also to be partially divested by the birth of other children.

Then followed a clause called the survivorship and accruer clause; the effect of which was to give to the surviving children both the original share of any child, who being a son died under twenty-one, or being a daughter died under that age without having been married, and also any share which had accrued to him or her under the clause under consideration. For example, let the property be £40,000, and let four children be born: the eldest when born takes an interest in the whole £40,000; but on the birth of the second his interest is cut down to $\frac{£40,000}{2}$, or £20,000; and when they are all born, each takes a vested interest in $\frac{£40,000,}{4}$ or £10,000. Now, suppose one of them to die under twenty-one. His £10,000 is divided into three equal shares of £3,333 6*s.* 8*d.*, one of which survives to each of the other children. Suppose one of the survivors to die. Then, not only his original £10,000, but also his £3,333 6*s.* 8d., has to be divided between the other two, who take an additional share of $\frac{£10,000 + 3333 \text{ 6s. 8d.}}{2}$ =£6,666 13*s.* 4*d.* So that the total share of each of the two children who survive and ultimately live to attain twenty-one is the original share of £10,000; together with the share accruing on the death of the first child, £3,333 6*s.* 8*d.*; and on the death of the second child, £6,666 13*s.* 4*d.*; in the whole, £20,000—exactly the same as he would have taken under the more modern trusts.

An error is sometimes made by persons ignorant of the real meaning of the survivorship and accruer clause. They add this clause to the ordinary trust for children at twenty-one, &c., which is utterly useless. (3 Dav. Prec. 789; 4 Martin by Davidson, 436; and *Re Collings' Trusts*, L. R. 1 Eq. Ca. 498.)

Exclusion of eldest.

Occasionally, when a large landed property is settled upon the marriage in the usual manner (*post*, p. 328), it is wished, *in the event of there being more than one child*, to exclude the child who succeeds to the land from taking a share of the settled personalty.

In this case the power of appointment is declared in favour of the children "other than an eldest or only son *or daughter* for the time being entitled to the first estate tail under the limitations of an indenture, &c.," describing the settlement of the land. The words in italics in this and the following paragraph would be inserted if the limitations to the sons were followed by successive limitations to the daughters in tail or tail male. In such a settlement there are different methods of declaring the trusts in default of appointment. In the more modern method, which can hardly be said to have yet come into general use, the trusts are declared for the children at twenty-one, &c., in the usual manner, "other than the first or only son, or any other son or sons who, before his or their respectively attaining the age of twenty-one years, shall become entitled, *or any daughter or daughters who, before her or their respectively attaining that age, or marrying under that age, shall become indefeasibly entitled* to the first estate tail;" followed by a gift (in default of any child becoming entitled under the preceding trusts) to such of the excepted class of children (*i. e.*, any son who before attaining twenty-one becomes the eldest, or any daughter who before attaining or marrying under twenty-one becomes in the position of an eldest son owing to all her brothers, if any, having died without having barred the entail, and to the death of one of her parents, so that no other brother can be born) as being sons shall attain twenty-one, *or being daughters shall attain twenty-one, or marry.*

In this scheme, if there be any younger children,

an eldest son takes no share of the personalty, but a younger child who attains twenty-one, or being a daughter marries under that age, and subsequently becomes entitled to the first estate tail, takes a share in the personalty exactly as if it had remained a younger child. In the other scheme, which is an adaptation of the survivorship and accruer clauses, a younger child does not lose any share to which it is entitled at the instant of becoming the eldest, but is not entitled to any part of the shares subsequently accruing. See as to the effect of a resettlement, *Collingwood* v. *Stanhope*, L. R., 4 E. & I. Ap. 43.

(γ). When an appointment is made to a child, or the issue of a child, the child is not excluded from taking a share in such part of the fund as remains unappointed, a result which would generally be contrary to the intention, as it would create inequality. Suppose, for instance, a man had five children, and that the settled fund was £50,000, and on the marriage of a daughter he appoints £10,000 to her and makes no further appointment, then, if there was no hotch-pot clause, she would take one-fifth of the unappointed £40,000; *i. e.*, another £8,000, or £18,000 altogether. The usual intention of the donee in exercising a power of appointment is not to create inequality, but to make a fixed provision when necessary, as on the marriage of a child. To prevent inequality a clause, called a hotchpot clause, is usually inserted; this modifies the trust for equal division in default of appointment by declaring, that no child to whom a share is appointed shall, in default

Hotchpot clause.

of appointment to the contrary, take any share in the unappointed part without bringing the appointed share into hotchpot, *i. e.*, until each of the other children shall have received a share equal to his.

When the power of appointment extends to the issue of children, the hotchpot clause should be framed so as to require the shares appointed to such issue, as well as to the children themselves, to be brought into hotchpot.

Advancement.

(δ). By the advancement clause, power is given to the trustees, with the usual consents, and at the usual discretion, to apply for the advancement in the world of any child part of the share to which, if it attained twenty-one, it would become entitled on the death of its surviving parent. The money might, for instance, be wanted to purchase a commission in the army, or to pay a premium on articling a boy to a solicitor. It will be observed, that until the death of one of the parents the trustees would be unable in the absence of the power, to make any advance out of capital, owing to the wife's being unable to bind her life estate where she is restrained from anticipation, and where she is not, owing to her inability to bind her contingent reversionary interests in remainder expectant on her husband's death; and also that even if one of the parents were dead, so that these difficulties did not occur, the trustees could not, in the absence of a power, advance any part of the trust funds for the sake of establishing a child during its minority. In the older forms, the power was confined to sons, but it ought to be extended to daughters, as it is quite impossible to say that they may not want it. The father may be ruined, and the daughters may have to earn their own livelihood; and in this case the clause may be of the greatest value.

The power of advancement as usually framed does not extend to an appointed share; and therefore if an appointment directs the advancement of the appointee this cannot be done during the lifetime of both parents for the reasons given above: to obviate this difficulty Mr. Davidson suggests (4 Dav. Prec. 237) that the power of appointment should authorize the insertion in the instrument by which the power of appointment is exercised of a provision, overreaching the interests of the mother, for the advancement of the appointee. The same object may be effected by authorizing, in the advancement clause itself, the application of "part of the share appointed to any issue" for its advancement.

(ϵ ζ). The object of the maintenance and accumulation clauses is to enable the trustees, after the death of the husband and wife, to apply the income of the share to which each minor is presumptively entitled for its maintenance, and to accumulate the surplus. The Trustees and Mortgagees Act, 23 & 24 Vict. c. 145, contains clauses which are intended to supply the place of these clauses. The words of the Act appear to be so large as to comprise the interest that any infant would take in default of appointment under a settlement framed in the usual manner. Maintenance and accumulation.

The trusts in favour of the children appear to Modifications in the trusts for children where the father takes a protected life interest.

require some slight modifications in the cases where the husband's interest is determinable on his bankruptcy, &c., and where there is added a discretionary trust in his favour. First, as to the usual power of appointment.

Assuming that the settlement is in the usual form, where the husband's life interest is made determinable on bankruptcy, &c., the trusts for the children are made to arise "after the death of the wife and the failure or determination of the trusts declared in favour of the husband." It appears that, after the death of the wife and the cesser of the husband's life interest, he cannot exercise the power of appointment so as to affect the interests of any child who has attained a vested interest. I say, appears, for the decision in *Haswell* v. *Haswell*, 28 Beav. 26, 2 De G. F. & J. 456, where Lord Romilly's decision was confirmed by Lord Campbell, is not approved of by Lord St. Leonards (Sugden Powers, 261), and not followed by Lord Hatherley, then V.-C. Wood, in *Wickham* v. *Wing*, 2 H. & M. 436, a case which may be distinguished as relating to real estate; while Mr. Davidson (3 Prec. Con. 648, n.) approves of the decision in *Haswell* v. *Haswell*, but is of opinion that it would not apply to the case where there is a discretionary trust in favour of the husband after his bankruptcy.

The ground for the decision in *Haswell* v. *Haswell*, where the wording was rather peculiar, is that after the death of the wife and determination of the husband's interests the trustees had nothing to do but to distribute the shares actually vested. While the argument *contrà* depends upon the rules, which we have not considered, as to the time at which powers may be exercised.

In this conflict of opinion, it becomes necessary to use language which will determine the question one way or the other. Mr. Davidson is of opinion that in the case where there is no discretionary trust in favour of the husband the power should not be made exerciseable by him after the determination of his interest, but that where there is a discretionary trust in his favour he should be able to exercise it. Having regard, however, to the frame of an ordinary settlement where the husband can exercise the power of appointment, in spite of having alienated his life interest, it appears, on the whole, to be the wiser course to allow the husband to exercise the power, in spite of the determination of his interest.

The power of maintenance should be made exerciseable during the husband's lifetime after the determination of his interest; and as this power may become of the greatest importance in settlements of this nature, it is advisable not to rely on the statute, but to insert the power expressly. And as a father is *primâ facie* liable to maintain his children, a declaration should be added that the trustees may apply the funds towards maintenance without reference to the father's ability to do so.

As to the power of advancement. Where there is a discretionary trust, the effect of which is not far different from an inalienable life interest, for the husband, it is clear that the power of advancement ought to be made exerciseable at all times during his lifetime with his consent. And there appears to be no valid reason against this course being adopted where there is no discretionary trust: for the husband will probably, in spite of his bankruptcy, be the most proper person to determine whether any, and what, advances should be made for the benefit of the children.

*Clauses of the Fourth Class.*

Ultimate trusts of the husband's property.

The general rule is that, subject to the interests of the husband, wife, and issue of the marriage, property brought into settlement on the part of the husband is made to revert to him, so that he can dispose of his interest in his lifetime or by his will, while the wife's property follows a different rule; for if it were given to her absolutely, subject to the interests of her husband and issue, it would be a reversionary chose in action which would belong to the husband were he to survive her; for the purpose of avoiding this, the custom is to declare an ultimate trust for the wife absolutely if she should survive the husband (thus giving her a chose in action which cannot by any possibility fall into possession during the coverture, and which, being given to her by her marriage settlement, cannot be disposed of by her under Malins' Act), but if she should die in his lifetime, for such persons as she should by will appoint; and in default of appointment, for her own family according to the statutes for the distribution of the effects of intestates, so as to exclude her husband.

Ultimate trusts of the wife's property.

Sometimes the power of appointment is omitted, and the trust for her own family alone is inserted. This appears to be a little hard, as, in the event of her having no children, there appears no reason for prohibiting her from leaving any part of her property to her husband; and in cases where he wishes to misbehave, the existence of the power may give the wife a strong hold over him. Sometimes the ultimate trust, in case of the wife surviving, is declared for her next of kin, according to the statute; this is most improper, as it prevents her from making any settlement of her own property on a second marriage, and she becomes poorer than if she had never been married. The reason why the power of appointment given to the wife, in case she dies before the husband, is to be exercised by will, but not by deed, is that a will is always revocable, and that, therefore, whatever pressure may be put on the wife by the husband or his creditors to dispose of her property in their favour, she is unable to bind herself irrevocably at any time during her husband's lifetime.

**Effect of husband's death on wife's will made under the power of appointment.**

As the power of appointment is usually framed, it only comes into operation if the wife dies before her husband; thus producing the strange effect, that the death of the husband renders his wife's appointment void. In all cases, therefore, where a wife has made a will under such a power, she ought to re-execute it; or, rather, to make a new will immediately after her husband's death. A very slight change in the usual form would, however, obviate the difficulty. All that would be necessary would be to give the wife a general power of appointment by will, whether she survives the husband or not.

"Next of kin." In declaring the class who are to take in default of appointment by the wife, the phrase "next of kin" is sometimes used. This is improper; as next of kin means the nearest blood relations of the same degree. Be careful also not to say "the persons who would be entitled thereto under the Statutes for the Distribution of the Effects of Intestates as if she had died *unmarried;*" it should be, "as if she had died *without ever having been married.*" For the word "unmarried" is considered to mean "not under coverture at the time of her death." So that, while it excludes the husband, it does not exclude minor children surviving the wife. Any share which any such child takes passes on its death under age to its administrator—*i. e.*, the husband, if he should survive it; so that ultimately he might take a share of the wife's property, to the exclusion of her relations.

"Unmarried."

*The Clauses of the Fifth Class* consist of—

(α). The power to appoint new trustees.

(β). The clauses for the indemnity and reimbursement of trustees.

The power to appoint new trustees. Never trust a sole trustee.

(α). As it is possible that, before the trust funds are finally distributed, some of the trustees may die or wish to be discharged, it is necessary to have some means of appointing new trustees; for it is of very great importance to take care that the number of trustees should not fall as low as one, or that if it does another should be appointed immediately; so as not to allow the trust funds to remain in the name of a sole trustee. The reasons are the following:—The trustee is at law the absolute owner of the trust property; and in most cases he can, with very small risk of detection, sell it and apply the proceeds to his own use. I believe that this form of fraud is almost unknown so long as there is more than one trustee, as a trustee wishing to commit a fraud is most unwilling to run the risk of asking the other to concur with him. I believe, also, that in the great bulk of the cases where this fraud is committed, the trustee is under the impression that he will be able to replace the trust funds very shortly, so that no one will be the worse.

The author desires to impress on the reader the great danger of trusting a sole trustee, and the importance of urging most strongly on his clients not to delay the appointment of a new trustee as soon as there is only one left. There is, he believes, hardly any man of middle age who does not know amongst his own personal friends of some family that has been ruined, or at least sustained very serious loss, by having trusted a sole trustee.

Where the trust moneys are invested in the public funds, or the stock or shares of any public company, security may be obtained by means of a *distringas*.

A *distringas* is, in form, a writ issued out of the Court of Chancery, for the purpose of restraining **Distringas.**

the transfer of the stock. It can be obtained, as a matter of course, by any person interested in the stock, on his, or his solicitor, making an affidavit that he is interested in the fund.

The effect is to prevent the transfer of the stock, without eight days' notice to the solicitor who put on the distringas.

The objection to a *distringas* is the dislike that people have to doing anything which appears to show the slightest suspicion of their trustees; so that a *distringas* is not often made use of in the case of a marriage settlement, except in the case where the interest of the *cestui que trust* has been incumbered; in which case it is a matter of course for the incumbrancer to put a *distringas* on.

With the view of avoiding frequent appointments of new trustees, the modern practice, now generally adopted, is to appoint three or four trustees originally. It is inconvenient to have more than four, as the Bank of England refuses to allow stock to stand in the names of more than four persons, in the absence of special circumstances.

An alysis of power. The power to appoint new trustees contains four sub-clauses.

1. The equitable power of nominating new trustees.
2. A declaration that on the appointment the number may be increased or diminished.
3. A direction for the transfer of the trust funds to the new and continuing trustees.
4. A declaration that any new trustee may act before the transfer is made.

1. The equitable power of nominating a new trustee in the place of one dying, being abroad, or wishing to be discharged, or refusing or becoming incapable to act, is generally vested in the intended husband and wife, and the survivor of them, and after the death of such survivor, in the surviving or continuing trustees, (with power to a retiring trustee to act for that purpose), or the executors or administrators of the last surviving or continuing trustee.

2. In the absence of the second sub-clause, the two following questions would arise on any attempt to exercise the power:—

What number of trustees should be appointed.

First, may less than the original number be appointed? The universal opinion of conveyancers was that this was improper, and that a title depending on such an appointment was bad. But in *Re Poole Bathurst's Estate*, 2 Sm. & Gif. 169, where two trustees had been appointed in the place of three, and in *Emmet* v. *Clark*, 3 Gif. 32, where three trustees were appointed in the place of four, a title depending on the appointment was forced on the purchaser. The point appears, however, to be still so doubtful, that, if possible, the full number should always be filled up. Sometimes you will find it quite impracticable to do so. The trusts may be very complicated, and you may be unable to find enough persons to fill up all the vacancies. In this case, when you appoint a new trustee, take care to appoint each new trustee in the place of one who has died, &c., so that upon a future occasion, when you have found other persons willing to undertake the trusts, you may be able, should it become necessary, to fill up the full number.

Second, may more trustees than there are vacancies be appointed? The rule (as laid down by Lord St. Leonards) is the following :—"If the power clearly require that only one person shall be substituted in the place of another, of course it must be complied with. But under a power in the common form, or general in its terms, it seems, upon both principle and authority, that more than one person may be appointed to fill a vacancy by the death, &c., of one of the old trustees."

When the Court appoints trustees, it does not consider itself bound to the original number.

3 & 4. The third sub-clause is merely directory; the fourth was originally inserted owing to the old doctrine, that a trustee could not act till the transfer had been completed, but this doctrine appears now to be overruled. (See 3 Dav. Prec. 178; *Noble* v. *Meymott*, 14 Beav. 478.)

Statutory power.

Where reliance is placed on the statutory power of appointing new trustees, 23 & 24 Vict. c. 145, § 27, the second sub-clause should always be inserted, and in practice it is in most cases convenient to name the persons who may exercise the power.

Indemnity and reimbursement of trustees.

($\beta$). The clause for the indemnity and reimbursement of trustees contains the following sub-clauses :—

1. A declaration that the trustees shall be chargeable only for such of the trust funds as they actually receive, notwithstanding their signing any receipts for the sake of conformity.

2. That each of them shall only be answerable for his own acts and defaults.

3. That no trustee shall be liable for dispensing with the investigation of the lessor's title on lending money on or purchasing leaseholds, or for lending money on or purchasing hereditaments with less than a marketable title, or for the deficiency of any investment, or for any other loss, unless the same happens through his wilful default.

4. A power to the trustee to pay his expenses out of the trust property.

The first two and the fourth of these sub-clauses only express the general rule of Equity, and the insertion of them gives no additional protection to the trustees. The Act 22 & 23 Vict. c. 35, § 31 (Lord St. Leonards' Act), enacts, "that every deed, will, or other instrument creating a trust, either expressly or by implication, shall, without prejudice to the clauses actually contained therein, be deemed to contain a clause in the words, or to the effect following, that is to say," the words being those usually contained in the first, second, and fourth sub-clauses. In the author's opinion, it is advisable to omit these three sub-clauses, as a trustee perusing them might possibly be led into error as to what he is allowed to do. The third sub-clause should be retained.

**Solicitor trustee.**

Having regard to the rule of equity that no trustee is allowed any recompense in respect of the time and trouble that he expends in the execution of the trust, it follows that a solicitor who is a trustee and acts as solicitor to the trust is not allowed more than costs out of pocket; it is a usual and convenient practice in cases where a solicitor is appointed trustee to introduce a provision authorizing him to receive remuneration just as if he had not been so appointed. (*Broughton* v. *Broughton*, 5 De G. M. & G. 160; 2 Tudor Lead. Ca. in Equity; note to *Robinson* v. *Pett.*)

### PART II.—STRICT SETTLEMENTS.

The author has treated the subject of strict settlements more briefly than its importance requires. He has done so for two reasons: *first*, the discussion of all the points likely to arise in the preparation of a strict settlement would require a treatise for itself; and *second*, it is, in his opinion, unlikely that the beginner will have to prepare one. He has, therefore, only pointed out a few of the more obvious questions which arise, and refers the student to the works of Davidson, Peachey, and Prideaux for a fuller discussion.

Object of strict settlement.

A marriage settlement of real property in the ordinary form, commonly called a *strict settlement*, has, in the most simple case, where the intended husband is seised in fee of the property, the following principal objects:—*First*, to make provision for the wife; this is effected by securing the payment to her of two annuities—the one, payable during her husband's lifetime, called "Pin-money;" the other, payable after his death, called a "Jointure." *Second*, to provide for the payment of gross sums of money, called "Portions," to such of the younger children of the marriage as attain maturity. *Third*, to provide that the property charged with these provisions for the wife and younger children should go as a whole to the eldest son.

Contingent remainders.

The student who has mastered the chapters "Of a Reversion and Vested Remainder," and "Of a Contingent Remainder," in Williams's Real Property, will observe, that if the limitations contained in a marriage settlement are to the use of A., the intended husband, for life, with remainder to the use of his eldest son in tail, the remainder is contingent; it is not ready to come into possession on the determination of A.'s life estate, for A. may die before a son is born. The instant that any son is born his remainder becomes vested, for it then becomes ready to come into possession on the determination of the prior estate. Till lately, the fact of the son's remainder being contingent had an important bearing on the frame of the settlement; for, suppose the common case of limitations to A., an unmarried man, for life, remainder to his first and other sons in tail, remainder to C. in fee, if A., before he had a son begotten, had conveyed his life estate to C., it would have merged in the fee, and the contingent remainders limited to the sons would have failed for want of any particular estate to support them. To prevent this catastrophe, it was the custom to insert a limitation, as follows:—"And after the determination of A.'s estate, by any means, in his lifetime, to the use of [trustees] and their heirs during the life of A., upon trust to support the contingent remainders hereinafter limited." The estate limited to the trustees was always ready to come into effect upon the determination of A.'s estate; and, if it ever took effect, would last till A.'s death, when his eldest son's estate would have become vested, even if he were *in ventre sa mère*, for a posthumous child took as if he had been born in his father's lifetime. Butler Co. Litt. 298*a*. (n. 3).

Cannot now fail by the forfeiture, &c., of the preceding estate.

"The Act to Amend the Law of Real Property," 8 & 9 Vict. c. 106, enacts, that contingent remainders existing at any time after 31 Dec., 1844, shall be capable of taking effect, notwithstanding the determination by forfeiture, surrender, or merger of any preceding estate of freehold; and has therefore rendered it unnecessary to insert this limitation to trustees in the case above stated.

Trustees to preserve sometimes still required.

An enormous blunder is sometimes committed by persons unable to construe the Act, which does not give any effect to a contingent remainder which is unsupported by a preceding estate of freehold. All that it does is, to prevent its being destroyed by the destruction of the preceding estate. Let us consider the three cases of a gift to A. for life, remainder to A.'s eldest son in tail; a gift to A. for life, remainder to B.'s eldest son in tail; and a gift to A. for ninety-nine years, if he should so long live, remainder to his eldest son in tail,—where the son in each case is unborn at the time of the settlement. In the first and second cases, the contingent remainder is well created—it is supported by an estate of freehold, and nothing that A. can do will destroy it; but there is a great difference between the two cases—for in the first case, as any son of A. must be begotten in his lifetime, his estate must be ready to take effect on A.'s death, and therefore cannot fail. In the second case, it is possible that B.'s eldest son may not be begotten till after A.'s death, in which case, as his contingent remainder would have become unsupported on A.'s death, he would not take anything. In this case, it would still be necessary to limit an estate to the trustees during B.'s lifetime, in remainder after A.'s life estate, to support the contingent remainder. In the third case, the contingent remainder is badly created, and can therefore never take effect, unless a freehold estate is limited to trustees during A.'s lifetime.

Terms used for securing annuities and gross sums.

At law a termor is merely the bailiff of the freeholder, so that the insertion of the limitation of a term, either before or after any limitation of an estate of freehold, has no effect on the seisin of the freeholder; but the termor has the right to the rents and profits of the land during his term, and if he be made unimpeachable of waste, he can cut timber, open mines, &c. For these reasons, when an annuity or a gross sum of money is intended to be charged on the settled property, the usual and convenient course is to limit a term to trustees upon trust "out of the rents and profits, or by the sale of timber or minerals, or by mortgage of the same premises, or any of them, for all or any part of the term; or by all or any of the ways and means aforesaid, or by any other reasonable ways or means" to raise the annuity or gross sum and their costs. They are also directed to "permit the person or persons for the time being entitled in reversion immediately expectant on the said term to the said premises therein comprised, to receive the surplus of the rents and profits of the same premises." Formerly, a proviso was inserted for the cesser of the term as soon as the trusts were fulfilled; this is not now necessary, owing to the provisions of 8 & 9 Vict. c. 112. (See Dav. Concise Prec. Ap. II.)

Annuity. Where an annuity is secured in this manner, it is rarely necessary for the annuitant to call on the trustees to act; as it is to the advantage of the person in possession to keep down the annuity, so that he may not be disturbed in the possession of the land.

Gross sum. Where the object of the term is to provide for a gross sum of money being raised, it has to be carried out by means of a mortgage of the term—a mortgage in which, according to the forms in general use, no power of sale can be inserted. As the tenant for life in possession is bound, as between himself and the remainderman, to keep down out of the rents and profits the interest on any charge bearing interest (*Kensington* v. *Bouverie*, 7 H. L. C. 572)—he is generally willing to concur in the mortgage for the purpose of covenanting with the mortgagee to pay the interest accruing due during his life. Occasionally, he is willing to covenant to pay the principal; when he does so, it should be provided that, as between himself and the mortgaged property, the latter should primarily bear the debt, but that the mortgagee should not be affected by the proviso.

Having regard to the difficulty that there may be

in finding a mortgagee willing to advance money on the security of a mortgage not containing a power of sale, unless the income of the estate far exceeds the interest on the mortgage debt, it is desirable, in all cases where this is likely not to be the case, to insert a power of raising the sum secured by the term by a mortgage of the inheritance, with power of sale.

**The position of the limitation of the term.** Where it is intended that an annuity—pin-money, for example—should be paid during the lifetime of the tenant for life, the term is made prior to his estate for life, so that he is entitled to the possession of the estate, subject to the obligation of paying the annuity; if it be intended that an annuity or gross sum, such as a jointure or portions, should become payable after his death, the term is limited in remainder after his life estate; so that the tenant in tail is entitled to possession, subject to the charges being paid. Care must be taken not to insert the limitation of the term subsequent to the estate tail, for in that case the charges could not be raised during the existence of the estate tail, and the tenant in tail could, by executing a disentailing assurance, [the effect of which would be to enlarge his estate tail into an estate in fee simple] destroy the term, and prevent the money intended to be secured by it from ever being raised.

As we shall see, the usual practice is to limit a term to trustees to secure the wife's jointure in remainder after the husband's life estate, with remainder for another term to other trustees to secure the portions; the effect of this is, to secure the payment of the jointure in priority to the portions. In cases where there is any difficulty in finding a sufficient number of persons fit to act as trustees, and where the value of the property is so great that there can be no difficulty in keeping down the jointure after payment of the portions, one term may be made to serve for both purposes.

Analysis of strict settlement. Here follows an analysis of the most simple form of strict settlement, viz., when the intended husband is seised in fee:—

Parties: A. B. intended husband (1); C. D. intended wife (2); P. T. & Q. T. trustees of powers (3); P. M. & Q. M. trustees of pin-money term (4); K. J. & L. J. trustees of jointure-term (5); M. P. & N. P. trustees of portions-term.

Recitals: (1.) The intended marriage.

(2.) Narrative recitals where necessary, showing the state of the title.

(3.) Agreement for settlement.

Operative clauses:

1. Grant to P. T. & Q. T. and their heirs.
2. Parcels, general words, all estate.
3. Habendum to P. T. & Q. T. and their heirs; to the use of "A. B. and his heirs until the said intended marriage, and from and after the solemnization thereof"
4. To the use of P. M. & Q. M. for 99 years (the pin-money term).

5. To the use of A. B. for life.
6. To the use that C. D. shall receive an annuity for her jointure secured by powers of distress and entry.
7. To the use of K. J. & L. J. for 200 years (the jointure-term).
8. To the use of M. P. & N. P. for 600 years (the portions-term).
9. To the use of the sons of the marriage successively in tail.
10. To the use of the daughters of the marriage as tenants in common in tail, with cross remainders between them.
11. To the use of A. B. in fee.
12. Trusts of the pin-money term.
13. Trusts of jointure-term.
14. Trusts of the portions-term, with the auxiliary trusts and powers.
15. Declaration as to receipt and application of rents during minorities.
16. Power to husband to jointure a future wife.
17. Power to husband to charge portions for the children of a future marriage.
18. Power of leasing for 21 years.
19. Power to grant building leases.
20. Power to grant mining leases.
21. General power to grant leases.
22. Power to grant licences to copyholders.
23. Power of enfranchisement.
24. Power of sale and exchange with auxiliary trusts.

25. Covenant to surrender copyholds to the use of P. T. and Q. T. upon trusts corresponding with uses of freeholds.
26. Assignment of leaseholds to P. T. and Q. T. upon trusts corresponding with uses of freeholds.
27. (If these leaseholds be renewable.) Trusts for renewing the leaseholds, and for raising money on mortgage for that purpose.
28. Receipt clause.
29. Power to appoint new trustees.
30. Indemnity to trustees.
31. Covenants for title.

It will only be necessary to consider some of the operative clauses.

Consideration. 1. The grant is expressed to be made "in consideration of the said intended marriage and in pursuance of the said recited agreement."

Parcels. 2. It often happens that the title is not investigated very strictly; so that it may possibly happen that some part of the property intended to be settled is omitted in the particular description of the parcels; for the purpose of guarding against this, a few sweeping words are often inserted for the purpose of conveying all the settlor's property in certain counties or parishes.

Pin-money term. 4. The object of the pin-money term is to provide an income for the wife during the joint lives of herself and her husband, to be applied by her for her own private purposes, such as dress, &c. But having regard to the importance of making an inalienable provision for the support of the family it is a matter for consideration in some cases, whether the income so secured to the wife might not with advantage be made larger than is necessary for these purposes. It is suggested that where such a course is adopted, the amount of the pin-money might, within fixed limits, be left in the discretion of the trustees from time to time. The term is limited to the trustees to commence from the solemnization of the intended marriage, "upon the trusts," &c., "hereinafter declared," &c., "concerning the same." The statement of the limitations is not interrupted for the sake of declaring the trusts of the term. In a subsequent clause, the 12th, the trusts of the term are declared to be to raise an annuity of £—— "to be considered as commencing from the solemnization of the said intended marriage, and as accruing from day to day (*ante*, p. 275), but to be payable on (the usual quarter days) "in every year to the said" intended wife for her separate use without power of anticipation. Then follows a declaration that the first payment is to be made on the quarter day next following the marriage, and that the trustees can raise and retain or pay the costs incurred in respect of the trusts of the term.

5. The estate for life of the intended husband is usually made unimpeachable of waste (Tudor's Leading Cases on Real Property; note to Lewis Bowles' case.) Where the intended wife is intended to take

the first life interest in the land, an estate is generally limited to trustees during the joint lives of herself and her husband, or for a term of years determinable on the death of either; and by a separate clause the trusts of the estate vested in the trustees are declared, being trusts which in effect vest in the trustees the whole management of the property, subject to the wife's control, and to the duty of paying the rents and profits to her for her separate use, without anticipation.

**Jointure rent-charge.** 6. The jointure is generally secured by the limitation of a rent-charge with collateral powers, a plan which may sometimes be adopted in other cases for the purpose of securing an annuity.

**Rent-service.** Before the statute of *quia emptores*, if a man (Co. Litt. 142*a*) made a feoffment in fee-simple, with or without a deed, he might have reserved to himself and his heirs a rent in fee-simple; this would have been rent-service, the feoffee would have held his land of the feoffor by the service *inter alia* of paying the rent; and if he neglected to do so, the feoffor might have distrained of common right. After the passing of the statute, this could no longer be done, as no service could be created on parting with the fee. **Rent charge.** Since the statute, if an alienation be made by deed, and by the same deed the feoffor reserves rent, with power to distrain in case of non-payment, the rent is called a *rent-charge* (Co. Litt. 141*b*), because the land is charged with it, and by virtue of the deed he can distrain for it. If the clause of distress be omitted, the rent is a mere rent-seck, that is rent for the recovery of which no power of distress is given either by the rules of common law or by the agreement of the parties. A power of distress is given by 4 Geo. 2, c. 28, § 5, to the owners of rents-seck. Although the effect of this statute is to render it, strictly speaking, unnecessary to insert a power of distress when a rent is created, still it is invariably inserted, except where it is reserved on the creation of a term, or where the rent-charge is created for the purpose of qualifying a man to vote, or to hold some office, such as the office of a magistrate. (*Dodds* v. *Thompson*, L. R., 1 C. P. 133.)

**Frame of limitation of jointure rent-charge.**

The limitation of the jointure rent-charge consists of three clauses: by the *first* of which the annuity is limited in full for (*the intended wife's*) jointure and in bar of all dower and free-bench, words which are inserted for the sake of indicating clearly that the jointure is to bar the wife's dower (*Stat. Uses*, §§ 6 to 10), and also to bar in equity her free-bench, which, as copyholds are not within the statute, is not barred at law; by the *second* clause, a power of distress is limited to the jointress in case the jointure shall ever be in arrear for twenty-one days; and by the *third*, a power is given to her, if the jointure is ever in arrear for forty days, to enter and take the rents and profits until the arrears of her jointure and her costs are satisfied. The powers of distress and entry cannot be exercised over lands subject to leases either in existence when the settlement was made, or made afterwards by virtue of the powers in the settlement: and probably for this reason it is the invariable custom to secure the jointure collaterally by a term of years limited to trustees. If the jointure be not paid, the trustees will force the tenants to pay their rents to them; this they can do, for they are the assignees of the reversion expectant on the determination of the terms created before the settlement, and they are the reversioners expectant on the determination of the terms created by grants of leases under the powers contained in the settlement.

Variations in the manner of creating the jointure.

As the payment of the jointure is sufficiently secured by the term, it appears that the clauses in group 6, limiting a legal rent-charge, with powers of distress and entry may, where brevity is an object, be safely omitted. Occasionally, on the other hand, the term is omitted, and power is given to the jointress, or to her executors after her death, to limit the term, a power which may probably never be exercised.

Jointure rent-charge not inalienable.

As a jointure rent-charge is not inalienable by the wife during her husband's lifetime, the position of a wife for whom provision is made after her husband's death by a jointure appears to be less secure than that of a wife for whom provision is made by a marriage settlement of personalty. Advantage may, however, sometimes be taken, for the wife's benefit, of her power of alienation. Suppose a case where the jointure is secured on an estate to which the husband is entitled in fee-simple subject to the jointure. The husband wishes to mortgage it, and the intending mortgagees require the wife's concurrence, so as to make the mortgage free from the jointure. She may stipulate that, in consideration of letting in the mortgage before the jointure, a fresh jointure of larger amount, subject to the mortgage, should be given to her, or that some provision should be made for her children, and in either case the release of her jointure would be a sufficient consideration to support the transaction.

8 & 14. I give an analysis of the modern form of the trusts of the portions term.

**Analysis of the trusts of the portions term.**

(α). Direction to the trustees if there shall be any younger child or children to raise after the death of the husband

(β). If there be but one such child, the sum of £——, to be paid to such child being a son at his age of twenty-one years, or being a daughter, at her age of twenty-one years or day of marriage, which shall first happen, if the same shall happen after the husband's death; and if the same shall happen during his lifetime, then immediately after his death

(γ). If there be more than one such child, an amount variable with the number of children, to be paid to them as the husband, &c., shall appoint, but not before twenty-one in the case of a son, or twenty-one or marriage in the case of a daughter

(δ). In default of appointment, to be divided equally between the children for whose portions the same shall be raised, but to be payable [*similar directions to those in clause β*].

(ε). Hotchpot clause.

(ζ). Power to trustees to raise for maintenance of minors after the death of the husband such yearly sums as he shall appoint, and in default of appointment, such yearly sums as the trustees shall think fit, in either case not to exceed interest at the rate of 4 per cent. on the child's then expectant portion.

(η). Advancement.

(θ). Provisoes in what events the sums advanced are or are not to be taken into account in estimating total sum raiseable.

(ι). Power for the tenant for life to require the portions to be raised in his lifetime.

(κ). Power to secure a portion on the land to the person entitled to it instead of actually raising it.

(λ). Power to trustees in case it is desired to raise portions during the lifetime of the tenant for life to limit a term during his lifetime for that purpose, with a declaration that the tenant for life shall as between himself and the remainderman keep down the interest on any money so raised.

(μ). Declaration that subject to these trusts and to the right of the trustees to raise their costs the surplus rents and profits shall be received by the reversioner.

These trusts will be readily understood by the

student who studies the analysis; in considering the reasons for the insertion of the clauses he must bear in mind the following points:

*First*, portions are intended to be secured for every "younger" child, by which is meant every child except the one who succeeds to the estate; so that if the eldest child be a daughter, and a son succeeds to the estate, she is, for the purpose of receiving a portion, considered a "younger" child. The definition of the class of younger children given in the clause varies slightly in the different forms; it is perhaps most convenient to frame it so as to exclude any child, who though originally a younger child, becomes, if a son, entitled to the first estate tail before attaining twenty-one, or if a daughter, and the daughters take successive estates tail, *indefeasibly* entitled to the first estate tail before attaining twenty-one or marrying; but to include a younger child, who, being a son, attains twenty-one, or being a daughter, attains twenty-one, or marries, and subsequently dies in its father's lifetime. When the class of younger children is defined in this manner, it will be held to include a younger child becoming eldest in his father's lifetime, but prevented from succeeding to the bulk of the estate, owing to a disentailing assurance executed by his father and elder brother. (*Macoubrey* v. *Jones*, 2 K. & J. 684.)

Where there are cross limitations in tail between the daughters, it appears immaterial whether they are to have portions or not in the event of their succeeding to the estate, unless there are subsequent limitations to collaterals.

Amount of portions.

*Second,* the amount of the portions is generally made to depend upon the number of the younger children; care should be taken not to fix this amount too large as compared with the net rental of the estate, after the discharge of prior incumbrances, if any. In fixing the amount it must be remembered that the costs of raising the portions are payable out of the estate. (*Michell* v. *Michell,* 4 Beav. 549.) Where the prior charges are heavy, it is desirable that the payment of the portions should be secured collaterally by the tenant for life effecting an insurance on his life as suggested by Mr. Twopeny, 3 Dav. Prec. 367.

Where the limitations to collaterals take priority over the limitations to the daughters of the tenant for life, the portions are often made larger in the event of his having no son who succeeds to the estate.

*Third,* when are the portions to be vested; and

When are portions vested, when payable.

*Fourth,* when are they to be payable. In considering these two latter points, we must bear in mind the following rules of interpretation of trusts for raising portions:

General rules.

(*a*) If a portion or legacy payable out of land is made payable at a certain age, on marriage, or other event personal to the person to be benefited, and such person die before that time arrive, the portion or legacy is not to be raised out of the land.

(*β*) If the payment be postponed to the happening of an event not referable to the person to be benefited, but to the circumstances of the estate out of which the portion or legacy is to be paid, such as the death of the tenant for life, then it will be raiseable after the death of the tenant for life, although the term out of which it was to be raised had not arisen in consequence of the person to be benefited not having been *in esse* at the time of the death of the tenant for life. (*Evans* v. *Scott*, 1 H. L. C. 57.)

($\gamma$) When portions are charged on land by a person in *loco parentis*, either by will (*Jackson* v. *Dover*, 2 H. & M. 209,) or settlement, and the instrument is ambiguously expressed, or if it contains conflicting and contradictory clauses, so as to leave uncertain the period at which, or the contingency upon which, the portions are to vest, the court leans strongly towards the construction which gives a vested interest to a child, at the time when it stands in need of a provision, usually as to sons at the age of twenty-one, and as to daughters at that age or marriage. (*Howgrave* v. *Cartier*, 3 V. & B. 85.)

Practice.

The usual practice is to make the portions vest in each "younger" child (as above defined), who being a son attains twenty-one, or being a daughter attains twenty-one or marries under that age; but to make the portion of each child payable either at the death of the tenant for life, or at the moment when it becomes vested, whichever shall happen last, and to give a power to the tenant for life to require it to be raised during his lifetime.

Is the receipt of trustees sufficient to discharge a mortgagee?

It will be observed that the trusts of the portions term contain no receipt clause. This was omitted before the statutes supplying the absence of a receipt clause came into operation: so that the mortgagee advancing money on a mortgage under the power, was obliged to see to the application of his money, or, in other words, he could only pay it on the receipt of the persons entitled to the portions. The practice of causing those persons to join in a mortgage for raising portions for the purpose of giving a receipt has continued to the present day, although if for any reason it is impossible to make them parties, the money actually raiseable may be safely paid by the mortgagee on the receipt of the trustees alone.

Can the whole of the portions be raised where some only are due?

It is convenient for the owner of the estate to have the total sum that can be required for portions raised as soon as the first portion becomes payable, for otherwise the trustees may be obliged to make as many mortgages as there are portions. It appears very doubtful whether the whole of the portions can be raised at once in the absence of an express power (*Sheppard* v. *Wilson*, 4 Ha. 392; *Gillibrand* v. *Goold*, 5 Sim. 149; *Leech* v. *Leech*, 2 Dru. & W. 568), which accordingly is sometimes inserted.

10. The effect of giving cross remainders in tail

between the daughters is to make the land go as nearly as possible as if an estate tail, which had never been barred had been given to the father and he and all his sons had died. Cross remainders in tail.

The gift might run as follows:—"To the use of the daughters and the heirs of their respective bodies in equal shares as tenants in common." So far as we have gone, the intention is to divide the estate into as many equal parts as there are daughters, and to give one share to each daughter. The form continues—"And if and so often as any of the said daughters shall die without issue, then, as well as to her original share as also as to the share or shares which shall have survived or accrued to her or the heirs of her body, to the use of the others of the said daughters and the heirs of their respective bodies in equal shares as tenants in common." This latter part of the clause gives the cross remainders. The reader will observe that its effect is, on the death of any daughter and the failure of her issue, to divide both her original share and any additional share which she or her issue may have taken (in other words, all which she or her issue is *then* entitled to, between the other daughters in equal shares in tail. The final part of the clause is —and if "all the daughters but one shall die without issue, or if there shall be but one such daughter, then as to the entirety of the premises to the use of such one or only daughter and the heirs of her body." So that if all the daughters but one die without issue, that one takes everything.

It may render it easier to take an example. Let the daughters be A., B., C., and D.; then they each take an original one undivided fourth share in tail. Now suppose D. to die without issue, her original fourth is divided into three parts, one of which goes to each of her sisters, A., B., and C., each of whom now has her original $\frac{1}{4}$ and also $\frac{1}{3}$ of D.'s original $\frac{1}{4}$, and you will find that $\frac{1}{4}+\frac{1}{3}$ of $\frac{1}{4}=\frac{1}{3}$, the share to which each is now entitled.

Suppose now that C. dies without issue, her share (both her original $\frac{1}{4}$ and her accrued $\frac{1}{3}$ of $\frac{1}{4}$) is divided into two parts, each of which $=\frac{1}{2}$ of $\frac{1}{3}$. One of these added to the share to which B. or A. is now entitled, $\frac{1}{3}$, gives $\frac{1}{3}+\frac{1}{2}$ of $\frac{1}{3}=\frac{1}{2}$, and so if B. dies without issue, A. takes $\frac{1}{2}+\frac{1}{2}=1$, the whole.

In limiting cross remainders in tail, care must be taken that the accruing shares, the additional share or shares which any daughter or her issue succeeds to on the death of any of her sisters without issue, are given over together with her original share.

Management during minorities.

15. Difficulties would occur in the management of the property, if an infant became entitled to possess it. To obviate this, a clause is inserted directing the trustees to enter during the minority of every infant tenant for life (if the frame of the settlement admits of such) and tenant in tail by purchase, with very extensive powers of management; with directions, after payment of all outgoings, and maintaining of the minor, to accumulate the residuary income for his benefit should he attain twenty-one; but, if he should die under age, then the accumulations are to

be applied as if they had arisen under an exercise of the power of sale. If the limitations extend to females, the power is made exerciseable during the minority of any male, and minority and discoverture of any female.

The power for management extends to the felling of timber or underwood; erecting, pulling down, and repairing buildings; draining, insuring, making allowances to tenants, and accepting surrenders of leases.

Occasionally, by accident, the trust for accumulation is not restricted to the minorities of tenants for life or in tail *by purchase;* but is extended to the minority of all tenants in tail. In this case the trust altogether fails, as it is void for remoteness—*i. e.*, as offending against the rule of law against perpetuities.

**Rule against perpetuities.**

The rule against perpetuities—which is fully discussed in the notes to *Cadell* v. *Palmer*, in Tudor's Leading Cases—is generally stated as follows:—"Property cannot be rendered inalienable for a longer period than a life or lives in being, and twenty-one years afterwards." Or, perhaps, more properly, we may state it thus:—"Every disposition of property purporting to regulate its devolution at a time more remote than twenty-one years from the death of the survivor of several persons *in esse* is absolutely void." For the purposes of the rule, a child *en ventre sa mère* is considered as being in existence.

When we apply the rule in practice, we must remember that *possible*, not actual, events are contemplated.

Suppose, for instance, that a testator leaves property on trust for his unmarried daughter for life, remainder on trust for any husband whom she may marry, remainder to such of her children as shall be living at the death of the survivor of husband and wife. The gift to the children offends against the rule; for the class who are to take may not be determined till the death of the husband, who may be unborn at the death of the testator.

The reader will easily see that the trust for accumulation during the minorities of all tenants in tail offends against the rule. It is an attempt to regulate the devolution of property on the death of any tenant in tail during his minority, an event which may possibly happen after the lapse of any time.

The Thellusson Act.

Before the passing of the Thellusson Act, the accumulation of the income of property, and the suspension of all enjoyment of it, might have been directed for the same period as the suspension of its alienation—*viz.*, for a life or lives in being and twenty-one years afterwards. In the year 1796, Mr. Thellusson gave real estates to the value of £5000 a-year, and other estates which he directed to be purchased with the residue of his personalty, amounting to £600,000, to trustees upon trusts for accumulation during the lives of all his issue male living at his decease, and the survivor of them. To put it shortly, he directed his property to be accumulated during the lives of every one of his descendants whom he could possibly have known. The validity of this trust was determined; and immediately the

Act 39 & 40 Geo. 3, c. 98, was passed, for the purpose of preventing such unnatural dispositions being made for the future—posthumous avarice, as it has been called by one of the judges. By this Act, the period of accumulation is restrained to one of the following periods :—

Period of accumulation restrained to one of three periods.

1st. The life of the settlor.

2nd. The term of twenty-one years from his death.

3rd. During the minority or respective minorities of any person or persons who shall be living or *en ventre sa mère* at the death of the settlor.

4th. During the minority or respective minorities of any person or persons who, if of full age, would be entitled to the rents and income directed to be accumulated.

The second section restrains the operation of the Act, by providing that it shall not extend to any provision for the payment of the debts of the settlor, or any one else, nor for raising portions for the children of the settlor or any person taking any interest under the settlement, nor touching the produce of timber or underwood.

It will be observed that no trust for accumulation will be good which was bad before the Act. But a trust for accumulation which does not offend against the rule as to perpetuities, but is too large having reference to the Act, will only be void *pro tanto*. The accumulation will go on so long as the Act allows, and then will cease.

Power to lease under the Settled Estates Act.

18 to 21. At common law a tenant for life can make leases for no term longer than for his own life. In the absence of any power in the settlement, a tenant for life may, under 19 & 20 Vict. c. 120, s. 32, if the settlement be made since the 1st of November, 1856, grant leases of any of the settled land, except the principal mansion-house and demesnes, for twenty-one years, to take effect in possession; the lease to be by deed, at rack-rent.

By virtue of the same Act, building, repairing, or mining leases of land comprised in *any* settlement, can be granted with the authority of the Court of Chancery.

Power to lease inserted in settlements.

It is, however, the practice to insert powers of leasing, so as to enable leases for twenty-one years to be made during the minority of infant tenants in tail, and building and mining leases to be made without the necessity of applying to the Court. The proper method is, to authorize the donee of the power to appoint by way of lease. Where the power is exercised, the term takes effect exactly as if it had been limited by way of use in the original settlement. Mark the distinction between such a power and a power of leasing vested in trustees to whom land is conveyed in trust for sale. In the latter case, they are at law absolute owners, and as such can lease. But, as granting leases would be inconsistent with their duties as trustees for sale, equity would not allow this to be done. The insertion of the power to lease in this latter case, merely operates as a declaration that equity shall not interfere with the trustees

Nature of the power.

in granting a lease; they grant the lease out of their estate, the power operates in equity only. On the other hand, when land is in strict settlement, no one—(subject, at least, to the powers given by modern Acts of Parliament)—can grant a lease, either at Law or in Equity; the power is one which operates by virtue of the Statute of Uses. So that, when the lease is granted, the tenant becomes possessed by force of the statute, without entry.

**Donees of power.**

The powers of leasing are generally made exerciseable by tenants for life while in possession, and by the trustees of the settlement during the minority of any person who, if of full age, would be entitled to the possession. The powers of leasing usually inserted are—1st, a power to lease for twenty-one years at rack-rent; 2nd, a power to grant building leases for ninety-nine years; 3rd, a power to grant mining leases for forty years.

The powers are made exerciseable by deed, and it appears to be convenient to direct that the leases should take effect in possession, or within six months from the date of the appointment.

**Building property.**

Whenever it is probable that the estate may become extensively available for building, it is proper to insert more extensive powers than the common power to lease for ninety-nine years. In this case it may be advisable to make the power quite general, so as even to allow a fine to be taken, such fine to be paid to the trustees of the power of sale, and to be held by them upon the same trusts as if it arose under the power of sale: and the donees of the power, who in this case should be the trustees, should be authorised to dedicate part of the property to the public, or to appropriate it for churches, chapels, public parks, &c.

It is extremely convenient to have a power to accept surrenders of leases and to grant new leases, taking into consideration the value of the surrendered lease in estimating the rent. It is clear that if this be done under the common power to lease at rack-rent, the renewed lease would be bad, as of course the rent reserved is less than rack-rent.

**Best yearly rent.** The direction that the best yearly rent must be reserved does not mean that the largest offer is to be accepted without reference to the eligibility of the tenant. (*Doe* d. *Lawson* v. *Radcliffe*, 10 East, 278.) The word "rent" in a power may be construed to mean not merely money, but any return or equivalent adapted to the nature of the subject demised; thus, a render may be reserved under a mining lease instead of rent, unless from the general frame of the power it appears that a money rent alone was contemplated. The wisest method is, in all such cases, to state distinctly what may be reserved; thus, "the best rents, tolls, duties, royalties, renders, or reservations, by the acre, the ton, or otherwise," appears to cover every possible case. When a lease is granted which is invalid owing to some deviation from the terms of the power, it will, under 12 & 13 Vict. c. 26, and 13 & 14 Vict. c. 17, be considered in equity as a contract for the grant, at the request of the lessee, of a valid lease, with such variations as may be necessary for the purpose of bringing it within the terms of the power.

22. The power to grant licences to copyholders, the donees of which are generally the same as the donees of the ordinary powers of leasing, consists,— Power to grant licences to copyholders.

*First.* Of a power to authorise copyholders to commit specified forms of waste:

*Secondly.* A power to licence copyholders to grant leases:

*Thirdly.* A power to fix, during the term comprised in the licence, the sum which shall be considered as the annual value for assessing fines:

*Fourthly.* Proviso that no fine shall be taken for granting a licence except the customary fine, that the old rents, &c., shall be reserved, and that the licence shall be entered on the Court Rolls of the manor.

It is, to say the least doubtful, whether, in the absence of any special power, a tenant for life of a manor could not grant licences for the purposes provided for in the first two clauses. (See also 21 & 22 Vict. c. 77, s. 3.) But in practice they are always inserted. The third clause is the one of real importance; for as the fine on admittance to a copyhold is estimated by reference to the rack-rent at the time of estimation, persons claiming under a copyholder who had granted a building lease would, in the absence of the clause, have to pay a fine, not on the rental to which they were entitled, but on the rack-rental of the house.

23. The powers to enfranchise copyholds, and to Donees of

powers to enfranchise, sell, and exchange.

sell and exchange, are generally made exerciseable by the trustees, but during the lifetime of the tenant for life, with his consent. In the author's opinion, the power to enfranchise copyholds may safely be omitted, as the enfranchisement may be made very cheaply under the Copyhold Acts. The prudent copyholder will always prefer to take an enfranchisement under the Acts rather than one under the power, for when an enfranchisement is made under the power, any charges affecting the manor are let in upon the enfranchised lands; while if it is made under the Copyhold Acts, such charges do not affect them.

Enfranchisement under Copyhold Acts preferable to one under power.

Power of sale.

24. The power of sale, with its ancillary trusts and powers, contains nine clauses.

Liberty to sell.

By the *first*, liberty is given "to the trustees and the survivor of them, and the executors and administrators of such survivor," during the life of the tenant for life, with his consent in writing, and during the minority of any son of his who would, if of full age, be entitled to the possession or receipt of the rents and profits, at the discretion of the trustees or trustee, to sell or exchange the premises. This is a mere equitable power given to persons who have no interest in the land. Express permission is given to sell by public auction or private contract, the clause following closely the corresponding clause in the power of sale in a mortgage (*ante*, p. 161). It should be observed, that although the custom is to authorise the power to be exercised only during the lifetime of the tenant for life and minority of the tenants in tail by purchase, the power would be good

General power does not offend against the rule against perpetuity.

if authorized to be exercised at any time; for as any tenant in tail can, by barring his estate tail, prevent the power from being exercised, the power, limited in the most general form, does not offend against the rule against perpetuities.

Power of revocation and new appointment.

By the *second* clause, power is given to the trustees, for the purpose of carrying out the sales, to revoke the old uses and appoint the property to a purchaser, subject to any then existing mortgages and leases. This power takes effect as a declaration of a use, and when exercised, the uses declared in the appointment are fed out of the seizin of the grantee to uses in the settlement.

Reinvestment in land.

The *third* clause contains a direction to receive all monies arising on a sale or enfranchisement, and to reinvest them in the purchase of land.

To be conveyed upon the uses of the settlement.

The *fourth* clause directs that the land purchased or taken in exchange shall be settled upon the uses and trusts declared by the settlement or under any exercise of the powers of jointuring or charging portions, or as near thereto as circumstances will admit, "but not so as to increase charges or powers of charging."

Renewable leaseholds.

The *fifth* clause directs that if renewable leaseholds are purchased or taken in exchange, proper provisions shall be inserted in the settlement of them for their renewal, and that fines on renewal shall be defrayed out of the premises, so that the persons beneficially entitled shall contribute towards the fines in the proportions laid down by the rules of equity. Seton on Decrees, p. 518; 3rd edition.

Power to raise monies on mortgage.

By the *sixth* clause power is given to the trustees to raise money on mortgage for the purpose of defraying the fines on renewal, or any money payable for equality of exchange, or for procuring the enfranchisements of copyholds.

To discharge incumbrances.

By the *seventh* clause power is given to apply any monies arising from any enfranchisement, sale, or exchange towards the discharge of incumbrances.

Interim investment.

By the *eighth* clause the trustees are directed to invest any monies arising from any enfranchisement, sale, or exchange, until it is applied as aforesaid, in the government funds or real securities, and to apply the income as if it were the rents arising from hereditaments actually purchased with the monies. As the real intention is that the monies should be reinvested in land, it is not advisable to authorise any interim investments which are likely to give a high rate of interest.

Receipt clause.

The *ninth* and last is a receipt clause.

The whole of these long clauses, with the exception of the earlier part of the first, giving liberty to sell and exchange, may be safely omitted in simple cases, and reliance may be placed on the provisions of 23 & 24 Vict. c. 145; and in the absence of a power of sale the settled property can be sold under the provisions of the Leases and Sales of Settled Estates Act on application to the Court of Chancery.

Donees of power when there are undivided shares.

Sometimes owing to the settlement containing limitations to the daughters in tail with cross remainders, or for other reasons, an infant may become entitled to an undivided share while the persons entitled to the other shares are *sui juris*. It requires some consideration as to who are to be the donees of the powers during the minority.

The power of management during minorities (*ante*, p. 342), is usually made exerciseable by the trustees in respect of the minor's share, and they are directed to exercise, "or concur in exercising," the power as to that share. It would appear convenient to add a few words to the power as usually framed, so as to authorise the trustees to delegate their power to the adult owners of the other undivided shares.

Two schemes are adopted with respect to the powers of leasing; sometimes the power after the death of the tenant for life is restricted to the shares of the minors, so that the concurrence of the adult co-owners is necessary: and sometimes the power is vested in the trustees so long as any share belongs to a minor.

It must be remembered that it is extremely inconvenient in practice to require many signatures to a lease, so that where the shares may arise in respect of there being cross remainders, a case in which there may be very many co-owners, it appears more convenient to vest the leasing powers in the trustees during the minority of any one entitled. On the other hand, if the necessity for the provision arises from the property settled being itself an undivided share, the former scheme appears unobjectionable.

The powers of enfranchisement, sale, and exchange, may most conveniently be vested in the trustees, so long as any undivided share belongs to a minor, but may be made exerciseable only with the consent of the adult co-owners.

Copyholds. 25. Where the settlement includes copyholds, the settlor sometimes covenants to surrender them to uses corresponding to the uses of the freeholds; this is however incorrect, for it is, to say the least, doubtful whether all the powers that affect the freeholds can by law be made to affect the copyholds. The proper plan is to covenant to surrender the copyholds to the use of the trustees "Upon such trusts, and with and subject to such powers, &c.," as shall correspond with the trusts, &c. declared concerning the freeholds, "as nearly as the different quality of the premises and the rules of law and equity will admit, but not so as to increase charges and powers of charging." Bearing in mind that the parties may omit to have the surrender made, the settlor should covenant to stand possessed of the copyholds until the surrender upon the same trusts, &c., as if the same had been actually surrendered.

Leaseholds. 26. Leaseholds are assigned to the trustees upon trust to pay the rent and perform the lessee's covenants: and subject thereto, upon such trusts, &c., as shall most nearly correspond to the uses of the freeholds. If the form stopped here, the first tenant in tail coming into *esse* would become absolutely entitled to the term; for words which confer an estate tail in real, give an absolute interest in personal property. (See Tudor's Leading Cases, *Leventhorpe* v. *Asbie.*) A declaration is therefore inserted, that they shall not vest absolutely in any person made tenant in tail *by purchase* unless he attains the age of twenty-one years; but, on his death under age, shall devolve as if they had been freeholds of inheritance included in the settlement. The reader will see that unless the words *by purchase* are inserted, the direction would be void for remoteness.

30. The covenants for title are entered into with the grantee to uses; they then run with the land, for the benefit of all persons claiming under the settlement, or any exercise of the powers contained in it. They are similar in form to those inserted in a purchase deed. Covenants for title.

The advanced student may consult, besides the works already cited, Fearne on Contingent Remainders, Sugden on Powers, and Butler Co. Litt. 327 a (n. 2, II.).

## PART III.—NEGOCIATION AND PREPARATION OF A SETTLEMENT.

When a gentleman becomes the accepted suitor of a lady, some general information is given by him to her relations as to his fortune and expectations; while they give him similar information as to her position. A detailed statement of the lady's fortune is afterwards furnished by her solicitor to the gentleman's solicitor, including in the term "fortune" not only that which actually belongs to her, but also the property intended to be settled on her behalf. The gentleman's solicitor then prepares the "Proposals for the Settlement." This document contains a statement Negociation. Proposals for the settlement.

of the nature and amount of the property proposed to be settled on behalf of the gentleman, a copy of the statement of the lady's fortune, the nature of the provisions that the gentleman's solicitor thinks proper to have inserted in the settlement, and the names of trustees proposed on behalf of the gentleman, leaving a blank to be filled up by the lady's solicitor for the names of the trustees on her behalf—the general rule being that an equal number should be nominated on each side. In case any part of the property is held by title—as, if it be land, or an interest under a marriage settlement—the proposals should also state what title or evidence of title is proposed to be shown. The proposals are considered as forming a basis for negociations, and as, therefore, being liable to be altered by the lady's advisers.

Tact required in the negociations.

There is, perhaps, no duty ever performed by a solicitor that calls for the exercise of greater tact and discretion than the negociation of a marriage settlement; it must be remembered that it is impossible, if unreasonable propositions are made, to defeat them by the threat of breaking off the negociations; and that the clients are generally so ignorant of the nature of a settlement, that they are unable to see the objects which their advisers are aiming at.

Points for consideration in negociation of settlement of personalty.

The more important points for consideration in the negociation of settlements of personalty are the following:—

1st. What amount of capital is to be brought into settlement on each side.

2nd. Who is to take the first life interest in the wife's fortune. Is the husband's life interest to be made determinable on bankruptcy, &c.; and, if so, is there to be a discretionary trust in his favour. Although it is the invariable custom to give to the husband the first life interest in his own fortune, it may deserve consideration, in a case where he is engaged in trade, whether it may not be proper to give it to the wife; or, if this be objected to, whether it might not be given to the wife subject to a discretionary trust in favour of the husband (*ante*, p. 297).

3rd. Are the trusts for the children to be in the usual form, or is an eldest son to be excluded in the event of his succeeding to an estate.

4th. If the settled property is reversionary, how is an immediate income to be provided.

5th. Is the husband to insure his life.

6th. What investments are to be authorized.

7th. Is the after-acquired property of the wife to be settled; and, if so, are any special provisions to be made in the event of her marrying again.

There are also a few minor points to be attended to. Care should be taken that all the property belonging to the gentleman and lady is not settled; for it must be remembered that they will probably have to furnish a house, and to incur other large expenses in the first year of the marriage; and, even if the gentleman has already a house and establishment, he will have to pay for the settlement, and it is desirable that he should have something in hand to meet abnormal expenses. Care must be taken not to settle such large sums on the issue of the intended marriage as to be unfair towards the issue of any former marriage of either the gentleman or lady; and if such issue be unprovided for, it is but reasonable to make some provision for them.

Is land to be put into strict settlement or not.

Strict settlement.

Where the property to be settled is land, a preliminary question arises, Whether it is to be put into strict settlement, or to be settled as personalty (*ante*, p. 272). In the former case, the only questions for consideration by the lady's advisers are the amount of the pin-money, jointure, and portions; the order of the limitations in tail being generally left to the discretion of the husband's advisers. Care should be taken not to charge the estate with so large an amount for portions, when compared with its value (*ante*, p. 338), that it will have to be sold when the portions become payable. In case the property is already incumbered, it deserves consideration whether it may not be advisable for the gentleman to insure his life, for the purpose of providing, in part at least, for the portions. (See Mr. Twopeny's remarks, cited 3 Dav. Prec. 367.)

Where the gentleman has an estate intended to be put into strict settlement, and the lady has a fortune consisting of personalty, it used to be the practice, unless her fortune was very large indeed, not to settle it, so that her husband took it *jure mariti*, provision being made for her by means of pin-money and a jointure charged on his estate. The modern practice in such a case is to settle the lady's fortune upon the usual trusts of a settlement of personalty, with the variation that if more than one child attains a vested interest the eldest child is excluded. In cases where the old practice is followed a large jointure should be stipulated for, otherwise, on her husband's death the widow may be poorer than if she had never been married; as in that case she would have retained her own fortune, and might have purchased an annuity with it.

Lady's solicitor prepares the settlement.

The lady's solicitor has the duty of preparing the settlement. This rule creates some inconvenience in the case of a strict settlement, for, as the gentleman's solicitor knows the circumstances of the estate, he is better able to advise as to the necessary powers for management, &c., than the lady's solicitor. In the common case of a father tenant for life, and his son tenant in tail, joining in cutting off the entail and making a fresh settlement on the marriage of the latter, the difficulty is usually provided against by proposing on the gentleman's behalf that the re-settlement should contain powers of jointuring and charging portions; in this case the resettlement is prepared by his family solicitor, while the deed by which the powers of jointuring and charging portions are exercised is prepared by the lady's solicitor (*post*, Chap. XIII. "Resettlements").

Case of a family resettlement on the marriage of a son.

Occasionally, when the gentleman is likely to be

Power to

raise costs of settlement. short of ready money at the time of his marriage, a clause is inserted in the settlement directing the trustees to raise and pay the costs of the negociation and preparation of the settlement out of the trust funds.

Costs of a marriage settlement. The practice is for the husband to pay the lady's solicitor his costs of the negociation and preparation of the settlement, on the grounds laid down in *Helps* v. *Clayton*, 17 C. B. N. S. 553, where it was decided —*first*, that the liability of the husband is not an original liability towards the lady's solicitor, but only a liability to reimburse the expenses of the settlement which the lady or her father or person *in loco parentis* may have incurred; *secondly*, that as between the lady and her father, the solicitor is *her* solicitor, so that she is liable to the solicitor, although the father may have actually instructed him, and all that she has done is to execute the settlement; and *thirdly*, that a settlement is a necessary for a female infant, so that she can enter into the contract of retainer to a solicitor to act for her in the negociation and preparation of it.

Costs as affected by the Married Women's Property Act, 1870. A question of considerable nicety has arisen, viz., whether a man marrying since the Married Women's Property Act, 1870, 33 & 34 Vict. c. 93, came into operation escapes this liability; by the 12th section of the Act it is enacted, that "A husband shall not, by reason of any marriage which shall take place after this Act has come into operation, be liable for the debts of his wife contracted before marriage, but the wife shall be liable to be sued for, and any property belonging to her for her separate use shall be liable to satisfy such debts as if she had continued unmarried."

The author, with some hesitation, advances the opinion that the Act has not altered the incidence of the liability; and that whether the instructions to the solicitor are given by the lady herself, or by some person acting *in loco parentis* for her, she, and after her marriage her separate estate, is liable to the solicitor; and that while her husband remains liable to indemnify her or her estate, he is also directly liable to her solicitor. Assuming that the author's opinion is incorrect, and that the Act has made some change in the nature of the husband's liability, it is probable that the change in the law would not cause any change in the existing practice; and, having regard to the fact that, if the settlement be in the usual form, and the wife's separate estate is subject to a restraint on anticipation, the only funds out of which she could pay her solicitor would be the income from time to time actually paid to her, it is probable that the Courts would in some way or another fix the liability of paying him on the husband.

It might be advisable, till the question is settled one way or the other, to insert more frequently the clause alluded to at the top of the last page.

# CHAPTER XII.

## WILLS.

Difficulty in framing a will.

THE preparation of an intricate will is perhaps the most difficult task ever performed by a draftsman. A will does not take effect from its execution, but from the death of the testator, and accordingly the draftsman has to consider not only the circumstances of the testator at the time when the will is prepared, but also what they may possibly be at the time of his death. It follows that nothing but experience and a well cultivated imagination will enable even the accomplished lawyer to settle an intricate will in a satisfactory manner.

Folly of testators who make their own wills.

In spite of this, many testators insist on making their own wills. A man ignorant of law would be considered, and perhaps would acknowledge himself to be, a madman, if he were to purchase a house and attempt to prepare the conveyance himself; and yet this task is easy compared to that of preparing a will which would properly provide for his wife and children,—a task which he would undertake without hesitation. It is very difficult to find words sufficiently strong to express one's sense of the folly and selfishness of a testator who prepares his own will; I say *folly*, because of the very strong probability, amounting to a certainty, that he will fail in expressing his intentions correctly, and *selfishness*, because for the sake of saving himself the costs of having his will properly prepared, he runs the risk of entailing on his family the expenses of legal proceedings for the purpose of putting some meaning on his words,—proceedings which often give rise to irreconcileable family quarrels.

A testator is generally anxious to make a just will, but ignorant of the schemes usually adopted for the disposal of property. The advice to be given to him should be founded upon the principle that he should endeavour to make a perfectly just will, one on which he can look with satisfaction on his death-bed, that all family quarrels should be disregarded, and that he should not act under the influence of caprice. The testator should be advised to make a list of his property, stating its probable value. He should be asked if he is in the habit of saving or of living up to his income, as in the former case his residuary legatee may be benefited to a much larger extent than he intends; his marriage settlement, if any, should be inspected; where he states himself to be the owner of land, it should be ascertained whether this is really the case, or whether he is only tenant for life; the circumstances of his family, by which I mean not only the number, but also the position of the children or other issue should be inquired into. (See a detailed list of questions, 2 Jarman on

**Suggestions to a solicitor taking instructions for a will.**

Wills, Appendix.) A testator should be discouraged from making an intricate will; it is sufficient if he makes a will that is proper under the existing circumstances of his family; it is unnecessary, as in the case of a settlement which cannot be altered, to provide against every possible contingency, for if circumstances change a new will may be made. A testator whose circumstances warrant his taking much trouble in the disposal of his property should be advised to reconsider his will with respect to the altered circumstances of his family, after the lapse of every few years, and with respect to the amount of the gifts contained in it, in case of a loss or accession of fortune.

Clauses that should not be inserted.

Before passing to the consideration of the usual clauses of a will, I will point out some clauses that ought not to be inserted. In old wills we often find a long statement of the testator's opinion on religious subjects, sometimes even going to the extent of making a bequest of his soul to the Almighty; the practice has now become excessively rare, and is of course never adopted where the will is prepared under professional advice.

Statement as to religious belief.

Gift of a shilling to the heir.

There is a popular belief that if a testator disinherits his heir-at-law he is bound to leave him a shilling, hence the phrase "to cut off an heir with a shilling." This is one of the many instances where the old Roman law has been handed down by tradition. According to that law, as modified by Justinian (Inst. Lib. ii. Tit. xviii. *De Inofficioso Testamento*), a will which was at variance with the dictates of natural affection was called "inofficious," and accordingly if the heir being within a certain degree was entirely disinherited, he could bring the action "*de inofficioso testamento*" for the purpose of setting aside the will; but the smallest gift to the heir would prevent him from bringing the action. I need not point out that as there is no action analogous to that "*de inofficioso testamento*" in our law it is unnecessary to mention the heir when it is intended to disinherit him, and as the gift of a shilling would appear an insult, it ought never to be inserted; for the like reason it appears to be inadvisable to state the reasons which have caused the testator to leave his property away from the heir; unless indeed the reason for doing so is that the heir is already, in the testator's opinion, sufficiently provided for.

**Directions as to funeral.** A testator should be discouraged from expressing any wishes as to his funeral *in his will*, as it often happens that from a feeling of delicacy the family neglect to open the will till after the funeral. The testator had better state his wishes in a letter addressed to his executors, with a direction that it is to be opened immediately after his death, unless indeed he is satisfied with making a verbal statement of his wishes to one of his relations.

**Funeral expenses.** It appears that the executors, who cannot be certain at the time of the funeral how the testator's estate will turn out, will be allowed reasonable expenses according to the testator's condition in life out of the assets, even as against creditors: and that where they do not either expressly or implicitly give orders for the funeral they will be liable in their representative character for such expenses; but that where they give orders for the funeral, or adopt the acts of another person who gives such orders, they will be liable personally to the undertaker, with the right of recouping themselves their reasonable expenses out of the assets. It follows, that, where there are any doubts as to the sufficiency of assets, the executors should be careful not to consent to an order for an expensive funeral being given, even with the consent of the residuary legatees, for as in case of deficiency of assets they will only be allowed their reasonable expenses as against the creditors, they will on that being the case have to pay the rest of the expenses out of their own pockets. (Williams on Executors, part iii., b. ii., c. i., s. 1, and part iv., b. ii., c. ii., s. 1.)

Precatory trust.

Occasionally the testator, in giving a life interest to his widow, expresses a wish that she will provide for or educate the children: as a general rule, he wishes to impose only a *moral*, not a *legal*, obligation on her. The Courts, however, lean to the construction which renders the expression of the testator's wishes imperative, and as creating a trust, which is called a *precatory* trust. (See Hawkins, Const. of Wills, p. 158.) It is of importance, therefore, to ascertain whether the testator really means to make the provision for his widow subject to a trust in favour of the children, or whether, as usually happens, he does not wish to do so. In the latter case, care should be taken to add a few words showing that no legal obligation is intended to be imposed on her. It is worth while noticing that if the widow's life interest be made subject to a trust for the maintenance of the children, and the fund be divisible, subject to the life interest and the trust for maintenance, among the children attaining twenty-one, &c., in the usual manner, the effect may be to prevent the widow and the adult children entitled in remainder from making a title to the shares of the latter. (*Berry* v. *Briant,* 2 Drew. & Sm. 1.)

It is obvious that the device of giving a legacy imposing a moral but not a legal obligation on the legatee to apply it in some particular manner may be used for various purposes. A provision can be made in this manner for an improvident child, or land can be applied for charitable purposes. In all of these cases it appears advisable not to state the real intention of the testator in the will, but to leave with the will a letter (not attested) addressed to the legatee stating the wishes of the testator. The greatest care must be taken not to inform the legatee during the testator's lifetime of his real intentions, as if the legatee be informed, a trust will be created contrary to the intentions of the parties, and that even where the result would be to make the testator's intentions fail altogether; as for instance, if land is given in trust for a charity, the result is that the devisee holds the land in trust for the testator's heir-at-law. (*Wallgrave* v. *Tebbs,* 2 K. & J. 313.) Letter left with will.

The following scheme is understood to be generally Letter

providing for superstitious purposes.

adopted to make gifts, which might be void as being gifts for superstitious uses or as offending against the Statute of Mortmain, for the purposes of the religion of one of the principal denominations in this country. The testator devises or bequeaths the property to two or three of the clergy of his own denomination, selecting respectable people whom he does not know personally, and he carefully abstains from communicating his intentions to them; he leaves with his will a letter addressed to them stating what he wishes to have done with the gift, and also a letter addressed to their ecclesiastical superior informing him of the circumstance. So that it is impossible on the one hand for them to suppress the testator's wishes and retain the gift for their own use without their conduct becoming known to the superior, and on the other hand for any one to establish that a trust is created which might be invalid as offending against the law.

Although it would be impossible to give any detailed analysis of a will that would be of any use to the reader, I subjoin an analysis that will indicate the general arrangement.

1. Commencement.
2. Specific legacies.
   (α.) Absolute.
   (β.) Settled.
3. General legacies.
   (α.) Absolute.
   (β.) Settled.

4. Specific devises.
    (α.) In fee simple.
    (β.) In strict settlement.
5. Residuary gift.
6. Trustee clauses.
7. Appointment of executors.
8. Testimonium.

A will generally commences with a description of the testator, and it should be remembered that if he has lived in different places in different parts of his life, so that it is probable that he is described in documents relating to his property by various descriptions, it is convenient to mention them all; and if, as often happens in London, the name of the street or the number of the house in which he lives has been altered, it is convenient to refer to the alteration. Example: "I, A. B., formerly of ——, then of ——, but now of No. 10, John Street, which was formerly known as No. 20, James Street, in the parish of ——, in the county of ——," the clause proceeds "do hereby revoke all wills, codicils, and testamentary dispositions heretofore made by me, and declare this to be my last will and testament." Commencement.

It is proper always to insert a clause of revocation, for cases have occurred where a document entitled "a last will and testament" has been admitted to probate *conjointly* with a former will, a result generally not in accordance with the testator's wishes. The clause of revocation is occasionally placed at the end of the will, which may in this case begin "This is the will of ——." Revocation of prior will.

"Will," "devise," "testament," "bequeath."

Strictly speaking, the words "will" and "devise" refer to real estate, "testament" and "bequeath" to personalty; and although in practice the word "will" is used for "testament," the skilful draftsman always employs the words "devise" and "bequeath" correctly.

Specific legacy.

The legacies generally follow the commencement of the will, specific preceding the general legacies: a specific legacy is a gift of a specified part of the testator's estate, as "the watch that I usually wear," "my dog called Jack," "the sum of £10,000 consols standing in my name on the day of the date of my will;" while a general legacy does not amount to a gift of a particular thing—thus, a legacy of £100, a diamond ring, a horse, are general legacies. The distinction between them is of importance, for, on the one hand, a specific legacy fails if the subject of it does not belong to the testator at the time of his death; on the other hand, it does not abate with the general legacies on a deficiency of assets. A general legacy must be purchased by the executors, if necessary; but on a deficiency of assets is liable to fail.

General legacy.

Demonstrative legacy.

A demonstrative legacy is a general legacy, charged on a particular fund; as a gift of so much money, "to be raised by the sale of my stock." It is a general legacy in so much that the legatee is entitled to have it raised, even if the fund out of which it is to be raised should fail; on the other hand, it is so far specific that it is not liable to abate with general legacies on a deficiency of assets, while the particular fund exists out of which it is directed to be paid.

Where the testator is married, it is convenient for him to bequeath his household stores and goods, furniture, books, plate, &c., to his wife; or, if he be unmarried, but keeps house with other members of his family, to them. Almost every conceivable form of words has been used for this purpose, and the decisions on the meaning of the words employed are numerous. Where brevity is an object, the better course appears to be, not to attempt to enumerate the various classes of objects, but to give "all the chattels in or about" the house "at the time of my death, other than money or securities for money." **Household goods.**

If the testator is likely to have a considerable stock of wine, or of other consumable articles, they may form the subject of a separate gift. A specific gift for life of consumable articles vests them absolutely in the first tenant for life; but if they form part of a residuary gift, they must be sold in due course of administration. **Consumable stores.**

Sometimes the furniture, &c., in a house is bequeathed to the testator's widow for life, and is directed either to be divided among the children, or to go to some particular child at her death. In this case the questions occur—*first*, is an inventory to be taken or not; and, *second*, is the tenant for life to keep the furniture in repair. **Settled furniture.**

In the absence of any directions on the subject, it appears to be the duty of the executors to require an inventory to be made, as otherwise there is a risk of some confusion occurring, at the death of the tenant for life, between the settled chattels and her own property; perhaps it is the better course in ordinary cases to direct in the will itself that this should be done.

If, owing to the property being small, or for any other reason, the testator considers it unnecessary to require an inventory, the will should state so explicitly. Generally, directions should be given for insurance by the tenant for life, and possibly for repairs; but when this is the case, the executors should be expressly exonerated from seeing that the insurances are kept up and the repairs made. It is convenient, where power is given to let a house containing settled furniture, which on the death of the tenant for life may go to different persons, to give power to let the house and furniture together at a gross rent (*ante*, p. 239), with power for the trustees, if necessary, to apportion the rent as between the owners of the house and the furniture.

Personalty to accompany freeholds in strict settlement.

Leaseholds.

Occasionally it is desired to cause personalty, such as leaseholds, or personal chattels such as plate, pictures, &c., to accompany freeholds in strict settlement. The method of doing this is to vest them, in the case of leaseholds, in trustees upon trusts corresponding to the uses of the freeholds, so far as the rules of Law and Equity will permit; the trusts being similar to those described (*ante*, p. 355).

Heirlooms.

Personal chattels settled so as to accompany freeholds in strict settlement are sometimes, though incorrectly, called heirlooms. Heirlooms, in the strict sense of the word, are extremely rare. They are such goods and personal chattels as by custom pass to the heir instead of the executor. I am unable to give any instance of an heirloom, except, perhaps, the ancient jewels of the Crown. It appears, however, that monuments, &c., &c., set up in memory of the deceased in the church or churchyard, his Garter (and possibly all his insignia), belong to his heir in the nature of heirlooms. (Williams on Executors, pt. ii. bk. ii. ch. ii. s. iii.)

Where a testator gives instructions that certain chattels are to be made heirlooms, he means that they are to be enjoyed by the same persons as are entitled to certain property in strict settlement, either under his will or otherwise; or by the person who for the time being shall be the holder of an hereditary title.

The difficulty in carrying the testator's wishes into effect, arises from the rule that generally those words which confer an estate tail in realty, give an absolute interest in personalty. So that if the chattels were bequeathed to the trustees upon such trusts for the persons taking the land under the settlement as should most nearly agree with the estates that they took in the land, the first tenant in tail (whose estate is indefeasible) coming into *esse*—*i.e.*, in the common case of settlement on A. for life, with remainder to his first and other sons successively in tail, with remainder to B. for life, remainder to his first and other sons successively in tail, the first son of A., not of B., who is born, would become absolutely entitled to the chattels, and on his death under age they would pass to his administrator. To prevent this, a declaration is inserted that they shall not vest absolutely in any tenant in tail by purchase, but on his death shall devolve as if they had been freeholds. The words "by purchase" are inserted to avoid offending against the rule as to perpetuities. It will be observed that on the death of A.'s eldest son under age, the chattels either pass to his issue in tail, if any, or to the next remainderman in tail, if there be no such issue. In the former case they vest absolutely in the issue. (See the notes to *Leventhorpe* v. *Ashbie* and *Wyld's Case* in Tudor's Leading Cases.)

Business. Where the testator is in trade, it will be proper to give special directions as to his business. It must be remembered, *first*, that executors who carry on the testator's trade without express authority given by the will commit a breach of trust (*Kirkman* v. *Booth*, 11 Beav. 273); and, *second*, that executors who carry on the testator's trade, either with or without such authority, cannot escape personal liability towards the persons with whom they deal (*Lucas* v. *Williams* (No. 1), 4 De G. F. & J. 436, and *Lucas* v. *Williams* (No. 2), 4 De G. F. &. J. 439); and for this reason it is desirable when the testator's trade is bequeathed to any person for his own benefit to make him the executor so far as regards the trade: or, if there be any doubt as to whether the residue of the testator's property will suffice to satisfy his debts other than trade debts, to appoint the legatee executor jointly with the general executors for the purposes of the trade only. Bearing in mind that one executor alone can give receipts for debts due to the testator, the legatee of the trade can

Special executor.

practically act (if the second plan be adopted), without any interference from the general executors; and, on the other hand, they can interfere if it becomes necessary to do so owing to the deficiency of the testator's general assets. If it is intended to settle the testator's business, this must be done by bequeathing it to trustees on trust to carry it on. It is hardly necessary to point out the great difficulty that there is in finding trustees willing to undertake such an onerous trust.

Partnership.

Where the testator is in partnership, it is proper to authorize the executors to make arrangements with the continuing partners as to the method of winding up the business; or, if the articles authorize the testator to nominate a successor, and he desires to nominate trustees to succeed him, he should give them full power to act (within the limits provided by the Articles of Partnership) for the benefit of his estate.

Sometimes the testator's business or share in a partnership is bequeathed charged with an annuity or other provision for his widow.

Annuity.

An "annuity" is a "legacy," so that a direction to pay legacies out of any particular fund charges the annuities on that fund also, unless the contrary intention appears.

Where the testator wishes to make the bequest of an annuity, he should provide from what fund it is to be payable, and whether it is to be charged on the corpus or on the income only. If the annuity be charged on land, it may be limited as a rent-charge, and secured by means of powers of distress and entry, and by a term of years; or it may be secured by the term of years only, by either of which means it is secured on the corpus of the property. If the annuity is to be secured on personalty, either of the following methods may be adopted: the annuity may be charged on the income of the whole residuary estate, with power to the trustees, if part of the residuary estate is wanted for division, to appropriate such part as they may think fit to answer the annuity; or the trustees may be directed to appropriate at once a sufficient sum to meet the annuity, with power to apply the income of any part of the residuary estate to answer the annuity till appropriation. If the annuity be large compared with the probable income of the residuary estate, it may be advisable to charge it on the corpus; and, at all events, it should be charged on the corpus of any special fund set aside to meet it. It will rarely be advisable to authorize the trustees to purchase a government annuity for the annuitant; but in cases where the annuity is small this may be a convenient course. It must, however, be borne in mind that in the latter case if instead of *authorizing* the testator *directs* the trustees to purchase the annuity, the annuitant has the option of receiving in lieu of his annuity the sum which would be required for the purchase. It will be remarked, that when the annuity is payable out of the whole or an appropriated part of the residuary estate, it necessarily defers the final distribution till the death of the annuitant.

The time at which the annuity is to begin, and

the date of the first payment, should be mentioned; in the absence of any special directions, the annuity is held to commence from the testator's death, except possibly where it is payable out of residue; but the first payment, even if the annuity be directed to be paid quarterly, will not, in the absence of a direction to the contrary, be actually payable till the expiration of a year from the testator's death, at which time the whole of the payments accruing during the first year will have to be made. (*Storer* v. *Prestage*, 3 Madd. 167. See 4 Dav. Prec. 92 n.)

Generally speaking, a gift of an annuity is construed to mean an annuity for the life of the legatee, but as the rule is subject to numerous exceptions (Hawkins, Const. of Wills, 125), it is better to state so distinctly.

Provision is often made for a testator's widow or unmarried daughters by way of annuity to determine on marriage, or in the case of the daughters on their marrying under a certain age without their guardian's consent: it is necessary, therefore, to consider the doctrine of conditions in restraint of marriage.

Before we do so, let us consider the difference between conditions precedent and conditions subsequent (*Egerton* v. *Earl Brownlow*, 4 H. L. C. 1); a condition precedent is one which must happen before the vesting of an interest, as if I give £100 to A. if he comes to London: the condition of coming to London must be performed by A. before he becomes entitled to the £100, and on its performance he becomes entitled to the gift; on the other hand, a

Conditions.

condition subsequent is one which divests an interest already in existence; thus, suppose I give an annuity to A., and declare that it shall cease if he comes to London, here, if he performs the condition, *i. e.*, if he comes to London, the annuity ceases. A good example of a condition subsequent is afforded by the proviso for re-entry in a lease: in that case, if the condition is performed by the lessee committing a breach of covenant, his estate is divested, for the term ceases.

A condition may be subsequent as to one interest and precedent as to another. Thus an annuity may be payable to A. B. for life, subject to the condition that if he does some particular thing, changes his religion for instance, it shall be payable during the rest of his life to C. D. Here the condition is subsequent to, or divests, A. B.'s interest; it is precedent to or must happen before C. D.'s interest vests.

Conditions in restraint of marriage.

There is an important difference with respect to conditions in restraint of marriage according as the subject matter of the gift is realty or personalty; in the former case the rules of common law, and in the latter case the rules of civil law, apply.

Where the subject matter of the gift is land.

In cases where the common law applies, *i. e.*, where the subject matter of the gift is land or a charge on land, the rules are the following:—*First*, a limitation or gift until marriage is good and is determined by the marriage; *second*, a general condition, whether precedent or subsequent, in restraint of marriage, is bad as opposed to public policy; a rule subject to the exception that a general condition subsequent restraining a widow from marrying again is good, (*Newton* v. *Marsden*, 2 J. & H. 356); *third*, where the gift is subject to a condition precedent of marriage with consent, the condition must be performed to entitle the devisee to the estate; *fourth*, where the gift is subject to be divested by a condition subsequent on marriage without consent, a breach of the condition will divest the estate; *fifth*, a condition imposing a particular restraint on marriage, by which is meant a condition not to marry under a certain age, or to marry or not to marry a particular person, or even a person of certain particular classes, is good, whether the condition is precedent or subsequent.

**Where the subject matter of the gift is personalty.**

In cases where the rules of the civil law apply, *i. e.*, in cases where the gift is personal property, the rules are the following:—*First*, a gift until marriage is good and determined by the marriage; *second*, a general condition, whether precedent or subsequent, in restraint of marriage is void, subject to the exception that a testator can annex such a condition to a gift to his own widow, though *apparently* not to the widow of any other person; *third*, a condition precedent requiring marriage with consent is satisfied by marriage without consent; *fourth*, a condition subsequent directed against marriage without consent is considered to be *in terrorem* only, and has no effect; *fifth*, the third and fourth rules are subject to the exception following, in each of which cases the condition, whether precedent or subsequent, must be followed strictly; (*a*), if there be a gift over on marriage without consent; (β), where the marriage with consent is one of several alternative conditions, as where the bequest was subject to the condition precedent of attaining a particular age unmarried, or marrying under that age with consent; (γ), where the condition is directed against marriage under a certain reasonable age without consent; (δ), where the legatee takes another legacy on breach of the condition; *sixth*, a condition imposing a particular restraint on marriage is good. (Hayes and Jarman's Concise Forms of Wills, by Eastwood, 381; *Scott* v. *Tyler*, 2 Tudor, Leading Cases in Equity.)

Gifts for charitable purposes.

Where gifts are made for charitable purposes, care should be taken, having regard to the Mortmain Act, to direct that they should be paid out of "such part of my personal estate as may by law be bequeathed for charitable purposes," and having regard to the fact that the debts and the expenses of administration have to be paid rateably out of the pure personalty and mixed personalty, it is proper to add "and preferably to any other payment thereout." (*Beaumont* v. *Oliviera*, L. R. 4 Ch. Ap. 312.)

Real estate.

The owner of a landed estate may adopt three different schemes of disposition: he may give it absolutely to the devisee, he may put it into strict settlement, or he may settle it on trusts resembling those in a settlement of personalty.

Devise in fee.

In the *first* case, several different plans may be adopted for vesting the legal estate in fee simple in the devisee; the testator may make (α) a devise "to A. B. and his heirs," (β), a devise "to C. D. and his heirs to the use of (or in trust for) A. B. and his heirs," ($\gamma$), a devise "to the use of A. B. and his heirs," and in either case the words of limitation may (7 Will. 4 & 1 Vict. c. 26, s. 28), though they should not, be omitted. If it is really intended that A. B. should take an equitable estate only, the devise may be "to E. F. and his heirs, to the use of C. D. and his heirs, in trust for A. B. and his heirs," or, "to the use of C. D. and his heirs in trust for A. B. and his heirs." The best plan in either case is to devise directly "to the use of" the person intended to take the legal estate.

The rule that a devise "to C. D. and his heirs to the use of (or in trust for) A. B. and his heirs," vests the legal estate in A. B., is subject to the exception, that the legal estate is vested in C. D. if any trust or duty is imposed on him the performance of which requires that it should be vested in him. For example, (Hawkins, Const. of Wills, p. 140) a devise to trustees on trust *to pay the rents and profits* to A., vests the legal estate in the trustees, because they must receive before they can pay, while a devise to trustees upon trust *to permit A. to take the rents and profits*, vests the legal estate in A., as no trust or duty is imposed on the trustees. As a further illustration, consider a devise to trustees upon trust *to permit B.* (a married woman) *to receive the rents and profits for her sole and separate use;* here it is necessary, for the purpose of carrying out the testator's intention, that of protecting the woman, that the trustees should take the legal estate, and accordingly they do so.

Devise in strict settlement.

In the *second* case, the devise in strict settlement follows very closely the form of a marriage settlement, with the following exceptions: (*a*), as it is unnecessary to raise a seisin on which the uses are declared, the devise had better be made directly to the uses; (*β*), the usual form of a gift in tail is "to the use of A. B. in tail," instead of "to the use of A. B. and the heirs of his body;" (*γ*), the successive limitations in tail are generally introduced by the words "with remainder," instead of the words "in default of such issue;" (*δ*), bearing in mind that the will speaks from the death of the testator, and that therefore time has to be calculated from that moment with respect to the rules against perpetuities, a proviso may be inserted cutting down the estate tail given to any person born in the testator's lifetime to an estate for life, with remainder to his children successively in tail.

Debts.

In cases where a devise is made in strict settlement, and any doubt exists as to whether the testator's personal estate will be ample to satisfy his funeral and testamentary expenses, debts and legacies, it is a convenient course to limit a term in his realty to the use of trustees in trust to raise such sum of money in aid of the personal estate as may be required for such purposes.

Executory and executed trusts.

Sometimes a testator directs land to be purchased, and to be settled for the benefit of certain persons, or of a certain class of persons. The question, which is sometimes of great nicety, then arises, has he left it to the trustees to discover from his general expressions what uses and trusts are to be inserted in the settlement, or has he definitely stated such uses and trusts? Has he been, as it is sometimes called, his own conveyancer; to use technical language, are the trusts *executory* or *executed?* The question, which is sometimes of considerable nicety, is discussed in the notes to *Lord Glenorchy* v. *Bosville*, 1 White and Tudor's Leading Cases in Equity. As to the form of the settlement, see Hayes and Jarman's Concise Forms of Wills, by Eastwood, p. 388; *Stanley* v. *Coulthurst*, L. R. 10 Eq. Ca. 259; *Thompson* v. *Fisher*, L. R. 10 Eq. Ca. 207, and the cases cited in the authorities referred to. Generally speaking it is more convenient to frame the will so that the trusts are executed, but occasionally, when it has to be prepared in a hurry, this cannot be done; in the latter case the order of the limitations should be stated with at least the same degree of accuracy that they would be in carefully framed instructions for a will; any powers for the benefit of any particular person or class of persons, such as powers to jointure or to raise portions, must be specifically mentioned, while it is only necessary to mention generally those powers which are to be inserted for the management of the estate, such as powers of leasing and sale.

In the *third* case, where the land is to be settled upon trusts resembling those of a settlement of personalty, it should be devised to trustees upon trusts for sale, and the trusts should be declared of the proceeds. This plan should always be adopted where the scheme of the will is for the division of

Land to be divided.

any particular landed estate between the testator's children (*ante*, p. 272).

Land in foreign country.

The practitioner must not attempt to make a devise of land situated in a country where the law is different from the law of England: for the questions whether such land can pass by a will, and if so what must be the manner of executing the will, and what construction will be put on any technical words employed in the will, are regulated by the law of the country where the land is situated. If, therefore, the testator has such land, the proper course is for him to dispose of it by a separate instrument in conformity with the law of the place where it is situated.

Residue.

A gift of residue, whether the word "residue" be used or not, is construed so as to pass all the testator's property not otherwise effectually disposed of. It follows that lapsed and void legacies pass under the residuary bequest; and (in wills made since the passing of the Wills' Act) lapsed and void devises pass by the residuary devise. The result is, that, even where a testator believes that the gifts in his will have so far exhausted his estate as to leave but little to fall into the residue, it may happen, owing to the death of some of the objects of his bounty, or owing to his saving money, that the residuary gift may eventually become of importance: for this reason it requires some consideration as to whom the gift of residue should be made. In the ordinary case of the executors being the persons to whom the testator leaves the bulk of his fortune, it is convenient to make them the residuary legatees, as doing so may save trouble in making up the accounts of the testator's estate.

As a general rule, if any devisee or legatee dies in the lifetime of the testator, the gift to him lapses and fall into the residue. This rule is subject to the following exceptions :— **Lapse.**

*First.* Where any person to whom any real estate is devised for an estate tail, or an estate in quasi tail, dies in the lifetime of the testator, leaving issue who would be inheritable under such entail, and any such issue is living at the death of the testator, the devise does not lapse, but takes effect as if the death of such person happened immediately after the death of the testator (7 Will. 4 and 1 Vic. c. 26, s. 37). **Devise in tail.**

*Second.* A gift to one of the testator's issue is sometimes prevented from lapsing by 7 Will. 4 and 1 Vic. c. 26, s. 33, which enacts, that "Where any person being a child or other issue of the testator, to whom any real or personal estate shall be devised or bequeathed for any estate or interest not determinable at or before the death of such person, shall die in the lifetime of the testator leaving issue, and any such issue of such person shall be living at the time of the death of the testator, such devise or bequest shall not lapse, but shall take effect as if the death of such person had happened immediately after the death of the testator, unless a contrary intention shall appear by the will." **Gift to testator's issue.**

The effect of this section is not to substitute the issue of the deceased legatee or devisee for him, but to render the property left to him *his own* property, so that it passes by his will, or, if he die intestate as to it, goes to his heir or administrator, as the case may be, being in either case liable to his debts in due course of administration.

But the rule does not apply where the gift is to a class, as to "such of my children as attain twenty-one," and a member of the class dies, for in that case there is no lapse, as no child dying before the testator is included in the class. For example, suppose a testator having a son John and other children bequeaths £10,000 to John and £20,000 to be divided between his, the testator's, children. John dies in the testator's lifetime, leaving issue, and some of his issue survive the testator. The legacy of £10,000, which would have lapsed had John not come under the saving contained in the section, passes under John's will, or to his administrator, as the case may be. As to the £20,000 there is no lapse, the will speaks from the testator's death, at which time John was not one of his children, so that no part of it is given to John, or passes by his will.

"A very nice point (says Romilly, M. R., *Re Mason's Will*, 34 Beav. 497) may arise on the statute, as to whether the will of a legatee who predeceases his father, the testator, is to be construed according to the event, or whether it is to be construed as if the legatee had survived the testator;

or, in other words, as if the testator had predeceased the legatee."

Occasionally, where it is desired to prevent the provision made for a child coming under the operation of the Act, his issue is substituted for him in the event of his death in the testator's lifetime: the class of issue who are to take may conveniently be limited to those alive at the testator's death.

*Third.* Where the subject of the gift which lapses is a share of residue it does not fall into residue, but remains undisposed of. This peculiarity of a lapsed share of residue not falling into residue may be exemplified by the case where the "residue" of residue is given. Thus, to take the case supposed by Mr. Hawkins [Constr. of Wills, p. 43], "If the testator gives £10,000 out of the residue of his personal estate to A., and the *residue* to B., and the bequest to A. fails, the gift to B. will not in general carry the £10,000 bequeathed to A., which will consequently be undisposed of." This is not generally intended, and some words should be introduced to restore it to the residue, properly so called, on A.'s death in the testator's lifetime. Share of residue.

The wishes of testators and the circumstances of their families are so different, that it is extremely difficult to lay down any rule as to what is the most usual method of making a provision for a testator's wife and family: perhaps in cases where the property is of a moderate amount and children are young, the best plan is to vest the residue in trustees upon trust Provisions for testator's family.

to pay the income to the testator's widow for life, and after her death to divide the capital among such of the testator's issue as she shall appoint, and in default of appointment, upon trust for such of the testator's children as, being sons, shall attain twenty-one, or being daughters shall attain twenty-one, or marry under that age, or marry *with the consent of their guardian* under that age.

In this scheme no provision is made for the children during the widow's lifetime; so long as she remains unmarried she may, in most cases, be safely trusted to provide for them, but there exists the possible risk of her contracting a second marriage without making such settlements as will secure to her the enjoyment of her life interest. Several plans may be adopted to guard against this. Her life income may be made determinable on a second marriage, in which case it would be proper to give her an annuity, to commence on her remarriage; or an express power of maintenance and education may be given to the trustees, to arise on her remarriage, and to override her life estate.

If this scheme be adopted, and any one of the children attains a vested interest, no lapse will take place; on the other hand, if a son marries under twenty-one, or a daughter marries under twenty-one without consent in cases where consent is required, and either son or daughter dies under twenty-one leaving issue, such issue is unprovided for—a result which is probably intended, but which can be remedied if the widow think fit by an exercise of the power of appointment. It is proper also to make some disposition of the residue in case no child attains a vested interest, for if this is not done, the residue will in that event be undisposed of, and will pass to the widow and children, according to the statutes of distribution; and on the death of any child its distributive share will pass to the widow, if she be alive; so that in the result, if the widow should survive all the children, she will become entitled to the whole property.

When at the time of the testator's death most of the children are adults, sometimes the foregoing scheme is adopted, with the variation of giving to each child an immediate legacy, or an annuity during its mother's life: and having regard to the possibility of a child marrying and dying in the testator's lifetime leaving issue, a clause may be added substituting such issue for their parent, so that they will take the share which their parent would have taken if he had survived the testator. In doing so, if the vesting of the shares of the child's issue is to depend on their attaining twenty-one, it must be distinctly specified that the issue who are to take must be "in existence at the testator's death," otherwise the rule against perpetuities will be offended against. Perhaps the better course in most cases is to substitute the "children," instead of the "issue," of any child dying in the testator's lifetime, for their parent.

It would, perhaps, be convenient in the case under

consideration, to declare that any sums of money which the testator should in his lifetime advance or covenant to advance to any one of his children on his or her marriage should be taken towards satisfaction of the provision to be made for such child.

Perhaps, in the case that we are discussing, that of the testator having adult children, the best way of providing for the widow is to give an annuity, and the use of a house and furniture, to her for life; and to render such part of the testator's fortune as is not required for such purposes immediately divisible among the children.

Settled legacies.

Sometimes, where the scheme of the will is to provide for the daughters, either by means of legacies or by shares of residue, their legacies or shares are settled: in this case, the trusts declared concerning each legacy or share may follow closely the usual trusts in a settlement of personal property, with the exceptions—*first*, that, if the daughter be unmarried at the date of the will, it is more convenient to give her a power (to be exercised while not under coverture by deed, and while under coverture by will) to appoint a life interest to any husband who may survive her, than to give him a life interest in the will itself; *second*, that the trusts for the daughter's children should not be confined to those by any particular husband; and, *third*, a power may be given to the trustees, to be exercised with the consent of the daughter in contemplation of her marriage, by deed, to revoke the trusts declared concerning her share, and to make a different declaration of trusts for the benefit of herself, her intended husband, and her issue; the object of the power being to enable a bargain to be made for a settlement by the husband on the occasion of her marriage.

Testator's marriage invalid.

Occasionally doubts may exist whether the testator's marriage is valid or not, or whether some or all of his children are illegitimate; it is extremely painful to the feelings of the family that any statement of the doubts should appear on the will, which, on its admission to probate, will become a public document; the plan adopted in this case in making gifts to the widow or children is to describe the person who is the object of the testator's bounty so clearly that (even if it should be proved that the super-added description of "wife," "son," "child," &c., should be incorrect) there can be no doubt who is meant.

Gift to woman to whom the testator is not lawfully married.

In the case of the wife, a gift by will to a person with whom the testator has undergone a marriage ceremony, and with whom he has always lived as husband, by the description of "my wife," appears to be a sufficient designation of the person to entitle her to take the gift, even if the marriage be entirely void. (*Re Petts*, 27 Beav. 576; *Pratt* v. *Matthew*, 22 Beav. 328.) On the other hand, if the testator has a real wife alive, so that the words "my wife" would describe her, a description of the person passing as his wife by her Christian name as "my wife Sarah," where his real wife's name was Elizabeth, would be sufficient. (*Dilley* v. *Matthews*, 2 N. R. 60; *Doe* d. *Gains* v. *Rouse*, 5 C. B. 422.)

Gifts to illegitimate children.

The case of gifts to children of doubtful legitimacy, or where, though they are clearly bastards, the testator wishes to conceal the facts, presents very considerable difficulty to the draftsman, owing to the strong leaning that the courts have to construe any such words as "sons," "children," "issue," as meaning *primâ facie* legitimate sons, children, or issue. It follows as a corollary that a gift to the children of a person who at the date of the will has illegitimate children only (a fact well known to the testator) will pass nothing to them, but will be construed to mean his legitimate children which may possibly be born afterwards. It appears impossible to provide in any manner for bastards unborn at the date of the will.

There are a few exceptions to the general rule, which are discussed in Hawkins's Construction of Wills, 80.

It follows that a gift to his "children" by a testator who has illegitimate children only at the date of his will passes nothing to them, as there is always the possibility of his having legitimate children. If, therefore, the testator wishes to provide for an illegitimate child of his own, or of any other person, he must mention the child by name, so as to show clearly whom he means, or he may describe a class as bastard children.

Where some or all of the testator's children are bastards, but it is thought desirable to conceal the real fact, the best course appears to be to mention all the children *nominatim* the first time that they are mentioned as a class: thus, "I give to my children, John, aged eight years, Thomas, aged four years, and Mary, aged one year." In subsequent parts of the will, when mentioning them as a class, it will be sufficient to describe them as "my said children." For the effect of using the word "children" only in the subsequent part of the will, see Hawkins, Constr. of Wills, 84.

Bearing in mind that a gift cannot be made by will to a bastard unborn at the date of the will, it appears proper that a testator whose marriage is invalid should immediately after the birth of each child make a codicil providing for it. There are several methods in which this can be done. If the testator wishes to provide for his bastard children as a class, probably he might declare that in his will the phrase "my children" should mean John, aged eight years, Thomas, aged three years, &c., now residing with me at ——. Then on the birth of another child, Mary, he might declare by codicil that the phrase "my children" in the will should mean John, Thomas, and Mary.

Whenever a gift is made to a bastard under the age of twenty-one years, a gift over should be made on the event of his death under twenty-one, so as to exclude the title of the Crown.

Here follows an analysis of the clauses providing for the testator's widow and young children out of residue:— **Analysis of clauses providing for widow and young children.**

1. Gift of residue to trustees upon trusts for conversion.

2. Direction to pay funeral and testamentary expenses, debts, and legacies, out of proceeds, and to invest the residue with power to vary securities.

3. Direction to pay income to wife during life.

4. After her death to stand possessed of the trust funds upon trust for such of the testator's issue as she shall appoint.

5. Trust in default of appointment for such of the testator's children as being sons attain twenty-one, or being daughters attain that age or marry.

6. Hotchpot, advancement, maintenance, and accumulation clauses.

7. Trusts in default of any child attaining a vested interest.

8. Power to postpone sale and conversion, with directions as to intermediate income.

9. Appointment of guardians.

Frame of gift of residue and trust for conversion.

There are two different manners of framing the gift of residue to the trustees and the trust for conversion; sometimes the gift of realty is separated from that of personalty, and each gift followed by a trust for conversion; but the better, though more unusual, plan is to make a mixed gift of the residuary real and personal estate, followed by the trust for conversion. Where copyholds are to be converted, it is convenient to give the trustees a power of appointment over them, for if this be done, and the trustees can sell before the lord can seize for want of a tenant, the purchaser is entitled to be admitted without any admission of the trustees or of the testator's heir. The power of appointment should be followed by a declaration that it is given to the intent that the trustees shall sell the land.

The trustees are directed, out of the proceeds of the sale and conversion and the testator's ready money at the time of his death, to pay the testator's "funeral and testamentary expenses and debts and the legacies bequeathed by the will or any codicil thereto, and to invest the *residue of the same moneys.*" The student may possibly inquire whether *the residue of the same moneys* is not a "residue of residue." This appears not to be the case, for the property originally given to the trustees is really residue plus the amount required for payment of funeral and testamentary expenses, debts, and legacies, and the true "residue" is not ascertained until they have been paid, or in other words is "the residue of the same moneys." The trusts for investment, the power to vary securities, and the trusts for the wife and issue of the testator follow closely the forms in settlements of personalty (*ante*, chapter XI.), with the exception that the wife's life interest is not, generally speaking, given to her separate use, and therefore require no further discussion; the maintenance and accumulation clauses may, in most cases, be omitted in reliance on the statutory powers.

In case the children provided for are not the testator's own children, it is (in cases where their parent is poor) proper to add to the maintenance clause a provision that the trustees may maintain the children without reference to their father's ability.

Ultimate trusts.

The frame of the ultimate trusts in default of the children taking must depend upon circumstances. If the testator has brothers and sisters, the trust may be for such of them as survive the testator, and the children, living at the testator's death, of such of them as die before the testator, equally *per stirpes*. If some of the testator's children have already or have nearly attained twenty-one, the ultimate trust may, in cases where the property is small, be omitted: for the only case in which it will ever take effect, is the unlikely one of no child attaining a vested interest; and it must be remembered that should all the children die during the testator's lifetime he may probably make a new will.

Guardian.

It appears proper, in most cases, to constitute the widow, during her lifetime, and after her death the trustees for the time being, the guardians of the infant children. Although a father cannot appoint guardians for his illegitimate children, the Court will usually appoint the person named by the reputed father as guardian. (*Peckham* v. *Peckham*, 2 Cox, 46. See Hayes and Jarman, Concise Forms of Wills, p. 239 (n.), 6th edition.)

Conversion.

It is the duty of the trustees, in the absence of directions to the contrary, to sell all personal property to be enjoyed in succession, and to invest the proceeds, as provided for by virtue of 23 & 24 Vict. c. 38, and the General Order of the Court of Chancery of 1st Feb., 1861. This rule will be applied both in favour of and against the tenant for life. Thus, if the property be leaseholds, they must be sold to the prejudice of the tenant for life; while, on the other hand, a reversionary interest producing no income must be sold and the proceeds invested, so as to produce an income for the tenant for life.

For these reasons it is important—where a considerable part of the testator's property consists of leaseholds, or of some other security of a wasting nature, or of reversionary interests—to say distinctly whether they are to be sold or enjoyed in specie.

**Failure of objects of conversion.**

Occasionally, where the testator has directed land to be converted into money, or money to be invested in land, in the event a partial intestacy occurs, and the questions arise—Does the heir at law or next of kin take the property the trusts whereof have failed? and does the person taking it take it in the state in which it happens to be at the time when the failure occurs? Let us suppose, for example, that a testator having real property directs it to be sold, and the proceeds to be held upon trusts for his wife and children, similar to those mentioned at p. 393, but that he omits to declare any ultimate trust should no child attain a vested interest. Here the question would arise, would the land or the proceeds pass to the person who was the testator's heir-at-law at the time of his death, his eldest son, suppose: or would it pass to the persons who would become entitled to it under the Statutes of distribution had it been personalty: *i. e.* to his widow and infant children. All the cases may be tabulated thus, *where the figures have reference to the cases deciding each point*:—

| Nature of Property directed to be converted. | Into what it is to be converted. | To whom the Interest undisposed of goes. | Does he take it as *Personal* or *Real* Property. |
|---|---|---|---|
| Money. | Land. | Next of kin (1). | *Personal* (2). |
| Land. | Money. | Heir (3). | If failure of trusts be total, *real* (4): if failure be partial, *personal* (5). |

(1) *Cogan* v. *Stephens*, 1 Beav. 482.

(2) *Reynolds* v. *Godlee*, Joh. 584.

(3) *Ackroyd* v. *Smithson*, 2 Br. C. C. 503.

(4) *Smith* v. *Claxton*, 4 Madd. 484.

(5) *Jessop* v. *Watson*, 1 My. & K. 665; and *Smith* v. *Claxton*, 4 Madd. 484.

Power of leasing and management.

Where the residue is given on such trusts that no person *sui juris* immediately becomes the owner of it, and part of it consists of real estate, it is proper to insert a power of leasing for twenty-one years, and possibly more extensive powers of leasing and management.

Occasionally, powers are given to the trustees to retain investments held by the testator at his death, although they are not such as are authorized for fresh investments.

The *trustee clauses* consist of—

Trustee clauses.

1. Power to executors to determine the subject matter of specific bequests, to apportion blended trust funds, and settle questions.

2. A receipt clause.
3. A power to appoint new trustees.
4. Clauses for indemnity and reimbursement of the trustees.
5. Devise of trust and mortgage estates.
6. Appointment of executors.
7. Power to executors to arrange and compromise.

All of them, except the 1st, 5th, and 6th, may be omitted in reliance on the statutory powers given by 23 & 24 Vict. c. 145. (See *ante*, p. 316.)

The reason for making a devise of trust and mortgage estates is to avoid the inconvenience that might possibly occur owing to the legal estate in them descending to an infant heir. The propriety of the practice, which was once doubted, appears to be settled.

**Property in different countries.**

Where the testator has personal property situated in different countries, or in England and one of the colonies, it is convenient to appoint different executors, with respect to the property situated in the different places. In such a case, if the property is to be vested in trustees, it is desirable to authorize some trustees to act in respect of the property in England, and others in respect of the property in the colony. Either of the following plans may be adopted—*first*, different sets of trustees may be appointed for the property in the different countries or in England and in the colony; there is a disadvantage in adopting this plan, where part of the property is in one of the colonies, owing to the fact that colonists often leave the colony and return to England; so that frequent appointments of new trustees of the property in the colony may become nccessary; *second*, the trustees for the time being in either place may be authorized to act with respect to the property there as if they were the only trustees, with power to the trustees in either place to give a power of attorney to those in the other place to execute leases, conveyances, &c., in their names, without being responsible for any loss occasioned by any improper exercise of the power.

Codicil. A codicil should never be used for the purpose of making extensive alterations in a will, on account of the very great difficulty in framing the dispositions made by it so as not to be inconsistent with those of the will; but it may be properly employed for such purposes as substituting one person for another as trustee or executor, giving a legacy to a person not taking any benefits under the testator's will, or altering the amount of a legacy given in the will, in which latter case care should be taken to state expressly whether the gift made by the codicil is in addition to, or in substitution for, that made by the will, the rule of construction being that, in the absence of special directions, the legatee is entitled to both gifts (Hawkins, Constr. of Wills, 303). It appears hardly necessary to mention that no draftsman ought ever to attempt to prepare a codicil to a will unless he has the will before him.

# CHAPTER XIII.

## PART I.

### DISCLAIMER.

"THE law is not so absurd as to force a man to take an estate against his will. *Primâ facie*, every estate, whether given by will or otherwise, is supposed to be beneficial to the party to whom it is given. Of that, however, he is the best judge, and if it turn out that the party to whom the gift is made does not consider it beneficial, the law will certainly by some mode or other allow him to renounce or refuse the gift." (*Townson* v. *Tickell*, 3 B. & Al. 36; *Peacock* v. *Eastland*, L. R. 10 Eq. Ca. 20.) In practice the only case of disclaimer is that by a trustee or executor; it will be convenient to consider these cases separately.

The words "disclaim" and "renounce" are used indifferently with reference to property and an office.

A person who has once accepted a trusteeship will not be allowed afterwards to disclaim any of the trust property, for the very fact of his accepting the office indicates his willingness to accept the property, which, when it has once vested in him, can only be taken out of him in the appropriate method. Similarly he cannot afterwards renounce his office merely by refusing to act; his *cestui que trusts* must acquiesce in his throwing down his office, or a new trustee must be appointed in his place, or he must be removed by a court of competent jurisdiction. It follows that the only case in which a trustee can disclaim and renounce, is where he has never from the moment of his appointment had the intention of accepting the office.

Although it appears impossible to force a trustee to execute a disclaimer, the usual course in cases of importance is for him to execute a deed poll, whereby "it is witnessed that he the said A. B., hath renounced and disclaimed, and by these presents doth renounce and disclaim" the trust property and the office of trustee, the past tense being employed in addition to the present, as it expresses the facts correctly.

The disclaimer has no operation at law, it appears to be merely a convenient way of solemnly asserting the intentions of the person disclaiming. Care must be taken not to insert a conveyance by the person disclaiming, for as this would show that he had accepted the trust-estate, it is clear that he could not effectually disclaim it. (*Nicloson* v. *Wordsworth*, 2 Swan. 365.)

The advanced student may enquire how it is possible for the trustees of a strict settlement, who, according to the modern form take no estate in the land, to renounce their office so as to disable themselves from executing the powers of sale, &c., which are powers *simply collateral,* and as such cannot be extinguished by the act of the donee. (Butler, Co. Litt. 342 b). If, however, we look at the intentions of the parties as expressed in the settlement, we find on the construction of the whole settlement that the powers of sale, &c., are to be exercised by the persons who, for the time being, fill the office of trustees; it appears to follow that on the renunciation, *ab initio* of his office, by a person named as trustee, he cannot execute any power annexed to that office.

An executor who has not acted can renounce by a formal proceeding in the Court of Probate; formerly, if there were several executors, and one renounced, and the rest proved, he might afterwards have proved; so that if an executor, who had proved, died, leaving another, who had renounced, surviving, the representation did not belong to the executor of the deceased executor. (*Cottle* v. *Aldrich,* 4 M. & S. 175.) The rule is now changed by the 20 & 21 Vict. c. 77, s. 79, which enacts as follows: "Where any person after the commencement of this Act renounces probate of the will of which he is appointed executor, or one of the executors, the rights of such person in respect of the executorship shall wholly cease, and the representation to the testator and the administration of his effects shall and may without further renunciation, go, devolve, and be committed in the same manner as if such person had not been appointed executor."

Where the same person is appointed executor and trustee of personalty, he cannot renounce the office of trustee and accept that of executor. (*Mucklow* v. *Fuller*, Jac. 198.)

## PART II.

## RELEASES.

IT is the usual practice on the final adjustment of accounts between a trustee or executor, and his *cestui que trusts* for them to execute a release to him under seal. Disputes sometimes arise as to whether the trustee or executor is, strictly speaking, entitled to anything more than a simple receipt for the monies handed over by him. The doctrine is laid down in *King* v. *Mullins*, 1 Drew, 311, by Kindersley, V. C., in the words following:—

" I am of opinion that in the case of a declared trust; where the trust is apparent on the face of a deed; the fund clear; the trust clearly defined; and the trustee is paying either the income or the capital of the fund; if he is paying it in strict accordance with the trusts, he has no right to require a release under seal. It is true that in the common case of executors, when the executorship is being wound up, it is the practice to give executors a release. An executor has a right to be clearly discharged, and not to be left in a position in which he may be exposed to further litigation; therefore he fairly says, unless you give me a discharge on the face of it protecting me, I cannot safely hand over the fund; and therefore it is usual to give a release; but such a claim on the part of a trustee would, in strictness, be improper, if he is paying in accordance with the letter of the trust. In such a case he would have no right to a release."

It appears to follow that in the common case of the trust monies having been resettled, the trustees or executors of the original settlement or will are entitled to a release under seal, from their *cestui que trusts,* though they are entitled only to a mere receipt from the trustees to whom they pay the monies. (*Re Cater's Trusts,* 25 Beav. 366.)

Dealings should be at arm's length.

It is always desirable that the person giving the release, and the trustee, should be advised by different solicitors, and that the dealings between them should be at arm's length. This is of the utmost importance where the trustee stands in such a relation to his *cestui que trust,* that the latter is unlikely to exert himself so as to form an independent judgment as to the propriety of the transactions in respect of which the release is given. (*Rhodes* v. *Bate,* L. R. 1 Ch. App. 252; *Lyon* v. *Home,* L. R. 6 Eq. Ca. 655.) Suppose the trustee to be a father, and the *cestui que trust* to be his son, just come of age, living at home under his father's control, it is not to be supposed that the son would be able to form any independent judgment unless he has the advice of an independent solicitor. Suppose that the trustee and *cestui que trust* stand towards each other in the relationship of solicitor and client, similar reasoning would apply; and, accordingly, in either of these cases, the release would be liable to be set aside by a Court of Equity, on the application of the *cestui que trust,* unless the latter had been advised by a different solicitor.

Form of release.

The release is effected by an indenture between the *cestui que trusts* and the trustee: which (owing to the doctrine that, where the release contains any recitals, the operative words will be construed as having reference only to the matters set forth in the recitals) should contain very full recitals setting forth the title of the parties giving the release, and the facts in respect of which the release is intended to be granted. In cases where the accounts are too long to set forth in the deed, they may be made up in a book, and signed by the parties, while the release contains a recital that the releasing parties have examined and are satisfied with the accounts. If any breaches of trust have been committed, they should be designated as breaches of trust.

Recitals.

Sometimes there is difficulty in determining at what point of time the recitals should commence. If a release be given to the original trustees of a settlement, the recitals will of course begin with the settlement itself, but when new trustees have been appointed, so long after the date of the settlement that many changes have occurred in the *cestui que trusts* and the trust fund, it is not very easy to frame the recitals in a satisfactory manner. The duty of the draftsman is on the one hand not to encumber his deed by long statements of circumstances that occurred before the new trustees were appointed, and with which they are therefore not concerned, and on the other hand to insert such circumstances as are necessary to render his story intelligible.

The witnessing clause runs as follows: "that in pursuance of the said agreement, and in consideration of the premises," the *cestui que trust* "doth hereby release the said trustee, his heirs, executors, administrators, estates and effects from the said" [ ] *or,* "in respect of the said" [ ] "and all actions, suits, accounts, claims, and demands for or in respect of the same" [ ] "or for or in respect of anything in anywise relating to the premises." Operative clauses.

Where there is any doubt as to the title of the *cestui que trust,* the deed also contains a covenant by the *cestui que trust* to keep indemnified the trustee, "his heirs, executors, administrators, estates and effects from all actions, suits, claims, and demands, by X. Y., in respect of," &c.

Sometimes the bulk of the trust funds is handed over by the trustees, who retain such part as has not yet become payable; in this case the generality of the release may be qualified by a proviso that it shall not extend to the funds remaining in their hands.

If anything remains to be done by the trustees, as for instance, to surrender copyholds, a proviso is inserted that the release shall not operate till they have done so.

The release is drawn by the solicitor to the trustee, at the cost of the trust estate, and approved by the solicitor of the *cestui que trust*. There is sometimes a little practical difficulty as to costs, as the trustee may feel unwilling to part with the trust fund until his costs are provided for, and the amount cannot be exactly ascertained till the deed has been executed. Generally the *cestui que trusts* agree to pay the costs, and nothing is said about them in the deed: at other times the amount is estimated as nearly as can be, and is stated in the deed to have been retained by the trustees in respect of their costs.

The trustee should be careful to ascertain, before he hands over the trust funds, that all legacy and succession duties have been paid.

## PART III.

### APPOINTMENTS OF NEW TRUSTEES.

A new trustee may be appointed (*α*) by the Court of Chancery acting under "The Trustee Act, 1850," 13 & 14 Vict. c. 60, or "The Trustee Extension Act, 1852," 15 & 16 Vict. c. 55; (*β*), by a person duly authorised to do so by the instrument creating the trust; (*γ*) if there be no such person, and if the instrument creating the trust was executed after the 28th August, 1860, or being a will or codicil was confirmed or revived by a codicil executed after that date, by the surviving or continuing trustees or trustee for the time being or the acting executors or executor or administrators or administrator of the last surviving and continuing trustee or the last retiring trustee (23 & 24 Vict. c. 145, s. 27.)

The instrument of appointment.

We will confine our attention to the two latter cases. In framing the instrument of appointment which is generally an indenture, although in most cases it is not absolutely necessary that the instrument should be under seal, we must show by appropriate recitals (*a*), either that a power of appointing new trustees exists by virtue of the instrument creating the trust, and who are the present donees of it, or who are the present donees of the statutory power given by 23 & 24 Vict. c. 145, (*β*.) what the property is of which the new trustee is to be appointed, (*γ*) that such circumstances have occurred, such as the death, incapacity, or unwillingness to act of a trustee, as enable the power to be exercised. It is convenient if possible to endorse the instrument of appointment on the instrument creating the trust, so as to obviate the necessity of reciting it. If this be done, it will be unnecessary to recite in any subsequent appointment also effected by indorsement, any of the acts recited in the earlier appointment, for a person reading an instrument indorsed on another is presumed to read not only the latter instrument, but also everything indorsed on it. It is usual, though not absolutely necessary, to recite all the changes of investment that have been made since the trust was created, so as to show that the property which will be transferred to the new and continuing trustees properly represents the original trust funds.

Should be indorsed on the instrument creating the trusts.

Recitals.

Operative clauses.

The operative part of the instrument consists (a) of the clause appointing the new trustee, and sometimes (β) of clauses transferring the trust property. The first of these clauses by which the donee of the power "in exercise of the power for this purpose by the [*within written indenture*] given to" him, *or* "by the joint operation of the [*within written indenture*] and of the act 23 and 24 Vict. c. 145, intituled 'An Act to give trustees, mortgagees, and others certain powers now commonly inserted in settlements, mortgages, and wills, given to him, and of every or any other power in this behalf him enabling, doth hereby appoint A. B. to be a trustee in the place of C. D. for the purposes of the [*within written indenture*]" appears to require no discussion.

Clause appointing new trustee.

Should the assignment of the trust property be contained in the instrument of appointment?

The question whether the trust property should be assigned by the instrument of appointment requires detailed consideration. *First,* where the trust property consists of personalty which is transferable by delivery, such as furniture, by deed in a statutory form as a railway debenture, or in some special statutory manner as consols, a recital is inserted in the instrument of appointment that the property is intended to be forthwith transferred into the names of, or assigned to, the new and continuing trustees, and an agreement and declaration is inserted that the trustees shall stand possessed of it after the transfer or assignment, "upon the trusts and with and subject to the powers, provisoes, agreements and declarations applicable thereto by virtue of" the instrument creating the trust. The transfer of the trust property is made in the appropriate manner immediately after the execution of the instrument appointing the new trustees.

*Second.* If the trust property is of such a nature that it can be transferred by a deed in the ordinary form, it is possible to effect the transfer by the instrument of appointment itself; and, as a general rule, this may safely be done in cases where immediately before the transfer is effected the instrument creating the trust forms a link in the title to the property; on the other hand, if this is not the case, the transfer should be effected by an independent instrument containing no statement of the property being affected by any trusts, so as to avoid complicating the title to the property by giving notice that it is trust property.

Suppose, for example, that the trust property is a chose in action, which was assigned by the same instrument as that by which the trusts were declared concerning it, or is a mortgage bequeathed in trust; in either case, the instrument of assignment, or the will, is a link in the title to the trust property; and no further complication of the title will be occasioned by making the transfer in the instrument by which the new trustees are appointed.

For another example, suppose that the trustees of a settlement have lent the trust monies on a mortgage, which was prepared according to the ordinary form, not disclosing the fact that the money advanced was trust money (*ante*, p. 151), in this case it would introduce needless complication into the title of the mortgagor if the mortgage were transferred by the deed appointing new trustees of the settlement; the transfer is properly effected by a separate deed (*ante*, p. 179); if there were several mortgages they would all be transferred by separate deeds, so that when any one of them was paid off, the mortgagor could have handed to him all the deeds affecting his own property.

Exception to the rule.

The rule is subject to the exception that where the trust property consists of land, held upon trusts for sale, purchased under the usual power to invest in land in a settlement or will of personalty, and the conveyance on the purchase by the trustees was made to them upon the trusts declared by the will or settlement, it is usual, where new trustees are appointed, for the conveyance of the land to be effected by an indenture, bearing even date with the appointment of the new trustees, and endorsed on the original conveyance in trust. By this indenture the land is vested in the continuing and new trustees in fee simple "upon and for the trusts and purposes and with the powers applicable thereto by virtue of the said Indenture of Settlement (or will)." A covenant against incumbrances by the conveying parties is added.

Land conveyed on trusts for sale.

Where the trust property is land conveyed in trust for sale by a deed of even date with the settlement (*ante*, p. 272), the new trustees of the land are not appointed by virtue of the power contained in the settlement, but by virtue of that contained in the conveyance in trust for sale. The deed of appointment may conveniently be endorsed on the conveyance in trust for sale. The operative clauses consist of, *first*, the appointment of the new trustees, *second*, a conveyance of the land to the new trustees and their heirs "to the use of the [*continuing and new trustees*], their heirs and assigns, upon the trusts and with and subject to the powers, provisions, and declarations subsisting therein or applicable thereto, by virtue of the within-written indenture," *third*, a covenant against incumbrances.

Strict settlement.

The form of the appointment of a new trustee of a strict settlement will depend upon whether he is to be a trustee of one of the terms or of the powers, and in the latter case, whether the old trustees have or have not an estate in the trust property, the former being the rule in old settlements, where the trustees of the powers were usually the trustees to preserve contingent remainders, the latter being the rule in modern settlements.

To take these cases in order—

Trustees of a term.

*First.* Where a new trustee of one of the terms is to be appointed.

The operative parts consist of the appointment of the new trustee, an assignment by the old trustees of the term to the new and continuing trustees, "upon the trusts," &c., "subsisting therein by virtue of" the settlement, or to adopt the more usual and lengthy form "upon the trusts, &c.," "which would have been now subsisting in the same premises by virtue of" the settlement, "in case this indenture had not been executed, and the said [*new trustee*] had been originally a party to and trustee to the within-written indenture instead of the said [*retiring trustee*], and the name of the said [*new trustee*] had accordingly been in the said indenture inserted throughout instead of the name of the said [*retiring trustee*]," and lastly, a covenant by the continuing and retiring trustees severally against incumbrances with the new trustee.

Trustees to preserve.

*Second.* Where a new trustee of the powers is to be appointed, and the old trustees are the trustees to preserve contingent remainders.

Here the form is similar to that in the first case, except that the freeholds are granted to the [*new trustee*] and his heirs, habendum to the [*new trustee*] and his heirs to the use of the [*continuing and new trustees*] and their heirs for the estates limited to the [*original trustees*] by the [*settlement*] upon the trusts, &c., as in the more lengthy form in the first case.

Occasionally there is an express direction in the power that the transfer is to be carried into effect by a revocation of the old uses, followed by a new appointment. In this case two deeds are necessary. By the first the new trustee is appointed, and the old trustees revoke the uses, &c., "now capable of taking effect," and appoint the premises to a provisional trustee in fee to the intent that he may forthwith convey the same unto the said [*continuing and new trustees*] in fee to the uses, &c., to which the premises would now stand "limited, in case this indenture had not been executed, and the said [*new trustee*] had been originally a grantee to uses and trustee in and under the said indenture of settlement, and accordingly the name of the said [*new trustee*] had been inserted throughout instead of the name of the [*retiring trustee*]," and lastly, there is a covenant against incumbrances. By the second deed [endorsed on the first] the provisional trustee conveys in the terms of his trust.

*Third.* Where a new trustee of the powers has to be appointed and the trustees of the powers have no estate in the settled freeholds, the operative part consists merely of the appointment itself. **Trustees of powers taking no estate.**

In either the second or third cases, if there be any leaseholds vested in the trustees upon trusts corresponding to the uses of the freeholds, they must be assigned in the deed of appointment; if copyholds are vested in the trustees on trusts corresponding to the uses of the freeholds, the deed of appointment must contain a covenant to surrender them, and the surrender must be made immediately after the execution of the deed of appointment.

The costs of the appointment of new trustees and the transfer of the trust property are properly payable out of the *corpus* of the estate, although in practice they are often paid by the tenant for life (*Carter* v. *Sebright*, 26 Beav. 376). **Costs.**

It may be remarked that whenever on the appointment of new trustees it is convenient to endorse one instrument on another, the draftsman will remember that as all the deeds are prepared by the same soli- **No difficulty in endorsing the appointment.**

citor, there is not that conflict of duties between solicitors which often interferes with endorsing one deed on another.

## PART IV.

## DISENTAILING DEEDS.

General explanation.

The student is referred to Williams's Law of Real Property for a general explanation of the method of barring an estate tail. On reference to the "Act for the Abolition of Fines and Recoveries and for the Substitution of more simple modes of Assurance," commonly called "The Fines and Recoveries Act," 3 & 4 Will. 4, c. 74, he will find that a tenant in tail can dispose of the lands entailed for an estate in fee simple or any less estate as against the issue in tail, and all persons whose estates are to take effect *after the determination or in defeasance of* his estate tail.

These words require some explanation; suppose that the limitations be to A. for life, with remainder to B. in tail, with remainder to C. in tail, with remainder to D. in fee simple; with a proviso that if B. inherits a peerage, E. shall (subject to A.'s life estate if he be living) become entitled in fee simple: then if B. (but during A.'s lifetime with his consent given in the manner prescribed by the Act) executes a disentailing deed before he inherits the peerage, he can dispose of an estate in fee simple (subject to A.'s life estate if he be alive,) as against his own issue, as against the remainder men C. and D., and as against E., whose estate would have arisen in defeasance of B.'s estate tail.

Disposition to be enrolled.

The disposition by the tenant in tail may be effected by any assurance, not being a will, by which the tenant in tail could have made the disposition if his estate had been " an estate at law in fee simple absolute : " and must be enrolled in Chancery "within six calendar months after the execution thereof."

Protector.

When the estate tail is preceded by " any estate for years determinable on the dropping of a life or lives or any greater estate not being an estate for years," then the owner of such preceding estate, or, if there be more than one such estate, the owner of the first of them, is called the protector of the settlement ; in certain cases the Lord Chancellor is protector ; and the tenant in tail cannot without the consent of the protector acquire more than a base fee ; the rule being subject to the exception that if the tenant be entitled to the reversion or remainder in fee immediately expectant on the determination of the estate tail, the consent of the protector is not required.

Base fee.

When an estate tail has been turned into a base fee, the person who would have been tenant of the estate tail if it had not been barred can enlarge it into an estate in fee simple by a disposition under the Act; if there be a protector his consent is required.

Who is protector when more than one

It must be remembered, that where more than one estate sufficiently large to qualify the owner to be protector precedes the estate tail which is to be

estate precedes the estate tail? barred, the owner of the *first* of such estates which exists at any time is then the protector. Let the limitations be to A. for life, with remainder to his first and other sons successively in tail, with remainder to B. for life, with remainder to his first and other sons successively in tail. Suppose that A. is alive, and B.'s eldest son wishes to bar his estate tail, then A. is the protector. Suppose, on the other hand, that A. is dead, and that he has left a son; then such son would be the protector, as regards all the remaindermen in tail.

Consent of protector how given. The consent of the protector may be given in the disentailing assurance itself, or by a separate deed executed on or before the day on which the disposition is made. If the consent is given by a separate deed, the latter must be enrolled, either at or before the time when the disentailing assurance is enrolled.

Copyholds. A legal tenant in tail of copyholds can disentail by surrender; an equitable tenant in tail, either by surrender or by a deed, which has to be enrolled, within six months of its execution, on the rolls of the manor. (*Gibbons* v. *Snape*, 1 De G. J. &. S. 624.) The consent of the protector may be given by a deed entered on the Court rolls; or, if the copyholds be conveyed by surrender, the consent may be given by the protector himself to the person taking the surrender.

Money. Money subject to be invested in the purchase of lands can be disentailed, in the same manner as if the lands had been actually purchased.

We will now consider the frame of the disentailing assurance. **Frame of the disentailing assurance.**

In the very simple case where a tenant in tail in possession desires to acquire the fee simple no recitals appear to be necessary, in the disentailing assurance he "grants and disposes of" to a grantee to uses the parcels, described either "as situated in" [*certain parishes*] "of or to which he is seised or entitled at law or in equity for any estate in tail male, or in tail under" [*the instrument creating the estate tail*], "or otherwise howsoever," habendum to the grantee and his heirs, "freed and discharged from all and every the estates or estate in tail male, or in tail, either at law or in equity of him, the said [*tenant in tail*], and all remainders, reversions, estates, rights, titles, interests, and powers to take effect after the determination, or in defeasance of such estates or estate in tail male or in tail, or any of them, To the use of the said [*tenant in tail*] his heirs and assigns for ever."

Sometimes the parcels are described still more generally, avoiding all reference to the instrument by which the estate tail is created.

Where the protector refuses to give his consent, the tenant in tail can only dispose of a base fee. It appears proper in this case to insert such recitals as will show the nature of his interest in the property.

It should be observed that, when a base fee and the remainder in fee belong to the same person, and there is no intermediate estate in existence, the base fee does not merge in the reversion; but is, *ipso facto*, enlarged into as large an estate as the tenant in tail could have created with the consent of the protector.

The student is referred to Shelford's Real Property Statutes for a full exposition of 3 & 4 Will. 4, c. 74.

## PART V.

## RESETTLEMENTS.

WHERE the protector gives his consent to an estate tail being barred, he generally does so in contemplation of a re-settlement. I will suppose that he is tenant for life in the settlement, an analysis of which is given, *ante* (p. 328), that his wife is still alive, that he has a family, that his eldest son is about to be married, and that he has agreed to give his consent to the son's estate tail being barred, on condition of a re-settlement being made.

**What are fair terms of resettlement as between father and son.**

It requires some consideration to determine what are fair terms for the resettlement as between father and son; on the one hand, if the son survives the father, he will be able to acquire the fee simple; on the other hand, he is unable during his father's lifetime, without his father's consent, to bar the remainders after his own estate tail; he can make no provision for his wife during his father's lifetime, nor having regard to the possibility of the failure of his issue, can he make any certain provision for her after the death of the survivor of himself and his father, nor if his estate be in tail male (so that the base fee which he can acquire without his father's consent, will determine on the failure of his issue male), can he make a provision for portions for his younger children, which will be available for his daughters on the failure of his issue male; he has also nothing to live upon during his father's lifetime. It is generally considered fair as between father and son, that in consideration of the former charging his life estate with an annuity for the son during the joint lives of himself and his son, and with a jointure for the son's intended wife should the son predecease him, the son should agree to cut down his own interest to an estate for life, with remainder, subject to a jointure for his wife and portions for his younger children, to his children successively in tail, with similar remainders in favour of his brothers and their children, where by the use of the word *children* I mean to indicate that it is a matter for discussion whether the limitations should be so framed as to exclude or admit the son's daughters, and if they are admitted, whether they are to take successively in remainder one after the other, or concurrently as tenants in common in tail with cross remainders between them. Sometimes the son agrees to increase the jointure for his mother or the portions for his brothers and sisters.

Where the terms of the resettlement are of the nature above mentioned, supposing that the amount by which the mother's jointure or the portions for the son's younger brothers and sisters is increased is not excessive, there appears to be no appreciable risk of its being set aside by a Court of Equity, even if the son has no independent advice; assuming always that the solicitor employed for both parties carefully explains to him the nature of the transaction: I use the word *explain*, for merely reading the deed over to an unprofessional person is not considered sufficient explanation to satisfy the rule. In that large number of cases where the son has already begun to contract debts, and it is consequently desired that the resettlement should seriously restrict his interests, as, for instance, by making his life estate determinable on alienation, or where it is wished to raise money for the father's benefit, it appears absolutely necessary that the father and son should deal with each other at arm's length, and that they should employ different solicitors. (*Houghton* v. *Houghton*, 15 Beav. 278; *Dimsdale* v. *Dimsdale*, 3 Drew. 551; *Hartopp* v. *Hartopp*, 21 Beav. 259; *Jenner* v. *Jenner*, 2 De G. F. & J. 364.)

Three deeds made use of.

The disentailing assurance and resettlement can be carried into effect by one deed: this is, however, never done in practice, as the expense of enrolling a long deed is considerable: sometimes two deeds are employed, the one being the disentailing assurance, the other the resettlement: more usually, however, where the protector joins for the purpose of consenting to the disentailing assurance, owing to the conflict of duties which arises between the solicitor of the son's intended wife, whose duty it is, as between her and her intended husband, to prepare the deed containing the provisions for her, and the solicitor of the protector of the settlement, whose duty it is to see that the terms of resettlement agreed to by the protector are carried out, three deeds are employed, *first*, the disentailing assurance; *second*, the resettlement which provides an annuity for the son during his father's lifetime, and contains powers for him to charge the property with a jointure for his intended and any after taken wife, and portions for his younger children, and also contains the limitations agreed upon between the father and son; and *third*, a deed by which the son exercises the power of appointing the jointure and portions, and assigns his annuity during his father's lifetime, and demises his life estate to trustees to secure pin-money for his intended wife.

The student may enquire whether when the bar of the estate tail and the resettlement are effected by different deeds the effect of the disentailing assurance may not be to confirm any prior voidable estates created by the tenant in tail (3 & 4 Will. 4, c. 74, s. 38); the case of *Crocker* v. *Waine*, 5 B. & S. 697, decides that this is not the case.

The powers appendant to the father's life estate should be preserved.

It must be remembered that some of the powers contained in the father's settlement, such as the powers of leasing and of giving consent to the exercise of the power of sale, are *appendant* to his life estate, and therefore cannot be exercised after he has alienated or charged his life estate without the consent of the alienee (*Alexander* v. *Mills*, L. R. 6 Ch. App. 124), or of the persons entitled to the charge; unless indeed the father's right to exercise them be reserved either implicitly or expressly at the time when the alienation or charge is effected. It will be observed, that when the resettlement and the deed charging the pin-money and jointure for the son's intended wife have been executed, both the son and his intended wife and her trustees will be incumbrancers on the father's life estate. It would be highly inconvenient if it were necessary for them to concur in every exercise of the powers appendant to the father's life estate, and therefore the right of exercising them is expressly reserved to him.

The disentailing assurance.

By the disentailing deed, the father, "so far as relates to his life estate," grants, and the son, "with the consent of" the father, "as protector of the settlement," grants and disposes of, unto A. B. and his heirs, [*parcels*] *habendum* to A. B. and his heirs, "subject and without prejudice to the uses and estates limited" by the father's settlement "which are prior" to the son's estate tail other than the father's life estate, and "to the powers annexed to such preceding uses and estates, and the uses and estates limited in exercise of such powers," the latter words have reference to the mother's jointure and the several terms in the father's settlement, and the powers annexed to them. The deed proceeds: "But freed and discharged from the said estate in tail, &c.," to such uses as the father and son shall jointly appoint or as the son shall, after the death of the father, appoint, and in default, to the subsisting uses of the father's settlement.

It will be observed, that until the joint power of appointment contained in the disentailing assurance is exercised, the father's life estate is not alienated or charged, and that consequently, until the joint power is exercised, he can exercise all the powers appendant to his life estate.

The resettlement is effected by a joint appointment by father and son to the uses, &c., thereinafter declared—the uses being, in the case that we are considering, to the uses of the father's settlement till the solemnization of the son's marriage, and afterwards to the use that the son and his assigns may, during the joint lives of the father and son, take a rent-charge, &c., then follow powers of distress and entry, and a term to trustees for the purpose of securing the rent-charge; and subject thereto, and to the trusts thereof, to the use of the father and his assigns for his life in restoration of the former life estate limited to him by (the father's settlement), with remainder to the son for life, with remainder to his sons successively in tail, with remainders over. Powers are given to the son to charge a jointure rent-charge secured by powers of distress and entry in favour of any wife whom he may marry, and to limit a term for securing it collaterally (the amount of the jointure, in case the son dies in his father's lifetime, being often made larger on the father's death), and to charge portions in favour of the son's younger children, and to limit a term to secure them. The resettlement also contains the usual powers of management, leasing, sale and exchange, &c. The resettlement.

In a subsequent part of the resettlement is contained a declaration that nothing therein contained shall prejudice the powers contained in the father's settlement, and appendant to his life interest, or such of them as it is intended to preserve, and that the uses, &c., contained in the resettlement shall be overreached by any exercise of such powers, and that all lands to be purchased with moneys arising under the father's settlement shall be settled to such of the uses of the father's settlement as shall be capable of taking effect.

The deed providing pin-money, jointure, and portions.

By the third deed the son exercises the powers given to him by the resettlement of charging a jointure and portions, and limits terms to secure them. It will be observed that no provision is made in the resettlement for the pin-money of the intended wife; this is effected by the son's assigning his annuity during his father's lifetime, to trustees, and by his demising his life estate to them for the purpose of securing the payment of the pin-money. When this is done a declaration must be inserted, that the demise of the son's life estate shall not interfere with the exercise of any powers contained in the resettlement which are appendant to that estate.

Demise of son's life estate effected by bargain and sale.

It will be observed that if the son were to effect the demise to the trustees by means of a demise operating at common law, they would only take an "interesse termini" (*ante*, p. 25.) To prevent this from being the case, the son for a nominal pecuniary consideration "bargains and sells" his life estate to the trustees for a term determinable on his death:

thus raising a use in their favour, which, as the interest intended to be passed to them is not a freehold, takes effect without the deed being enrolled.

Analysis of operative clauses in resettlement:—

1. Appointment by father and son of (parcels) to the existing uses, &c., "until the solemnization of the said intended marriage, and from and after the solemnization thereof."
2. To the use that son shall receive, during the joint lives of himself and his father, an annuity secured by powers of distress and entry.
3. To the use of trustees for 200 years, to secure the son's annuity.
4. To the use of the father for life, in restoration of his old life estate.
5. To the use of the son for life.
6. To the use of his sons successively in tail.
7. To the use of the father's second son for life.
8. To the use of the second son's sons successively in tail.
9. Similar provisions for the other sons and their issue.
10. Ultimate remainder in fee.
11. Power to son to jointure any wife, and to give her the usual powers of distress and entry, and to limit a term to secure the jointure.
12. Power for subsequent tenants for life to jointure (as in last clause).
13. Proviso that no jointure shall be a charge

unless the appointee and his issue come into possession.

14. Estates not to be liable at one time for more than a certain sum for jointures.

15. Power for son to charge portions and to limit a term for securing them.

16. Power for subsequent tenants for life to charge portions and to limit a term for securing them.

17. Proviso that no portion shall be a charge unless the person charging or his issue come into possession.

18. Estates not to be chargeable with more than a certain sum for portions.

19. Declaration as to receipt and application of rents during minorities.

20. (Clauses 18 to 28, pp. 327-328.)

21. Declaration that powers of leasing, granting licences to copyholders, enfranchising copyholds, sale and exchange, in the former settlement shall overreach the uses of the present settlement.

22. The trustee clauses, 29 & 30, p. 328.

23. Covenants for title, the father covenanting so far as regards his life estate, and the son as regards the reversion in fee.

Analysis of deed providing pin-money and jointure for the wife, and portions for the younger children.

Parties:—

A. B. intended husband (1); C. D. intended wife (2); P. T. and Q. T. trustees (3).

Recitals:

1. The intended marriage.
2. The resettlement, showing that A. B. takes an annuity during the joint lives of himself and his father, that he is tenant for life in remainder, and that the powers of jointuring and charging portions are vested in him.
3. The agreement to secure the pin-money and to charge a jointure and portions.

Operative clauses:

1. Assignment of annuity to P. T. and Q. T.
2. Bargain and sale of life estate in remainder for a nominal pecuniary consideration to P. T. and Q. T. for ninety-nine years, if A. B. and C. D. should both so long live. (*Ante*, p. 31.)
3. Declaration that the trustees shall hold the annuity and the term upon trusts to raise pin-money for C. D.
4. Charge of jointure, with usual powers of distress and entry.
5. Appointment to trustees of the lands charged with the jointure for a term to commence on the death of A. B., to secure the payment of the jointure.
6. Charge of portions, with maintenance in the meantime.
7. Limitation of term to commence on the death of the survivor of A. B. and his father to secure the portions.
8. Covenants for title by A. B. with trustees.

9. Declaration that, notwithstanding the demise of his life estate, A. B. may exercise all the powers in the resettlement appendant to his life estate.

In the scheme of resettlement that I have pointed out, no provision is made for the son's children till after the death of both the son and his father, so that, if the son dies in his father's lifetime leaving a young family, they may be unprovided for. In most cases the risk may be run, for probably their mother will support them out of her jointure, and if she dies they will have the benefit of any personal property settled on her marriage. Should, however, there be no such property, they will be dependent on the bounty of their relations. If it is thought necessary, a power may be inserted in the resettlement, enabling the son to charge the estate after the death of himself and his wife during his father's lifetime, with sums for the maintenance of the children, a power which he will exercise by the third deed.

# APPENDIX.

"The Attornies' and Solicitors' Act, 1870," 33 & 34 Vict. c. 29, authorises a solicitor to make an agreement with his client as to the amount and manner of the payment for his services. Having regard to the probability that in many cases arrangements will be made between solicitors and their clients for the remuneration of the solicitor, to be calculated according to the value of property dealt with, the Council of the Incorporated Law Society has proposed the following scale of commission for adoption :—

## SCALE OF COMMISSION

*Proposed by the Council of the Incorporated Law Society for the Remuneration of Solicitors for their skill, labour, and responsibility in respect of Loans and Sales, exclusive of all disbursements and of Solicitor's charges for searching and registering in register counties; but inclusive of all charges for negociation.*

*The Commission charge is not to include journeys out of England, or any extra work occasioned by changes occurring in the course of the business, such as the death or insolvency of a party to the transaction, nor is it to include any business of a contentious character, nor any proceedings in any Court, such as an application for a vesting order, or payment of money into Court on a Chancery Sale.*

No scale can be made applicable to every case; but in ordinary cases the following scale of fees appears to the Council of the Incorporated Law Society to be fair and reasonable between solicitors and their clients. A commission is a remuneration for skill, labour, and responsibility, and should be regulated by the extent of that skill, labour, and responsibility; but while it seems impracticable to fix the rates of commission absolutely, it is nevertheless hoped that the scale now framed will be found of essential service to the profession, and enable parties, having due regard to circumstances, to fix rates in the great majority of cases.

## Scale of Commission on Freeholds, Leaseholds, and Copyholds.

| *Loans.* | Mortgagor's Solicitor. | Mortgagee's Solicitor. |
|---|---|---|
| £500 . . . . . | A sum equal to ¾ of the Mortgagee's Solicitor's allowance | £15, i.e., £3 per cent. |
| And in addition, After the first £500, for every £100 up to £2,000 . . | Ditto ditto | £2 per cent. |
| And in addition, After the first £2,000, for every £100 up to £10,000 . . | Ditto ditto | £1 per cent. |
| And in addition, After the first £10,000 . . | Ditto ditto | ½ per cent. |
| *Loans under the Drainage Acts, on County and Borough Rates, Dock Dues, and for other purposes under Statutory powers, and Securities of a like nature.* | The Council is not prepared to suggest a scale for the remuneration of the Mortgagor's Solicitor on this class of securities. | *At the rate of ½ of the allowance of the Mortgagee's Solicitor for Freeholds, Leaseholds, and Copyholds.* |

Fractional parts of £100 to be reckoned as £100.

SCALE OF COMMISSION—*continued.*

| *Sales of Leaseholds, Freeholds, and Copyholds.* | VENDOR'S SOLICITOR. | PURCHASER'S SOLICITOR. |
|---|---|---|
| £500 . . . . . | £15, i.e., £3 per cent. . . . . | Same as Vendor's Solicitor. |
| And in addition, After the first £500, for every £100 up to £1,000 . . | £3 per cent. . . . | |
| And in addition, After the first £1,000, for every £100 up to £5,000 . . . | £2 per cent. . . | |
| And in addition, After the first £5,000, for every £100 up to £50,000 . . | £1 per cent. . . | |
| And in addition, After the first £50,000, for every £100 . . . . . | ½ per cent. . . . | |

Fractional parts of £100 to be reckoned as £100.

The Council is not prepared to suggest a scale applicable to loans or sales below £500.

Where the same solicitor acts for both mortgagor and mortgagee, he should have the mortgagee's solicitor's allowance, and one-fourth of the allowance of the mortgagor's solicitor.

Where a loan on mortgage forms part of a sale and purchase transaction, and the same solicitor acts, the solicitor shall be entitled to half the allowance for a mortgage in addition to the allowance for a sale and purchase.

The Council leave open the question as to what commission should be received by a solicitor who acts both for the vendor and purchaser.

Sales in lots to be treated as separate transactions if lots are sold to separate purchasers.

## SPECIMEN TABLE.

### FREEHOLDS, LEASEHOLDS, AND COPYHOLDS.

| | Loans. | | | Sales. | |
|---|---|---|---|---|---|
| | Mortgagor's Solicitor. | | Mortgagee's Solicitor. | Vendor's Solicitor. | Purchaser's Solicitor. |
| £ | £ | s. | £ | £ | £ |
| 500 | 11 | 5 | 15 | 15 | 15 |
| 1,000 | 18 | 15 | 25 | 30 | 30 |
| 2,000 | 33 | 15 | 45 | 50 | 50 |
| 3,000 | 41 | 5 | 55 | 70 | 70 |
| 4,000 | 48 | 15 | 65 | 90 | 90 |
| 5,000 | 56 | 5 | 75 | 110 | 110 |
| 6,000 | 63 | 15 | 85 | 120 | 120 |
| 7,000 | 71 | 5 | 95 | 130 | 130 |
| 8,000 | 78 | 15 | 105 | 140 | 140 |
| 9,000 | 86 | 5 | 115 | 150 | 150 |
| 10,000 | 93 | 15 | 125 | 160 | 160 |
| 15,000 | 112 | 10 | 150 | 210 | 210 |
| 20,000 | 131 | 5 | 175 | 260 | 260 |
| 30,000 | 168 | 15 | 225 | 360 | 360 |
| 40,000 | 206 | 5 | 275 | 460 | 460 |
| 50,000 | 243 | 15 | 325 | 560 | 560 |

# INDEX.

THE END.

BRADBURY, EVANS, AND CO., PRINTERS, WHITEFRIARS.

CPSIA information can be obtained
at www.ICGtesting.com
Printed in the USA
LVHW032000130323
741532LV00002B/372

9 783382 119645